ADVANCE PRAISE FOR *Go Home*

"At the heart of Sohrab Homi Fracis's poignant new novel, *Go Home*, is the question of one's place in the world, the answer never more ambiguous or fragile than for the immigrant or exile, when a person's condition of homelessness is in transition, neither here nor there. Given the cultural moment, I'm grateful to Fracis for his highly topical reexamination of the American Dream, a still reliable but never easy remedy for all those yearning to reinvent themselves beyond the constrictions of tribe and nation. And in *Go Home*, assimilation, sometimes a wretched exercise, can also be a hilarious and uplifting affair."

— Bob Shacochis, author of *The Woman Who Lost Her Soul* (Dayton Literary Peace Prize) and *Easy in the Islands* (National Book Award)

"I read *Go Home* with great pleasure and lots of empathy for the displaced and somewhat mystified but always lovable Viraf and his misadventures in America. The author's (and Viraf's) powers of observation as well as the period he covers — Deadheads and Pintos, great fun — are distinctive qualities of his engrossing account of the immigrant experience."

— Diane Johnson, author of *Le Divorce, Persian Nights*, co-scriptwriter of *The Shining*

"*Go Home* is the story of one man's journey to build a cultural bridge across continents, crossing waters that are unsettling and unsafe. While Fracis sets the novel during one of the most turbulent decades in both India's and the United States' history, his writing also offers insight in today's tense climate. Beautiful prose, wise and witty."

— Susan Muaddi Darraj, author of *A Curious Land* (AWP Grace Paley Prize, American Book Award) and *The Inheritance of Exile*

"This is a beautiful novel about leaving home and moving to America, old world to new, and the courageous spirit of beginning a new life. With his accurate eye and marmalade-like descriptions, Sohrab Fracis's characters come alive. *Go Home* fulfills the promise of his Iowa Short Fiction Award."

— Deepak Singh, commentator for NPR, BBC, and author of *How May I Help You? An Immigrant's Journey from MBA to Minimum Wage*

PRAISE FOR *TICKET TO MINTO: STORIES OF INDIA AND AMERICA*

"Splendid Debut. Fracis' book...won the prestigious Iowa Short Fiction Award."
— *India Today International*

"Recent novels and story collections by authors such as Akhil Sharma, Chitra Divakaruni, Amitav Ghosh, Manil Suri, and Jhumpa Lahiri (a Pulitzer winner) have won wide critical acclaim.... The latest to join that impressive roster of authors is Sohrab Homi Fracis.... Fracis writes beautifully about the dizzying excitement, fear and insecurity that one experiences when living in a foreign land."
— Carmela Ciuraru, *The Hartford Courant*

"Not all writers need 200-plus pages in which to demonstrate sophistication, subtlety and complexity. Fracis's 12 short stories reflect a wide range of influences—from the somber realism of Somerset Maugham to the hip, colloquial humor of Junot Diaz.... Readers will recognize...the work of an impressive new talent."
— *Publishers Weekly*

"Stunning in its breadth and scope of language and description.... This is a fresh voice in South Asian fiction.... One can grow tired of Rushdie wannabes, mother-in-law stereotypes and village parodies. Fracis's writing is brutally honest, exposing sinew and nerves and getting at the heart of the matter."
— Michelle Reale, *India Currents*

"One more star in the literary firmament of Parsi fiction. Into this arena dominated by expatriate writers like Rohinton Mistry, Bapsi Sidhwa, and Boman Desai enters Sohrab Homi Fracis.... Underlying a poignant and sympathetic tone...is a strange and uncanny streak of violence as the protagonists try to come to terms with themselves."
— Firdaus Gandavia, *Parsiana*

"Distinctive, visceral, and original.... The Indians in the stories are a diverse lot—Hindu, Muslim, and Parsi. Recommended heartily..."
— S. Pathak, *Choice Magazine*

"Reading *Ticket to Minto* was an emotional and intellectual joyride I did *not* want to end. Here is a writer who leaps headlong into the creative furnace—daring, energetic, fresh! This collection of stories will haunt me for years to come."
— Susan Power, *The Grass Dancer* (PEN/Hemingway Award)

GO HOME

Sohrab Homi Fracis

KNUT HOUSE PRESS

ISBN-13: 978-0692761465 (Knut House Press)
ISBN-10: 0692761462

Published by Knut House Press, PO Box 52727, Lafayette LA 70505, USA (knuthousepress.com). Book design and cover art by Knut Knudson. Author's portrait by Noli Novak.

Acknowledgments: This novel was written with the help of a fellowship at the Sewanee Writers' Conference and artist's residencies at Escape To Create and Yaddo. Excerpts of *Go Home* first appeared in *Slice Magazine*. ("Distant Vision"), *South Asian Review* ("Country Roads"), *Crossborder* ("New World, Old World"), *Bridge Eight* ("Caught a Whale"), *Fifth Wednesday Journal* ("The Summer of the Strike"), *The Normal School* ("Hood").

"And all the voices, all the goals, all the yearnings, all the sorrows, all the pleasures, all the good and evil, all of them together was the world."

— Hermann Hesse, *Siddhartha*

"If I knew the way, I would take you home."

— Grateful Dead, "Ripple"

CONTENTS

Hear Me

1981 was a bad year for a Parsi to come to America. The Iran hostage crisis had left Americans with a smoldering resentment of foreigners. "Go home!" Viraf was told. But where, exactly, was that?

The violence he met was the small kind. When newsmen on distantvision spoke of serial killers, it cheapened the petty violence that fell to Viraf. Yet no violence felt small on the receiving end. It rocked him.

If only he'd heeded the warning to fix a taillight, he might have managed his fateful clash on Porter Road. Could have looked for the police instead of reasoning with rednecks—a slur he hadn't known then. Still fresh off the boat and seasick, he didn't know redneck from Deadhead.

In his mind he often saw what his peripheral vision had missed: the big American's hand swinging around in an elliptical, inescapable arc that tracked toward the side of Viraf's head.

Did the cowboy's eyes note the glasses over the Indian's? Did the maniacal eyes recognize that, to the side of the Gandhian specs, the shortsighted eyes couldn't see? Standing up close, rasping his words, did the cowboy know the "stupid wop" would stand there unsuspecting, until the hidden hand sent him staggering toward the second man's fists?

Slowed down, it was such a veteran, almost clever, brawler's trick that it fascinated Viraf even as it tormented him, reminded him what an easy target he'd been.

How absolute strangers could hate him, he didn't entirely know. But he knew the distance that stood between strangers. "Do you hear me, you goddam dago?" the Bronco's driver had bellowed, as if across a chasm.

And Viraf would hear that raging voice for the rest of his life.

PART I

NEW WORLD

CHAPTER 1

Columbus Discovered America

Victoria Terminus, three miles from the Adajanias' flat in South Bombay, was an amalgam of brownstone, neo-gothic buildings erected by the British a century ago: monstrous pillars and towers pocked with gargoyles. Behind the façade stretched a dozen concrete platforms under corrugated roofs. The railroad spread north, south, and east—west of Bombay there was only the Arabian Sea.

As the family Fiat turned into a parking area crammed with boxy cars, Viraf felt throughout his growing frame the clamor of transition. It was an odor in the smoky, dust-laden air. The Indian Institute of Technology was a thousand and five hundred miles away, across the breadth of the country. Reaching it would take the Howrah Express two nights and the intervening day.

Their coolie's mouth was as red as his shirt from chewing paan. He'd spurned the use of a trolley for just one person's luggage: the olive bedding-roll was on his head and the VIP hardtop in his hand. His other hand steadied the bedding while clutching an air bag. Burdened as he was, he led Viraf and his parents at an unsteady trot through a crowd beneath giant departure boards, rushing toward gates or trudging out of them. It was a good thing Mamaiji, grieving for Grandpa Rustomji and bitter at the automated world, had refused to come along. She'd known the day would come when her grandson would leave home. And she didn't think he would ever return.

On Platform 12, people bunched around reservation lists on the bogies. His mother Behroz now trailing, they passed the first class and air-conditioned bogies, then began to check the second class. His father Aspi was of the opinion that other students would travel second class and so should Viraf. It made sense, though the family traveled AC to neighboring hill stations. Second class all the way felt like a sub-adventure.

The list glued to the fifth compartment finally acknowledged his reservation. The coolie spat a bloody stream of paan onto the platform before entering. Soon he'd crammed the bedding-roll under a lower berth in the compartment. Then he cast around for space to put the suitcase, but the rest of the metal floor was taken up by assorted pieces of luggage beneath seated men. Viraf stood by in the open corridor, while his father, still on the platform in his stone-gray safari suit, peered in through the window bars.

The coolie squatted in khaki shorts and reached between the men's feet to accommodate the suitcase. The middle-aged passenger at the other window watched with a critical look on his angular, chai-colored face. Speaking in Hindi, he repeatedly stopped the coolie from moving any of his bags. His clothes were wash-drab but neat on a lean frame, shirt tucked into beltless pants that stopped well above leather sandals. A befuddled look spread over the coolie's mustached face, but he obediently turned away from the man's luggage again and again. Viraf, feeling his own impatience mount, could see through the open window the slow tightening of his father's mouth, the faint gathering of his eyebrows.

Then the passenger directed the coolie to take the suitcase around the corner to the next set of berths. The coolie mopped the sweat off his face with a cloth and started to straighten. Viraf backed into the corridor to make way.

"Vaha hi rakho." His father's voice sounded quiet as he reversed the stranger's command through the bars, pointing the bag down at the seated passengers' feet. But Viraf heard clearly the old tensions in the voice, knew immediately the stretched look on the sunburnt face—that old devil Ahriman, the Spirit of Darkness, was on the verge of taking over. And Viraf's stomach tightened.

The coolie, his thin hairy legs still bent, looked helplessly at his two directors.

"There is no place, you can't see?" the seated man at the window said.

"Yes, I see," said Aspi Adajania, still dangerously controlled. "I've been seeing now for ten minutes."

Viraf caught sight of his mother, alerted by a new charge in the atmosphere, drifting into the frame behind his stocky father, only their upper halves visible through the window.

"But what are you saying, when you come late like this?" The tone was sharp. "I should move my bags?"

Viraf could tell the man thought he was in a routine argument where he had the logical and territorial upper hand. And for the moment, it seemed as if his father was engaged in pure argument, too.

"There is place for everybody's luggage."

"There is also a proper way to do things!"

But the debate was over.

"Bas," said Aspi, holding up a hand to the man and turning again to the coolie, his right index finger gesturing the bag down sharply, his upper lip climbing. "I've listened too much."

"What you've 'listened too much?'" The man seemed more offended by this turning away than by anything that had been said. "Who are you to tell me you've 'listened too much?'"

Aspi turned back. In an instant his face filled with blood, and he began to roar at the man, his features distorted, his hand shaking visibly and stabbing the air: "You want to see who I am? I'll show you who I am! I'll break open your head!"

The stranger's eyes flew open for a moment, taking in this violent apparition so shockingly out of control, like some animal prodded repeatedly through the bars of a cage, except that Aspi was on the outside. Then the eyes closed again and averted themselves. The man lifted his hands, palms down, and pushed down thrice.

"What are you becoming so angry?" The critical expression was rearranged into a mask; the voice had lost its edge. "We are civilized adults, not little children to start fighting like that."

"Yes, yes, yes." Aspi had clearly left civilization behind and was practically foaming at the mouth. "You see, I'll break your head!"

Shaking his threatened head as if dazed, the man quickly gestured to the coolie to fit the bag underneath. "Rakho, bhai, rakho. Bhagwan jaané what the world is becoming."

"Bas avé, darling." Viraf's mother had both her hands on his father's arm, pulling it down and wheedling him away. "Come on, now, that's enough."

Something in her placid tone and unperturbed expression struck Viraf—she seemed pleased with his father's un-Gandhian behavior. What had happened to her invocations of Ahura Mazda, the Spirit of Light, at the Princess Street fire temple?

Viraf's suitcase was finally stowed, and the coolie shook his head, wanting more than five bucks. But his dad had told Viraf what to pay. So he stood firm, despite the wounded expression on the man's swarthy, stubbled, perspiring face.

"What, sahab?" The question was put in a street version of the formal Hindi taught at Campion but not too well absorbed by the boys. "Brought you so far. After that, both sahabs wasted so much of my time with their fighting."

"Yes, yes, that's okay," Viraf said, also in Bombay Hindi, adjusting his uncomfortable new aeronautical specs. For the first time in his life, he'd have to watch his allotted money for months at a stretch. "It's enough."

A resigned look replaced the wounded one, the five-rupee note was accepted with a perfunctory salaam, and the coolie left to search for other passengers.

Viraf hung the air bag across from his father's vanquished adversary, who stared out onto the platform. On his way out through the corridor, he noticed Imtiaz Ahmed, a former classmate at Campion, settling in. Imtiaz, too, had made it through the JEE, Joint Entrance Exam to five IITs around the country. Smart fellow, always in the top three. On the platform, Viraf found Behroz and Aspi chatting with Imtiaz's parents.

"My God, what a crush outside," Mrs. Ahmed, in a blue and green sari, was saying. "I hope our driver finds a good place."

"Oh, our driver is very good." Viraf's mum had on a knee-length dress in butterscotch, its hem safely above the paan-streaked platform.

He couldn't see what driving well had to do with finding parking space and was surprised to hear her praising the family driver, old Satput Singh, for a change. But Mrs. Ahmed had turned to him with a big smile. "Viraf, look at you, all grown up and ready to go to college! I want to see who's taller, you or Imtu, when he comes out."

Viraf smiled back at her, trying to think of what to say.

"Viraf is taller, I think," Mr. Ahmed said, the brown plastic of his glasses enclosing tiny gold highlights. Just then, Imtiaz stepped out of the bogie, holding the side-rail. "Come over here, Imtiaz, and stand next to Viraf."

Sporting upswept hair and a mustache, Imtiaz looked tolerantly at his parents. He uttered a quick "Hullo uncle, hullo aunty" to the Adajanias and a casual hi to Viraf, then strolled across and stood shoulder to shoulder. Viraf, glancing sideways, had to lift his gaze to meet his classmate's dark eyes.

"Same," Mr. Ahmed said, wagging his head sagely. "Only little more to become six-footers, you two."

"No chance," Viraf's dad said, unrecognizably calm now, his safari suit the same one he'd worn to the Pfizer construction site earlier that day. Its color, he'd often said, was mael khau—a dirt-eater. "Better keep doing your pull-ups in Kharagpur, Viraf, if you want to catch up with Imtiaz."

Viraf was five-nine-and-a-half in the morning, stretched by a night's sleep, and five-nine in the evening, after a day's compression. He'd measured himself every Sunday against the doorjamb, pencil in hand, ready to scratch a line if the book on his head topped the highest mark. The old ones, at four feet and up, were rungs of a tiny ladder that had taken years to climb.

Making the penultimate mark at five-nine, he'd been eager to stand beside his father—a little over five-eight—to see if he felt taller. He timed his entry at breakfast for when Aspi folded the *Indian Express* and stood up. At first it felt no different, especially if he made the error of checking the top of his dad's head. Eyebrow level, on the other hand, needed no lifting of his gaze.

"Taller than you now, Dad! Five-nine—I'll show you the mark," he'd said with some trepidation. Whenever Viraf acted too big, Aspi always made it known who was boss on the fifth floor of Seth Building.

Once, at lunch, he'd advised his father with the smugness of an expert on how to open a new bottle of Dippy's Tomato Sauce. Wedging the bottle-top between the hinged end of the dining-room door and the doorjamb made twisting the cap off easy.

"Columbus discovered America," his sister Soona said slyly, and "Don't teach your pop how to suck eggs," added Aspi Adajania. It was a curious image, his father cracking the top of an egg then sucking on it like a mongoose, and Viraf had made up his mind to try it himself. That was a year ago, but he still hadn't ventured into Louise's kitchen.

At the time, he'd been distracted by the sight of his father re-gripping the stubborn bottle in his brawny fists, knuckles standing out, then tearing the cap off with an explosive grunt. Sauce splattered onto the dinner mat, whiffs of tomato mixing with chicken-broth vapors.

"And don't go making dents in our doors," said the elder Adajania, breathing hard but brushing aside his wife's hands to wipe the stains himself. "Have some common sense."

But this time Viraf's father smiled mildly at being overtaken, lifting plastic reading glasses to rub his nose. A normal nose, unlike the Persian beak on Grandpa Rustomji, whose memorial portrait Mamaiji touched reverently every day.

"It's how it should be, Viraf," his father said. "Same way, one day you'll take over from me at Adajania Construction. Plus, don't worry, still one or two inches for you."

That would stop him short of six feet, but it was all right. Little more than a year ago he'd feared he wouldn't reach five-six, doomed to remain a shorty for the rest of his life.

And now, at five-nine, he was leaving home and setting out into the world. The one-eyed, snub-nosed giant pulling the train blew a blast that shook the platform. Their maroon bogie lurched, launching them all into a panicked confusion of hugs and byes and best-of-lucks. Then Imtiaz and he went for the rear door, pacing alongside so when they stepped up they could hold on to the side-rails and hang outside and wave.

This they did at length despite desperate motions from Mrs. Ahmed to get in, as the Express gained momentum. The roof opened above them into a gray evening sky, a confusion of rails stretched in all directions, and their parents' figures, still waving, dwindled then disappeared as the train rumbled around a bend.

CHAPTER 2

Don't be a Stranger

Before the Bronco blew into his world, before the world went bad, the blackened Madras Mail steamed from Viraf's mind in Longwood Gardens of Pennsylvania.

IIT was still in his rearview, the day he tripped with Doug and Alison. They set out from Newark under glimmers of sun, Doug's massive old Galaxie floating out of First State Apartments, then humming along SR 2. Viraf leaned forward in the plush, stained backseat, Ali's marmalade hair whipping at his face. Doug, with his free hand, waved a perforated page like a sheet of miniature stamps. Across its white blotting paper, an outline of Donald Duck in faint yellows and blues looked out at them, bill open, as if about to go "Wak!" Ever since Bernie returned from his Laguna Beach gig, then went into hiding with such cartoons for company, Viraf had sensed an excitement among his neighbors.

Light freckles across her nose bridging broad, ruddy cheeks, Ali snatched the sheet from Doug and twisted toward Viraf. The air, whisking in through her window, carried a banana scent—her perfume changed daily, it seemed, each day a different fruit.

"I'm going to show Vir how," she said.

"Yeah, it's real hard," Doug said, bobbing his head ironically and, with it, the hair down to the base of his neck. He looked the part of lead guitarist for the Moles. And with his beard of pulled gold, he resembled a blue-eyed Christ.

"See these, Vir?" Ali yelled over the rushing air, ignoring Doug, and pointing to the perforations. "Each little piece is one hit."

She and Doug lived in the apartment next to the one he shared with Nitin. It was vicariously exciting evidence of the sexual freedom he'd heard so much about. People did, in fact, live together without getting married. Having a girlfriend here automatically meant sleeping with her, without having to hide it. In Viraf's first month at the University of Delaware, he and Ali had sometimes crossed on the way to or from campus. She'd say hi as she passed, making little of what Americans called eye contact. But once Doug invited his new Indian friends into the apartment, she'd gone surprisingly fast to flirtation.

Viraf was twenty-two, only months in America, and she'd knocked him out. She was America. Young, fair, and pretty. Different. Unconsciously seductive.

Or was it conscious? One weekend, Nitin and he had gone over after their poorly cooked dinner, to find Doug seemingly alone behind the kitchen counter. Except that they'd heard him speaking, as they knocked and came through the routinely unlocked door.

"Talking to yourself, Doug?" Viraf said, at which someone peeped out from behind the kitchen column. Swiftly the face withdrew, but not before he recognized it. "Ali, why're you hiding?"

"Hi, Vir." Her face re-emerged, brightly flushed, a partly flustered, partly mischievous look on it. When she stepped out from behind the column, he saw why. She was in only her underwear: skincolored bra and panties. After a moment's hesitation, she came straight at him, startlingly, for a hug. And not a distant one. Even as he felt her warm body against his, he could see an expectantly grinning Nitin behind her. But when she released Viraf, leaving a tingling along his entire front, she turned for the bedroom.

As she vanished, he observed that Doug wasn't exactly grinning. When she'd joined them again, she was in jeans and a modest top.

In the car now, she tore off a hit along the perforations, opened her mouth, placed the tiny rectangle flat on her tongue for him to see, and closed.

He looked for signs of high on her face, like after a pull on Bernie's bong. But her expression didn't change. Then she was tearing off two more strips. She held one out between fingernails, translucently coated, more adult than the rest of her. They touched his fingers—long and brown, his mother said artistic—and then the hit was in his hands.

He rotated it gingerly, squinting through his specs' reflections, finding no more than a single, faint, ocher line on one side. The word *acid* made him think hydrochloric, sulfuric, like in chemistry lab at Campion. Lucy in the Sky with Diamonds... Even Doug, now downing his hit, hadn't known what the letters really stood for. "Prime stuff, man, Vir. California acid. The purest thing."

Bernie Weingartner, with whom Doug had once tried to make the big time in

LA but wound up disillusioned and broke, had come in from Laguna Beach last Saturday in crosshatched flannel and worn jeans, carrying a bag of pot. That night, it was packed into the bowl of Bernie's bong, to similar praise. Apparently, anything from "out West" was prime stuff.

And bubbling up through browned water, it was smooth but heady. They lolled around Doug and Ali's living room, listening to Bernie talk about his Laguna Beach gig. Goatee waggling, he raved about the ocean, about giant blue-whale murals on beach-house walls, about San Juan Capistrano and the swallows that came every year, how he'd fed the pigeons, how fucking tame they were, settling fatly on his shoulders and eating grain from his hands. Anything but about why he was back.

It was hard to tell from Doug's half-closed eyes if he wished he'd gone, too, or if he'd known it wouldn't last. It had surprised Viraf at first to learn that Doug, a smart guy in general, was a high-school dropout. Another sign, though, of American freedom. You could say "fuck school" here and still get along. He'd dropped out, Ali said, because he'd believed so utterly that the Moles would make it.

Viraf hadn't heard about the acid until Thursday, when he said, sure, he'd go with them to Longwood. Doug's hair shook with the emphatic movement of his head: "It's the perfect place."

So here he was. In flux between gray and blue, Ali's eyes were still on him. Just a piece of paper—why look like a wimp? He centered it on his tongue, and it began to dissolve.

Not a whole lot of taste, not even the blandness of copybook paper. He'd once torn off and chewed a blue-lined piece, when his mother said eating paper would make him stammer. Now, as the hit melted, he braced for the lightheadedness that came with booze or grass. But nothing came. Ali smiled, then pivoted in her seat without a word. The Ford surged ahead, and he looked out on the road slipping behind them.

Funny word, wimp. Like fat Wimpy stuffing burgers into a bulging mouth, in Popeye comics he and Soona read when they were kids. He shifted uneasily in the car seat. He'd been flattered when Doug shortened his name to Vir.

"Veer's a Hindu name," he said, "meaning brave."

Then Nitin explained the difference between Hindus like himself and Parsis like Viraf.

"So you're really from I-ran, huh?" Doug had said.

Viraf considered the literal meaning. He'd heard that pronunciation before.

The first time, he was walking along Main Street, books in hand. The stretch from UD to First State was increasingly familiar yet eternally strange: the old Deer Park Tavern, behind its red-and-white porch, where the Moles had set up a gig now that Bernie was back. College Barbershop and its peppermint swirl of a barbershop pole. Happy Harry's, the drug store, misleading term for a chemist's, where, forget about Band-Aids, you got liquid skin in a bottle called Nu-Skin and the cashiers were college girls who sang a cheery "Enjoy your night now," though they'd never seen you before in their lives.

He was no longer surprised by older strangers passing by who nodded and smiled and asked, "How you doin'?" He smiled back and replied without slowing, despite the buzz among foreign students that this was superficial friendliness: anything outside the standard "Good, thanks" was met by a glazing of the eyes and an uneasy retreat. But that suited Viraf. Nothing wrong with good manners, and this took it to a new level—when did someone on Bombay's footpaths even greet strangers? Where it mattered, at the apartments, though the undergrads kept to themselves, Doug and Ali had never turned away from him. Almost as if they knew how it felt to be kept at a distance. One of the phrases they liked to use when even a week passed without meeting was "Don't be a stranger."

Now, as he walked along, a large car faded yellow coasted in his direction. As it neared, two heads stuck out of the windows, one accompanied by a hand that seemed to wave at him. He smiled and almost waved back, when he realized it wasn't a wave and they were saying something, shouting the same words over and over. Then they were passing, slowly, and above the car's motor he could hear them.

"Go home, you fuckin' I-rainian!"

The strangers were male, maybe his age or younger. The one in the rear seat, whose hand was gesturing him back to a country he'd never seen, had a shock of brown hair over the forehead. And in a second or two, the car and its voices receded.

At first, as he walked on past Klondike Kate's, past the flower shop, the Chinese Laundromat, and Bings Bakery without an apostrophe, he busied his numb mind with the pronunciation, adding it to the *schedules*, *laboratories*, *dociles*, and *routes* for which he'd been corrected. American pronunciation wasn't limited to English words. "Oh, Booda?" Bernie said when Viraf mentioned Buddha in a rambling discussion of world religion. The Dalai Lama was the

Dolly Lama. *Allah* he pronounced as *Aluh*, whereas Will Thompson, the black teaching assistant at UD, said *A La*. Zoroaster put Bernie in mind of Zorro, and Ahura Mazda of Star Trek's Uhura.

Even the alphabet sounded different: you had to aspirate your Ps to say *pigheaded* or have it heard as *bigheaded*. Punctuation had changed: call it a *period* now, not a *full stop*. Spelling was tricky: *color*, not *colour*; *practice*, not *practise*. Familiar words meant something else: *gas* was petrol; *fags* were homosexuals. Jam was jelly, and jelly was Jell-O. You couldn't trust your own words to mean what they used to: don't say *torch*, say *flashlight*. The wrong choice brought you strange looks and embarrassment: don't ask for the bathroom or toilet or WC, ask for the restroom or the men's room. And if English speakers were unsettled, what was it like for those foreign to the very language? What must it do to them to be fluent in their own tongue yet tongue-tied in conversation? To have sophisticated thoughts in their heads but sound like a two-year-old?

The thought of restrooms generated a twinge in his bladder. He turned onto First State Drive. Fall was changing Newark, sharpening its air, turning its trees red. At times they took his breath: trees still equaled green for him, so used to Bombay's heat and humidity and only the hint of northern cold in Kharagpur. Just off the driveway a sour gum stood thirty feet tall, one of the first to turn red. Its broad, long branches were on fire almost to the ground. He stooped through its fragrant shade. Distantly, as he emerged, came the rattle of washers from the laundry room. A car pulled into the parking line as he cut across to Building H.

He let himself into the apartment. Nitin was still at college, so he didn't bother to shut the bathroom door, just let out a heated stream. In the kitchen he fried two eggs. He'd become a better cook since flying across the ocean to a land of no servants. Then he yanked on the plastic blinds and stretched out on the couch. No TV set on a research assistant's stipend, no distantvision. And class assignments could wait while he replayed the encounter on Main Street.

Doug was steering the Galaxie off SR 2 and onto SR 52. It brushed past Wilmington, then fields turning green, loamy smells blowing through the windows. No signs of a high yet, and Viraf's anxiety seemed unfounded. Doug and Ali were chatting about her painting class at UD and her favorite art form, pointillism. Viraf had been pulled into her impressionistic landscapes and portraits, breaking down to thousands of varicolored dots.

And there were her funnier paintings.

"What's the latest ghoul look like?" Doug was saying, in grubby T-shirt over faded jeans.

"What a terrible thing to call my cuties." *Her* cotton top was clean against the yellowing car seat. "Vir, would you call my little creatures ghouls?"

Hobgoblins was the word that had come to mind when he first saw them, pointillistic Yodas floating in seas of pointillistic light.

"Quite ghoulish," he said. "And not so little. But you should see the stone gargoyles on Victoria Terminus in Bombay."

"Ooh, Bombay. Why, are they good?"

"Ya, in the same way." Reptiles and baying hounds, from what he could recall. Too high on VT's dome to see clearly. "Not very prepossessing, but you would like them."

"Well, I'm going to sulk now, thank you." And she turned to the front again.

He couldn't decide if he liked her coquettishness better than Maya's quiet, behind which had lurked so much unrest, back in Kharagpur. Or Ali's almost consciously sweet Delawarian accents—which he'd thought were generally American—over the lilting South Indian.

"Not very what?" Doug said. But his grin said the question was rhetorical: he and Bernie got a kick out of Viraf's vocabulary. Nitin, on the other hand, told him to stop showing off.

The car slowed through tidy little Pennsylvania towns, Centerville and Fairville, all wooden houses, brick schools, churches, antique stores, and gas pumps. Then it sped up again, and directions for a ski area pointed east. Not something they'd have seen in flat Delaware—they must have been climbing imperceptibly.

Go home, you fuckin' I-rainian....

He let himself sink into the car seat.

Not home to India, his South Bombay stomping grounds: Marine Drive, Churchgate, Mahatma Gandhi Road, Cuffe Parade, Eros, CCI, Colaba. Not to Seth Building and his loved ones: Mum, Dad, Soona, Mamaiji—best not to even think of Maya.

No. Go home to Iran. To a place he'd never seen.

Go back a thousand years.

Reverse his ancestors' voyage into the unknown, after the Arab invasion put Zoroastrianism to the sword. In wooden dhows, half a millennium before

Columbus embarked for India, they'd sailed the Arabian Sea. Iran to India, Pars to Gujarat, migration in his blood.

There would be no going home, no going back ever for the Parsis. Centuries of settling and moving and starting up again. Sanjan to Navsari, Navsari to Udvada, Udvada to Bombay. And now, after hundreds of years, India to America. Old World to New.

Not to flee, this time. Nor to settle. The idea was simple: see the world, have some fun, get a degree along the way, then go home. He'd even said as much, under Why I Want To Pursue Graduate Studies. Imtiaz had sniggered; you weren't supposed to say so. But Viraf was the first to receive, nestled in the mail on Patel Hall's mess table, a foreign-stamped letter of acceptance.

Bad timing, it turned out. The Iran hostage crisis had just ended with Carter's term, after four hundred and forty four days of deepening enmity brought Reagan to power and fifty-two American hostages home. In his final year, Viraf barely scanned the political section, too used to handing the papers over to his dad. He knew the pro-Persian shah had fled, leaving the mullahs in power. Or that Carter had organized a boycott of the Moscow Olympics. His father hated the intrusion of politics into his world of sports, just as when Black September took the Israeli athletes at Munich hostage. Yet when black athletes went political in Mexico, he was awestruck by their black-power salute.

Viraf knew that Lennon, imagining brotherhood, was shot by a madman hearing voices. Or that Reagan, who'd played a cowboy in old movies, was shot by a fan of Jodie Foster. Or that a billion people, including Viraf, watched Prince Charles marry Lady Diana on distantvision. The wedding of the century had only made him think of Maya. He'd read of two jumbos colliding not in the air but on a runway in the Canaries. Six hundred passengers went up in flames. In Guyana the leader of the Peoples Temple ordered a thousand disciples to drink cyanide. And they obeyed!

But, of all things, the seizing of the US Embassy in Tehran by a radical Muslim student group had slipped Viraf's notice. So when he applied for a US visa, he was taken aback by a hostile interview at the American Consulate on Warden Road.

The central question was this: "How do we know you won't stay on after the master's?"

"I don't want to stay on," he said out of pique. Imtiaz, armed with a scholarship from Columbia, would have his interview soon and was set on getting his Muslim arse out of Hindustan. Maya and Rangan, who'd both failed to get a schol, envied Imtiaz and Viraf. So going abroad seemed the next great adventure.

But waking at five to stand in an already long line at the gates, then sitting for hours in the waiting room, fueled Viraf's ambivalence about even studying abroad. Finding his place in the world wasn't necessary—he already knew where that was. Or thought he did. And yet, he was surrounded by people who thought differently. Anxious young mothers in churidars or saris with babies on their hips kept calling to their children. Intermittently, people were summoned to windows to be screened. Some went behind a door for the final interview, clutching forms, to emerge downcast or jubilant. By the time it was his turn, he was ready for either outcome.

"I'm going to join my dad's construction company," he said. "Here in Bombay—that's what the degree is for: civil engineering. I already have a share in the ownership."

His claim drew a look from the brown-bearded official at a desk heaped with applications. "Did you bring proof of that?"

"Yes." Suddenly conscious of his father's foresight, he fought an urge to ask this rude foreigner for proof *he* wouldn't stay on in India. The assumption, apparently, was that anyone would prefer America. A country from which he now had standing instructions to go home.

A scrutiny of his papers ensued. Then a tanned hand reached for his passport.

Flipping it open in the afternoon sun, blinking at a raspy stream of Fiats, Ambassadors, and BEST buses, he saw a visa in pretty reds and greens stamped across an entire page. And like magic he was transported to a new world.

CHAPTER 3

Long, Strange Trip

On the radio the Doors sang, "Oh, show me the way to the next whisky bar." Doug and Ali were talking below the road noise. Viraf resettled the specs pinching his Persian nose. All was normal, and the Ford floated along.

It turned west on US 1. When Doug gave him directions, Viraf felt the need for a compass. Oh for simple lefts and rights.

A mile later they took the exit for Longwood Gardens. The parking area spread wider than a cricket field under the climbing sun, colors glinting off car-tops, windshields exploding in white. Viraf had to shade his eyes. The gardens, said a pamphlet that came with the tickets, were once the country home of the du Ponts. He'd expected it to be the size of Hanging Gardens, but he saw greenhouses, towers, lakes, fountains, gardens, and meadows around an absolute webwork of trails. People in holiday-wear with cameras consulted signposts. The high laughter of children reached him in spurts.

"Wow," he said, checking the pamphlet. "This says it's three hundred and fifty acres!"

"Yeah." Doug sounded unimpressed. "Let's hold off on the greenhouses for when it gets better."

"Meaning?"

"Oh, nothing."

It irritated him, this withholding of knowledge already hinted at.

"I vote for the fields first." Ali shifted her weight on sandaled feet. Minus a summer tan her legs were blotchy, more naked, in shorts. "The rest of the world's headed for the arbors and gardens."

So they turned past an open-air theater, its hedges cut in blocks like giant green monoliths. Skirting the du Pont manor, they struck out into the meadows, leaving the road and tourists behind. Viraf's Adidas, bought streetside in Darjeeling, now picked up dew from Longwood grass.

The field abutted a garden, a tart-scented, pointillistic blur. But again

Doug said it would be better later. So they turned away and took a road called Forest Walk, until they came to a field edged with trees. And suddenly Viraf knew that something had changed.

"Wait a minute," he said, and stopped.

Doug and Ali stopped as well, some veiled expression in their eyes. Viraf looked back up at the trees. What had he seen? Just regular green trees now, not as tall as the sour gum in First State.

"Nothing. I don't know," he mumbled, shaking his head. And they walked on.

He kept his eyes on the trees. They seemed fine, but when he glanced over at Ali, he saw a smile pull at her mouth. Quick as a flash, he looked up at the trees—and jolted to a halt.

"My God!" he said.

This time the trees had not changed back.

Where before they'd stood upright, now they were stunted and uneven: crooked, flattened, their misshapen branches spreading like bonsai.

Where once they'd been as green as a hill-station in monsoon, now they were a pale, shifting purple. Lavender fringes crackled around them like bottled lightning.

And everything around the trio had taken on these violet hues—the grass was tinged with it, and the sky. His jaw went slack; what kind of world was this? What gates had been opened by the little pieces of blotting paper? He whirled toward Doug and Ali.

But their faces had changed, too—not even the people here were the same. Their faces were pond reflections that warped and shifted, dream images crackling with energy. As if the spirits of light and darkness were knocking around inside their skulls.

He slid his glasses on top of his head, but the effect was only heightened, and now the shifty versions of Doug and Ali were laughing. They'd never said what it was like, just waited till he was here in this dizzying underworld. It must have always existed beneath the surface of what he'd assumed was a clear, unchanging reality.

"What do you think?" It was Doug, his Jesus face shifting, hands flung wide to an unreal horizon.

"I didn't—" Hearing the cracked uncertainty in his voice, he tried again. "Why didn't you say it was like this?"

They laughed again, Ali's voice rising above Doug's.

"How could we?" she said. "Look at it! Would you have believed us?"

Viraf dropped his glasses back down and looked around: pink trees, lilac grass, shimmering plants. A fountain splashed over an artificial lake in the distance, but its waters were violet light. She was right—he'd have laughed at the idea. Too fucking ridiculous. He made an all-out effort to focus, to see clearly...and things seemed to straighten out, thin, return to normal. Gray water, white froth, blue sky, white clouds, green grass, green trees. The old world was still there behind the new one, if he tried hard enough.

"Look at our faces," Doug said. And Viraf turned to see identical smiles pulling at their mouths.

"Now feel your own mouth."

He put a hand to it—the smile was there. A bemused one, in his case.

"That's why we call it the land of the electric grin. It's so impossible and gorgeous, you can't stop. Tomorrow, your face muscles are gonna ache from it."

Sure enough, the purple land was waving before his eyes again, and it astonished him. He was struck by a thought: *this* was what Jimi Hendrix meant by "Purple Haze," the song they'd blasted so often in Patel Hall's common room. Imtiaz and Rangan would look up from the carom board to shout, "'Scuse me while I kiss the sky!" Then Rangan would top it with an air drumroll.

But who'd have imagined, back there, what Purple Haze meant? What would they say now if they knew? Rangan and Maya in India, and even Imtiaz at Columbia, seemed a long way off in this seductive new land of the electric grin.

With Ali in the lead, they crossed a flanking path onto another meadow, where wild flowers grew and the smell of honey rose hot in the air. Magentas, light blues, deep blues, brick yellows, pinks, all tinged with lavender and bordered in violet—no pure white flowers anymore. She dashed around to pick a bunch, their long uneven stems crisscrossed beneath her fist.

"Are we allowed...?" His question dried up at sight of her shrug.

She plunged her face into the bunch, mushing it around, petals shearing from the flower-heads that sprang up around her cheek and eye. Then she offered the disheveled bouquet to him, a Biblical move in this Garden of Eden. He angled forward to inhale, but the fragrance, too sweet, pushed him back. A purple bee in black stripes buzzed slowly past his ear. Tracking it, he saw its malevolent, thousand-eyed ant's head and filmy, roseate wings at a hundred points of flutter.

"Check this out," Doug said, shaking haloed hair over the back of a fluorescent T-shirt, then walking across their line of vision with an exaggerated stride, arms swinging freely.

He was leaving a trail in the air! Like flicker-action picture books. Like Flash, the Scarlet Speedster, streaking through panels of DC comics they'd rented in Bombay. Doug's secret identity was out, quick-change into radiant costume and all: Superhippie. Distant relative of the druggie but exotic flower children in beads, sandals, torn jackets, long skirts, frayed jeans, and yellowed pajamas who hung around the Taj and Stiffles at Apollo Bunder. Superhippie, leaving a trail in the air as he sped off to do a hero's business. Or was it a super-villain's?

"How are you doing that?" Viraf shouted, and he thought his voice echoed. "How are you moving so fast?"

"I'm not," Doug said, parading the other way, loose-limbed and six-foot-plus, electric smile on his face. "You're seeing it slow. Real slow."

"Or real fast," Ali said, her voice eager but tinny and high. Petals hung off her ear and the sleeveless shoulders of her top. "You're seeing every split-second."

She spun around on open-toed sandals, an American Kali of many hands and red heads. Petals spilled off her in lavender arcs.

Viraf's head, too, had started to spin. Once more, as they followed signs for Hourglass Lake, he tried to focus, to still the waviness, panicking when it didn't happen, making second efforts enough to burst his head, then finally a glimpse of steady lines, straight lines, the unviolet world. But it was harder to hold on to, and things just purpled over. They were going deeper into Doug's perfect place, and Viraf had lost sight of the old world. Maybe forever. His head was spinning too much to try again.

"Doug," he said, hearing the strain in his voice. "This will go away, ya?"

"Oh, yeah," said Superhippie, striding along in faded lavender jeans. "Just let it happen; don't fight it."

The echoing blitheness left him suspicious. He took a quick look at his Seiko. 10:55 and the sun almost on top of them. All this walking out in the open, and now the heat—he felt dizzy, tired. Doug spoke again, but his voice boomed and whispered, distorting the words. He pointed to a tall shrub, almost a tree, its stems sprouting pods and branches in the hundreds. They made their way over. Head whirling, Viraf steadied himself against an off-center bole, thankful for the shade. Fat, finger-length pods covered in lavender fuzz swayed inches from his face.

Taking one in his hand, feeling the silkiness of its fur, he sniffed at it. A slurred question came out of him: "What's this?"

He heard Ali begin, her tone teasing: "Don't you know?"

But before she could tell him, his vision was drifting over Longwood. It floated high above the trails and visitors—no one seemed to notice, as if he wasn't there. A faint snatch of conversation reached him and faded. Then he was looking down on a vast network of tracks sweeping into an old station and out of it. Chains of maroon bogies extended past the platforms, trailing massive engines. The world was either converging on or setting out from the junction.

Longwood was far gone.

The odor was not of pods but the coal at Kharagpur Station. He was on a bicycle, pedaling up a flyover. Imtiaz, alongside, thumbed his clanger at other cyclists. Viraf could barely hear it over the growl of trucks. An overloaded lorry like these had deprived him of a grandfather and doomed Mamaiji to a bitter widowhood. Gray crows on a parapet took off and flapped along, then settled again, cawing. Their eyes held a beady anger. One dipped its body and lifted its head, then opened its beak—to address him, he thought, but they whizzed by it.

Sweat streaked the back of his neck as he pumped, and he looked over the parapet at the starburst of tracks. Then they were rolling down the gradient. He straightened up and free-wheeled, half a length behind Imtiaz. Now that the truck noise had receded, he could hear his heart pump.

"What time is her train?" he shouted, the air snatching at his words.

Imtiaz looked over his shoulder, and hair blew across his face. "5:30, she said."

She said. They must have called each other over the holidays. A part of Viraf flinched. Another part flared.

His silver-and-black Seiko showed a quarter past five. "Better speed up, then."

They bent to their pedals, shooting down the flyover to wind through the railway bazar. Masala smells streamed from a local dhaba. A high-voiced little girl ran crying across the lane, her buttonless dress turned as brown as her. Viraf clutched his brakes for an instant, falling forward, then pushed at the pedals again.

They swung past the gate for the Northeastern Railway Workshops. It reminded him of *Atlas Shrugged*, each door one half of a giant cutout figure, feet apart, arms stretched to the walls—whether to topple them or hold them up or keep them from closing in, Viraf could never tell. On the figure's massive shoulders, in place of a head, was the iron wheel of a train.

Coasting into the station compound, they stood their bikes up, chained the wheels, and dashed inside, not bothering with platform tickets. Beneath their feet, the dirty cream pavement shuddered as a train left its platform. Two steps at a time up the overhead bridge to a sign for Platform 6. They galloped down halfway before it was clear that the Mail had not yet arrived. Finally, they stopped to exchange a look and continue at a sober pace.

On the grainy concrete, they drifted toward the end where Maya's AC compartment would come to rest. There were hardly any townspeople or even coolies around.

"It's coming," Imtiaz said, and Viraf saw it, too, larger by the moment, suddenly audible, sh-sh-sh-sh then a long whistle. Years since he'd seen the steam engines of his childhood, but here it came, a coal-black locomotive shrouded in smoke, pulling its load of dust-covered cars.

Sh-sh-sh-sh growing louder, and now the clash of levers, rush of wheels over wooden ties. The great circular nose bore down on them, deceptively quick, and they backed off from the edge as it swept past with the momentum of a juggernaut. Its powerful clankings deafened him; the thick, dizzying smog came over them like the breath of a dragon. Then a great whoosh of emanations, and it ground to a stop. Slowly the fog around it lifted, revealing a web of pipes over a massive cylindrical core. And the giant engine stood before them, rumbling as if sharing their anticipation, shifting uneasily back and forth.

CHAPTER 4

The Great World Illusion

Through the steam that encircled the brooding Mail, he could see Maya stepping down from the AC bogie with her luggage. Strangely, she was naked. They ran toward her, waving and shouting her name. He took in the sweep of her flank, the black feathered groin, the curve of her thigh, the brown swell of her breast, and the indigo nipple, before she turned to them. Fully clothed passengers crossed behind and in front of her, but then he could see her face again, the dark lips and rounded nose. Her eyes widened under black eyelashes, though he couldn't tell if it was at both of them or just one. But when they reached her, her hesitant smile was aimed at him.

"Viraf. Imtiaz. I didn't know you were coming."

"I told you on the phone." Imtiaz sounded surprised.

The dark eyes broke away from Viraf's to look into his rival's.

"I know," she said. "Still..."

"How was the rest of your hols?" Imtiaz put his arm around her bare shoulders and pulled her to him. Viraf winced to see her breast squeezed up against his old friend. But she pulled away and took a step back.

"Very nice. I didn't want to leave."

That was a change from her usual complaints about strict rules at home before she came to IIT. She was only allowed to go out with her parents or brothers, while they, still in school, could come and go all the time. Things must have loosened up once she was on her own a thousand miles away, where she could have been up to anything without their knowledge. Which she had. So she hadn't felt like coming back? Kharagpur was a dump after a big city like Madras, but a statement like that would send Imtiaz a message.

And he got it.

"Didn't want to see me again or what?" he said, affecting a humorous tone and nodding as if knowingly, narrowing one eye in an uneasy wink.

"No, no, not like that." She smiled again and put a small brown hand to the back of Imtiaz's, catching it in mid-gesture. Again Viraf felt a stab of jealousy. "In fact, guess who came to see me in Madras?"

"Who?" he asked, jumping in. "From Kharagpur?"

She turned to him, letting go of Imtiaz. But now, in a sleeveless white top and butter-brown jeans, she was fully clothed! Small pearl earrings dangled from her ears in strings of three, all perfectly and artificially round.

"Ya," she said. "Try to guess first. Come on."

"Must be Kamini." Kamini Garg was her best friend in the women's hostel.

"Ya, some hopes she'd come all the way there, from her precious Delhi."

Imtiaz had fallen silent, so Viraf continued. "Okay, then, the hall warden came after you? What did you jhaap from SN Hall?"

"Nothing, you loony." He smiled at that, and her South Indian singsong lilted all the more. "You two should know more than anybody else. See now, there he is, such a slow-coach."

They followed her gesture with their eyes. Stepping down the walkway was Rangan, he of the "Purple Haze" drumroll. But strangely subdued now, head at a wary, almost apologetic angle.

Viraf's mind was in a dozen places, and Imtiaz's mouth was open. "*Rangan* stayed at your place in Madras?"

"Not *my* place." The pearl earrings began to swing. "Obviously, he was staying with his rellies. My mum and dad didn't know him, first, so no chance he could stay with us."

"Otherwise," Viraf said pointedly, "you wouldn't have minded."

She struggled for a response. Then Rangan was with them, avoiding their eyes, even hers. In tennis shirt and slacks, hair all in place. She gravitated to his side and linked her arm with his, locking fingers. He brightened and looked around with a tentative smile.

"I was looking all over for you buggers. Should have told me you were coming here."

"Didn't know you were so desperate to come." Imtiaz's urbane tone had acquired an edge. "You never told us about your trip during the hols."

"We're hardly two days back in Kharagpur." Rangan's mouth had dropped at the corners. He'd seemed preoccupied, Viraf realized, ever since their return. "I was going to tell y'all, but you kept talking about yourselves all the time."

Viraf could feel his temper mount. "So you can tell us now; nobody's talking. You had a good time?"

Rangan's face tightened as he glanced at Maya. But her gaze had gone inward, her mouth was closed. "None of your business," he said.

"Ya, Maya?" Imtiaz said, a rare strain in his voice. "None of *my* business, too?"

Everyone's business but Viraf's anymore. Finished, he now knew with deadening finality, the days when it was just the two of them on evening walks. In blue jeans and canvas shoes, turning off the campus roads once no one could see. When he kissed her, her face was a blur against his glasses, so he closed his eyes. Her breasts pressed against him. The dark lips opened, and her skin had the fragrance of warm milk.

Now those lips were shut, as the Mail pulled away and Imtiaz railed at her: "How come you're saying nothing? What happened to those things you used to call me, all those things you said? Big excuses about your parents and all that shit... Now you coolly let Rangan see you in Madras, and all of a sudden you're holding his hand and saying the same things to him?"

That was too much for Viraf. "Same things she said to me, before you came after her with your tongue out and she wagged her arse back at you."

It stopped Imtiaz in mid-rant. He looked nonplussed.

"Relax," Rangan said. "She can do as she likes."

Taking courage from that, she shot back at them: "Just because you felt all those things about me, coolly you assumed I felt the same way! Both of you. And after you said whatever *you* wanted to say, if I didn't say things back, then you were angry with me, like little boys."

They were silenced by this revelation, and her voice rose: "You think I was seeing Rangan only after he came to Madras? I'd have let him come just like that?" Rangan kept his eyes on her, studiously avoiding theirs. "If one of you had come to Madras, what would I have said to my parents? See, this is my Parsi boyfriend? Or, here, I have a Muslim boyfriend, aren't you happy?"

Viraf's vocal chords froze. That was how she'd thought of him—the gora Parsi, too different from her. Just like orthodox Parsis who wouldn't marry non-Parsis. Their excuse was Jadi Rana's stipulation against inter-marriage, in exchange for sanctuary a thousand fucking years ago.

His eyes and ears were pulling Viraf back into the moment. Imtiaz was speaking, his face in a knot, his voice hoarse with betrayal.

"You bloody prostitute!"

And before they could close their mouths, he slapped her across her face.

The weight of it snapped her head sideways, rocking her into her bags. She screamed and stumbled over them.

Then Viraf and Rangan were upon him, grabbing his arms. Rangan was shouting: "Have you gone mad, you bastard? Have you gone mad?"

And Viraf wondered, too. His parents had told him and Soona pointblank it was cowardly for men to hit women. Imtiaz had been brought up just as well by Mr. and Mrs. Ahmed. Nor was he the kind to go after someone weaker. During freshers' ragging he'd out-boxed Viraf yet held off as much as he could.

Now he made no further move at Maya, nor did he try to shake his rivals off. Finally Rangan went to her. She'd straightened up, her hand at the side of her face. He put his arm around her, and she leaned into him, clearly in shock.

"Stupid fucker," Imtiaz said. Viraf stopped settling his specs and tightened his hold, thinking Rangan was next. But there was a spent note in the voice of his old friend. "Only reason she'll open her legs for you and not us is because you're Hindu like her."

Rangan started back at them, but Maya clung desperately to him. She was crying, saying something, tears trickling down her cheek into her mouth, her teeth very white.

Viraf tried hard to tell what she was saying, but there was something in the way now, he didn't know what. And her voice had changed, gone higher, lighter. It had turned into Ali's.

"It's a pussy willow," she was saying teasingly.

Inches from his nose, coming slowly into focus, was a fat silken pod. Covered in lavender, it hung from brown, crisscrossing stems. Between them, like shafts of light from the head of a saint, streamed the Longwood sun.

His eyes awash, he straightened shakily from the pod. There they were, Doug and Ali, smiling the electric grin at him in the purple land, its trees still encased in violet lightning.

He stole a look at his Seiko.

It read 10:55.

They set off again toward Hourglass Lake. A part of him now accepted without a word the trails they left in the air, while he considered his voyage in spacetime. It hadn't felt like a memory or daydream, even if it could all have fitted into a second. He'd been all over again in a three-dimensional, fully peopled Kharagpur that he could feel, smell, and taste. Maya had been right in front of him, and then she wasn't.

His head and eyes ached. Along the move to America, with all its attendant disorientation and never-ending adjustment, there had been stretches when he hadn't thought of her at all, and moments, within range of some pretty American's charms, when he'd imagined himself free of the longing and bitterness that had alternately possessed him. He'd thought himself open to another girl entering his life. That would serve Maya right, as would his succeeding in America. But his return to her, willy-nilly, from this fractured new world said he'd been fooling himself, and it was making him physically sick. He had the dread feeling now that forgetting her wasn't even possible, that her dark Indian beauty and the lilt of her voice would fill his head all of a sudden when he least expected it, for the rest of his life. And each time she would deceive him and be lost.

A clock tower in the distance chimed eleven. His glasses had slid down his beak until they hooked on the back of his ears. He put a finger to the center of the frame to push it up.

Ali still had the flower stems in her hand, stray petals hanging off her hair and shoulders.

"Pussy willow... Why's it called that?" He tried to ignore the feelings of vertigo and a throbbing need to stop, just sit down where he was, close his eyes, and be still.

She chuckled. "Couldn't you tell?"

"Ya, I know," he said quickly, wishing he hadn't asked.

"Well, now," Doug said, his tongue flicking out and around his upper lip, brushing the blond hairs, eliciting giggles from Ali, "what're we talking about here? Haven't you heard of cat's whiskers?"

Viraf laughed uneasily with them, but their faces were moving around again, and this time the effect was lewd. The Longwood air seemed sexually charged now. Its three-way dynamic reminded him of Mohan Bhagia's casual talk of orgies.

CHAPTER 5

The Love Temple

At UD, of a dozen Indian students senior to Viraf and Nitin, they'd found two especially worth examining. Ritesh Thadani, a light-skinned, clean-shaven Bombayite, was the cat, clearly Americanized by his two years in the US of A. Not only had his English accent undergone a marked shift, so his "aunts" and "can'ts" were now "ants" and "cants," but even more remarkably, his Hindi interjections had an American twang. He got ribbed for that by the rest of the bunch and took it good-naturedly.

"I don't know, yaar," he'd say, when the newcomers wondered how his speech had changed so drastically. The chummy expression was obviously meant to indicate his continuing membership in the Indian club, but its stylized pronunciation simultaneously signaled his Americanization. "It just happens. It'll happen to you after a while."

The idea intrigued them, that the way they'd spoken all their lives would be mysteriously transformed.

But Ritesh sounded like a caricature of Americans they knew, rather than the real thing. Mohan Bhagia, on the other hand, flabby and dark enough that his mustache almost blended with his skin, spoke as unselfconsciously as if he were still in Hyderabad. Below loose charcoal T-shirts, he wore pants so tight they were probably the ones he'd brought over from India.

Both fellows were heavily into tennis on the public courts—passing up unexpectedly free facilities was not the Indian way. And there any similarity ended. Were Viraf to have guessed at which of them was popular with women, he'd have picked Ritesh. But the cat turned out to be something of a loner, often found eating alone in a restaurant or studying at a desk in Morris Library. "Too much work, guys," he'd say. "Writing a thesis is really a drag."

As for Mohan, it was not like he had a woman on each arm when they ran into him, but he was always either headed for a weekend party or coming from one. And from what he nonchalantly let drop, he went to some wild ones.

"Didn't come home till early morning," he said, one Saturday afternoon on campus, when asked why he looked so bleary-eyed. "Japanese girl at a party wanted me to lick her pussy the whole night."

He was obviously aware of the envy the statement evoked, but he said it as if he wished the inconsiderate girl had not imposed such an onerous task on him.

Nitin was always begging Mohan to get him into such a party and always being told, Ya, ya, no problem. "All Oriental girls?" he asked. Viraf knew he had a thing for a pretty Korean in his TAs' office at the electrical department. But she kept him at arm's length.

Mohan shook his head authoritatively. "All kinds. Lots of American girls, lots of swapping. I was in a group with three-four of them, but afterwards this chick never let me go. Bloody went to sleep between her legs in the end."

They were standing where the campus lawn, a long strip called the mall lined with brown-bricked college buildings, reached Main Street. Off to the left, Viraf could see students laughing around tables on the red and white porch of the Deer Park.

"Lucky bugger," Nitin said. "Eating all that pussy."

Mohan lolled his tongue and shook his head. "Too salty, man."

Viraf had the feeling that Nitin would have been happy to get some pussy even if it tasted like garlic. And despite his occasional brooding over Maya, he wouldn't have minded some himself.

But "picking up" women was new to them. They'd had a hard time getting women to dance with them at the Deer Park. Neither Bombay nor Bangalore had bars. The few exclusive discos, such as Studio 29, were a recent innovation from the West, where party groups reassembled to dance.

The girls Nitin asked politely refused. Short, stocky, and dark, he couldn't decide whether to put the rejections down to his height, his looks, or even his well-schooled Bangalorian accent. Ironic, now, how some Campionites used to make fun of what they called "vernacular" Indian accents. Viraf had met with just as little success, though he'd tried less often if he was with Doug and Ali. In his case, height couldn't account for it. He'd reached five-ten-and-a-half, a decent height. His sharp Persian features were closer to the mainstream than Nitin's rounded type, and if skin-color was the problem, his stood out less than Nitin's, especially in the bars. As for his Bombay Jesuit-school accent, well, that was a mixed story.

Around Doug and Bernie's flower power friends, several of them semivegetarian, Viraf and Nitin's command of English inspired mild surprise, even admiration, as did their grad student status. Their accents, too, prompted smiles and wondering imitation from the women: "'Aa'm not sure of dat'— that's cute." But it reminded Viraf that he sounded different. And on occasion, the approval was based on an illogical assumption.

"I'm so proud of you, Viraf," Megan Ross once said in her New Castle County accent, lifting a slice of pizza topped with broccoli, sun-dried tomatoes, and black olives, while a folk singer, Emmylou Harris, sang sweetly on the stereo.

Megan and her boyfriend Taylor lived in a small home out in the countryside, not too far from Porter Road. Their Irish wolfhound, Galahad, was so huge that, stretched out on the hardwood floor, his flank lightly heaving, he spanned more than the length of the couch. Unlike Doug, Bernie, and even Ali, who'd visited New York a couple of times, they had never been outside New Castle County and had no desire to ever leave it.

"Oh, thanks. Why?" Viraf had asked, touched by the softly spoken and unexpected compliment.

"Not even a year in America and your English is so good," she said, obviously in earnest.

"Mm," he said, deflated. "Actually, I mainly spoke English from the time I was four years old."

That was the year his sister had returned from her first term at Presentation Convent prattling exclusively in English, her Gujarati forgotten, to the mixed amusement and dismay of their trilingual parents. And before long, Viraf's Gujarati had fallen off as well, replaced forever by English. In the years that followed, their father would periodically start up dinner conversations in Gujarati, trying to draw the children in, only to be stonewalled. When he pressed too hard on one occasion, Soona burst into tears. Muttering about their disrespect for tradition and the lack of support from their mother, he'd given up, baffled.

"Oh," Megan said, disappointment washing over her thin, expressive face. "I really thought you'd picked it up so fast."

What could he say to that? Her intentions, he knew, were good-hearted, so he told her about Soona at Presentation Convent, and she'd brightened again.

But when he opened his mouth to women in bars, even those who'd smiled and looked receptive, something shifted in their eyes, and it was not admiration. Then every hard consonant he uttered, every long vowel, every idiomatic word, stuck out like a wart next to their smooth enunciation. He began to stumble over his phrases, to pause and think them through before trusting them to the air, knowing all the while that his cause was already lost.

And he was convinced that something else was at work, something that didn't come into play for Nitin. Sometimes when the women looked at him, Viraf thought their eyes stopped at his specs, didn't see through to his eyes. So many men in India had glasses that he hadn't considered them a handicap with women. But here he heard phrases such as "old four eyes" around the department, which had its share of bespectacled profs.

At Longwood now, on a wooden walkway that wound between green rushes, he wasn't sure if he needed new glasses or if he should take Ali's expressions at face value. Every time he turned in her direction, she snaked out her tongue at her upper lip, ruddy without lipstick, and shook with the giggles. Then Doug's tongue came out as well—at both of them. Viraf had given up on trying to still the electric world, and it was hard to separate the shifting of their faces from the faces they made. All in fun, of course. Or was there an underlying intention?

"Okay. I know," he said finally, venturing a nonchalant smile and a knowing nod.

"What?" they asked, apparently delighted. About what, though? That he was in on the joke? Or that he was on to their plans?

"I just know," he said.

But he didn't.

The walkway led onto a small wooden bridge across the narrow part of the lake, like a belt at a woman's waist. They stood on it, hands on the rail, looking over into brackish water. Its deep reflected green was lined with froth, and the act of looking down was making him giddy again.

"Maybe if we stay after dark," Ali said, "we could go skinny dipping."

There it was, the clue. Funny little euphemism. So opaque were the waters, it was hard to picture his body breaking the surface.

"Yeah," Doug said. "Like at Lums Pond."

They'd talked of it before, a state park on the outskirts of Newark.

"Won't they close Longwood down at night?" Through all the depression and dizziness, the thought of swimming naked with Ali was doing things to his prick.

"Yeah," she said. "We'd have to hide." Her smile was pure excitement, but he couldn't tell if it was adrenalin or lust.

The taller rushes at the other end bent over like genial listeners. On gravel again, they followed signs to the Italian Water Garden. Concrete basins spouted fountains around pools spouting larger fountains. And the water that shimmered in the air was still violet.

At the far end, in the company of other people again, all leaving trails, they walked above archways and waterfalls. Past lily pads afloat on oily lakes, they came to a small, open structure called the Love Temple. It was shaped like a birdcage, an iron-barred dome over Grecian columns, and they stood under it for a while.

"We could hide in the Love Temple," Ali said.

It was only the most conspicuous place in the park.

"Oh, yeah," Doug said. "Might as well wave a sign to say 'come get us.'"

They moved along but soon spotted arrows for either the lake or the garden. So they strolled by the fountains and arches and waterfalls and lily pads—and came to the Love Temple once more. They all laughed, and Doug and Ali's tongues wriggled out again. Then they set out on a different route and almost split their sides when eventually it brought them back a third time, as if unavoidably, to the giant birdcage.

This time, Viraf was the first to snake his tongue around his lip, and now with all three of them at it, the people walking by must have thought they were either sex-crazed or delirious. But it was all a joke, just a joke, and his laughter was half relief, half disappointment.

Sometimes Ali was hard to figure out, but he knew she was serious about Doug. One winter morning, finding their door unlocked, he'd barged into the apartment only to see that the living room and kitchen were empty

As he hesitated amidst a scattering of her drawings on the floor, Ali's voice, sounding drowsy, came out of the bedroom. "Are you back already?"

"It's me, Ali," he said. "Sorry, the door was open."

"Oh, hi, Vir." The pitch had gone up. "Doug's gone to work. I'm so lazy, I'm still in bed."

"Ya?" He peered around the doorway, ready to back off if necessary. She was turned on her side, facing him, under a powder-blue fleece blanket. Her bare shoulders and arms drew him as if on a leash into the room and toward her. He was conscious of leering.

In response, an enormous smile spread across her face. As he settled onto the edge of the bed, she pulled herself up so she was sitting against a faded old headboard, one hand yanking the blanket up to her neck. "Vi-ir," she wailed, her face almost as red as the hair that tumbled around it, but either pleasure or amusement or excitement or some blend of those emotions still fueling that smile. "I'm *naked* under this blanket!"

"You are?" he said, maintaining the man-about-town tone and the amused little smile. He saw how the fleece had shaped itself around her breasts.

"Yes, I am," she said with a wiggle.

"And so?"

"So nothing. It's embarrassing!"

That was probably his cue to leave, but he was literally having a hard time doing that. It was too delicious a feeling, to be so near her and have her talk to him without her clothes on. "Why? What's wrong with being naked?"

"Nothing...when I'm by myself." Then, with a sly cock of the head. "So what do you think of women who pose for girlie magazines?"

"I like them a lot—as long as they're not my girlfriend." And unavoidably he was reminded of Doug. The room smelled vaguely of him. Or maybe *she* smelled vaguely of him.

"See?" she cried in mock outrage, still flushed, the blanket shifting tantalizingly. "Men are such hypocrites. That is such a double standard, Vir. Aren't you ashamed of yourself?"

And so they'd stretched it out for a while, in more or less innocent thrall with the situation, caught in its balance between push and pull. It was almost a perfect place.

But the blanket, not so different from the cover of water, seemed to represent what stood less flimsily between them: their relationships with Doug. He was damned if he'd do to another friend what Imtiaz had done to him, and Rangan to Imtiaz.

At the bars, too, Ali's loyalty was evident. Viraf, unable to feel anything near that intimate familiarity with other women there, had been ever ready to say fuck it, just relax and dance with Ali instead. She seemed happy to rotate among Nitin, Doug, and himself. And on the floor she had fun with the numbers, meeting his eyes. But two songs in a row was her limit, reduced to one if a slow dance came on. Unless she was dancing with Doug.

When the Moles had a gig and Doug was up on stage at Deer Park or the Stone Balloon, she was reluctant to dance, except when they needed more people on the floor. She talked less, too, just watched his fingers walk the fretboard, pealing out an angst he didn't express in words. She said he talked to her about it, though. Before he'd even known her, she'd been a groupie and had caught his eye at gigs, or so he'd told her when they met after a show.

The double life Doug led intrigued Viraf: short-order cook by day, lead guitarist by night. Who was to say that the Don Henleys and Robert Plants and Grace Slicks and James Taylors they'd listened to back in India hadn't also done their stints at a Seasons Pizza? And who would have thought it, back there, where a cook was a cook, a musician a musician. But Doug spent most of his time in the Seasons kitchen, preparing Philly cheese-steaks or Reuben sandwiches for a paycheck, while The Mamas and the Papas played incessantly in his head. He never griped about it, hardly mentioned work other than to say unemployment was an unholy 10% these days, so he was glad to have the job. But the occasional night gig must have been a release, his version of the California limelight.

Among all the heightened senses the acid had imparted, one seemed strangely dulled: nobody felt hungry, none of the ravenous cravings that grass induced. The day wore on without a word about food, and Viraf didn't care. He did care that the shifty lavender world had taken complete hold of him; it was no longer on and off. The two at his side, he was starting to think, had been in it all along, and once he'd been inducted, he was here to stay. Like in "Hotel California." The Moles had played the Eagles number at Deer Park.

Ali had gone ahead again, her bottom shifting above speckled legs. A pink brick road lined by flowerbeds led them to a circular pool. On cardboard labels were the flowers' names: wax begonia, Japanese knotwood, globe amaranth, angelona, Madagascar periwinkle. They seemed to mirror the brick. But ringing the pool was a swath of field daisies, and their petals too were a light shade of pink, their centers a deep mauve. It was too much for him.

"Doug," he said, "it's not going away. And I swear my head's spinning."

Doug turned, the smile on his face. This time Viraf was sure it wasn't on his—the purple land was a seductive but disorienting new world. It was not his perfect place.

"It'll go—just take it easy and enjoy it."

"But when? It's afternoon now."

On Doug's face something shifted within the shifting, and abruptly there was a note of impatience in his voice. "You're too uptight, man. Why don't you just let it happen?"

Viraf looked away. "But what the hell's 'happening'?"

After a step or two, he heard Doug respond. "Here's what it is: it's your engineer's mind. You're logical. And this isn't logical—so don't go analyzing it. Don't fight it; that's what's messing you up. Just go with it."

Said the spider to the fly. But it made sense, and once again Viraf pondered the intelligence of this high-school dropout.

"Sounds logical," he said.

And the smile came back on Doug's face.

So from the rose arbor to the peony garden, from the square fountain to the main fountain, from Peirce's Park to the cow lot, from the topiary to the conservatory, the day stretched like a week. But eventually the clock tower chimed four, as they went in the greenhouse. And at the Silver Garden there were pine-needled cacti that shone like silver. Something in Viraf's head was starting to loosen.

The feeling of being trapped in a twilight zone began to lift, giving way to a blanketing numbness. By the time they walked out past the Chimes Tower, back to the Ford collecting heat in the parking lot, he'd begun to feel what Taylor or Megan would have called mellow.

His Jesus face no longer shifty, Doug winked and said he'd take them on a ride before heading home. He swung the Ford onto a perimeter road. Hemmed in by trees, it was a narrow two-way that dipped and turned so it was hard to tell what lay ahead.

With their windows down, the old Galaxie surged through the rises in a warm rush of air that lifted him, then swept him along. He lowered his window and fell back in the seat. Branches covered in green seemed to swing in on him, so he closed his eyes to a sensation of floating, an absence of ballast.

He must have looked like he was out. Ali kept her voice down, and he barely heard her over the car noise. "Maybe we should've given him just half a hit."

It felt good to know she was worried.

"Yeah, maybe." Doug's voice blended with the sounds, then came through again: "...thought he...bad trip, for a while there."

More road noise and the feeling of being pressed against the side on a turn. He opened his eyes. They crested a hill and a black pickup was suddenly upon them, sweeping over the top along the center of the road. Doug yanked the wheel and they flew past, almost scraping, their tires churning dirt. A light dizziness closed Viraf's eyes again.

When he opened them, the left side of the road had cleared to a stretch of farmland. Scattered horses, their graceful necks dipping and lifting, grazed a yellowed pasture around a wooden ranch. The house was white, and there was a quiet, unhurried quality to the scene. He shut his eyes, felt the car coast to a stop, then make a slow U. It picked up speed again, and he let himself float.

CHAPTER 6

Country Roads

As his first fall at Newark started to shift into winter, Viraf found the walk to campus increasingly cold. Soon, his assistantship dollars were being spent on sweaters and jackets. Before it turned really cold, Doug said, he had better get a car.

When he wondered how he could afford a car on an RA's stipend, he was surprised by Doug's talk of getting a used car. He could remember his father ordering the spotless new Ambassador, and he assumed the older Fiat was also bought new. Sometimes his mother recalled the "little chicken" they'd first owned, a gray Austin—driven, apparently, until it "conked out." The same fate awaited the Fiat and the Amby.

The idea of selling one's possessions or buying someone else's was unheard of in Bombay. But here, people held what they called "yard sales," where they unabashedly assembled their junk on their front lawns to sell for small change. And they routinely sold their cars to get newer models. Once they had licenses, Viraf and Nitin could visit used-car dealerships in Wilmington or check the paper for people advertising their cars.

That weekend, Doug was too busy with band practice and work shifts to drive them to Wilmington. But he took them to a local neighborhood where someone had advertised a '71 Pinto for $700. Creek Bend was row upon row of pastel wooden houses, behind lawns turning yellow with the weather. The extent to which American houses were made of wood still amazed Viraf; all the emphasis in IIT on reinforced concrete and steel structures, he wrote to his father, would go to waste here.

In a PS to his mother's reply—which took a month to reach, but international calls were ridiculously expensive—his father said it didn't matter, there'd be plenty of RCC work for him in the Bombay-Thana area when he joined Adajania Construction. Cyrus Uncle's son, Percy, fresh out of Poona Engineering College, was already helping at the new Pfizer site. Viraf made a mental note to avoid that site, if it was still under construction when he went back.

If he went back.

He'd begun to wonder where his place in the world really was. There were grounds, he now saw, for the questioning at the American Consulate. All his certainty about going home had turned into a big question mark. Increasingly, his memory of India, no matter how nostalgic, had the consistency of a watercolor in contrast to the thick reality around him.

As winter approached, though, the Newark landscape was no longer dense with foliage. They swung past a line of naked trees that Doug could only identify as "shade trees, maybe birches." Ali would have known; she'd identified the sour gum for Viraf. Doug cruised along a street that dead-ended in a circle of homes. A cul-de-sac, he said, pulling into the driveway of a canary-colored house.

There was a crisp, clean chill in the air, like at a hill station, when they got out of the Galaxie. Parked outside an open garage was a rust-colored car.

"Puky color," Nitin said, hopping in place to stay warm.

"Nah, that's an orange-brown that a guy can drive." Doug took a walk around the long-nosed vehicle. "Not too many nicks or dings."

"Dings," Viraf said, liking the word, shivering in the filtered daylight.

The middle-aged man who came to the door could have used some of Doug's hair. He'd been the Pinto's only owner, he said, in its ten years on the road and 138,000 miles.

"That's good," Doug said, turning to Viraf. "Single-owner cars stay in better shape."

Still, in the presence of the owner, Viraf's anticipation was diluted. The Fiat and Amby had been all their own, never belonged to others. This car had been a part of another person's life for a decade. In its own lifespan, Viraf would be just a postscript.

"Got all the maintenance receipts in the glove box," the man said. "Oil change like clockwork."

No Satput Singh here, to change the oil.

Viraf drove it around the block, adjusting to a gear stick on the floor instead of the column. Other than that and keeping to the right instead of the left, driving in the States was easy: everyone in their lanes, obeying signs. In Bombay, you could hardly tell there were lanes. No one thought of them, just about barging ahead. Even Satput Singh, mild and preternaturally calm, knew how to push through BEST buses, taxis, scooters, lorries, handcarts, cycles, and pedestrians all darting in every direction. Aspi, on the other hand, was like a monsoon cloud at the wheel, and it was only a matter of time before he burst out in gaalis at drivers who cut him off.

Viraf had learned by just driving around with Satput Singh at the side. The taciturn old Gurkha had his ways of letting the chhota sahab know of his opinions: he dug his fingers into the seat when Viraf braked too hard; fell to one side when he took a sharp turn; looked behind them when he stopped on a climb; and hovered over the hand-brake when he pushed in the clutch. The RTO test, in comparison, was a walk in the park.

He offered $500 for the Pinto. Its owner said he'd split the difference, so Viraf wrote a check for most of his monthly stipend and followed Doug back to the apartments. An inspired Nitin on the passenger seat was already planning visits to dealerships.

As they left the former owner behind, Viraf's sense of proprietorship grew. It sounded throaty, his first car, as he shifted gears. He liked the projectile, almost rocket shape formed by the long hood and sloping hatchback. He liked the two-door design and folding seats; he liked the tan upholstery and matching carpet. Most of all, he liked that it was his.

They pulled into the driveway past the sour gum, whose long arms stretched nakedly. Its once-glossy leaves, now crinkly and brown, were scattered everywhere. The girl in the apartment directly across Doug and Ali's peeped around her front door.

The apartment functioned as something called a halfway house, for mentally ill people being eased into the mainstream. One of the two women in it had developed an attraction to Nitin and Viraf—it was a matter of debate whom she liked most. Bright-eyed but inarticulate and chubby, she often came outside her door just when one of them entered the building, smiling broadly at him and saying incomprehensible but clearly flirtatious things. Even her name, offered seductively, was hard to decipher at first, except that it started with an L.

Neither of them, they confessed to each other, knew what to say or do other than smile back. Her vulnerability prohibited a snub. To go along with her advances, on the other hand, seemed vaguely distasteful, smacking of desperation.

"But she's young and screwable, yaar," Nitin once said. "I'm honestly tempted."

Viraf had lifted his shoulders to say, Do what you like, and it seemed to dampen Nitin's lust.

Now all three of them smiled and said hi, then went through Doug's door. Ali was waiting for him and pulled on a sweater.

"Vir just got a car," Doug said.

"Oh, I wanna see it!" The sweater was a girly pink and the perfume du jour something like peach. "Where'd you get it?"

"In Creek Bend," Viraf said.

"Single owner," Doug said. "Took real good care of it."

"Fantastic price, Ali," Nitin said. "We Indians know how to find a bargain."

They streamed out, past a chubby, smiling Lynette in a thigh-high dress. Viraf had heard she was saving every penny she could for when her time came to fly the coop.

In the driveway, they followed the line of cars until they came to the Pinto. When they pointed it out, Ali ran at the car and began to circle it, her hair a prettier shade of the paint job. All of a sudden, she stopped.

"You bought a Pinto?" She gestured at the logo, remarkably untarnished after ten years.

"It's a Ford." Doug sounded defensive. "A Ford's a Ford. They go forever—check out my ol' Galaxie."

"What's wrong with buying a Pinto?" Viraf said.

For a second, no one spoke. Where the back-end of the driveway met a railroad embankment, a freight train began to rumble past.

"You don't want to know," Ali said, her eyes skipping away.

There it was again, one of those strange American idioms. He'd asked the question; obviously he wanted to know. He shifted his gaze to the flatcars trundling by, past a patch of woods and on into the distance.

Where did the tracks go, he wondered. If you kept on past Deer Park, what lay beyond? Well, he'd find out now—his knowledge of Newark was no longer limited by his feet.

"What do you mean?" Nitin said, curiosity lighting his dark features.

Doug made a dismissive gesture. "Not important. Some owners sued Ford, claiming a defect. I wouldn't worry; this baby's been taking that Creek Bend guy around for ten years."

"It has?" Ali said. She peered in at the dashboard, shading her eyes. Viraf pulled out the keys and let her in. "Oh, yeah; one hundred and thirty eight thousand, five hundred and twelve miles!" And she looked up from the tan seat with a smile that took his mind off it all. "Pay no attention to my babbling—you're fine. How much did you pay for it?"

She went back into cheerleading mode over the price, then left with Doug in his car. As Nitin and Viraf went in, he could still hear the freight train rumbling by.

Lynette was half out her door and said hi with a little wave. They waved back and ducked into their apartment.

"Let's find a new place for dinner," he said, yanking on the blind to let in light. "Some place we can't walk—now that we have a car and all."

Mamaiji, who'd cursed all cars and lorries after Rustomji's death, would have overflowed with warnings. But Nitin was all for exploration. "Ya, cool. Wilmington jaana hai?"

"Nai, I want to see where Main Street goes. On the other side."

That evening, past campus and the tavern, they came to a fork in the road. To the right, SR 896 would take them into Pennsylvania. To the left lay I-95 and the city of Baltimore. Straight ahead, Main Street would become SR 273.

"Toss a coin," Nitin said.

"Coins have three sides?" It was a never-failing pleasure to ease into the fragmented old monotones. And speaking or thinking in Hinglish, Hindi, or Gujarati was like crossing over into familiar parallel universes.

"Heads we go right, tails we go left. Then keep doing that every time there's a branch."

Viraf laughed, peering into the dusk. "You'll end up back in India like that. Like Columbus discovered America thinking it was India. I just want to go beyond Main Street before it's dark—so we go straight."

"It's your car, bhai. Drive."

Viraf put the Pinto in gear. The campus slipped behind as they picked up speed. A sign said Newark Country Club, and the road opened up into fields that proved the world was flat after all. At the horizon the sun began to set, bathing the countryside in orange. In fourth now, the Pinto settled into a steady drone. He switched the headlights on, and the dashboard lit up. Nitin leaned over, pulling his seat belt with him, to twiddle with the radio. The UD station crackled for a bit, then Wilmington stations came through on FM.

There was no FM in India. Viraf had no idea they were listening to AM on Sundays, when his dad switched on their silvery Bush transistor, extended the antenna, and tuned over to BBC for Western classical. The gradations along which, like magic, stations built, blared, then disappeared were SW and MW. Short Wave came from foreign lands, whereas Medium Wave was either national or local: All India News, Binaca Hit Parade, and so on.

Mamaiji, who remembered when there was no radio in India, would ease herself off his parents' double-bed, on which the family sat after lunch, and shuffle away to the balcony. When Behroz reminded her of Papa's love for Indian classical on Akashvani, or Voice in the Sky, she waved this off as only proving her point. His fatal affinity for the mechanized world had reduced him to an akashvani himself.

Nitin had stopped on a Dover station that called itself Continuous Country. For Viraf, who hadn't heard of "country music," the name evoked a national American station to which his father occasionally listened: Voice of America. But this was not a news station. The songs it played had what Rangan, in Kharagpur, had contemptuously termed a dhin-chak beat, mimicking a simple alternation between the snare and the cymbals.

Rangan abhorred dhin-chak numbers, whatever the melody, despite his own inability to master the more complex beats he admired. When Imtiaz pointed out that Ringo's beats were often dhin-chak, Rangan cited Keith Moon as a non-dhin-chak drummer. A group such as Dire Straits that indulged in dhin-chak was saved from his scorn only by the masterful off-beats on "Skateway."

The headlights illuminated signs that said the Pinto was leaving Delaware and entering Maryland.

"Man, whole state full of Marys," Nitin said.

"Like Bharat," Viraf said. Bharat was India's ancient Hindu name and a popular name for Hindu men. "Country full of Bharats."

The deejay announced a singer Viraf had never heard of, George Jones. He sang a slow, smooth, more or less dhin-chak love song about a man whose former girlfriend said he'd forget her in time. He replied simply that he'd love her till he died. The song was called "He Stopped Loving Her Today." Dover began to fade, and Nitin switched to a Wilmington rock station. A local Clapton favorite called "Willie and the Hand Jive" was on. When the Moles played it at the Stone Balloon, the waitresses hopped up on the tables, wagging their hands at the waist.

He couldn't recall having heard that number in Kharagpur, but "Cocaine" was standard when they made do with grass from the chai stall. Its bass made their walls quake. Precisely when Rangan was most transported, Imtiaz would open his eyes slyly to say, "Dhin-chak!" And Rangan, the champion of British rock over American, couldn't deny it.

That argument—Pink Floyd or the Eagles, Jethro Tull or Steely Dan, Traffic or CCR, the Stones or Dylan—raged between them to the end of their final year. Each was certain he was right and couldn't understand how the other could be so lacking in judgment, it was so obvious his own brand was better.

By the time Viraf returned to Bombay for hols and his mother put on her favorite LPs—Jim Reeves, Nat King Cole, Skeeter Davis, Connie Francis, Trini Lopez, Mohammad Rafi, Harry Belafonte, Lata Mangeshkar, Don Williams, Mario Lanza, and others—he felt ashamed for ever having liked them. That Soona still cared for them was a sign of how little she'd learned at her commerce college.

CHAPTER 7

The Rising Sun

The Pinto whizzed past townships named Fair Hill and Calvert, its headlights lighting roads to where they petered out in the dark. The dim shape of a large shack came into view on the right, behind an electric signboard. Viraf slowed. Letters in red said $1 PITCHER OF DRAFT and $2 SHRIMP BASKET. The line at the top said THE RISING SUN.

"Look," he said, pulling off the road. A road sign gave mileage to a town called Rising Sun.

"'House of the Rising Sun.'"

"'It's been the ruin of many a poor boy....'" Nitin was no Eric Burdon, but he could keep a tune.

"'....And, God, I know I'm one.'" Viraf parked to the side of a pickup in the dirt lot.

When they entered, his first impression was that the place was very quiet, almost asleep. It seemed in a haze; then he noticed the scattered customers smoking, steeped in that eerie silence. Heads didn't turn to acknowledge them so much as eyes shifted their way.

The man behind the far end of the counter regarded them steadily as they wove between tables, but he didn't approach. Two men at the bar turned back to their drinks. Their flannel shirts looked roughened by wear, and so did their faces. These were no college boys. Viraf heard the diffidence in his voice as he ordered, and the raspy tones of the man who said he'd bring it out to them.

They picked a table and considered their surroundings. The room was dim and spare, unpretentious. A dank tone of blue dominated. Only one piece of it was metallic: a faded jukebox against the wall. And the customers were all men. More than one had a light, scruffy beard. A newer metal item—his own glasses—framed the scene.

"No women," he said, keeping his voice down.

Nitin's head made a quarter-revolution and swung back. "Also no blacks."

That was true, though Nitin could have passed for one. Once, when he'd been turned down at Deer Park, he worried that the woman might have confused him for a black man. Not that they'd seen many blacks in Deer Park or, for that matter, Newark. Will Thompson, in the teaching assistants' office, was the one Viraf saw regularly. Doug and Bernie had a black musician friend who'd jammed on Megan's unpolished old piano, while everyone gathered around. But privately they spoke of the rise in crime by blacks and of trusting habits giving way to a need to lock their homes and cars: not even the enormous background presence of Galahad, who was neither bark nor bite, felt like protection to them anymore.

The man came around the counter with their pitcher of Miller draft and baskets of heavily breaded shrimp. He set it all down without a word and left. They clinked mugs. The shrimp were crunchy. Viraf reached for a squeeze bottle of ketchup next to mustard.

"Bloody prawn, why do they call it shrimp?" Nitin said, putting one in his mouth.

This was their habit between themselves, to point out the strangeness of American ways. "Even tomato sauce is ketchup. And who takes straight mustard like that? Goes up your nose."

A customer in scuffed jeans and worn boots walked to the door with a rolling gait. There was something mythic about the image. It reminded Viraf of the cowboy movies he'd loved as a kid, in the back rows of Sterling and Excelsior. They'd changed with him as he grew. First, dusty scenes of wagon lines plodding west, carrying hopeful, industrious settlers, arrows rained on them by ululating Red Indians with savagely painted faces. Then the Clint Eastwood films, the jaded, slow-talking gunman with a rock-hard face walking warily among Mexican hoods; long-striding horses, the thunder of hooves over wide open mesas; gunfights and the blistering draw. And finally, his favorite, the Trinity series, starring blue-eyed, stubble-faced, unshakably good-natured Terence Hill, who'd winked at the Eastwood genre and made fun of it with huge helpings of burp-inducing spaghetti.

When they were done with the shrimp, Viraf poured them another mug and eyed the jukebox. "Ole Turkey Buzzard" played in his head. After the Adajanias saw *Mackenna's Gold* at Eros, he'd driven Soona crazy with its theme song about circling desert buzzards "just a-waitin'" to descend upon a comatose Gregory Peck. She'd never liked how Parsi bodies were picked to the bones by vultures, in the towers of silence. As if he liked it any better, morbid three-thousand year old method.

He'd shut up only after his father threatened him with "one tight rap" when he warbled the song in Mamaiji's hearing. But Mamaiji was the first to defend the practice, literally to the death, he was sure, on the grounds that it was absolutely natural and had worked fine, thank you, for centuries; why change to some new-fangled, mechanized nonsense like electric cremation? Just asking for trouble. She wouldn't even be talking about the religious side of it.

"*Mackenna's Gold* dekha, kya?" he asked Nitin, still keeping his voice down. The name reminded him of Doug's: McKenzie.

"Man, kya nude scene tha!" Nitin brightened at the recollection.

It was true. Barely eleven, Viraf had sat stunned as the half-breed Apache woman who was Omar Sharif's sidekick coolly stripped off her shirt and leggings, split the surface of a waterhole, and attached her taut body to a still-clothed Gregory Peck's. Viraf knew that his mother, watching silently, was wild that the rating was U for Universal, not A for Adult.

"Ya," he said, remembering Ali's semi-naked hug and her fondness for skinny dipping. "Deadly babe. With an old bloody guy like Gregory Peck... And Omar Sharif's an Egyptian, like Talaat in my office—how can he play a Wild West outlaw?"

"Hardly matters," Nitin said. "You think the girl was really Red Indian? How many Red Indians you see around here?"

None, he realized. The funny thing was, he'd remembered movie references to Red Indians and cowboys, even Mexicans and gringos, but another term had slipped his mind. He thought he'd never heard the term *whites* until arriving in America. Yet he must have, in the Westerns or in comicbooks like Rifleman. And in Mr. Pande's history class, when he'd railed at the British. Something about the white man's burden. It wasn't literal, considering their skin was really pink. And most of the blacks here were brown.

Nitin's mind was on skin, too: "By the way, there aren't just A movies here, but X and double-X and triple-X!"

"Huh." Viraf considered this over a swallow. "What does it stand for? The X in *sex*?"

"Unknown variable x equals what? We have to solve the equation—at Cinema Newark."

Near Brunswick Alleys, where they'd gone bowling when everyone had cash, stood a theater whose marquee occasionally touted the seductive rating.

"Just now I'm broke, yaar. Later on. Spent my whole check on the gaadi."

"Another check in two weeks, man, don't worry." Nitin made the same monthly amount for TAing, two hundred more than the car had cost.

Lowering his mug, Viraf smiled ruefully. Sometimes he wished he'd taken his dad's offer to fund his studies abroad. Getting a scholarship, instead, had been a matter of pride—for both of them. So he'd embarked from Bombay on an early-morning flight, with just $500 in foreign exchange from the Reserve Bank of India and $500 from the black market.

But there were two things he hadn't known: assistantships, as they were called here, left little in your pocket after your rent and meals. Secondly, you had to work for them: twenty hours a week on top of your coursework. It was a new concept for an Indian, working your way through college. Luckily, Dr. Reese, his puffy-nosed advisor, had not held Viraf's Persian beak to the grindstone.

Ed Reese doubled at the new computer science department, spending most of his week there. The only prof who taught construction management, he was used to being left out of the loop when his old department's assistants were assigned. So he looked pleasantly surprised when Viraf approached him, on the advice of their departmental secretary. In hearty tones and an accent that Viraf learned was a New York variety, Reese welcomed the heir to Adajania Construction. On the DEC-10, he announced, they would develop a simulator of construction projects to study their management.

Impressed, Viraf mentioned the computer project in his next letter home and was deflated to get no response from his dad. He found that developing a new program module every couple of weeks was enough to keep his advisor happy. The affable professor, whose frequent smile transformed a bloated face, seemed to understand Viraf's priorities.

A moody silence prevailed at the Rising Sun, as if its customers came for that, preferred it to conversation. But in that silence, for some reason, Viraf could hear the flatcars behind First State still rumbling along.

"I want to try out the jukebox," he said finally, and drained his mug. American beer, he'd found, was less bitter than Indian. "But it looks like it hasn't been played since the last century."

"Go ask the guy for quarters." Nitin looked as if the food and beer were settling him into the prevalent mood. "If he doesn't like you to play it, he'll tell you it's broken or that he doesn't have quarters. Then don't insist, because as it is I'm getting some bad vibes."

The man behind the counter said exactly nothing, rubbed at the side of his mouth with a large thumb, then made his way to the cash register and punched it open for quarters. He led the way to the heavy contraption against the wall and leaned over behind it until its lights came on. When he straightened up, he was taller than Viraf by half a head. Then he left Viraf to himself, apart from the eyes that had turned their way. This concerted silence was getting to him, so he was both eager to drown it in sound and guilty over ruining the quiet.

Tiny lighted panels invited him to select them. Some of the musicians he knew from Patel Hall days: Creedence Clearwater Revival, Bob Dylan, John Denver, Joni Mitchell... Some he'd come to know through Doug and company: Grateful Dead, Joan Baez, Gordon Lightfoot, Fleetwood Mac... And some he hadn't heard of: Harry Chapin, Dolly Parton, Willie Nelson, Bob Seger... But one name belonged to an automatically dubious set: Don Williams was among the singers on his *mother's* LPs.

Yet, something about the panel puzzled him: the song attributed to Williams was "We're All the Way." Viraf had often heard it...on an Eric Clapton cassette! It was a Clapton number whose chords he'd figured out on a fellow Patelian's guitar.

His quarters clinked through the slot. He selected the Williams' number and its flip side, a song called "Good Ole Boys Like Me." The 45 swung out to play, and he walked back, shrugging to Nitin's inquiring eyebrows. Familiar light scratches filtered out into the room, and the song began. A piano riff, a bass progression, and then a quiet, deep voice. Viraf recognized it; he'd heard only two other voices as deep and true: Gentleman Jim Reeves', his mother's favorite, and Paul Robeson's, which rolled like the rivers it described on his father's scratchy old 78s.

The lyrics, too, he recognized: "Don't put words between us we shouldn't say," they urged some woman, just as they had in Kharagpur. "Don't be actin' halfway, when you know we're all the way." But Williams' voice owned them so completely, Viraf couldn't recall Clapton's version. And there, as he listened closely, behind the voice, behind the piano, behind the slide and harmonica and bass guitar, there it was beneath it all, almost hidden yet unmistakable: dhin-chak, dhin-chak, dhin-chak...

It ran through "Good Ole Boys Like Me" as well. But as soon as he stopped listening for it, the song opened out into a story unlike those he and Soona had read, probably one that after a certain age she wouldn't have cared to read—there weren't any women in it. A man looked back on his past with a quiet sense of loss. And when he sang, "Those Williams boys they still mean a lot to me, Hank and Tennessee," Viraf knew Williams was singing of himself. He sang of his childhood, when he slept under a picture of Stonewall Jackson and was kissed goodnight by a father who drank but taught him a code of honor.

Into the boy's life, as they had into Viraf's, came the sounds of the radio and the words of writers such as Thomas Wolfe. A fatalistic refrain said, "I guess we're all gonna be what we're gonna be, so what do you do with good ole boys like me?" It could have been written by Mamaiji, helplessly spreading her hands at children who read of distant worlds and wanted to see them, instead of being contented with home. The boy in the song watched his friends burn up on booze and drugs, but he was too smart for that. He listened to the news and learned to speak like the newsmen. Then at eighteen, he "hit the road." Even so, the chorus sighed, no matter where or how far he went, Southern winds still blew inside his head.

The song ended, and the room turned silent again. But now it was the silence of men listening.

Nitin was one of them. "Deadly guys, reading Thomas Wolfe and all."

"Tennessee Williams," Viraf added. "And what a name: 'Stonewall Jackson.'" Not a figure Mr. Pande had covered in history class.

They downed the rest of the beer, put down a tip, and went to the cash register. This time, the big man behind the bar walked over to ring them up. There was a stolid dignity about him. His crinkled eyes regarded them, not unpleasantly, as he gave them their change. And when Viraf thanked him, he nodded and said, "Sure thing."

Outside it was dark, and now the cold was like no hill station's. They zipped up their jackets, fished new gloves out of pockets, and pulled them on. Viraf's padded fingers fumbled with the keys, so he was shivering by the time he got in and unlocked Nitin's door. The Pinto coughed on starting up. When he turned up the heat, it blasted cold air.

He shifted into reverse, but his foot jumped off the unfamiliar clutch, and the hatchback darted at the rear of the pickup to its left. For an instant he thought they would hit it and have to go back in to face its owner. But the Pinto squealed around it by a hair.

Then they were out onto an empty 273. Something hard was playing on the Wilmington station, obscured by the sound of blowing air, which gradually grew warm. Nitin turned the radio off. Viraf stepped on the gas, the sound of their wheels became audible, and soon they were flying through the dark behind their headlights.

"See how much you can do," Nitin said, gesturing at the speedometer.

Viraf pushed down on the pedal and felt the car surge. "Speed limit kya hai?"

"Who cares, on such straight roads. Fifty-five, must be, but it's an arbitrary number. Used to be seventy, Doug says, before the oil embargo. Same roads. Then the gas prices shot up, and they changed it."

The dial hand swung past sixty-five and seventy. He leveled off a hair under eighty, and for a while they rushed through invisible countryside.

CHAPTER 8

Value of a Life

That Sunday, Viraf decided he had better get to work on the next module for Dr. Reese. He could drive, now, instead of shivering down Main Street.

He yanked up the blinds, then whisked two eggs with a fork. This morning, his attention was diverted. The windows' bottom edge, in their sunken apartment, was just a foot above the grounds. So normally they looked out on a strip of grass, the driveway, and a row of cars from the eye-level of squirrels. Of which there were usually many. But today the cars were obscured by a steady, sideways drift of white flakes through the air, in self-renewing multitudes. All of it disappeared quietly into a white carpet.

As he whisked, there were sounds in the corridor outside his door and up the steps to the entrance. Boots appeared, roughing up the snow, then Doug, Bernie, and Ali came into view. They were bundled in heavy jackets and gloves, colored woolen scarves around their necks. Ali had on a knitted cap; her quilted kapok was an electric orange. Doug's camel-brown parka was edged with fur. He bent over in the driveway, scooped up snow, and mashed it together in his gloves. Ali had her arms up to the falling sky and was mouthing something when his snowball spattered against her ear. Viraf could hear her squeal through the windowpane. They started to pelt one another with the stuff, and Bernie's goatee turned so white he looked like a porcelain Chinaman.

Viraf dropped the bowl on the coffee table, yolk hanging from the fork. He grabbed his jacket, and was still zipping up when he threw open the entrance door to join them.

His shoes sank and crunched in the snow. Frigid air pricked his face, slicing up his nostrils and down his throat. Flakes settled lightly on his hair. Their mingled voices came at him at the same time as snowballs that splashed his jacket and then, as he stooped for ammunition, his head. His first snowballs were too loose, but compacted they flew better, and he nailed Bernie and Ali a couple of times. Doug was the champ, quick to duck and fire before Viraf could recover. By the time they were done with one another, icy streams ran down the back of his neck, and the metal hands of his glasses were cold. His ears felt frozen. But he was heated inside and panting and still saying things at the top of his voice.

Through slicked glasses, he saw the living-room window go up. Nitin's head and arms leaned out, low to the ground.

"Thanks for the egg," he said, plate in hand.

"You bloody thief." Then Viraf remembered his plan for the day. "Anyway, I'll see y'all later. I have to go do some work for Dr. Reese."

Amid loud protests from Doug and Ali, he made his way through the slush and over a still-deepening carpet to the Pinto, on whose hood lay more of the white stuff. He switched the wipers on and pulled out just as Nitin joined them. Ali waved and said something.

He rolled the window down.

"Drive safe," she said.

All of Main Street was turning white. The old people's home, the flower shop, Klondike Kate's, all had a coating that made them prettier, like on a Christmas card. Today there was no one seated outside, but the few in the hushed street looked different, bulky, hidden under layers. As the flakes continued to drift across his windshield, there was a slowed down, relative stillness to it all.

He came to Academy Street and, turning past the lab, coasted into the small, triangular parking behind Evans Hall. It was a space that would drift through his nightmares, but he didn't know that yet. Only one other car by the dumpster, on a Sunday. He shuffled over to the back door and let himself in with his key. The corridor was dark, but it felt warm inside. Upstairs, in the assistants' office, Will Thompson had pulled up the slats to let in light.

"Hey, man," he said, looking up from his desk with an ironic lift of the eyebrow. "Couldn't stay away from work on a Sunday?"

"Look who's talking," Viraf said, rolling out the chair at his desk.

"True. The wife was not happy when I said see-ya after morning service." He always just called her "the wife."

Will was the only married assistant in the department. The departmental secretary, Richard Danner, also married, had held him up as an example to the other assistants: "Mature, reliable, just a pleasure to work with." He'd put in a few years at a Wilmington company after his bachelor's, before coming back fulltime for a master's. A black man, he'd told Viraf, had to work twice as hard to get ahead, and he could use the leg up on colleagues with only undergraduate degrees.

"You go every Sunday, huh?"

"Oh yeah. Gotta go. None of them fire temples around here?"

Viraf shook his head. "I hardly went, even in Bombay—only when my parents took us on special days."

On Navroz or Papeti, when Soona and he were kids, they'd all pile into the Fiat for a five-minute ride to the Wadiaji Atash Bahram. Their mother bought sandalwood sticks from the Princess Street vendors, then they donned their prayer caps and went inside. Gigantic paintings of Zarathustra and other religious figures looked down from the walls of the outer hall. In the darkened inner sanctum, orange flames danced out of a great silver chalice.

"Anyway," he continued, "it's time to keep the project moving for Dr. Reese."

"Mm-hm. Good man, Reese. Something went down, though, between him and the chair. Don't know what."

"The department chair?" Viraf wasn't sure he'd ever seen the man.

"Yep. Probably to do with Reese doubling up at Computer Science. Got a little frosty between them, like the weather. So see you don't stick your head in that ice box."

Viraf mulled that over. "Okay. Thanks for the warning."

Will nodded. "Not the man to cross, Dr. Pickett."

They got down to work. It was easier to get it done without the other assistants around. They were an international bunch—Vietnamese, Saudi, Egyptian, Chinese, Swedish—and there was always talk to distract you. Or else there were undergrads consulting TAs. But on Sunday it was so quiet you could hear the heat grinding on.

By the time he had a new page of code, he'd begun to feel the missed breakfast. After debugging that segment, he was ravenous.

"Will," he said. "You had lunch yet?"

"Nah. Give me five minutes."

They decided to walk over to the Deer Park and went out the front. It wasn't snowing anymore, but the campus greens were ethereally white. Even the brown-brick college buildings looked like illustrations in a fairy tale.

"Beautiful," Viraf said. "In India, you have to go to Darjeeling or Kashmir to see snow like this." When he was very small and his grandfather still alive, the family had vacationed in those hill stations. Mamaiji had nothing against machines then, and had flown with them.

"It's cool." Will seemed less enchanted. "Give it a week. It gets slushy, dirty, freezes over. Then it's slippery as hell, but you've got to clear out your driveway—or dig out your car. And then drive that mother on slick roads."

Viraf glanced at him. He was lanky, but today his long overcoat filled him out. Even in snow and with his hands in the coat pockets, he walked with a swagger. The Cossack hat on his head put him well over six feet, and Viraf, chilled to his scalp, resolved to get one.

"I finally bought a car," he said.

"Yeah? Good time for that. What kind did you get?"

"Used car. '71 Pinto."

"'71?" Will lifted his ironic eyebrow.

This rattled Viraf. What was it about his car that drew these oblique questions? "Ya. Why?"

Will seemed to find that funny. A chortle issued from his mouth, with a frozen puff of air. Breathing one of his own, Viraf squinted at the cloud that dissipated quickly, replaced by another as he breathed out again.

"All right, man. I'm here to give you an education you can't get in the classroom. Not in no Du Pont Hall." Will flipped a thumb at its enormous pillars. He never talked like that around Danner or the profs. They tramped up the steps to Main Street. "Your Pinto a hatchback?"

Viraf nodded.

"A while ago, Ford got sued over a '72 hatchback. Big case all over the papers."

"My neighbor mentioned it, but he didn't tell me in detail."

"He should have. When this Pinto was rear-ended, it caught fire. Killed the lady driving it; almost killed the passenger. Boy in his teens."

"Shit!" He struggled to think how it must have felt to be trapped in that flaming Pinto. Deer Park's red and white stood out of the snow like a cake. They crossed the street to it. "But that was an accident, right?"

"Nope. Not the fire. That's what the law suit was about...and other cases, too. Turned out the tank is right where a crash will punch these bolts into it. Then the gas leaks—into the car. Now that's a good way to make a fire."

They reached the porch and stepped up. A couple of hardy undergrads were at an outdoor table. Against the front wall, a plaque proclaimed the tavern's history, dating back to the mid-1700s. The menus, he knew, had a longer version. The high point was a visit from Edgar Allen Poe when he'd lectured at the Newark Academy. Getting down from a carriage, he slipped in the mud and famously pronounced a mock curse on the Deer Park, just a log cabin at the time: "A curse upon this place! All who enter shall have to return."

A blessing for the inn, of course. Doug said Deer Park was the original Hotel California. Viraf couldn't help but think of Mamaiji, who out of bitterness had cursed all machines. A curse now fallen on her grandson. Maybe he, too, like Rustomji, was destined to die in a car—a rolling firetrap of a car.

Ironic for a Zoroastrian.

Inside, the restaurant was doing good business, and Will pointed to a corner table. A brick fireplace glowed not far from them, radiating heat, so they shed their winter paraphernalia. Viraf's glasses clouded over, and he looked away from the fire with a sense of foreboding instead of reverence. But the smell of hot food was all around, and he felt hungry again.

"Now get this." Will opened his menu. "The papers say Ford knew about the design flaw—surprise you what people will say in office memos. It would have taken them, per vehicle, the price of this dish here"—he tapped a finger on an entrée—"to fix the car before it went into production."

"Figure out what you want?" asked a waitress on cue, with her notepad. In lime T-shirt and white pants, her dirty-blonde hair in a ponytail, she was probably an undergrad working part time.

"Not yet." Will retracted the finger. "I'll get a soda first. Pepsi."

"Same here; no ice, please."

She left, and Viraf opened his menu. It outlined the tavern's history. In the 1760s, when it was an inn, Mason and Dixon stayed in it while surveying the line between North and South. George Washington spent a night there during the American Revolution—a landmark revolt against the British Empire with which an Indian could identify.

"So why the fuck didn't they fix it?" he continued. It was all very confusing, like so many things about this country. That fleeting relaxed feeling was gone. But his appetite was not; he decided on the Deer Park Pie.

"Yeah." Will leaned back. "They did a cost-benefit analysis. Like if somebody died, say $200,000 a case. If somebody got injured: less. If they got out safe: way less. At say a couple of thousand cases, that added up to fifty million." He smiled. "Then they said, what'll it cost to fix all the cars? Oh, about a hundred million.... Now, that's simple math: don't fix it."

One of Mamaiji's pet peeves had been the People's Car controversy. Indira Gandhi's son Sanjay had no automotive qualifications, yet he'd been handed the Maruti contract. And his Italian sister-in-law, Sonia Gandhi, was appointed Maruti's managing director. So she'd been forced to resign. But at least the Marutis themselves were safe, not deathtraps.

Viraf looked around. One of the showcases housed a brown-feathered rooster. A placard at its talons proclaimed it UD's original Blue Hen. Why blue, he wondered, and why hen? Not a fearsome image: the Fightin' Blue Hens. In another showcase, a stuffed Poe raven's beak was permanently open, as if to caw Nevermore.

Their waitress brought the drinks and asked if they were ready. Will ordered the special, Ginger & Lime Iron Hill Steak.

"All right," he said, after a sip from his Pepsi. "Now, you never know about juries, but this much I know: they don't think like corporations. When the jury put a price on this burned lady and the boy, you think it was two hundred thousand? Three hundred thousand?"

Viraf considered the value of a life—very possibly his life—while he took a sip. His glass was packed with ice. Even on a winter day, a drink without ice made no sense to the waitress. She probably thought he'd said *more* ice. "A million?"

Will stretched his legs at the side of the table. "That all?"

"I don't know," Viraf said, well aware he sounded irritable. "Ten million?"

"Try a hundred. More than a hundred. About what it would have cost them to fix the whole line. That's a record judgment...it put the fear of God in those corporate boys."

"Serves them fucking right." His mood was irretrievably ruined. "So I should just get you to crash into my car and let myself get burned. Then, if I stay alive, I'll be rich."

"You got a deal: fifty-fifty."

"Uh-uh. It's my skin, so I should take ninety, you take ten."

"If we're talking ten mill, all right. And I'll throw in a call to 911."

"Hmm." Viraf shifted in the wooden chair. "But to get that much, I'd have to die."

"All right, so we let you get burned this much...." Will held his forefinger and thumb an inch apart. Viraf noticed his palm was lighter than his face and arms. "And I'll settle for a million."

They shook on it. When Viraf first met Will, his immediate associations were both African and Caribbean. While some IITians had looked down on African students, they revered, to a man, the West Indies' cricketers who dominated the sport with their flair, speed, and power. Viv Richards, Rohan Kanhai, and Andy Roberts were gods not only to them but to all whose favorite movies featured Indian villains labeled kalia: the black one. Maya's dark-skinned sisters might have had a better shot at playing a movie heroine if they could have hit the hell out of a ball.

As for Parsi sports fanatics, his father spoke of a blond, German, turn-of-the-century strongman named Sandow in the same wonderstruck tones as he did of Jesse Owens. "Aw, Sandow!" he'd say, inflating his own substantial chest and deepening his voice. "What a neck! Like a bull's. 20 inches' neck, 20 inches' biceps!" Or, lifting his hand, as if from the center of an Olympics' stadium toward the stands: "Jesse Owens! Beat all the Germans—proved Hitler wrong! Beat a horse in the 100 meters!"

That last accomplishment seemed out of place, conjuring images for Viraf that could have appeared on the lurid covers of his mother's Mandingo and Drummond novels—her favorite movie ever was *Gone With The Wind*. But once Doordarshan, or Distantvision, brought global sports into Seth Building, his father's admiration still spanned a similar range. "What a champ!" he'd say, watching the golden Borg squeeze passing shot after passing shot between the sideline and a persistently approaching McEnroe. It was finally something Viraf could share with his father, a passion for racket sports. They hadn't known whether to cheer or cry when, in protest against apartheid, India refused to play South Africa and forfeited the Davis Cup finals.

Despite Viraf's boxing ineptitude during fresher ragging at IIT, he got caught up in his dad's excitement over the rumbles in Zaire and thrillers in Manila. When naming the hero of both wars—who'd fought an entire government to oppose a real war—Aspi was torn between the crisp, foreign sound of Cassius Clay and the very Indian sound of Muhammad Ali. He chose to eliminate neither in his exclamations. Viraf and his IIT pals sang along to the Kinshasa Band, hailing Ali's ability to float like a butterfly and sting like a bee. He was struck by the concept, one he'd never seen in comicbooks, of a black Superman.

He glanced at Will, whose reach on the tennis court when they'd played had felt like Elastic Man's. Here they were, talking about Pintos and law suits, while Will had no idea of the notions in his friend's head. Or did he? Maybe he was accustomed to such complicated appraisals. Maya had always felt it was the first thing people saw about her, her dark skin. And as surely as he'd once tried to reassure her, Viraf had given her reason to believe it again.

They'd often strolled down an avenue behind the institute, under drumstick trees and banyans. Great roots stood like crutches from the branches to the ground. When they turned toward a field, leaves rustled underfoot. As soon as they were on the grass, she slipped her hand into his. It aroused him more than when, in his second year, he'd slept with a town-girl. Earthy smells enveloped them. They sat on the grass and spoke of random things, skirting those uppermost in his mind.

"Movie's changing at Mahal this Friday," he said.

"Thank God; that stupid *Majnu ki Aulad* has been running so long." She plucked a blade and flipped it away. Behind her, the sun bobbed on the horizon, by the cream institute tower. "What's its name?"

"Can't remember—another old movie. Meena Kumari's in it."

"Ya? She's so beautiful, na?" And she cocked an eyebrow.

"Ya, quite beautiful." The veteran actress had passed away, so he was safe enough. And it gave him an opening. "But nowhere near you."

A smile twitched her lips. "Don't lie."

"I swear," he said, putting forefinger and thumb to his throat.

The sun set. The tower's windows reflected it, winking and stuttering like Morse code.

"You don't wish," she started, and hesitated before finishing the sentence, "that I was fair like her?"

It took him a second to adjust. "Fair?"

"Yes. Like all the North Indian girls. Like Kamini." She put a hand up to the side of his face. "Like you."

"That's humbug," he said. And her hand came down. He'd never thought of himself as fair, especially when half the Parsis he knew were lighter-skinned and made a big thing about it. "All that gora-gori BS—why're you swallowing it like that?"

"You don't know what it's like to be dark." She was looking down in disappointment. "Just like Kamini, no idea."

"As if Kamini looks so great with those pimples. Fair, unfair, what difference?"

She started to giggle. "Fair, unfair! There are also South Indian girls who are fair, you know? Look at Hema Malini and Sridevi—otherwise you think they could have become actresses?"

There wasn't much he could say to that, but why did it sound like an accusation? "First of all, Bombay isn't North India, okay?" It wasn't South India either, but probably best not to say so. That one day he'd use her insecurity to take revenge on her did not even remotely occur to him. "Secondly..."

He couldn't think of a second point. So he said, "Come here," and brought her close. The seconds passed, her hands quiet at his waist. Then she relaxed against him and turned her face up to be kissed.

After Rangan took over, it was a different story. Imtiaz and Viraf cycled to Anarkali's for dinner one day. It was a sultry evening, so open-air seating was a good idea. The huts near Gole Bazar were all playing the same station's movie songs, so as they passed each hut, the music lifted and fell. A herd of goats, scurrying the other way, challenged their slow-cycling skills, before they broke through and turned into Anark.

Once they stood their Heros up and locked the wheels, they walked over to the tables, only to find Rangan and Maya at one. And then it didn't seem such a good idea, but it was too late to turn around. Everyone waved grudgingly, and Rangan made a show of insisting that they join them. Maya, on the other hand, looked uncomfortable and fell to rearranging a red dupatta around her neck and shoulders. She had on a sand-colored salvar-kameez.

The discussion, apart from the Punjabi menu, centered around their job prospects, GRE results, and applications for scholarships. Getting recommendations from profs was a pain, they all agreed, and it was tough sensing which prof might give them a bad reco behind their backs. The chances of Rangan and Maya going abroad were low, they said: they wanted schols at the same university or wouldn't go at all. Touchingly, they'd applied to an identical set of colleges and were crossing their fingers.

When the waiter came, they ordered an assortment to share: matar paneer, chicken makhani, veg pulav, naan, and Maya's choice, fish curry. The men were tired of eating the mess hall's Bengali version day in and day out, but the waiter assured them that this curry was Punjabi-style like the makhani. It tickled Viraf to see how much, out of their parents' sight, the Hindus enjoyed their meats. Imtiaz, he knew, was not about to eat pork, no matter where. When the curry came, Maya wanted to know what kind of fish it was: pomfret?

"Fish is hilsa, memsahab," the waiter said, smiling apologetically. "In Bengal you know how much they like. Pomfret has to come from Calcutta, more expensive."

"Oh, God," she said, smiling back. "Okay. I thought Punjabi would be at least rawas or something, na?"

"Sorry, memsahab," he said, and left.

"Even hilsa is good for you," she said, spooning it generously over steaming pulav, well aware the men had little taste for the bony Bengali favorite. "Fish has lots of protein."

"And vitamins," Rangan said.

She looked approving. "The Bengali girls swear it's good for your complexion."

Viraf had a second to hold back. But Ahriman had slipped into him, and there was no stopping the impulse.

"Mm," he said, nodding. "No wonder you took such a big helping."

Her face collapsed. Her eyes dropped to the table cover. Rangan's lips tightened, but Imtiaz burst into wild laughter—he clapped Viraf on the back.

"Too good," Imtiaz said, between loud, systemic roars that brought looks from other tables. Like Viraf, he'd never forgotten her verbal slap in the face, and his reply with a physical one had caused him no remorse. Nor had she forgiven him. Sending the fish back to her, he said, "You should take more, Maya—it's good for your complexion."

For Viraf there was a small feeling of release, of having found some repayment. It was a soothing perspective that permitted generosity. He soft-pedaled his remarks to her, the rest of the evening. But she was quiet and withdrawn, her fish left untouched. And Rangan remained tight-lipped, even curt, so only Imtiaz stayed in high spirits and drove what little conversation there was.

Viraf's feeling of reparation lasted almost the rest of the term. By then, they all knew where they were headed—for the time being, anyway. When on better terms, they'd agreed that, wherever each of them landed, twenty-five years later they'd reunite at the Eiffel Tower. It seemed the perfect place.

For now, Imtiaz was triumphantly off to Columbia, Maya and Rangan still together to jobs in Bombay, and Viraf on his way to Delaware. He was no longer sure his little revenge had really meant much.

At Deer Park, the salami pizza pie was hot with melted cheese. And Will's ginger-lime steak oozed pink and brown juice. Viraf almost suggested they share, but didn't think Will would like to. People didn't do that here. They each got the dish they wanted, then stuck to it. At best, if they were a couple like Doug and Ali, they'd swap morsels, irritatingly, on a fork. Never a spoon, all kinds of dishes with just fork and knife. Even if your pie was dripping with cheese, you couldn't spoon it up.

Doug should have warned him about the Pinto up front. It made him look like a fool, not to mention put him in danger every single time he drove it.

They left tips for the waitress, who passed them on their way out, saying, "G'bye. Drive safe." A young guy in a Blue Hens cap was playing Asteroids. Nitin often freaked out over the sophistication of even the games in this country. They could hear the pa-pow, pow, pow as a tiny spaceship maneuvered within an asteroid belt, barely escaping the hurtling rocks, swiveling adroitly to zap them into bits. At the door the cold kicked in, and Viraf zipped up his jacket and yanked on his gloves.

The snow had stopped falling. But daylight was low—the air seemed darker without the flakes. Enough had accumulated on the sidewalk that their feet sank in. Viraf looked up, as they crossed, to find the sky was all gray. Shivering a little, he lengthened his stride. It felt as if something was winding down.

PART II

WORLD GONE BAD

CHAPTER 9

Cowboys and Indians, I

The times they were, quite literally, a-changing. Twice a year, Americans altered their clocks and watches to Daylight Savings Time. When the nights grew longer, they moved the time back an hour. When the days lengthened, they moved it forward an hour.

At the spring equinox in March, his mother's letter from halfway around the world reminded him, instead, of Parsi New Year. Make sure, she wrote, you get together and celebrate Navroz with other Parsis. What Parsis, where? He was the only Parsi among the Indian students and probably the only one in Delaware, for all he knew.

Dr. Reese wasn't well and had asked him to handle two Monday morning classes for him—return their mid-term exams and go over the solutions. Viraf wondered why Reese had not been given a TA for Engineering Systems, but he was happy to help.

He wanted to be ahead of the students, so he walked into Mitchell Hall at ten minutes to nine. Sure enough, only one student was already at his desk, blond head bent over, writing something. Stack of papers in hand, Viraf strode toward the teaching podium. He liked the idea of being up there, for a change.

"Engineering Systems?" he asked the guy, to confirm he was in the right place.

The student nodded. "I'm the only one left. We didn't think anyone was coming."

Viraf didn't know what he meant. Checking his Seiko, he said, "It's just ten to nine."

A subtle play of expressions crossed the student's face. His gaze shifted over Viraf to the clock on the wall. Viraf turned to see what it said, and for an open-mouthed moment thought he was still on acid time.

Then it came to him. Last October, he'd been floored by the idea that the time was something you could alter for your convenience. The trouble was, if you didn't own a TV and didn't have the car radio on when a deejay mentioned it, then your watch was still set the way it had been for the past half a year, while everyone else's had changed.

He turned back to the student, a slim guy in longish shorts—even the length of shorts was changing. Neither of them said another word. He fished out the guy's paper, then left him to it. It had struck Viraf that he could still make it to the ten o'clock class.

He dashed across the lawns to Evans and up to the classroom, then slowed to a walk, breathing hard. The students were still buzzing on stepped benches. A few even strolled in after him, and he started to feel better, more in control up at the professor's desk.

After they stormed the desk to get their papers, he went up to the green board and announced he'd go over the solutions for them. One of the guys promptly asked if he had to stay for that.

Viraf shrugged. "Not if you don't want to know the solutions."

Upon which, a great rustle arose as almost all of them gathered their books and hurried out. He was left looking uncertainly at just two girls and a guy spread around the benches.

It was all a bit unsettling.

On a Saturday night after Longwood, Viraf had been in the Pinto by himself, suppressing thoughts of its history. Nitin, who now owned a '68 Nova, was having dinner with a salesgirl he'd met in the bicycle store on Main Street. And the band had a gig at a Wilmington bar. They'd asked if Viraf wanted to come along, but he'd said he had work. It wasn't entirely true. He had a feeling the sheet of acid might be circulating after the gig, if not before.

Physically, he'd been fine after Longwood, though the floating period, coming down, had lasted well through the night. What hadn't left him was the shock of seeing the world that had stood so solidly around him all his life dissolve without warning into the shifting, purple land. And of feeling the eerie elasticity of time, on whose regularity, too, he'd thought he could depend.

So, rather than sit at home after dinner, he was out for a drive—and there was still light outside. Even now, after dinner, the streetlights were just coming on. This time, he drove east on 273. Above the open road, dark striations played against an inverted bowl of a sky that, in spite of his wheels, seemed to limit how far he could go. Soon the brown of night came over the highway, and he clicked on his headlights.

Overhead signs for Chestnut Hill and Ogletown had appeared and disappeared, when the wail of a police car made him jump. Blue and red flashes lit the rearview as he pulled over to the shoulder. The cop pulled over behind him.

He rolled down his window, as a state trooper in gray wearing a Stetson came up and bent over to peer inside. The flashing lights played on a silver badge and the clean-shaven face of a man in his thirties. His Stetson put Viraf in mind of the sheriffs in Westerns. He wondered if he should deny he'd been speeding. But he had no idea how to address the man, nor even if American policemen took bribes. Traffic cops in Bombay were notorious for it—you could buy them off or threaten them with fictitious family friends among their higher-ups. Imtiaz had claimed to have done both.

It felt like a few seconds before the cop spoke. "Did you know your taillight is out?"

So he hadn't been caught speeding. "My parking lights?"

"Taillight. One on the left."

"No, I didn't know." Presumably, the confirmation was on his face. "It isn't working?"

The cop shook his head, asked for Viraf's license and registration, and went off to the squad car. After a minute just sitting there, wondering when the light had blown and if there was a penalty for such a thing, Viraf found himself fidgeting. He got out and onto the shoulder to stretch his legs.

No sooner had he begun to pace, than a loud, disembodied voice, barely recognizable as the trooper's, startled him. It emanated from the police car.

"I need you to get back in and stay there!" it said. "You're starting to make me nervous."

Viraf quickly held up a hand and returned to the Pinto. It was a revelation that he could be viewed as a danger by a seasoned policeman. In fact, it was a revelation that he could be viewed as a danger, period, instead of an educated, presumably civilized young man.

When the owner of the still wary voice returned to the window, he handed the license and registration back with a printed slip of paper.

"I'll let you off with a warning this time. Get it fixed in the next ten days." He paused. "If we have to stop you after that, you'll get a ticket. Then you'll need to pay a fine or else show up in court."

"Okay, thanks, I'll fix it," Viraf said, relieved at getting off without a fine.

The state trooper strode back to his cruiser. It pulled out, no longer flashing, just a murky long shape in the night. Viraf put the papers in the glove compartment, eased out, and took the next exit back.

Within the hour, he'd forgotten the warning.

The next month, things were still changing. Nitin not only had a girlfriend, Judy the bicycle salesgirl, he'd moved out of First State and in with this relative stranger, into her rented house miles away. The speed of it all had taken Viraf by surprise. One week, they were still doing stag things like solving the unknown variable in an X-rated film, the next, Nitin was packing his stuff—not that there was a lot. He offered to find another desi student to move in, in his place.

Viraf said no, thanks, though he'd have liked to continue splitting the rent. Money would be twice as tight now, on the research assistant's stipend. But a part of him was bothered by the transitory nature of the people in his life. What had been the point of getting so close to Imtiaz and Rangan, not to mention Maya, only to end up so far away? So why let a new guy, another stranger, move in and have to learn all about him and have him learn all about you and try to be buddies and so on, only to eventually see him move along too.

Better to relax, have the place to yourself, and make an effort to get together with an already proven friend, even if not as regularly. In fact, that meant getting out of First State more often, for a pleasant drive to Judy's old wooden house in the countryside, south of Newark. Once you were past the university stadium on College Avenue, the road turned into rural 896, just one lane either way at 45 mph, dotted with quaint names like Old Cooch's Bridge and Iron Hill, after which the Deer Park had named its Ginger & Lime steak.

About when you saw signs for Lums Pond of skinny-dipping fame, you turned off onto Porter Road toward Judy's place, passing yards on which wooden deer pranced around windmills, American flags, and private wells. At some point, you bumped over railroad crossings, the road became Porter Station, and you realized what the name meant. If you were from Bombay, you made the connection to the red-turbaned coolies at Victoria Terminus. *Coolie*, in the West, was understood as a disparaging term rather than a profession. Porters, on the other hand, had roads and stations named for them.

So the trains that rumbled behind First State also rumbled near Nitin's new home. The weekend after Viraf helped them move, they invited him over for beef stew, corn, and chicken curry. In the evening light, as he pulled into their dirt driveway behind the Nova, the old house was all pale-blue boards under a grayer shade of shingles. Its winter roof sloped steeply like a Dutch hat, pocked by what Judy called dormer windows. She was only a bit taller than Nitin, her face round like his. They took Viraf up into a musty, cluttered attic, to show him the view from the dormers. The humidity fogged his glasses.

In the cool shadows of the living room, he sat on a faded couch wiping his lenses, as they took turns going in and out of the kitchen, still talking over the counter, she in accents and words that reminded him at times of Megan and at others of the men in the Rising Sun. Nitin had opened a couple of Millers, and they remarked on how differently American beer tasted than Indian. Eventually everyone settled at the kitchen table, the "vittles" steaming lightly in rainbow-striped stoneware. He hesitated when Judy asked if he'd say grace with them, but he nodded. Following Nitin's lead, he inclined his head with his hands in his lap, as she thanked God for the good food He'd sent them that night.

The curry smelled better than it tasted: no less watery than Nitin had ever made it in their incompetent and infrequent attempts to cook at First State. So Viraf could compliment the thick and meaty stew instead, confident his words were reaching the right person. He saw quick confirmation in her eyes, hazel like Bernie's, under a brown shade of hair.

Thanking Viraf, smiling easily, she was pleasant company. They compared her ten-speed bike with the Hero he'd ridden in Kharagpur—Indian bikes were mostly basic. Hers took her on marathon races to Philadelphia and back. Trophy cups bookended her fireplace mantel. But, however sporty and nice, she had just a handful of college credits and at the moment was taking no courses. He wondered how that would match up with a grad student, not to mention a high-caste Hindu who, nevertheless, had accompanied her to church that Sunday morning. Now he was digging into her beef stew, as he had into burgers at McDonald's.

The conversation continued in the living room, slowed by a double helping of Rocky Road that thickened Viraf's tongue. To make her laugh, he griped about Daylight Savings Time, and Nitin joined in, teasing her. Viraf considered getting a laugh out of his TAing fiasco, but decided against it—it just made him look like an idiot. Bad enough he drove a Pinto.

Eventually he was walked out by Nitin, who was clearly in a good mood about his new situation. They stood around, exchanging sexual innuendos over the sound of crickets. Then Viraf got in the Pinto, reversed it, and headed back along the approach.

*

The path looked narrower in his headlights, and in the quiet he heard the tires crunch dirt until he turned onto Porter and trundled over railroad crossings. In his head, he could hear those trains rumble. The empty road was lit more by the night sky than by intermittent streetlamps. It opened up as he came to the T-junction with 896. He slowed to a stop and looked left before turning.

There was a clear, straight view along his single lane, nothing coming. So he let out the clutch and made the right, then shifted into second and stepped on the gas.

He was moving up to third, when something blew by to the left, so close and fast its wind pushed the Pinto sideways. As it rocked back toward the center, he saw a dark van streak ahead, arcing across the yellow line into his northbound lane. It had barely missed him. Suddenly the van slowed, and he found himself catching up.

As he drew nearer, he could tell it was a dark shade of blue, almost black, its chrome reflecting even in nighttime. Resembling a large closed Jeep, it continued to slow. Its right wheels went off the road onto a dirt shoulder, until it had almost pulled over.

But when he moved up to pass, his wheels over the yellow line, it sped up and kept pace with him. Steel letters on its front panel read *Bronco*. As its open window came abreast, he saw the driver, a man about thirty with his head turned to him, and one of the passengers, a woman in her twenties craning around the man for a look.

The driver was mouthing something down at Viraf, his index finger stabbing over at the dirt shoulder. Two things started to happen inside Viraf: an unrest in his head and another in his stomach. The first made him gather his brows and gesture, What do you mean—you're the one who almost ran into me.

But the finger became more frenetic in its insistence. The third passenger leaned across the woman, a younger man mouthing something, and the queasiness in Viraf's stomach took over. The evening's good mood was gone, and the last thing he wanted was an ugly shouting match.

He kept going.

The Bronco shuddered ahead and pulled onto the road in front of him. Then it slowed to a crawl. He pulled around it and accelerated, but in seconds its headlights were right behind him, high beams reflecting into his eyes. The hulking vehicle inched closer to his bumper, and he had a vision of the rear-ended Pinto catching fire. He tried to pull away again, but the Bronco roared close on his tail.

They were approaching town through Four Seasons now, past eleven on a Sunday night, the roads empty and Newark at rest before the workweek. He tried to think of what to do. Leading them straight to First State didn't feel like a good idea. Even if he could get into Building H quick enough, they'd know exactly where he lived. Or if he tried to reason with them and they made a big thing of it—

But that was ridiculous: it was their fault in the first place; they must have been speeding like crazy. Or had it been his fault in some way? How slow was he moving after the turn? In any case, nothing had really happened, luckily for *him*, given the Bronco's size and the brilliant design of his gas tank.

Still, if they did kick up a row, then Doug and Ali or the UD guys on the second level might hear their fellow Americans cursing him, and he'd have to tell them about it the next day. Or right away, if they came out to check, dragged out of bed in the middle of the night. He'd look, for the world to see, like someone who couldn't even drive around without getting into trouble. Just the sort of fool who drove a Pinto.

As he eyed the rearview, the Bronco's headlights swung to the left and into his sideview, pulling alongside. Maybe he could swerve onto the I-95 exit coming up on his right and open up some distance before they could turn onto the highway. Maybe they'd say fuck it, at that point, and go home.

A trucklike grille and front end passed his line of sight. Then he was looking at them again, the trio he'd see for years, taking in more now in better light. The flannel and glimpses of denim... The smaller guy at the passenger window, brown-haired, clean-shaven... The girl's blond hair and something about her face, he wasn't sure what... The big man at the wheel, a darker shade of blond, second-day stubble on his face...

He leaned across the others to yell through the open window. Viraf rolled his down. The wind snatched at the man's voice, but phrases came through.

"...follow you anywhere, motherfucker...full tank of gas...gotta stop sometime..."

Viraf's throat tightened. In a flash he saw his father, possessed by Ahriman, shouting crazily at the Howrah Express passenger through the compartment window before his mother intervened. The Bronco dropped behind again, and he checked his fuel gauge—about a third left. So much for the thought of just driving forever.

He let the exit go.

Something was fogging his specs, and he rolled his window up. He was not going to get out of this so easily. They'd have to talk it out...the question was where. What about a police station? But where? And even if he could find one, would they be open so late? If they were, that was his answer. These crazy idiots could throw words around all they wanted to in front of the cops, and he'd never have to see them again. Nor worry about what anyone else thought.

And that was when he remembered the taillight. He hadn't fixed it, as the state trooper had told him to. Within ten days. He didn't even know how many had passed, but it was before the scramble of Nitin moving out. Back when the time had changed, the week after Longwood. Forget about ten days, it had almost been a month. Why the fuck hadn't he remembered?

He could vaguely recall considering where to take it, what kind of place would fix a taillight, et cetera. It was bound to be a cheap job, small taillight... probably just replace the bulb. He could do that himself if he knew where to get a new one. And now, instead, he was looking at a fine on top of everything. Who knew how much they fined you for such things, but the cop had sounded serious, something about showing up in court if you didn't pay. And he'd sounded anything but friendly. I don't like you foreigners, his tone had said; you make me nervous.

Even worse, what if... Maybe that explained what had happened: with only the right taillight on, maybe the Bronco thought the single light was a motorcycle, plenty of room to go by. So what? They were still going a hundred fucking miles over the limit. If not for that, they'd have seen him well in time; it wasn't that dark. But to the cops they'd simply deny they were speeding, whereas he couldn't deny the taillight. To the cops, then, he'd be the foreigner already breaking the law, despite a written warning. *He* was the one who made them nervous.

So it came down to handling it himself. Maybe that was for the best— going to the police would be like a green fresher in Patel Hall running off to the warden's office to complain about ragging. Best to just pick a place and get the argument over. The stadium complex was behind them now, and they were coming into the university area on South College. If not First State, then why not the other end of his daily route, a place he knew his way around? He could enter Evans Hall through the back door, if he managed to get there ahead of them. Not likely, they were sticking so close, but it was better than no plan. And someone would be there, working late. Even if it was Will or one of the foreign-student assistants, they'd understand.

Coming up to East Delaware, he made a right, and the Bronco stayed on his bumper. Impossible, now, to give them the slip. Better not even look like he was trying. He indicated the turn on Academy Street and onto the access lane for the lab. The road curved around to the parking behind Evans, a rough triangle with the department, laboratory, and storage for its sides.

But it was twilit and empty, no one there.

It looked different that way. Just the dumpster to one side.

For an instant of renewed hope, the Bronco was no longer in his rearview—maybe they'd wondered where he was leading them and decided to turn back. But it rounded the corner, parking quickly as he pulled up in the middle and cut the engine.

He got out, locking the door, and took a step toward Evans as the Bronco's doors opened. At the center of this concerted movement, the young woman sat still. In an instant he saw that her face, its broad, almost innocent prettiness, reminded him of Ali's. That put the little group in perspective, just another trio of young Americans like Doug, Ali, and Bernie. A sort of calm came over him.

The area was lighted overhead, illuminating the bigger man as he stepped down from the wheel and flipped his door shut. Its thud gave way to the sound of crickets and the scritch-scratch of boots over pavement. Faintly, in the distance, Viraf heard the rumbling of a freight train. Then the big American was in front of him, taller by inches, and he looked up into those blue eyes for the first time. They held his own, regarding him unblinkingly, even as he became aware of the second guy coming up to his right.

There was a controlled edge to the big man's voice. "What do you think you were doing back there?"

Viraf struggled to make sense of the question, feeling his forehead knot and his calm start to slip. "What was *I* doing?" he said, hearing the tension in his voice. "I was turning onto an empty road. How many miles were *you* doing?"

The stranger's voice took on a rasp, and he flipped a thumb at the Bronco. "See my car there? See the paint?" It was as if he hadn't heard Viraf's question. "You can see your face in it. One month off the lot...one month off the lot, and you woulda fucked up my new car!"

Viraf was transfixed by the widening blue eyes. "Listen, I didn't do anything to your car. Nothing really even—"

But those eyes had gone manic, and the voice that overrode his and froze it into silence had turned to a bellow: "You hear me? DO YOU HEAR ME, YOU GODDAM DAGO?"

Maybe he was paralyzed by the sheer rage, such apparent hate blasted at him. Maybe a part of him was confused, distracted by the unfamiliar word, trying to gather what he'd been called. Maybe his peripheral vision, uncorrected by his glasses as he stared into lunatic eyes, couldn't pick up a blur off to the side.

Whatever the case, the right hand of the big American must have begun its hidden, elliptical swing before the final word was uttered, must have been coming around as Viraf took in the absurdly rhetorical question. He was struggling for words, when something like a pile driver slammed into his head, and he was spinning. Then pain erupted from the left side of his jaw.

The blow unseated his glasses, sent him staggering toward the other man, who must have known what was about to happen as soon as the argument began. His fist drove into Viraf's stomach, doubling him up before he could bring his hand to his jaw. As his breath grunted out, the man grabbed his arms from behind and pinned them back.

The bigger man moved in, shouting, "Do you hear me, you stupid wop?"

His fist drove into Viraf's body as he twisted free. It hit his ribs at an angle, but he was off-balance, turning his head and lifting his hands to take the other man's blows on his arms, when for a moment his eyes fell on the woman in the Bronco. She was sitting there, upright, looking straight at him, drinking in the spectacle with a thin smile on her face.

It crushed something in him, that cold little smile.

The next instant, the second man's fist cracked home to the side of his face, sending his glasses flying. He reeled backward, unseeing, everything a blur through which the smaller, more relentless man reappeared, rushing him, cornering him against the dumpster ringing hollow against his back. It gave off a faint stench.

The man's knees drove up at Viraf's crotch again and again. He jerked reflexively away from them, fending them off, catching them on his palms and his thighs.

But his balls were already broken, and he was scrambling toward the rear door of Evans, hearing the slap of feet behind him and the big man's voice, "Let him go," as he reached the steps.

Then the blessed door in front, and fumbling for the key, listening for the feet to come up at him, stooping desperately to see the keyhole without his specs. Now he was in and slamming the door behind him, slumping against it to the floor, insipid trickles in his mouth, breathing raggedly in the dim, empty hallway.

His mind stayed blank as he looked into nothingness, feeling his heart pump, hearing his breath. A confusion of pain still coursed through him. Then a thought, and his heart began to pound. The Pinto.

He listened for sounds through the door and thought he heard something. Reaching up along the doorjamb, he dragged himself to his feet. What were they doing—slashing its tires? Kicking its sides in? Smashing the windows, the windshield, the headlights?

He put a shaking hand to the doorknob, but his muscles refused to turn it. The blood hammered in his ears, and he broke into sweat. He knew he had to go out and—and what? His mind shrank from finishing the thought. The hand would not stop shaking, but he turned it and yanked the door open.

They were gone. Only the Pinto in the lot, its rust coat untouched. He hobbled to it, looking for his glasses along the way. A slow walk around the car revealed nothing until he got to the driver's side: the sideview had been broken off. Kicked off, probably.

He picked it up in a daze and searched for his glasses, bending low to spot them. They turned up halfway to the dumpster, the lenses knocked out of the frame. They were glass, ground by Baliwalla & Homi, not the new, unbreakable plastic. Now they lay cracked and splintered, the metal frame mangled.

He picked up the frame, moving it to the hand that held the sideview. Looking down on them, he was hit by a fear that the Bronco might return. Leaving the broken lenses where they were, he stumbled to the car and unlocked it.

The Pinto started up as if nothing had happened. He put it in gear and crawled out of the inner area. With the car rolling toward First State, the fear dissipated, giving way to something else. Something like hate. If they showed up now, he'd ram their fucking precious new car. And run them over if they got out. The woman, too.

CHAPTER 10

Cowboys and Indians, II

When he awoke the next morning, he was aching in his jaw and thighs. His ribs and stomach felt bruised, as he dragged himself over to the bathroom. He had to get on his knees and peer into the toilet bowl, in order to check without his glasses, and the smell of his own shit made him sick. But he couldn't spot any blood. He washed his face, bringing his eyes close to the mirror: he looked tired, and a purple bruise had exploded on his right cheek. A spot on his tongue felt raw where his own tooth had stabbed it.

After a shower, he stretched out on the couch beneath the window line, and stayed there for hours. His myopic vision settled on a frayed area of fabric—it was a Goodwill sofa that Nitin and he had picked up for pennies, along with much of the spare furnishing. Mohan Bhagia, of the boasted campus orgies, had helped transport it to First State in his used pickup.

Behind the beige threads flitted images of the three Americans, in colors Viraf hadn't noted the night before: the faded reds and yellows of their flannel shirts, the flush of their sunburned faces, the plain white of the girl's top. All bathed in a yellow glow from the overhead lamp. He saw again their changing expressions, the intensity of the big man shifting into rage, the anticipation on the smaller man's face, held back at first though evident now, then the open aggression. And, over and over, the woman's smile.

In his mind, they reenacted their long dance, all four of them, from Porter Road to Evans Hall. He second-guessed his every scattered thought when reaching the decision to stop and talk, then acknowledged its logic, then questioned it all over again. Most of all, what had made him think he could reason with them or imagine they'd had the slightest intention to do anything other than beat him to a pulp for putting his fucking Pinto in front of their precious Bronco? Aspi Adajania would be justified in berating his son for yet again having shown a lack of common sense.

He heard again the man's unhearing insistence on being heard—Do you hear me? Do you hear me? And he heard the names he was called: dago, wop. He knew they were insults or slurs, but not exactly what they meant. The "motherfucker" part of it he knew wasn't literal, so he discounted it. But not the "stupid" part. He'd proved himself worthy of that one. A more unthinking, unseeing, sitting duck than himself, standing open-mouthed in front of the big American as that hand came swinging around, he could not imagine.

Time and time again he returned to a central question: where had that boiling hate and anger and contempt toward an absolute stranger come from? What lay behind it? How could it all have been inspired by an accident that never happened? The contrast between Satput Singh's self-control, when cut off on Bombay roads, and Aspi's vituperative outbursts had taught Viraf that there was a wide range of reactions. But even his father had never beaten anyone up for bad driving.

Although in Viraf's interest, his father's enraged, almost crazed threats at the offending passenger to Howrah seemed a better comparison at first, especially in light of what he'd thought was his mother's subtle approval. But threats, no matter how violent, with the recipient safe behind a wall were not the same as threats followed by an actual, all-out, two-on-one assault. Viraf had always doubted if, had push come to shove, his father would have climbed into the train and really laid a hand on the stranger, let alone tried to break his head.

In retrospect, the altercation had the sound of two warring bears standing up on their hind legs to bellow at each other until the smaller one dropped to his fours and prudently turned tail. At which point, Aspi had allowed himself to be led away without a murmur.

And even if Viraf had been right about the undertones in his mother's voice, about the thoughts behind her words, her actions were to calm his father and defuse the situation, once her son's interest had been served. She hadn't looked upon a bare-knuckled beating and smiled.

Tuesday morning, he opened the yellow pages to Opticians and Automobile Repair. Then he ventured out, with a quick wave to Lynette loitering around the stairway. After her housemate had moved on from halfway to all the way out, she'd seemed lost but more adventurous, taking strolls, waggling her head, and smiling vaguely at the shrubs. He left the Pinto where it was in the parking line and walked stiffly up the streets, feeling the sun start to loosen his aching body.

Inside the air-conditioned Delaware Vision Center, a thousand new frames looked out from their housing. The fuzzy woman behind the counter joked about the shape his old frame was in. Upon getting no response, she asked for his prescription. He didn't have one, so she signed him up to see the optometrist. Neither of them mentioned his bruise. After refraction, a blurry Dr. Hansen presented him with one prescription for glasses and another for contacts.

"Have you considered wearing contacts?" The voice was quiet, older.

"No." He shook his head. "In India they're a recent thing, mainly for women."

"Ah, India." The doctor appeared to be smiling. "I was wondering where you're from. Once you spoke, I thought maybe India, but I wasn't sure."

"Mm." Viraf was in no mood for small talk or the inability of Americans to tell where he was from. "What are the advantages and disadvantages?"

Dr. Hansen looked disconcerted at being called back to business, yet Viraf realized he didn't care anymore. He'd always given too much of a shit about what people thought and about fitting in. Doug said Megan was a pleaser, and Viraf, who'd never heard of that but understood it right away, felt it applied to a side of him that seemed pointless now.

All business now, the doctor said Viraf would have to clean the lenses nightly. But his vision with lenses right on his cornea would be better than through glasses on the bridge of his nose. And he'd have better peripheral vision, closer to the wide angle of an eyeball.

Only half listening until then, Viraf sat up and paid attention. If he could have seen out of the side of his eye, he might have picked up the stranger's oncoming hand before it hit him.

"Okay, I'll try them," he said, mildly excited.

Well, then, the doctor said, what kind would he prefer? The old hard lens was more durable, the new soft lens more comfortable, and in between was the semi-permeable. Oxygen could pass through it to the cornea. Once his inner eyelid hardened from wearing it enough, he wouldn't feel it any more than a soft lens.

So he opted for the semi-permeable, remembering how his fingertips had hardened from playing guitar, back in Patel Hall. The doctor set him up with a starter kit and demonstrated how to insert the lens. Thrusting this tiny, curved piece of plastic into his open eye felt so counter-intuitive, he backed off and took stock of it. It was tinted a bluish gray to make it easier to find if dropped.

But on the third try it was in and floating like magic, invisible on his dark pupil. The left lens went in easily and his bruise came into focus in the mirror. So did the doctor's silver hair and buttoned-down collar. Only now did Viraf note that the man wore glasses himself, in a conventional tortoiseshell frame.

"How come *you* don't wear contacts?" he asked.

Dr. Hansen took the glasses off and in the same forward motion presented the lenses for inspection: at the base of each was a smaller, semi-circular, separately cut portion, like a lens within a lens. "Bifocals. Won't be long before we have them in contacts. Come back in a year, and you might see this old man without glasses."

Viraf had to smile at that. He felt a momentary pang over the disrespectful way he'd addressed an elder.

Back out on South Chapel, kit in hand, he headed for the university, blinking at the sudden glare. But apart from the need to squint, everything around him, the street, the fire hydrant, the walls, the footpath, looked unusually sharp. There was a sense of being free of the old contraption that had sat on his nose for nine years of his life, digging into it, getting heavier, cutting into his ears, and making him dizzy. Maybe those bastards had done him a favor when they stomped on his glasses and crushed them.

Never had he seen so clearly.

He took the long way to Morris Library, avoiding Evans. The campus colors looked heightened—trees a glossier green, bricks a ruddier brown—as if brushed by a layer of sun.

He trudged up the steps of the building, past the robed bust of Mr. Morris, whoever he was, and over to the enormous unabridged dictionary lying open on a wooden stand. Half a million words and their meanings. The last person to consult it had opened outsized pages that wound around from *nucleiform* to *nurse*. Between them, the student might have looked up *nude* or *number* or *numskull* or *nuplex*, there was no way to know which. He or she might even have investigated the Hindi *nullah*. Viraf flipped to D and looked up *dago*.

Its root was the Spanish name Diego, and in English it meant "a dark-skinned person of Italian, Spanish, Portugese, or other Latin descent." It was slang, the dictionary added, and a "vulgar term of prejudice and contempt." Except for an emphasis on Italian descent, the entry for *wop* said practically the same thing. He abandoned the dictionary, leaving the page exposed. The next student checking the dictionary would never know if it had been opened for *wool burier* or *woozy* or *workaday* or even *word*.

When he stepped out on the lawns, his mood had darkened again, and the extreme brightness felt like a joke. The bastards had no idea who they were beating up. Just a dark-skinned foreigner who fit some established picture in their minds.

He remembered a bit of doggerel that Mamaiji, who'd picked up some choice little pieces in St. Joseph's Convent, would spout at breakneck speed if anyone criticized her: "Sticks and stones may break my bones, but words will never harm me."

Not true. Not even in India, where communal digs were cleverly derived from a minority's own lexicon, then ironically rendered with a pseudo-respectful ji: sardarji, bawaji. And here where his community wasn't known, he was a dago or a wop. Or if his lineage was recognized, he was a fuckin' I-rainian told to go home.

By the time he reached First State, the contacts felt scratchy when he blinked, and his eyeballs were heavy. An hour later he had to pop the lenses out and store them. Then he was back on the couch, surprisingly drained. Dr. Hansen had said he'd need to build up to wearing the lenses all day. Only now, feeling the lightness and relief against his eyelids, did he realize that improved peripheral vision came with a catch. Yes, he might spot an oncoming blow. But maybe he should have opted for the soft lens. If his eye were hit, wouldn't the lens cut into it?

His mind drifted to other times he'd been hit, in twenty-two years of life. During the initial ragging period at IIT, one of the seniors had ordered freshers to box, teaching them to hit and be hit for Patel Hall.

"What all can you do?" Milind, the slightly built senior, had said in a reedy voice. He, too, had arrived from Bombay on the Howrah Express. Because of his ordinary appearance Viraf thought of him as Milind the Everyman. "You want to join Patel Hall, the oldest and greatest hall in IIT, you should show you will be useful members. Patel is inter-hall champion in so many things. Our wing, by itself, has so many famous students. That is how we had the points to get A Top rooms in our final year."

Viraf had begun to see how seriously the Patelians took their immediate surroundings: prominent students were famous, in their microcosm of society.

"Who can box?" No one spoke. "Come on, try on these gloves."

Milind went to his concrete shelves, and out came two pairs of boxing gloves. The plush black cushions felt springy as Viraf tied one on. Milind ordered Rangan to help with the other glove, then sent him over to Imtiaz. Suddenly, Viraf's fists felt bulky and powerful. He held them awkwardly at his waist.

Rangan returned to his spot, and, in a row, the freshers awaited orders.

"Take off your specs," Milind said.

Viraf fumbled at his frame, the gloves tipping it before he thought he'd touched it. Bowing to slide it off, he cradled it clumsily between the puffy gloves, unable to feel the weight. Out of habit, he tried to juggle it into his shirt-pocket, but the senior ordered him to put it on the desk.

He felt his way to the desk. Back in line, he squinted at the faceless figures in a room without edges. His gloved fists now hung by his sides. The feeling of power had vanished, replaced by a fog and the beginnings of a headache.

The ground between his feet looked like concrete slab, but even that was too fuzzy to be certain. From an initial prescription of just 0.5 diopters, his glasses had grown thicker despite his obedient wearing, until, sitting uselessly on the desk, they measured 3.0. When Soona, who read as much as him, had to be tested, he was still doggedly wearing his black-plastic frame and already up to 1.5. She, worried about her looks, had refused to wear specs except in lectures or theaters. To his amazement and envy, her lack of reliance continued year after year and increased to where she hardly ever pulled them out of her purse. She never wore them around her boyfriends.

"Okay," Milind's voice said. "You two turn to each other."

Viraf turned toward Imtiaz and they lifted their gloves. Even three feet away, his schoolmate's sharp features were blurred, his black mustache a smudge.

"Now fight!"

A moment ticked by, then Imtiaz moved and they lumbered at each other, leading awkwardly with their lefts. Imtiaz's pushed through and padded off Viraf's shoulder. Self-consciously they stopped to check if Milind was satisfied.

"Hit properly, or I'll put your head in the brainwash," said Everyman, gesturing through his wall toward flushable toilets.

They promptly lifted their gloves, circled for openings, swung wildly and missed. Seen without glasses, those roundhouse rights seemed to come into view out of nowhere—as would a big American's years later. Then Imtiaz charged, and Viraf's tennis footwork, backpedaling for an overhead, kicked in to slip the gloves that ballooned in his face.

But the court here was tiny. His shoulders hit wall, and before he could slide off it, a glove slammed into his temple, ringing his head. It spun as if he were seasick.

Imtiaz stopped punching and waited for Viraf to move off the wall. Dizzily, he did so.

"Okay, Ahmed," Milind said. "Get back in line. Adajania, you are no good. Do Simpson's Chair."

And he gestured downward with his palm.

"Sir, I don't know what that is." The words came out slurred and thick.

"Bend your knees as if you're sitting. And stretch your arms in front."

Viraf attempted the position gingerly, his head still spinning.

"Lower. Your thighs must be parallel to the floor and your back must be vertical."

He lowered his arse and almost toppled backwards.

"Make your arms straight."

He teetered into position.

"Okay, no movement. Stay like that till I tell you."

Still giddy, he tried to lock the straining muscles of his back and thighs. No sooner did he manage a precarious balance than his outstretched arms began to ache. A hatred for his tormentor flared in his head. And fuck that Britisher Simpson, whoever he was. Viraf yearned for the good old Gandhi chair, crosslegged on the floor.

That shot to his temple from Imtiaz, five years ago, had rung Viraf's head, but it had been cushioned by a glove. And far from following up, Imtiaz—ancient enemy, future rival, and friend for life—had backed off immediately, risking disobediance.

The men in the Bronco had not been under orders. Nor had they limited the encounter to an honorable man-to-man. They hadn't even allowed him to set up for a fight, just taken him unawares, then jumped him while he was reeling and beaten him up. They hadn't wanted a fight any more than he had, just a one-way assault.

The blow from Imtiaz was the only other time he'd been hit as an adult, if you considered a seventeen-year-old an adult. Before that, in Campion's upper standards, students were largely exempt from the corporal punishment in lower standards. The Jesuit priests made young misbehavers stick out their palms for stinging cuts from a cane. One of the Scots, Mr. McAllister, bounced his knuckles off the top of your head in jocular fashion that belied how much it hurt and got you to play along with an exaggerated "Ow." When Mr. Gonzales, the drawing teacher, lost patience, he let fly with the duster, straight at the head of the little nuisance, whose reflexes didn't always save him.

Presumably, the need for punishment had decreased as they grew older because their behavior improved. In the tenth standard, though, Mr. Pereira, the physics teacher and general disciplinarian, bandy-legged and stocky and sporting an Elvis pouf, had caught Viraf slipping late into the assembly, after an extended session of table tennis.

Mr. Pereira had assumed a joking manner in front of the class: "Had a good game, Adajania?"

Out of a false sense of ease acquired from wearing long pants with the uniform and being "treated as an adult," Viraf grinned and said, "Yes, sir."

Mr. Pereira had rewarded his admission by slapping him across the face, erasing his smile.

At home, his father, who'd have cursed Mr. Pereira for a bloody makapau had Viraf reported the incident, was almost all bluster and no follow-through in his disciplinary methods. Almost. Their mother was always one to pass the buck to her husband when the children had to prepare for math and science exams. She usually waited till the week before to say, "Aspi, jaana, the kids' exams are next week, haa. Soona, Viraf, show daddy what your portions are this time. Aspi, please, you know they won't do well without you."

This would a) have an immediate, depressing effect on the siblings, who would gladly have managed without him, and b) light a slow fuse in Aspi Adajania, as it became clearer by the minute just how much he'd have to cover, let alone how much he'd forgotten and would need to relearn. "Behroz, why always last-minute like this? As if I don't get enough headache at work!" he'd erupt at some point. "And what have you two been doing the whole term? The whole term!"

When the kids came up with wrong answers, he'd lift a hand and vibrate it as if on the brink of hitting them, shouting, "What? What did you say?" Soona would then burst into tears or Viraf would cower from the hand. But it never actually fell.

Except once, for a different reason. It happened before the Adajanias received a telephone line. Without a phone to let Behroz know of their whereabouts, the kids were expected to come "straight home" after school, on the school bus. Back up on the fifth floor, safe from the hordes of kidnappers apparently just scouring the streets for little children, they were encouraged to stay there and be bookworms—the kind of people their father the sportsman didn't like, even as he built bookshelf after bookshelf to encase them.

One evening, though, Viraf had been too tempted by the sounds of his classmates at play in Campion's back gardens after school. Gilli danda, football, rounders, or just catch with the hard red cricket ball, all of these normally had to end for him with the afternoon break. From the back gardens the group had moved to the grassy Oval to play some more. And from the Oval, it was a short walk to where a couple of them lived, in the flats across from the Cricket Club of India. Reassured by the area's familiarity, he tagged along—even his parents couldn't think there were kidnappers around their beloved CCI.

After the group finally dispersed, he rushed over to Churchgate only to see long lines of people getting off work, waiting for the BEST buses. At that point, there wasn't much difference between waiting to catch a bus and just walking home, so he hurried along the footpath with Queen's Road on his right and the railway lines on his left, reassured by the remaining daylight and his fellow pedestrians, flushed with satisfaction from the unusual amount of activity. It almost dispelled his uneasiness over coming home late.

By the time he turned into the odorous gully below their building and entered the lift, he'd realized that his father would be back from work. Aspi usually left his office near Gowalia Tank around six and made it home through traffic before six-thirty. Now Jadhav, the ragtag liftman in his grubby shorts and vest, gave Viraf the eye as the lift clanked upward. Something was up.

When he got out, the front door opened before he could ring the bell, and his mother, looking harried and relieved and angry all at once, frantically asked what had happened and where he'd been all this time. His father had just returned from searching everywhere, she said, and was about to go to the police.

She stood aside. And in the middle of the hall, glaring, was his father, still in work clothes, lips compressed. No bluster this time, no angry words, no words at all. He just stood there until Viraf slowly stepped forward and looked up at him with open mouth. Then, for the first and only time, he hit his son. It was the "one tight rap" he'd always threatened to deliver.

It stood across the years, that one slap, as evidence that it could happen if the kids went "too far." When they were older, they accused him of being a harsh disciplinarian. "But I didn't actually hit you," he said, apparently aggrieved. "I just acted as if I was going to." And in some ways, after all, it was expected of him, even by them, a sign that someone was watching over them, doing what the head of a family was supposed to do, saying don't stay out of our sight in the dangerous city, when we have no idea where you are.

So one day when their cousin Percy boasted, within the adults' hearing, of how hard and often his father had to hit him, Viraf could boast right back of how his father had slapped him when he got lost. And out of the corner of his eye, he saw the slightest of smiles play over his father's mouth before it was gone. Then he felt sorry he'd let his dad off the hook, publicly applauded him for hitting his son, even though Viraf had really done nothing wrong. He'd just played with his friends, for a change, instead of being boxed up at home because they didn't have a phone like normal families.

So that was it—a grand total of three blows in twenty-one years. In the land of nonviolence. And now, in the space of minutes, he'd lost count of how many. From complete strangers who, too, had wanted to teach him a lesson.

But what? Don't turn onto the road in front of us or we'll beat you up? Or just this is our land and you don't belong here. You don't fit in. Go home. Go home, you fuckin' I-rainian, you motherfuckin' dago. You goddam wop. Do you hear us? Go home.

CHAPTER 11

Cowboys and Indians, III

The next morning, he drove the Pinto to Newark Auto Service on Cleveland, keeping to the slow lane, flinching every time a car passed. Barely two hours later he was on his way back, with functioning taillights and a sideview soldered back on by a mechanic in a grease-streaked overall—the man who fixed it sounded confusingly like the men who'd kicked it off.

If he'd taken the car in a week earlier, he might have been fine. Maybe the blown taillight had something to do with the near miss. Or if not for it, maybe he could have found a police station. His head hurt, thinking of the little things that could have kept the worst from happening. It reminded him of a phrase he'd heard Taylor tease Megan with, when she moaned over something too late to change: Shoulda, woulda, coulda.

He skipped classes and stayed home, the rest of the week. By Friday, he was keeping the lenses in over six hours a day. The calluses were still forming; there was always a point when he couldn't keep them in anymore. That evening, Doug knocked to ask if he'd like to accompany them to a weekend gig in Wilmington. Viraf called out to say he was tired and needed to rest.

Saturday afternoon, he could hear them, Bernie and Ali and the brassy voice of the Moles' vocalist Sean, dark-haired and hung with amulets, as they left the apartment. There was a knock, and Ali asked if he was up for Frisbee in the courtyard. By then the bruise was almost gone. Keeping his face behind the door, he said he'd join them if his work was done.

He did have to work, after all the classes he'd missed. But he wasn't getting much done. His concentration had evaporated and the lenses were scratchy, so he kept looking up from the books. Eventually he took the contacts out. He could read without them. A part of him was tempted to go to the lawn, just watch the Frisbee sail, the guys showing off and badgering Ali when she dropped it or threw a clunker. But another part no longer felt like making an energetic show of camaraderie, thinking up funny things to say, making small talk afterward. So he stayed where he was, and eventually heard them return. Still later, through the window, he saw them stream out of the building, on their way to the Wilmington bar.

The next morning, they were at his door again, with Megan and Taylor, refusing to take no for an answer. Nice of them, he knew. It was a while since he'd seen the couple. They were all heading out to Lums Pond for a picnic, and by now he was tired of sitting at home. So he managed a smile and, grabbing a bag of chips from the kitchen counter, followed them out to the Galaxie.

He climbed in the back with Megan and Taylor, while Bernie sat with Ali and Doug. They talked about the gig, how Sean had brought the house down with "Stairway to Heaven," how some groupies from Newark had tried to pull him onto the floor, how one of them had gotten so drunk that her friends had carried her out. Then for a while the chatter was about Wilmington itself, full of street names Viraf didn't know: Market Street, Rodney Square, Shipley Street, Martin Luther King Boulevard. Ali and Bernie, both from Wilmington, had varying opinions of its hot spots. Viraf tuned out, watching the campus flit by. They turned onto South College.

"Vir, do you know who Caesar Rodney was?"

In the rearview, Viraf noticed Doug had trimmed his beard to stubble-length. The face looked smaller without the beard, less chin than he'd thought.

"Hint: why's Delaware called The First State?"

That was the slogan on the gold-on-blue Delaware license plates. Sometimes he'd see an out-of-state plate: New York was the Empire State, Pennsylvania the Keystone State, New Jersey the Garden State, Kentucky the Bluegrass State, and so on.

"It was a Roman state?" That was the best he could muster, but it got a giggle out of the girls and snickers from the guys.

"Nope. Try again."

"No idea," he said, unable to keep the apathy out of his voice. "Just tell me."

"We were the first state"—there was a drop-off in Doug's exuberance before it picked up again—"to say yea to the Constitution! Rodney was Delaware's Speaker—he rode through a thunderstorm all the way from Dover to Philly at night, to cast our vote for the Declaration of Independence. And *our* vote put it through."

Viraf grunted. In the rearview he saw that the long blond hair had been trimmed as well. It barely reached the top of the driver's seat. There was something about the new look that made him glance away. Not so different from that of another driver, in a Bronco. He looked out as the stadium slipped by.

"Gotta know that, Viraf." It was Taylor now. A brown-haired, mild-mannered guy, he probably cut his hair and shaved only because of his job at Howard Johnson. *He* looked like he could have been a cousin of the younger guy in the Bronco. Even his name smacked of Porter Road. "How're you gonna be an American if you don't know Caesar Rodney?"

"Mm," Viraf said and turned back to the window.

The others chattered on. Cooch's Bridge, it seemed, was the site of an early skirmish in the Colonial War. The Stars and Stripes had flown in battle there for the very first time. And the Delaware Blues, a top regiment in the continental army, was nicknamed the Blue Hen Chickens—that was how the Blue Hens got their name.

The heavy old Ford surged along a narrowing 896. As they neared the intersection at Porter Road, he felt a tightening in his stomach. Stretches of greenery felt spooky, as if they'd registered subconsciously on that long, uneasy wind toward Evans. Things he couldn't have seen in the twilight—a trailer park, a grown-over cemetery, a rundown shopping center—were now imbued with a sense of foreboding.

When they came to the intersection, he imagined a deep blue mass hurtling toward them. His stomach cramped—he had an irrational urge to get out of the way. Then they were past the intersection, and a sign marked the miles to Lums Pond.

Tall, fragrant woods rose on either side as they turned into the state park. Doug pulled up at a small hut in the middle of the road to pay a dollar entry. The guard-bar lifted, and they cruised around shaded roadways to an open area. A wooden board said Pavilion Fishing in yellow letters. Viraf was the first out of the car, stretching himself, the bag of chips in his hand. He stood there in the sun, feeling better, letting it seep into his limbs. Picnic tables and grills were scattered around a tree, one of them occupied by a couple with three kids. A toddler, his hair still baby-thin, stood unsteadily on the wood-planks table.

Megan and Ali picked a table at the far end, closer to an elongated lake, and began to set things up from the Galaxie's trunk. Burger patties, hot dogs, and packets of buns; a bag of coal and grilling tools; paper plates and napkins;

ketchup and mustard; a plastic cooler. And Bernie's bong. He had the grace, at any rate, to lay it on its side, presumably in deference to the family.

Soon the smell of smoke and cooking meat rose from the grill. Doug the expert stood over the dogs and burgers, rotating them or flipping them with tongs, questioning the cohesion of the patties. One or two were threatening to come apart and fall through the grill. Megan, who'd prepared them, was promptly informed of his secret ingredient at Seasons Pizza for holding patties together: raw egg white. Helped the taste, too, he said. Viraf, looking on, was conscious of disliking the new stubbled look. It felt like looking at a different person, like back in Longwood.

The feeling, it turned out, was mutual. "Vir, what're you doing without your glasses?" Doug passed his free hand back and forth across Viraf's line of sight. "Can you see? Need help getting around?"

"Oh, that's right, Vir!" It was Ali. "I thought something was different. No glasses."

He cast around for what to say. Luckily the bruise was just a smudge now—if they noticed it at all, they probably thought he'd been hitting the books at night. "They broke," he mumbled. "I sat on them by accident."

"They just popped out, right?" Megan said, stretching her slim legs. "Those plastic lenses don't actually break, do they?"

"They were glass. I got them in India."

"Oh, they still make them out of glass there?"

What the fuck. He nodded anyway.

"Well, I think you look nice," she said, sounding kind but condescending, leaning forward to peer at him. "You have nice eyes, Viraf."

"Thanks," he said, glancing away to the knots and grains on the tabletop, splashed here and there by bird droppings. His nice eyes felt dry from the heat coming off the grill. Her eyes, the color of the lake fifty yards away, looked as cool as water.

"You look nice with your glasses, too," Ali added.

"Thanks," he said again. They were killing him with nices.

"So they broke when you sat on them, huh?" Doug had a more entertaining angle in mind. "None of the pieces stuck in your ass?"

"Mm," Viraf said, unable to dredge up a smile for that. His sense of humor seemed to have died.

"Do-ug!" Ali said.

"Just concerned for his ass, Ali. I'd ask about your ass, too, if you sat on pieces of broken glass." He turned back to Viraf. "So you're gonna get them in plastic now?"

"Actually," he said, and hesitated, embarrassed about the contacts. In India, they were worn by women to look good. "Glasses were such a pain, I'm trying contacts instead."

There was probably no more than a few seconds of silence as they digested the news. But it felt like a minute.

"That's great, Viraf," Megan said. "You look really nice in them."

He gestured impatiently. "It's not about how I look. Like I said, I had a hard time wearing glasses."

"Yeah? Wearing glasses?" Bernie sounded incredulous. "Like how?"

"They just..." Why did he have to explain everything? Couldn't they just accept what he said? "They cut into my ears and my nose and sat crooked and made me dizzy. Things like that."

"Oh, okay." Bernie pursed his lips.

"All right, guys. Come get it!" Doug flourished the tongs over lightly charred patties. They smelled good.

Viraf tore open his bag of Frit-o-Lay's, and they set to, wedging dogs into bus, squeezing mustard and ketchup, laying onion and tomato slices over the patties. With the bun around his patty, he had a hard time opening his mouth wide enough. It was easier to get around the hot dog, but the ketchup kept spilling out. A blob missed his T-shirt and hit his jeans before he could bring his plate under to catch it. He dabbed at the blob with a paper towel, but a stain had already spread. Warm juices in his mouth took his mind off it, and he fell to chewing in earnest. For several seconds, the only sound around the table was the crunch of chips.

"Sorry about the crumbly patties, you guys," Megan said, wiping her mouth. "You know Taylor and I rarely do meat. I mean, Galahad eats more meat in a week than we do all year. Viraf, are you okay with the meat? I thought Indians were vegetarian."

This was hardly her worst assumption, he knew. She'd amused him in the past by asking how he'd managed, with all the snakes and elephants in India. Or *how* was he able to beat someone as athletic as Taylor on the tennis courts?

But he had no patience for it anymore. His tone was abrupt, almost snappy. "That's orthodox Hindus—like Nitin's parents. Like I've said before, I'm not Hindu. I'm Parsi."

"That's right," Doug said, and now *his* tone had an edge. "Vir's really from

I-ran, didn't you know?"

The word had a shameful new connotation now, pronounced that way, and Viraf couldn't control his reaction. "That's Iran, pal. Ee-raan. Why is it so hard to pronounce it the way the Iranians do?"

"Hmm, let's see." Doug cocked his blond head. "Why *don't* we talk like the I-rainians? Because we're in America, maybe?"

"I didn't say talk like them." His voice rose. "I just said at least say their own fucking name like they do. And just so you know, my folks have been Indian for a thousand years—that's twice as long as Americans have been around. So if I'm really from Iran, then you're really from Scotland."

"Yeah?" The Jesus-blue eyes opened wide, staring into his like another pair had done last week. "So if you love India so much, why don't you go back?"

There it was again. Go home. Go home, I-rainian. Go home, Indian. Go home, whatever you are if it's not American.

"I will," he said. "As soon as I get my degree."

"Good enough. And just so *you* know, I'm not your 'pal.'"

"Ya, I can see that," he said.

"Stop it, you guys," Ali said, putting down her burger and spreading her hands. "What's wrong with you? It's such a nice day, and you're spoiling it for everyone!"

Megan looked pained. "Viraf, is something the matter? You don't sound like yourself."

Another one of their absurd expressions. "What does that mean, like myself?" She didn't even know if he was veg or non-veg, Parsi or Hindu. In fact, he was sure she had no idea what a Parsi was. "Who do you think this is, some alien who's taken my place?"

As a matter of fact, his official designation in the States was *temporary alien*.

"All right, take it easy," Taylor said, a protective warning note in his voice. "All she meant was maybe you're not feeling too good."

Viraf paused, struggling to keep his voice level. "I told you guys it was a tiring week. Sorry I've messed up your picnic, but I told you I didn't want to come."

"Yeah, you did," Doug said. "Too bad we didn't listen."

"Fuck you, Charlie." He pushed his plate away and stood up, noting their confusion. In IIT it was just another way of telling someone to piss off.

"Hey, guys. Hey, guys." Bernie had picked up the bong and was waving it at them. "Time for a peace pipe."

"Fuck you and your peace pipe," he said, and headed for the lake.

Sunlight bounced off the water. A few tables pocked a slope to the muddy bank. Up close, the water was inky but placid. It took a bend at the densely forested far shore. A *No Swimming* sign stood on a stake. He found a dry spot near some rushes and sat down. A bluish-gray heron whooshed out of the plants, startling him. It swooped over the benches with a loud croak, then swerved to a small inlet. From where it settled, a second later, a pelican took off, squawking angrily. Then there was silence.

He stared at the trees across the lake and their green reflections. The ground felt cool, the air clean. He dribbled his fingers in tepid water, then dabbed at the stain on his jeans. It remained a darker spot within the damp patch. After a while, a canoe floated along, eventually circling into the mouth. The boater's head was just a dot, but now it was hard to keep people out of his thoughts.

At one level, he was mad at himself for having come and, once he had, for losing his cool so badly. Something had gotten into him. At a deeper level, he was mad at them, but unable to pin down the reasons. He was the one who'd looked bad, ungrateful for their inclusiveness. Hard to blame them for wondering what was up.

He could simply tell them. But there was a powerful resistance in him. The shame of it, not only to have been unmanned by strangers, but to have to air the sordid matter in public. To people who thought they knew him, but who from then on would see him as a coward. Not Veer the Brave. Vir the Wimp. From I-ran.

Eventually his lenses began to bother him. He tried blinking more often to generate moisture. But they dried up again, and needed to come out. In the rush to leave, he'd forgotten the storage case. All he could think of was to reach for the water with his fingertips and moisten his eyes. He looked out over the lake to where its mouth opened up. The canoeist was gone. The water eased the irritation, so he repeated the move again and again.

At some point, he became conscious of a sound. It was Ali, looking down as if puzzled, summer dress pressed against her by a breeze, her legs less blotchy than in spring.

"You okay?" she asked eventually.

"I'm fine," he said. "Getting used to the contacts. I have to take them out after a while, and I forgot the case at First State."

"I meant in general."

Ahh, fuck. He wanted to tell her and didn't want to tell her. "I'm okay, Ali, thanks."

She looked hard at him, but didn't insist. "We won't be staying much longer—did you want to finish your burger? It's gone cold, though."

"That's okay, thanks." He got up and brushed at the seat of his jeans. "I'm not hungry."

They made their way to the table, where the bong was back on its side, its bowl still clean. But next to it were the remnants of a couple of joints, one in a roach clip, the familiar odor in the air. He felt it grab at his eyes, so he leaned over to get his unfinished plate. After dumping it in a trash can, he settled on the bench at an angle toward the lake.

The others, giggling about something, weren't conscious of him anyway. He caught references to skinny-dipping and hoped they weren't planning anything stupid. Apart from the sign prohibiting it, Dr. Hansen had instructed him not to swim with these lenses—they'd be washed out of his eyes. Just thinking of them fueled the irritation. If he were back in his apartment, he could have simply put them away.

Just when he was about to drop a hint, the others began to clear up and carry things to the car. He dumped the empty bag of chips and joined them. Doug wheeled them past the guard hut and onto 896. An increasingly familiar and unpleasant landscape rolled by. Viraf turned to look ahead as the Ford picked up speed toward Porter Road. As if they felt his tension, the talk petered out, and they bore down on the intersection in silence.

He looked for cars at its mouth. There were none—it was easy enough to tell in the daylight. Not as easy at night, he imagined, trying to picture it through the Bronco's windshield. Again he was filled with that sense of foreboding, a sick feeling that the inhabitants of Porter Road were not done with him.

Then they were past it, and he slumped in the seat. Staring at the ceiling, he could feel the edges of the contacts against his eyeballs.

After a bit, the talk resumed. Doug, rolling his window down to gesture at Iron Hill, said Washington had stayed at a farmhouse there while surveying the British army. Before or after crossing the Delaware, Bernie wanted to know. After, Doug said: the tide had already turned at Trenton, on the New Jersey shore, when they routed the Hessians.

"Hessians?" Megan, squeezed in between Viraf and Taylor, had to raise her voice over the rushing air.

"Yeah," Doug said, rolling the window up. "German mercenaries. Think about all the German names in Wilmington. Like Mark Schiller, you know him? Or Bernie—right, Bernie? Weingartner." Clearly derived from *wine gardener*, like porters and tailors. "Descendants, probably. We were down and out in Pennsylvania—could've been it for the revolution! But we took them by surprise on Christmas, crossing the freezing river at night and surrounding them, some of us barefoot in the snow. It was a rout...like a handful of American casualties to a thousand Hessian."

"Well, a hundred. Most of them surrendered," Bernie said. "After Rahl was shot."

"Yeah," Doug said. "Tell you what: they make the best Americans, Germans do."

Viraf had a feeling he'd be dragged into the conversation...some crap about the making of a good American. The American Revolution against British rule had always resonated with him. But this talk of shock attacks was leaving him in uneasy sympathy with the Brits.

"So how's your Pinto, Viraf?" It was Taylor, leaning forward to look across Megan.

Ah, the Pinto... As in 'See how you've got a car, now that you're in America.' That was a joke. Their old Fiat was better than a Pinto, never mind the Amby.

"How do you think it is?" he said, his voice uneven and bitter. "It's a piece of junk that catches fire and kills its passengers. Ever think of telling me, Doug?"

Dead silence.

"You know what?" It was Ali, turning around to face him, those eyes finally cold, the normally flirtatious voice hard. "Doug didn't have to go out of his way to help you—he could've left you to *walk* all over town, looking for a car. You were the one who needed the car, so what stopped you from looking into it?"

Too much truth to deny. He hadn't even thanked Doug for helping him. But how should he have known to check it out? You never needed to "look into" Fiats or Ambies to know they were safe. Anyway, it didn't matter. It was not okay for foreigners to be critical, even in the land of free speech. He knew that by now. Should have known it all along, predestined to be the minority voice wherever he went.

"Nothing," he said. "That's what I should have done."

And he turned back to the window. His right thigh pressed up against Megan's thigh in the process, and he felt it move away. As if he'd wanted to touch her fucking thigh; she could go ahead and press up against her live-in boyfriend. He should have known what these women were like all along, instead of thinking they were so great. Fucking stupidity. Those Eagles' games he'd watched on Doug's 19-inch set, trying to figure out what was going on, stop and start, stop and start, but mind-blown by the cheerleaders, dancing and high-kicking and jumping every time the players beat one another's brains out. "Man, you can see their undies!" Nitin had said, once back in their apartment. And he'd whooped, "Yeah!" like that was such a great thing, women showing off their underwear in public.

The weekend they'd hooked up with Imtiaz in New York, he'd taken them to a bar, and a hostess had come by, sweet and innocent but in a low-cut, swimsuit kind of costume cutting up her crotch and her ass. She sat next to them on the bar stools and got them to buy her some exorbitantly priced champagne. Turned out to be a college student! Just earning her way part-time, she'd said, while studying photography.

And what crazy shit in that X-rated double feature he and Nitin had watched, open-mouthed, a month ago at Cinema Newark. Female prisoners, in the first, fucking around in the showers and forcing a new inmate to have sex with them. The second in 3-D, a motorcycle gang in black leather roaring off the screen into the audience, invading an open-air wedding to pass the terrified bride around and strip her of her lacy white wedding gown before gang-raping her on the banquet table. It had an apocalyptic feel to it, the spirit of darkness overpowering the spirit of light. Too weird, yet they'd been rooted to their seats by the confusing sensation of being disturbed and aroused at the same time.

The red 3-D glasses reminded him of the contacts, which were making his eyes throb now. Blinking didn't help anymore. And they were barely past the skating rink, just coasting along. He felt trapped inside with the others—no escape. Not even when they reached the apartments; they'd be next door every day, day after day. And wherever he went, only Americans all around him.

The one possible reprieve, still a month away, was the summer break. Mum's letter said Soona was finally getting married to Mehernosh, and Mamaiji, who'd been sick, wanted to see him there. Mamaiji's aversion for cars was starting to seem sensible, more than a bitter old woman's way of keeping her grief alive.

He hadn't been too sure he'd go, what with the price of an air ticket. But now he would. He'd go home. Home…how good that sounded. The Ford made the turn smoothly onto Delaware, and his aching eyes followed the campus slipping by. But in his mind he saw Marine Drive, sea waves lapping against the breakwater, hundreds of Indians on the sidewalk as evening fell and the Queen's Necklace lit up. He'd take it slow toward Nariman Point, a slashed-open coconut in his hands and a popping-hot makkai bhutta rubbed with chili and lime.

It would be sultry like only Bombay could be, the breeze filled with spray. He'd have on a cotton shirt, old jeans, and Kolhapuri chappals slapping against the pavement. The corn would burn his mouth and the coconut water would cool it down. Brown-skinned people like himself would pour out of Churchgate to the sea, the women in saris or dresses to their knees. He'd blend with the crowd as far as Talk of the Town, where he, being the privileged one, would turn off toward CCI.

There he'd pick a table by the pool, order bhel and chutney sandwiches, and wash them down with lassi. Then he'd stretch his legs in a soft-bottomed wicker chair, cross his ankles, and wait to be joined by his family.

CHAPTER 12

Going Home

"Go Big Red" emblazoned on its sides, a Trailways bus rumbled him north a month later on I-95. Beyond Wilmington and Philly, it passed crop fields dotted with barns, silos, and black-and-white cattle, on its way into the great city. Eventually it docked at Port Authority. Entering America after dark almost a year ago, he'd spent the night near the bus terminal, on a bunk bed at the 34th Street Y. Sloane House had been packed with foreigners and students. Now it was early evening, and he went straight to the bustling subway, lugging his suitcase aboard a train to JFK.

The space around the Air India counter was a little India: middle-aged women in saris fussing over children, black-mustached men with their top shirt-buttons open, huge piles of luggage by their sides, the air thick with Indian accents. Loitering at the edge of it all were two familiar faces—the UD seniors, Mohan Bhagia and Ritesh Thadani. Ritesh, the Americanized but lonely cat, was going home for good, thesis done, degree in hand, while Mohan of the tight Indian pants and pussy-licking fame had a job lined up in Philly. Mohan had driven his old friend to New York to see him off. Mohan still sounded like a hep Hyderabadi, and Ritesh like an American caricature.

"Good beard, yaar," Mohan said.

And Ritesh agreed: "Yeah, great beard!"

Viraf had grown it about a month ago. For some reason he'd deeply wanted a change. As soon as it acquired the density to make him look bearded and not unshaven, he'd felt a click of recognition, as if this was how he should look. That Ali hadn't cared for it only confirmed that impression.

The old friends hugged self-consciously at the gate, making sure no Americans noticed. Viraf shook hands with Mohan and promised to look him up in Philly. An hour later, the *Emperor Chandragupta Maurya* thundered down a runway, then rose as light as smoke toward their motherland.

Once it leveled off, Viraf exchanged seats with the passenger next to

Ritesh. Between ogling air-hostesses in silk saris, tuning in to sitar-and-tabla, and salivating over Mughlai dishes, they talked about finding one's place in the world. Ritesh was excited about his return, but wasn't doing it out of a preference over America. He missed having his family around, he said, that intimacy and support structure he'd had all his life before joining UD.

In the cool of the cabin, the lights dimmed for a few hours meant to replicate the long night blanketing the world below. They clicked their seats into maximum recline. Viraf, having put his contacts away, barely managed a wink before the hostesses swished by with breakfast. The jumbo dropped thirty thousand feet to glide into Heathrow. The ten-hours' stopover felt interminable, so they splashed their faces in the men's room and took off on foot to the approach roads.

Beyond the terminal, they entered clean streets lined by brick homes with gabled red roofs. It was an overcast day of cobblestone lanes and sausage-and-eggs beside Pakistani restaurants. They had pub-stool conversations with ruddy English people who seemed very interested in how India was doing after independence. It surprised him that he could like the English and that they could like him. But back at the airport, while others filed through without a glance, the boarding officials stopped them both, unzipping every pocket of their carry-ons and rummaging the bottoms, then dismissively left the repacking to them.

After refueling at Dubai, the airplane dipped a last time to coast over brown flatland. As it settled onto a runway, they exchanged telephone numbers. Ritesh headed for the red channel with cartons of Rothmans and a bottle of Johnny Walker. Viraf waved on his way out through the green channel and, without warning, hit a wall of heat. An endless expanse of earth tones filled his vision, and the old vertigo of disorientation swept over him in reverse.

Then his heart jumped. At the crowded exit stood a smiling, sunburnt man in a stone-colored safari suit, a slim woman in a peach sari, and a tall girl in a shorter skirt than he remembered her ever wearing. There was a round of hugs and squeals of approval and disapproval over his new beard and vanished glasses. His suitcase was lifted by a khaki-clad, thin-mustached driver half Satput Singh's age. Cataracts had begun to cloud the old Gurkha's vision and rendered his driving so tentative that he'd retired with his family to his ancestral village in Nepal.

As they trudged toward the parking area, the sight of rows of boxy Fiats and

Ambassadors renewed that sudden depression in Viraf. He tried to suppress it and failed. The new driver, Govind, pointed them to the blue Amby.

"You brought pictures of your Pinto?" His father's voice sounded higher; he looked smaller around the chest and shorter. Clearly shorter than Viraf. "What is its color?"

"Like rust," he said. "Orange-brown. I'll send you pictures from there."

"Takes bloody years to get your letters, Viraf. Good car?"

He hesitated. "Ya," he said. "Barely paid six hundred bucks for it, so can't expect too much."

"Six hundred bucks?" Soona said. She still didn't wear her glasses. "Dollars, na? That's like eight thousand, nine thousand bucks, haa, don't forget."

"Where's my Impala, mister?" his mother said. The driver opened the Amby's trunk and hefted Viraf's VIP into it.

He chuckled at the old joke as he settled into the front, recalling the fabled Impala of his childhood—a pearl-colored import with long tail fins floating in and out of the Cricket Club of India. When still a schoolboy, he'd promised to buy her one out of his first pay packet. But his grandmother, permanently embittered by Rustomji's fatal crash on the Western Ghats, said don't spend your money on a car.

Looking at the pay scale, now, for civil engineers fresh out of grad school, a used Impala might be possible—if you ignored the overseas shipment and import tax. Not that Mum seriously expected him to come through on it. She had an amused look on her fair, angular face every time she reminded him of his promise. And the more aware of the size of the commitment he became, the more her smiles turned to laughter. By the time he finished school and went off to IIT, he too had begun to play the promise as a joke.

"First I have to make more than an assistantship, Mum," he said now. "Then I'll get it for you."

"You can get your mum any car she wants, two-three years after you join us, don't worry," his father said. "So much business now we have, we're getting contracts even outside Bombay: Nasik, Poona, Goa!"

His mother promptly wanted to know why Aspi hadn't bought her a new car himself, if business was so good.

They emerged from the airport. A smoothly curving highway swept them past a three-story, naked statue of Mahavira in serene contemplation of twentieth-century runways. Then the stench of something rotting invaded Viraf's nostrils as they passed mile after mile of slums, people under tin sheets on garbage-strewn land. It was the land of no electricity and few grins. The opposite of a perfect place.

"Such a sight for travelers as soon as they arrive!" his mother said. "The municipality should really do something: move them to the outskirts, or put up a wall at least."

Once off the highway at Mahim, he could tell the new driver was more adventurous than Satput Singh. He lived dangerously between cars that hemmed them in, cutting ahead every chance he got, his horn blaring a repetitive note in the general cacophony. Buildings streaked with monsoon stains pressed in on them, and people crowded the sidewalks, breaking away to cross in front of them. It took an hour before the Amby rolled under the Princess Street flyover and turned into Seth Building's gully. By then, the sleep-deprived Viraf had a headache and a mild case of carsickness.

At the foot of the beloved yet suddenly dingy old building, Jadhav the liftman came running up in his dirty vest and shorts. With many a saluted "Salaam, seth," he grabbed the suitcase from the driver and lugged it up the threshold on spindly legs, past ragged, idly sprawling men. The family crammed into the wood-paneled lift, shoulder to chest, and it began its clanking, rickety ascent. Viraf's eyes were pulled to Jadhav's stubbled face: an eternally good-natured smile played about his mouth, but something about it and everything around it looked tired, pulled down and flaccid, as if he were on the verge of crying.

"He looks like he's sick or something," he said, with the slightest of nods in Jadhav's direction.

"I know," his mother said. "Shorty keeps nagging him—to ask for a raise. So much we're giving them both, plus the garage ka annex to live in."

Jadhav's wife, Saraswati, came in twice a day to clean the house and dishes. She was the only person in the building who rivaled his grandmother's tiny stature, beating it at barely four feet tall.

Despite his scant English, Jadhav had swiveled his head to listen, and, briefly, their glances met. His eyes were tired to the core under drooping brows, yet he offered the absurd smile.

Mamaiji was at the front door in her house dress, holding the ritual sagan nu ses tray. She got Viraf to step right-foot-first onto a leafy chalk pattern, and stretched desperately to do the achu michu over his bowed head with an egg and a small coconut. She cracked both at his feet, then drew a tili up his forehead, pressing the vermilion into his skin with her thumb.

She looked more wizened now, her skin wrinkled and dried like the husk of the coconut. Hugging him around his waist, she wanted to know how he'd survived so many days in the aeroplane. And was he satisfied now with his gallivanting or did he want to go back again?

"I have to go back for my studies, Mamaiji," he said, bobbing his head apologetically. "But I'm here now for a long vacation with you."

It was something of a theme. Louise, too, standing shyly in the corridor in a floral-patterned dress, her hair grayer than he recalled, asked in her stilted Gujarati if baba was back in India for good.

In some ways they had always been a pair, Mamaiji and Louise. Where Mamaiji despised and feared manmade mechanisms, Louise didn't particularly believe in them. In 1969, when his mother had taken the front page of the *Indian Express* to the kitchen to show Louise the grainy, black-and-white pictures of Neil Armstrong stepping out of a lunar module onto the riddled surface of the moon, Louise had laughed at the idea. Arré bai, she said; it's all bunk—do you really think a man can go up to the moon and stars? Not the stars, Louise, Behroz had said; only the moon—see: look at the pictures with your own eyes! No, bai, Louise said flatly after a skeptical glance; anyone can tell that is somewhere here on earth—how else could they take a picture of it?

Mamaiji, on the other hand, grieving for Grandpa Rustomji, and assailed by visions of overloaded lorries coming suddenly around the hillside to grind him into dust, had slipped into a state of despondency. She believed in the report only too well, and found it ominous in more ways than one. Not only did it mean that man had extended his meddling hand and ubiquitous machines into spheres that had belonged exclusively to Khodaiji, but it raised troubling questions about the whereabouts of Khodaiji Himself and also, by inference, of His good servant Rustomji.

Until then, she'd assumed that he was waiting for her in the heavenly Paradise that Zarthust saheb, over three thousand years ago, had told his followers was their ultimate reward. Ahura Mazda would have vanquished Ahriman, the sun would stand on high for thirty days, the Last Judgment would take place, and the souls of the righteous would be rewarded with the Making Wonderful. Yet, here were these photographs of the bleak, cratered surface of the moon, barren of any life other than bulky space-suited Americans hopping around it like bunnies.

She'd stirred herself for one of her increasingly rare excursions out of the flat, refusing the car and driver, but changing into a Gujarati-style, white sari and taking Behroz along for a short walk to the Princess Street fire temple. Behroz told them later Mamaiji had stuffed the great fire chalice with sandalwood stick after sandalwood stick, holding the hem of her sari over her nose to filter the smoke. She struggled with the tongs for minutes, repositioning the sticks and embers, sprinkling powdered ash over the fire.

Then all of a sudden, she put down the tongs, straightened up, and walked out of the inner sanctum without finishing her prayers. When Behroz caught up with her in the hall, it was obvious Mamaiji had been crying. But she insisted it was the smoke that had gotten in her eyes.

As for Louise, the Church of Our Lady of Dolour was right opposite the building, and ironically she had no problem believing in an invisible God. Early on Sunday morning, as Viraf settled into his old room and bed, he was awakened at five o'clock by the church bell, pealing out its summons incessantly to the entire sleeping neighborhood. Lying on the hard cotton mattress in the dark, instantly awake, he heard the sounds of Louise coming in from the kitchen balcony where she slept, shuffling to her bathroom, then up the corridor and out for morning service.

Once the bell ceased its insistent call, he could hear the soft whir of his ceiling fan and the intermittent clatter of trains approaching Marine Lines. For a dozy moment, he thought it was the freight trains behind First State. As he tried to drop off again and light began to seep through the wooden slats of his windows, the gurgling of pigeons fought a losing battle with the growing rumble along Queen's Road. Bombay was awake.

Washing up in his tiny old bathroom, he looked in the cracked mirror screwed into the wall and felt the surprise and approval that came with seeing his month-old beard, its aura of manhood. He snipped at it with scissors until satisfied with how it followed the lines of his face. When it had first reached a certain density, Ali had remarked, in the indirect way she had of conveying mild disapproval, that it hid his face. It wasn't too long since Doug had gone from his golden beard to the stubble look, so Viraf surmised she was responsible. In any case, he'd grown his out even longer, a black beard. But a point arrived when it became a bush, and he'd kept it down since then.

By the time he was out for breakfast, Louise was back, setting cups and a pot of tea on the black Jacobean table. The others were still in their rooms, except for Mamaiji in her kimono, seated in her spot at the near end of the table. For some reason, she seemed dazed and took a second or two to recognize him. Her hair, not entirely white, was straggly today, its strands clumped. Between sips of tea, she responded to his talk in a slurred voice and incoherent fragments.

Just as he started to wonder if he should call someone, his mother entered the dining room and went straight to a line of small, dark bottles on the sideboard.

"Come on, Mummy," she said. "Take your pills."

Louise brought in fried eggs with a plate of toast. Little yellowish pools of oil fizzed upon the whites of his egg, as he spread butter and jam on the toast. His father walked up, still in his sadra-lehga, said good morning to the group at large, poured himself a cup of tea, and took it into the hall, where he settled on the sofa under the window and opened the paper. Behroz asked if there was anything exciting in the news. Aspi shook his head, saying something about "those bloody Shiv Sena buggers"—he detested the militant Maharashtrian organization, whose symbol was the striped head of a growling tiger.

Mamaiji poked fitfully at her egg, crunching on the toast her daughter had spread. Behroz went off to Mamaiji's side of the flat and returned with a hairbrush. Perching on the arm of her mother's chair, she stroked the gray hair into a semblance of order, chatting past monosyllabic replies.

Then, as Viraf sopped up the yolk, Mamaiji's voice climbed back to full-strength, and her sentences were again startlingly crisp. Her head, which twenty minutes ago had drooped, was erect, the vacant brown eyes filled with light. It was as if Ahriman had left it, and Ahura Mazda re-entered. She polished off a second helping of breakfast and, when Louise came by to pick up their plates, strutted after her to the kitchen to conduct a loud argument.

"That's her big entertainment now," his mother said, as Mamaiji's strident tones drifted back through the corridor, "arguing with them the whole day about nothing. Louise doesn't get excited, so meek and mild she is, but shorty gives back as good as Mummy, just see when she comes in."

"What was going on with her before breakfast?"

"Oh God, you don't know what Dr. Udwadia said?"

He shook his head; clearly they'd both omitted certain things in their letters.

"Apparently there's not enough oxygen flow to her brain nowadays, God knows why. So he gave her medicine to boost the flow. Like magic it is, absolutely—you saw how much difference!"

"Ya," he said. It was as if a toy was winding down and someone had wound it up again. Oxygen... He took a conscious breath, inhaling the fried-egg aroma.

"She's fine after she takes the pills every day. But still she forgets everything two minutes after it happens."

Sure enough, crossing Soona with a red towel around her head, Mamaiji strutted back to her place at the table, obviously pleased with her showing in the kitchen. "Where's my breakfast?" she said in Gujarati, looking down at her empty place-mat and spreading her hands. Then in English, "Behroz, see, Louise hasn't made my breakfast."

Viraf chuckled; never mind breakfast, he could still feel the unaccustomed heaviness of dinner last night, the coconut of Louise's Goan curry still on his palate.

"Mummy," Behroz said. "You had your breakfast hardly ten minutes ago."

"Aaa, Behroz!" Mamaiji's tone could not have been more shocked. "Speak the truth and shame the devil!"

He started to crack up at the familiar ring of her St. Joseph's Convent aphorisms. She had a rhyme for every question he'd shot at her as a kid. Why? Because the sky's so high, and you were born in the month of July. So? Suck my big toe.

The worst one was, What? Basin full of snot. You're a nigger, I'm not. There were hardly any Africans in India, so, evidently, putting others down kept you up. If they were the dagos and wops, then it must follow that you were not.

"Mummy..." was all that Behroz could come up with, in the weary tones of someone who has said it all before.

"On my honor, Behroz!" Mamaiji put a hand to her heart, then reverted to Gujarati. "Where have I eaten anything today?"

Behroz got to her feet grumpily. "If you're not yet full, Mummy, just eat more, that's all; who's stopping you? But don't say you haven't eaten anything. That's what she tells people, you know?" She'd turned to Viraf. "When Mehru Aunty came to see her, she started complaining that we hadn't given her lunch. As if we were starving her!"

And she went off down the corridor to Louise, her voice trailing off. "Honestly! In her second childhood..."

"Viraf," Mamaiji said, turning helplessly to him, still in Gujarati, "my child, what did I say, you tell me. That I haven't eaten breakfast, that's all."

"Never mind, Mamaiji," he said, struggling with his rusty Gujarati at first, then giving up. "Don't worry about it; Louise will bring your breakfast out soon."

When Louise came by with an aromatic batch of eggs looking up like great alien eyes, he spooned two into Mamaiji's clean new plate, dashed them with salt and pepper, and spread another toast for her. She made satisfied sounds, cut smaller and smaller pieces to fork into her mouth, and nibbled at the toast for the next few minutes. Then she put her fork firmly down on her still very full plate and pushed it away.

"Bas," she said, in a voice of great conviction. "That's enough."

Making no eye contact whatsoever, she proceeded to the balcony.

CHAPTER 13

One's Place in the World

Unlike her grandson, Mamaiji knew her place in the world.

It was the balcony overlooking Queen's Road. In his childhood, he'd marveled at the hours she just stood there, contemplating the crazy traffic underneath. When the long half of the long and short of it, as Behroz called her parents, was reduced to nothing by a lorry on the Bombay-Poona run, a permanently embittered Mamaiji had cursed all machines and predicted that mankind would destroy itself with its own inventions. It would not have surprised her to learn that her grandson had been endangered by a speeding Bronco. Or, as she'd have thought of it, a Jeep.

Behroz, grief-stricken herself, reminded Mamaiji of how Papa had loved to fiddle with the latest gadgets. But the old lady was all the more convinced that had been their downfall. Had her Rustomji been content to live modestly like his forefathers, had he just walked to nearby places like the Parsi Gymkhana, instead of gallivanting all over the country after he retired, he would still be with them. And she would still have her life-partner, instead of having to be after the gunga every morning to change the garland around his black-and-white photo in the hall. In it, he was still young, his nose the family aquiline inherited by Viraf.

On holidays, the family often drove to the hill station of Mahabaleshwar. The road up the Ghats wound around the hillside in jalebi spirals, with no parapet or guardrail to keep them from going over. Aspi took the turns slow and smooth, which was a good thing, considering the number of times an oncoming car or teetering lorry suddenly rounded the bend on the narrow single lane, exactly as it had done when Rustomji died. It was a frightening sight now, Behroz said, to see a convoy of trucks grinding along in a cloud of dust. Even more so for Mamaiji, who refused to come along anymore.

She'd sworn never to enter a car again. Her sisters' flats were spaced too far around Bombay to walk there, so Mehru Aunty and Katy Aunty had to visit her. Even the Cricket Club of India was too far on foot, so she stopped accompanying the family there. The net result was that she rarely stepped out of Seth Building anymore. Her way of keeping tabs on the world was to stand patiently on their balcony, looking down upon the sprawl of concrete and humanity that stretched to the horizon on three sides of the flat and to the Arabian Sea on the fourth.

Queen's Road had been renamed Maharshi Karve Road after Independence, but people still knew it mostly by the old British name. At that early stage of his life, Viraf had not picked up on the uneasy silence his elders maintained on the subject of British times. History classes were still ahead of him, and for all he knew India had always governed itself. Independence Day was just a nice name for a national holiday every August 15, with colorful parades under the flapping Tricolor.

Standing on the veranda next to Mamaiji, the only grown-up other than Saraswati who didn't tower over him, young Viraf gazed out over South Bombay, thrilled by his vast perspective. Once he positioned his eyes between the balustrade's curlicues, he could see all the way down Queen's Road to where, past Churchgate, it flowered into the Oval maidan. Standing sentinel above the playfield, brooding over its swaying palms, was the Rajabhai Clock Tower. So sharp was Viraf's vision then, he could read the hands on the clock-face.

Mamaiji couldn't, but that didn't seem to concern her. Even the slim ladies' watch on the hand clutching his was seldom consulted. Her focus did not extend to the Oval, nor to Crawford Market on their left or the sea waves on the right. Instead, it was riveted on three manmade streams of traffic that flowed along Queen's Road, Marine Drive, and the railway lines in between. Her hand often tightened around his as Fiats, Ambassadors, Heralds, and the rare Jeep or Standard Companion grumbled through, five stories below, swerving around one another, honking at pedestrians.

"Government should have a law," she said; "make everybody walk again."

Secretly, Viraf felt that would be inconvenient for everyone except Mamaiji and the beggars, who had to walk anyway. After a while his hand felt numb inside hers, and his feet hurt from standing in place. Mamaiji was tall enough to support her weight with an arm on the railing, but he wasn't. And the scene that never ceased to enthrall her was already losing its appeal in comparison to the charms of distant worlds.

"I'm going inside to read, Mamaiji," he said.

"Go, baba," she said, releasing him with a little push and leaning both arms heavily on the railing. "Go read. All those books of yours... In the end they will take you, also, away from us."

Television, black and white on early Doordarshan or distantvision, was yet to arrive in India. But their mother had introduced Viraf and Soona to the pictures painted by words. Once Behroz was through deciding the day's menu with Louise, keeping accounts upon her return from the bazar, and being driven by Satput Singh for the family shopping, it was time for her to settle down to *Rebecca* or *Drummond* or *Peyton Place* or *Mandingo.*

The children's tastes, at first, ran to comics such as Spooky the Tuff Little Ghost, Little Lotta, Donald Duck, and Richie Rich, or fairy tales with drawings of the Seven Swans or the Little Mermaid or Puss 'n Boots. They read the illustrated *Panchatantra* and *Aesop's Fables* side by side.

But the horsey annals of Flicka and Black Beauty trained them to conjure their own pictures, luring them into detailed worlds that quickly became their own. Just as he would *be* the young Karna or Arthur or Sohrab of the ancient epics, Viraf *was* the young cowboy Ken, taming the filly Flicka on a ranch in Wyoming.

He was given to reading late into the night with the dim-light on, in spite of warnings from his mother that it was bad for his eyes. He didn't even know what that meant. She habitually forbade harmless activities on the grounds of unlikely and distant consequences: he shouldn't make faces, it seemed, because he would end up looking like that.

So he read more than ever, unconcerned for his eyes. Aspi grumbled about how his children were such bookworms. But he agreed with Behroz that the kids were safer at home than playing in Bombay's streets, where kidnappings were so common. And so he had his workers build more bookshelves for the kids.

In time, Caspar and Hot Stuff gave way to Archie and Veronica. Soona's tastes began to deviate from Viraf's: she read Wonder Woman and the romance novels their mother handed down to her. The brevity of Wonder Woman's costume caught his eye, but he, on the other hand, followed Superman and Thor, the Lone Ranger and Rifleman, Poirot and Sherlock Holmes, Tarzan and Beau Geste, Psmith and Jeeves, Scaramouche and Captain Blood.

The Persian *Shahnameh*, or Book of Kings, gave him the violent birth of an empire, the legend of Sohrab and Rustom pitting father against son to the death. The Arthurian legend gave him knights in armor, fair maidens to rescue, sorcerers casting spells, and fire-breathing dragons. Even Soona read the epics, drawn to the *Ramayan,* wherein Ram pursued Ravan to Ceylon to rescue Sita. And there was the war of all wars in the *Mahabharat* or Great India, pitting the Pandav brothers against their half-brother Karna.

It was a lot of reading.

So, for the first twelve years of his life, he could see without glasses. There were no frames, whether square, rectangular, or circular, to define what he saw of the world, just a wide open vista and constant, automatic clarity. That the sharpness of edges, the vividness of colors, the recognizability of objects was not a given, always to be relied on, that the specs he saw on many grownups and a few boys in school could someday descend onto his own nose—such an idea did not occur to him. He simply didn't question the way things were.

At Campion now, there was history class, which really meant Indian history, which really meant a long succession of foreign conquerors and rulers. Despite an unwarriorlike waistline, Mr. Pande kept a dashing Shivaji beard and mustachios. He smacked his lips over the names of his Maratha hero's nemesis, Emperor Aurangzeb, and Alexander the Great and Timur the Lame and Nadir Shah, whom Viraf didn't recognize as Iranian despite the Parsi first name. Persians, Arabs, Mongols, Greeks—all were lumped under the category of northern invaders.

The central theme was this: India once was a land of untold riches, so Nadir Shah and the rest were tempted to come pillage its cities of such treasures as the fabled peacock throne. The irony, understated in their textbook, was that the North Indians had themselves arrived as invaders and steadily driven the original Indians further and further south, some all the way into Ceylon. The demon Ravan in reality was probably a dark-skinned Southern king—fat chance Sita would go for him over Ram. Mr. Pande, too, had little to say about that.

But he and the text had plenty to say about the most recent invaders from the farthest away: the British.

"Till hardly ten, fifteen years before you boys were born, for nearly two centuries before the freedom fighters led us to independence, India was under the British raj. You think now about that."

The class was silent. From his third-row desk, Viraf could see the inscrutable or distracted or openly bored faces. Ten, fifteen years before they were born was ten, fifteen years before they were born. And yet, as the pause wore on, it struck him that not only Mamaiji but even his mum and dad would have been under the British—why did they never talk about it?

"Sir, what was it like?" he asked.

Mr. Pande smiled and leaned on the teacher's desk toward him. "We were all second-class citizens, my young bawaji. In our own motherland. Even I was too young to know what all was going on, but basically they were the big boss. So long as our forefathers slogged for them, England was fat and prosperous while India had famine. Famine, I tell you."

Viraf was quiet, assimilating the idea of his mother and father and Mr. Pande as second-class.

From the desk on his right, Robin Phillips, one of the three Anglo-Indians, spoke up. "Sir, Mr. Sethna says after the British left, the whole country has gone down the hill."

That was word for word what Mamaiji often said. His mother and father never responded, at least not in front of their children, so who knew whether they agreed or disagreed. But Mr. Sethna, the Parsi science teacher, frequently halted dictation or notes on the board to issue a diatribe against "those bloody ghatis" and what they were doing to the state of Maharashtra.

Mr. Pande's face tightened at Robin's remark, and he stood up. "Let us not talk about what other teachers say, in my class. Adi Sethna may think he is good at history, but he should just teach his science. How is your arithmetic, Phillips?"

Robin's gray eyes widened. "Okay, sir."

"Calculate for the class how many years India has been independent."

Robin looked glad of the chance to bend his head, black-haired like the others, and scribble some numbers.

"Twenty-four years, sir." It was 1971. The Indo-Pak war lay just over the horizon.

"Mr. Irani is teaching you well. Some other teachers, I don't know. Your parents had their silver anniversary?"

"My parents? No, sir."

Mr. Pande spread his hands. "Still one more year for India's silver anniversary. Only four elections so far. Wait at least till the diamond jubilee, Phillips, then if Mr. Sethna and I are living, we will see, down the hill or up the hill. You all will definitely be able to see." He shoved his wooden chair under the desk. "But what life we had during one hundred and ninety years of

British raj, you take this down."

He turned to the wall-wide blackboard and began to scribble at a furious pace, starting high and keeping the letters small.

Entertained by the classroom drama, Viraf opened his copybook to a clean page and readied his blue ballpoint. Looking up at the board, he was surprised to see that their emotional teacher, virtually tattooing the surface with his chalk, had produced some unusually illegible writing. Even the headings looked fuzzy, while the lines between them were unreadable.

Glancing around with a tentative smile, Viraf was amazed to find that everyone else was busy copying, looking up and down as if nothing was wrong. The pages in his neighbors' copybooks were filling up almost as fast as the board. He peered up at it again in utter puzzlement—the letters were definitely fuzzy. Then it came to him, and something plummeted within his stomach.

Straining to read and oppressed by a growing dizziness, he began to jot down only the headings: British East India Company... The Great Famine of Bengal... The Great Indian Mutiny... Savage Suppression... "The White Man's Burden"... Nonviolent resistance... Gandhi Arrested... General Dyer... Jallianwallah Bagh Massacre....

At that point, his head hurting, his eyes as dry as sandpaper, Viraf leaned over to Robin's desk to read more—at that distance, his friend's copybook was legible. It seemed General Dyer had marched fifty soldiers into the only entrance of a park in Amritsar, blocking it off for ten thousand unarmed men, women, and children gathered to protest the British rule. Without warning, Dyer had ordered his men to open fire on the trapped, unsuspecting crowd, cutting down thousands over the next ten, unrelenting, nightmare minutes, murdering four hundred peaceful protesters in cold blood as they screamed and milled around in terror.

Mr. Pande stopped writing and turned to face the class again. In ominous silence, he stood there, a portly Shivaji, as boy after boy finally put down his pen and lifted a face in some variety of shock.

"Phillips, my young friend," Mr. Pande said at last, very quiet. "You tell me now: it was better for Indians when we were under the British?"

"No, sir, I never said—" the hapless boy protested.

"Yes, yes, don't worry. When young people hear something from old people, naturally they think this must be correct. When they hear it from a teacher, even more. It's not your fault."

Someone slyly asked if Gandhi's nonviolent resistance was better or Shivaji's guerilla warfare against the Mughals. The voice sounded like Imtiaz Ahmed's. And Mr. Pande was off on a series of comparisons. But Viraf, staring straight through the side-wall, barely heard them.

That was his last week without glasses. The world would never seem the same again.

CHAPTER 14

Fortunate Son

On his first afternoon back, Viraf fell into a drugged sleep. Splashing his face, to counter an overpowering sleepiness at what in the States was three in the morning, hadn't helped. Shaking off the jet lag that evening, he descended the dark wooden stairs, past Jadhav and the men sprawled at the threshold under a thin cloud of ganja. He took the Fiat's keys from the new driver, Govind, and set out for CCI before he changed his mind about driving in Bombay. Sunday traffic was light enough that he got into the swing of it, as he passed the Parsi agiary and Kala Niketan's sari display, weaving and honking freely by the time he reached Eros. The junction seemed trickier than he remembered, having sprouted limbs in his absence.

At the light, one of the ragged beggar children around Churchgate approached the cars, and he pulled a rupee note from his wallet. Before the boy's salaam could leave his snot-covered face, a girl appeared at his heels, pleading, "Seth, seth, hum ko bhi do na," and behind her a one-legged man in grimy shorts, his stump obscenely unconcealed. Viraf was almost glad his oners were gone as he handed over a two-rupee note, before the light changed and the cars began to honk.

Apparently, the necessary layer of indifference had been eroded by his year away as an indigent foreign student. Bombayites, his family included, took pains to maintain that layer, with remarks such as "How many can you keep on giving?" or "It only encourages them to beg instead of working." But what realistic chance did an emaciated, half-naked, one-legged man have of getting a job?

He turned into the poolside parking lot. At the trellised white gate, he signed the guest register for two. Rangan had sounded happy to hear from him. The big news was that he and Maya were getting married. They'd set a date for the end of the year. In one way, that was good—there was no chance Viraf could return for it.

Passing through the gate was like going through a time warp. There, at the end of the clubhouse, was the cards' room, players hunched over their tables, and beyond it the cricket green. Straight ahead was the pool, kids splashing and yelling in the blue shallow. People reclined at tables around the perimeter. Behind it stood his beloved squash courts, hard-rubber balls resounding like gunshots. All so vibrant and relaxed; why did the sight depress him now?

He picked a table at the deep end and settled into a low-slung wicker chair. The pool held some of his oldest memories, not all of them good. When he was three, his father had let go of him in the shallow without a float. To a three-year-old, few depths were shallow. He thought he was drowning, swallowing chlorinated mouthfuls and snorting more up his nose. He'd flailed and clutched at his dad, who just backed away...until he began to scream. His father's embarrassment had been apparent.

But a hollow metal drum on his back had changed things. Some instructions on paddling, more practice against the sides, and almost magically he could untie the float and swim without sinking. The ability to float on his back, not paddling, relaxed, came later.

Monthly, his Campion class had visited the pool. By then he knew all the strokes, even the butterfly, but he wasn't inclined to race his classmates. Instead, he swam laps. Diving practice got him going: they'd line up behind the low board, run along it, and split the rippling water one after the other. Not as many cared to try it off the middle board. But eventually he managed it, and felt a certain pride.

As for the high board, the water so far below, so solid, he had to break through a mental barrier like the four-minute mile just to jump. Feet first, not only was he automatically balanced, but he didn't have to see that glistening surface coming up at him.

Now the high board seemed less daunting. But it had always looked safer from the poolside with his family. About five feet away sat another family that had heeded the government's Family Planning motto. "Do ya teen." Two or three. His father was fond of saying only uneducated people had too many kids, and they were the ones who could least afford them. Insinuating itself between the foursome was one of CCI's vagrant tabbies, this one gray and black, mewing seductively and nibbling pieces of samosa in a girl's hands.

"Look at him," a familiar voice said: Maya, with Rangan, stepping around the splashed pavement onto grass. Still blue jeans, but designer jeans, and heels instead of tennis shoes. "Hardly recognized you!"

He stood up and caught a look in those beautiful dark eyes as they took in his bearded, unspectacled face, a certain cock of her hips as she stopped to regard him. No automatic hugging between the sexes here, not even with an ex-girlfriend. He shook hands with Rangan, who looked as if a year away from mess grub had filled him out. It wasn't just the bulge at his beltline—there was something confident, even proprietary, about his bearing around Maya. They sat, and Viraf hailed a waiter.

He ordered and signed, the old membership number coming back to him as if he'd used it yesterday. Then there was a moment of taking stock before anyone spoke.

"Your old pada," Rangan said, looking around the club.

"Ya," he acknowledged. "Practically grew up in the place. I was remembering how we came here for swim class, in school."

"Your accent is different," Maya said, sounding intrigued.

"Accent?"

"Ya," she said. "Little bit Yank."

He chuckled at the irony.

"So tell," she said, and now there was the slightest edge to her voice, "did you like the complexions of American girls?"

He looked down, taken by surprise. She would never forget his insult. So easily spoken out of bitterness, but impossible to call back.

"Sorry," he said, looking up at her again, shaking his head, knowing it wasn't enough.

"Never mind," she said.

"So," Rangan said impatiently, "were the Yank chicks hot or no?"

He hesitated. "Ya. Pretty hot."

"Pretty hot!" they chorused, delighted by the American adjective, their *T*s hard in the way his, he realized, no longer were.

They wanted to hear stories, adventures in the US of A, and he found himself picking and choosing in his mind. He told them of the acid trip in Longwood Gardens, but he made it all funny and beautiful, like Doug's perfect place. They were in awe over the purpled trees and laughed over the shifting faces and flicking of tongues and circling around to the Love Temple. He told them of the time they'd driven to Philly in Doug's Galaxie to see the Moody Blues, bought tickets from scalpers—what a word, Maya exclaimed, just like the Red Indians!—outside the Spectrum, how in the parking lot before the show, Bernie had produced a homegrown snack, a box of chopped, dry mushrooms. Weird-looking, but he'd assured Viraf and Nitin they'd enjoy it.

That night, Viraf continued, the music was incredible, the fucking Moody Blues right in front of them, not a tape, playing "Eternity Road" and "Voices in the Sky" and "Tuesday Afternoon" and "Om." When "Nights in White Satin" began, the stage was wreathed in white smoke, and it was the most amazing moment in his life.

He'd kept saying so to Nitin, pounding him in rapture as the music swept over them, remotely aware that his friend wasn't as blown away as he ought to be. Back in First State that night, when asked about it, Nitin had spread his hands and said, "It wasn't *that* good, you know...."

Rangan rocked back in his wicker chair, laughing. "The mushrooms."

"Ya. Apparently, after one taste he quietly spat them out. Me, like an idiot, I took a second helping to be polite."

"Like Alice in Wonderland," Maya said.

"Jefferson Airplane's 'White Rabbit.'" Rangan ripped off an air drumroll. "Deadly drumming!"

They were satisfied: his America had lived up to their expectations.

Sipping lassi, Rangan and Maya spoke of their jobs at Hindustan Lever and Humphreys & Glasgow, already "fed up" with their bosses, but happy enough about the work. When they said "been," it sounded the way it was spelled, like *bean*. Whereas his *been*s were now closer to *bin*. It was a relief to note that his *can't*s hadn't changed.

The waiter returned with plates of sev puri, ragda patties, mutton samosas, and dahi batata puri, all drenched in chutney and masala. This was the best part of his trip: the desi food. Seeing young women in saris with their midriffs bared, a close second. He'd known how much he'd missed the first; the second surprised him.

Scenting fresh aromas at their table, the gray-and-black tabby picked its way over to rub against his legs. He glanced at its upturned face, and it mewed plaintively at him.

"How sweet!" Maya said.

He broke off a piece of puri, scooped the potato and curd, and held it out to the cat. It sniffed at the offering, then worked its mouth around it. Soon it was pleading for more, purring and rubbing its head into his hands. But when Maya lowered a heaped sev puri, even as he stroked it, the tabby turned its head.

She, too, petted it as it fed, bending and cooing, tipping her low wicker chair until her knees were in the grass. At first when he felt contact, he assumed it was her hand. But as he shifted along the fur, he had the sense it had felt too full to be a hand. He stole a look at her, but she had her head down and continued to coo. Then there it was again, soft and rounded, unmistakable, pushed against his hands and pressed into them.

Bringing his hands up, he straightened quickly, certain Rangan had seen what had happened right under his eyes. But, amazingly, those eyes were on his plate, hands busy with the food. Viraf sat there, simultaneously shaken and aroused. He could feel the bars of the Love Temple closing around him again, in the Garden of Eden. What on earth was wrong with the woman? Was she out of her mind? Shoving her breasts into an old boyfriend's hands right in front of her fiance? A mutual friend for whom she'd once dumped him? Cool as ever, still feeding and fussing over the cat as if she hadn't done a thing. And Rangan all smug about their wedding plans.

CHAPTER 15

Caught a Whale

Soona marrying Mehernosh almost didn't feel real, after all the years they'd been going out—no one said "dating" here—ever since they met at KC College. There had been an unspoken assumption within the family that, once she began to work and he started law college, it would dissolve on its own. Behroz introduced her to other Parsis from "nice" families—usually men in their thirties or late twenties already earning well—inviting the "boy's" family to CCI or being invited to their club, ostensibly to just socialize.

On the drive back, Aspi would praise the new fellow, comparing him favorably to "that pipsqueak" Mehernosh. It bothered him that said pipsqueak was an inch or so shorter than his daughter in high heels. It bothered Behroz and Mamaiji that Mehernosh's family flat was "a bit small," and what would they do once they had kids? It bothered Soona that everyone was so bothered. Even Viraf had had his problems with Mehernosh, working through the strangest form of jealousy. That this unknown bugger, as he'd thought of him at first, an absolute stranger, should waltz in and claim the affections of his lifelong sister hadn't made sense to him.

And finally it bothered Mehernosh, a quiet fellow in general, that no one thought he was good enough for Soona, and even more that it bothered her. There was nothing he could do about his height. But the thing about the flat was almost as unsolvable, given a) the lack of new housing in South Bombay, much of it already on land arduously reclaimed from the sea, and b) the absurdly high price for the rare empty flat. They could add themselves to the long waiting list for a Parsi Punchayat flat, but who knew when their names would come up?

So they argued and argued about it and walked away from each other, supposedly forever, a hundred times. And when it was Soona cutting it off, Viraf was fine. But when Mehernosh did the walking and Soona was all cut up, Viraf was mad at him. He hoped she'd learned her lesson and would finally do the sensible thing and forget about the fellow.

But time and time again they forgave each other, and as the years added up, so too did Viraf's estimate of Mehernosh's entitlement to his sister's affection. He could only imagine what the family would have said about Maya, had they decided to get married—it gave him some sense of what she'd struggled with. As for Soona, she started refusing dinners with the latest great prospect and shut her ears to her family's objections.

The breaking point came when Behroz and Mamaiji ganged up on her, bringing up the example of so-and-so's daughter who'd married so-and-so's son whose family owned such-and-such hotel and lived in a mansion on Malabar Hill.

"She caught a whale!" Behroz said, employing her favorite line.

"God, Mummy, you know what you're making her look like?" Soona said, making a face as if she'd bit into a lemon. "A prostitute! You want to turn me into a cheap prostitute?"

It reminded Viraf of the accusation an embittered Imtiaz had flung at Maya. As for the woman in question, no one could say she'd gone cheap, nor could Behroz know she'd been fishing. But clearly his sister was too mad and his mother too motivated to care about accuracy.

Behroz blanched and stuttered at that, literally shaking, and Mamaiji said, "Aaa, Soona, how can you say that? How your own mummy and daddy got together you know now, just like your grandpa and me, so happy we were. When you have your own daughter, you won't want to find the best boy for her?"

"But what do you mean 'best boy,' Mamaiji? Some stupid old creep just because he has lots of money? So Mummy can tell everyone I caught a whale? Ya, big *fat* whales, that's what they are."

"Don't be silly, Soona," their mother said, finding her voice, with a tremor in it. "When have we shown you a fat boy, you tell me. And thirty, thirty-two years is hardly old. More mature, only. You just go out with them, na, and you'll see."

"No, thanks, haa, you just drop that idea now." A firm expression had come over his sister's face. "I'm not going out with your whales. I've had enough of this business—don't talk about it again. My Mehernosh is all I want, and I'm quite happy with him, thank you!"

She flounced off into her room, leaving them shaking their heads. But after that showdown, they'd backed off.

*

So now here she was at the Colaba Agiary, in a lacy white sari draped the old-fashioned Gujarati style for probably the first time in her life, seated on the stage next to Mehernosh in a white daghli. The edge of her sari was drawn over the top of her head. On his was a glossy black phenta. Huge vermilion tilis adorned their foreheads, his a phallic exclamation mark, hers a female dot. Each of them held a coconut, and around their necks were colorful garlands. Viraf had not thought of them as beautiful, but they were.

The white-robed dasturji stood before them, intoning prayers in the ancient Avestan and tossing fertility rice grains at the couple. His assistant sat cross-legged, tending the sacred fire, its flames sending up fragrant blue tendrils to mix with the sea air. The stage was festooned in white and gold flowers, and behind it along the bay, ship lights flickered at the horizon.

Mehernosh's mother held a large silver ses tray with Behroz and Mamaiji, who had ventured out from Seth Building for the first time in years. When everyone set out, she'd refused to get in either car, insisting she would walk the seven miles. There was no way she'd let herself be driven by Aspi, with his awful temper, and she'd seen only too often from the balcony the new driver's habit of cutting out onto the road.

There was also no way they'd let her walk so many miles.

Proving her point about his temper, Aspi said let's just hire a ghoda-gaadi and she can smell the damn horse-droppings all the way. It looked like a stalemate, until Viraf asked her whether she'd go if *he* drove. She looked at him as if she'd never thought of that, then seemed to make up her mind. Apparently he'd passed her inspections, because she got in without a comment. Govind tagged along in the rear to handle the parking before he got the wedding food. Behroz said it would put some meat on his bones.

Though Viraf merged carefully onto Queen's Road, Mamaiji did a good imitation of old Satput Singh clutching the seat cover. When they picked up speed, she put out a shaky hand to the dashboard, and it struck Viraf that cars here didn't have seat belts. She was tense all the way to Churchgate. But past Eros, as the Oval slipped by she said, "My Rustomji was a very good driver, you know. If he was driving instead of his friend at the gym, they wouldn't have banged into the truck. But Behramsha Surti also died, so I can't say anything."

Now as the dasturji invoked the two family lines, she echoed him when he chanted the name *Rustom*. Eventually, he wrapped threads of sutar around the clasped hands of Soona and Mehernosh. Looking a bit moody, Behroz came up to the latest addition at Jamasji & Antia Solicitors with a jug in hand, and gingerly touched his shiny black shoes with drops of milk. Viraf found himself wondering when it would be his turn to receive that blessing.

Then, revealing a modern set of mind, the dasturji instructed Mehernosh to kiss the bride, and Mamaiji exclaimed, "See that fellow—ate up her whole mouth!"

In the next hour and a half, four hundred and fifty guests were seated bayside at rows of covered tables. Off banana leaves, they ate wafers, rotli and pickle, mutton gravy, rice pulav, fish in white sauce, dhansak, chicken curry, and lagan nu custard with their hands. Those who were waiting or had finished sat by the band stand, listening to godforsaken old hits like "Yellow Submarine" and "Wooly Bully." Male guests, featuring a fair number of whales in suits or daghlis, were a black-and-white backdrop for women bedecked with jewelry, the older ones in silk garas, younger ones in glittery chiffons.

Viraf, returning from endless rounds of shaking clean left hands along the tables and racking his brain to remember the name of this aunty or that uncle, made his way to where Rangan and Maya sat. In purple and gold, she was breathtaking, a matching purple bindi on her forehead. He almost regretted his inaction at CCI. But her demeanor was distant now, while Rangan rattled on about their wedding plans in Madras.

Soon they were joined by Milind the Everyman, their old ragger and then friend at IIT. With him was his pretty Maharashtrian wife, Veena. Ritesh Thadani from UD pulled up a chair. Viraf's lanky cousin, Percy, wandered over, clearly drawn by the sight of attractive young women in his cousin's company. Everyone was full of superlatives for the wedding feast, in anticipation of which they'd been salivating for days. But then the talk turned to city politics, and names were tossed around that Viraf had never heard before. Ritesh, the erstwhile Yank, was also at sea.

The big topic was that textile mill workers were on strike for better pay. They'd brought the industry to a standstill, running up losses in the crores of rupees. Clearly, Gandhi's homespun khaadi initiative was long forgotten. Samant and Chavan, the trade union leaders, were holding firm against the mill owners and the government. The stalemate was now months old. Workers struggling to survive had returned to their villages, awaiting a shift in the balance. The rest held daily protests at the gates, restricting the passage of inventory, until the government found a way to outlaw that and arrest them.

"Arré, you know, under Section 144, any big reception like this is basically against the law now," Percy said, preening a little in his Raymonds' pin-stripe, his sharp nose stirring misgivings about Viraf's own. "Aspi Uncle must have had to bribe the guards, na, Viraf?"

He shrugged and shook his head. "What do you mean against the law?"

Rangan spoke up. "The new law says maximum five people can gather in public."

"Five people?" Viraf and Ritesh chorused. It made no sense.

"Just an excuse to arrest the workers and the union leaders, yaar," Milind said, in the reedy voice of old. He'd had socialist leanings in Kharagpur, where his Calcuttan pals had Naxalite connections. "Like that only, they were able to lock up Salaskar and Budbadkar."

"But," Maya said, "Samant put out a call for Maharashtra bandh and still couldn't shut the state down. Isn't the strike weaker after that?"

"Arré, what weaker?" Percy said, leaning unctuously toward her. "You see now, they'll stop trying this Gandhi business. As if he was a saint. You read about those strikers, na, who threw petrol bombs at the loyal workers who were still going to their jobs? Bloody killed two fellows outright."

"No, yaar." Milind shook his head vigorously, his face as patchy as ever. "It's generally a peaceful strike. Exception proves the rule."

"Exception will become the rule," Percy predicted in dire tones.

Milind's wife seemed to shudder at that, in her silver-threaded pink sari. They paused to take in the sea air, then changed the subject.

To Viraf's dismay, his father suggested that he join Percy at a factory site, to get a jump on his future at Adajania Construction. Dr. Reese's site-management theories were pooh-poohed. College professors, his father said, knew nothing about real sites—once Viraf came home, he'd have to unlearn this theoretical nonsense and get down to practicality.

With the wedding behind them, those suggestions became concrete, quite literally. Viraf found himself in the Fiat on the road to Thana, thrice a week, though he could have gone just once, for all the experience he acquired. Percy's end of the project was barely underway; they'd only begun to survey one of the factory building sites. Blueprints in hand, the cousins outlined the RCC foundation with leveling instruments. Then they supervised as the ground was leveled or packed by a group of workers.

But after that, there was nothing to do but sit and wait for the transfer of wooden casting forms, once the foundation was poured at another site. Week after week, no one seemed in a hurry for this to happen. So week after week, Viraf sat in a makeshift site-managers' hut made of corrugated metal sheets, listening to Percy elaborate on his political views. Apparently, there were things he could say now that he couldn't in front of the Hindu group at the wedding.

"Where did you find those people, yaar?" he said, as if they were from another solar system.

"What do you mean? They're my friends."

"No, baba, I mean where did you meet them?"

Viraf shook his head, directing his gaze at the earth beneath their chairs, his eyebrows climbing. What was he supposed to do—repeat the name of his old college as though Percy didn't already know it?

But his silence was not going to shut his cousin down. "That Maharashtrian fellow was talking like a Shiv Sena type, haa, just be careful."

"Don't be funny," he said. "These are highly educated and broadminded people. Milind is a complex bugger, I'll give you that—he was a bad ragger at first. But after that he was all 'You just come to me and I will protect you,' and he really helped us out."

"Yes, baba, I know you went to IIT and all. But don't think none of the Shiv Sainiks and RSS are educated. And you know what they think of anybody who's not Maharashtrian, leave aside not Hindu: we are parjaat to them, man. Still foreigners. They don't want us here."

Viraf remembered his father's long-standing concerns about the militant Maharashtrian Hindu factions. "Those are small, extremist groups," he said. "In fact, good thing the Hindus are so tolerant and peaceful. Even our constitution says we're a secular democracy."

"Arré, what do you know how things are changing here? You remember the BJP?" Viraf nodded; Bharatiya Janata Party was new, with a Hindu nationalist platform, purportedly a party of the people. "You know how popular they're becoming? Not only Maharashtrians. The leaders are all kinds: Sindhi, Bihari, Gujarati even. You know here, in Thana, who won the Lok Sabha seat? BJP. How they beat Congress, do you know? That trade-union fellow, Samant, stood for election.... He never won, but he got lots of votes that would have gone to Congress. And the BJP candidate, Patil, is Agri caste, so he got all the Agri votes—and won."

"Agri?"

"Labor caste. SC-ST. Like our workers, when we did the leveling."

The acronym stood for Scheduled Castes & Scheduled Tribes. The workers were quiet and efficient, self-effacing, their wiry, dust-covered limbs burned by the sun. And here was Percy's news of an SC-ST voted into parliament.

"Just because BJP won," Viraf said, scuffing up dirt with his Volume Shoe from Christiana Mall and releasing earthy odors, "doesn't mean 'they don't want us here.'"

"Arré, baba, I'm not talking about your pals. How to tell you? Okay, listen. One day I was driving to our Nepean Sea site, taking the turn from Opera House to Peddar Road. How that railing is there for a divider you know? Bloody taxi-driver tried to squeeze between me and the railing. Next thing, he scrapes up my bumper and starts cursing through the window. I told him to fuck off; served him right for driving like a madman. Then the bugger pulls up on my side at the RTI light and runs around to my window, puts his hand inside, turns the handle, and yanks the door open. I'm trying to close it again; the bastard pulls me out and starts trying to hit me!"

Viraf's stomach had begun to churn. Seeing his mouth fall open, Percy rattled on.

"I'm holding onto his hands, wrestling him away, and what are the other taxi-drivers shouting to him? 'Maaro, saalé ko! Beat the bugger up!' Nobody's getting out, they're just watching the show. I was damn lucky, otherwise I would be dead today! Hundred meters towards Kemps Corner, there was a policeman on traffic duty. He saw and came running up, otherwise I would have had it. Even then, he should have put the bastard in jail like I was telling him. But he was also Maharastrian, a babu in half-pants, so he just took down the bugger's license and let him go. Never did anything afterwards. I told him I wanted to put the bugger in jail, but he said let him go, bhai, you escaped with your life, now let it be."

Viraf was silent, his head swimming, and Percy took that as a sign of reservations.

"You think I'm exaggerating, ask anybody about the Western Express Highway case. Three kids coming back from picnic at Madh Island had words with some truck-drivers. Next morning when they still hadn't come back, all their parents got together and called the police. They found the car on the roadside. All the kids in it—dead!"

Something clicked in Viraf's mind. He'd heard this story; it must have been making the rounds before he left for the States. But if it was true, why wouldn't his dad have read it in the papers and shared it with them? Maybe he didn't want to arouse painful memories for Mamaiji. Or maybe it had happened—if it had happened—when Viraf was in Kharagpur. And if it hadn't really happened, what made it such a widespread tale?

In any case, his cousin's personal story was gut-twistingly real for him. What did it say, about them and the world, that they'd had the same kind of encounter whole continents apart? And what did it say about himself that he couldn't tell his story even to Percy, who'd not only been able to tell his but had done it with gusto?

CHAPTER 16

The Other Side

After waiting on the wooden forms for weeks in Percy's scintillating company, Viraf managed to quit his visits to the Thana site. His father seemed under the illusion that work was moving along and the experience had been enthralling. A couple of inquiries about how the visits had gone, Viraf fobbed off with a "Fine."

In the meantime on weekends, he'd begun to "go out" with one of the Parsi girls his mother had introduced to him at the wedding. It turned out she was a distant cousin—he vaguely recalled her from birthday parties when they were kids. He suspected even this might freak the Newark bunch, let alone the fact that sometimes first cousins got married. With the community at only about 100,000 worldwide, most of those centered in Bombay for over a century, almost any two Parsis could find a common relative if they dug deep enough.

Her parents, bluff and hearty whenever he picked her up at their Cusrow Baug flat, were quite happy to have their daughter go out with a "nice Parsi boy" from a "good family" who'd gone to IIT and was getting his master's in America. All Open-Sesame signs that added up to "Go on, dikra, have a good time." In a way, though, that was exactly his reservation: that she might not have been interested had he not been a Parsi et cetera, like the American chicks who hadn't been interested in him at bars. Made it hard to tell how well she liked him apart from that.

Anyway, Jer was sweet and fun, so what the hell. It was good to be seen as a wholly viable option. One evening, they drove to the President Hotel at Cuffe Parade, and went to the Trattoria, where everything was pleasant at first. A doorman in red turban opened the glass doors for them, and they slipped into the air-conditioned cool of a lobby in white marble and polished granite, with plush sofas and oversized planters to green it up. There was a spacious serenity and sense of privilege, mirrored in the leisurely movements of well-dressed people, their wardrobes unaffected by the mill workers' strike.

The Trattoria was decorated in deeper wood tones, its lighting romantically low. Minutes after they'd ordered, a short, smartly suited maitre d' approached their table and stood there, a small but benign smile on his fair-skinned face, hands lightly clasped at his waist. Viraf's puzzlement changed to a sense that he knew this bare-cheeked but composed young man. Then he looked into a pair of gray eyes that hadn't changed in five years.

"Robin?" he said.

The maitre d' nodded. It was his Anglo-Indian classmate, Robin Phillips, who'd triggered Mr. Pande's diatribe against the British raj. So formally were his hands still clasped, that Viraf was caught between standing and remaining seated, but stuck out a hand anyway. They shook, and Robin spoke in an easy tone. He'd finished Catering College near Juhu and was climbing the management ranks at the President. After Viraf introduced Jer, he and Robin quickly caught up on other classmates, his only contribution being Imtiaz. They recalled their teachers, tacitly skipping Miss Fernandes's mini skirts in Jer's presence, eventually laughing over the feud between Mr. Sethna and Mr. Pande.

They fell silent together. After a second, Robin said, "I was in England for almost a year. London. Studying at Westminster."

"Wow," Viraf said, and Jer nodded appreciatively. "So why did you come back?" he continued, immediately embarrassed by his invasiveness.

But Robin's pleasant expression barely flickered. "Skinheads assaulted me on the footpath," he said, in the same even tone. "After I was released from hospital, I left college and came home."

Neither Viraf nor Jer knew what to say, though she made a sound and a sympathetic face. Viraf's face muscles had frozen. His heart was thumping.

Home, for Robin, had come to mean India. He seemed to sense an unspoken question in the silence, an obvious irony.

"Black hair," he said, gesturing at his fair, Anglo-Indian face. "Called me a Paki."

"Crazy bastards!" Viraf said at last, disgust and anger and empathy all pouring into the exclamation.

For the first time since the assault back in Newark, he felt an urge to tell the story, a feeling that here was someone who would automatically understand. But Jer's presence stopped him. And the urge passed.

The waiter came by with more breadsticks and butter. Robin instructed him to bring them a complimentary bottle of wine, then left with a lift of the hand and the subtlest of winks.

The wine was Italian and fruity. Jer, in a black dress and bluestone earrings, was definitely cute and into it, her lipstick transmogrifying to a shade of wine. Women with utterly black hair, he realized, was another thing he'd missed. Hers fell to her shoulders. Her Spaghetti Bolognaise arrived, and his Risotto Milanese, both smacking of garlic and onion, and there was wine in there, too. They ordered Coffee Cannoli for dessert, but continued to work on the wine.

He shook hands with a smiling Robin on their way out, putting his other hand to his classmate's shoulder. They emerged from the lobby into hot, humid dusk. He offered to bring the Fiat around to the entrance, but she said she'd accompany him to the parking area. She walked close enough that her curves brushed against his sides, and it was doing things to his dick.

"I'm tipsy," she said, bumping him intentionally.

"Yeah?" he said, eyeing her.

He opened her door, and they got in. The streetlight barely reached them. He put the key in without starting it, and when he turned to her, she was leaning conveniently. They kissed the flavors off each other's lips, getting close in the cushioned seat. Then they explored each other's mouths. It was the first time Viraf had kissed anyone since Maya, other than a greeting peck on the lips from Megan and Ali—and even those had felt potent when it was Ali. So he was really enjoying the moment with Jer, no specs in the way now, and the beard not a problem, when, suddenly, the car's roof seemed to crash down on them.

They jerked apart, utterly disoriented, their senses jangled. Someone was banging on the car, and Viraf's blood began to boil—it could not have felt more intrusive. In the streetlight, two men were at his driver's window. He piled out of his door at a scramble, only to find himself confronted by two smartly uniformed policemen. Not in the comical half-pants of Bombay's traffic cops, but long khakis.

Scowling but pulling up, he asked in Hindi, "Are you lunatics or what?"

"What do you think of yourself," one of them asked, his mustache trimmed flat, "that you can bring your bed into public?"

"Bed?" he said, outraged. Jer had stepped out and hurried around to their side. "What do you mean *bed*? And what are you saying, *public*? I'm in my car; who are you to tell me what to do inside my car?"

"Who are we?" the second man said, nodding ominously. "Come with us to the police station; we'll show you who we are. Don't you know there's a city ordinance against your English antics out in the open?"

"Where in the open?" Viraf shouted. "This is *my* car, do you understand? Do you know who Inspector Kamath is?" He'd snatched at any name for the purpose. "He is a strong friend of my father, so if you want your job, just shut your mouths and go away!"

But Imtiaz's strategy, if it still worked with traffic cops, had little effect on these men, who were evidently higher up on the ladder.

"Yes, yes," the mustached one said. "You can tell your Inspector Kamath. Now come on, both of you."

"Wait!" Jer said, speaking up for the first time. Turning quickly to Viraf she warned in English, "Don't say one more word." Then she turned to the cop, her face contrite, and began a series of conciliatory statements accompanied by pacifying gestures: it was completely their fault, they knew that; they'd done a very wrong thing, and the policemen were absolutely right to remind them of it; but they had not been thinking straight—they'd stupidly had too much wine in the hotel, and it had dulled their brains; all they wanted now was to go straight home; if the policemen would allow them to do that, they would be very grateful and would never again commit such an offense.

Viraf, still seething, tried to direct his glare at the pavement. It went against the grain to hear these false admissions of guilt, but he understood what she was doing, and he hardly wanted her arrested because of his pride and heightened sense of injustice. But however ridiculous the charge, the anger that had poured out of him was unsettling, almost shocking in its instantaneous climb to such white-hot temperatures. What on earth went on in his head, after the assault?

Finally the cops seemed to unbend. Without another glance in his direction, the mustached one, who apparently outranked the other, gestured toward the exit. "All right, go straight out of here!"

They did, though Viraf derived a tiny measure of release by gunning the car onto the road.

They drove in silence along the seaface, its salt air blowing in. Through the dusk they could see the beached and slime-streaked boats of the Koli fishermen, Bombay's original inhabitants when it was just a string of islands. On similar wooden dhows, the Parsis had set out from Iran a millennium ago. And now both communities were in decline, the Kolis squeezed out of existence by the development of every possible square inch.

He could no longer contain himself. "They couldn't have done anything to us for just kissing," he said, looking straight ahead.

She turned toward him. "No, you don't know what things go on in the police kholis nowadays: they beat the men up and do worse things to the women!"

"What?" he said. "Don't be funny. How can they get away with that? There would be a scandal."

"Arré, they can get away with anything. The lawful people don't care, because that's how they keep the criminals and goondas in check."

For a second, approaching the circular World Trade Centre, he was silent. Soona had taken him along for wedding shopping there, and the stores that lined its cavernous ring weren't drawing too many customers. Mr. Pande's hopes for India's economy still hung in the balance.

"That doesn't mean you have to tell them we're guilty when we're not," he pointed out. "Like we're bloody criminals for kissing."

"But they're correct, you know." Her voice took on a beseeching tone, as if she knew this wasn't going to play well with him. It didn't. "Even in the car, we were still outside our houses."

"So what?" he said, fuming again. "We were just kissing! As innocent as that. What the hell do they mean by shoving their pseudo morality down our throats?"

"They were just doing their work. You should try to see it from their side."

"Are you joking?" he said. "It's one thing to get out of going to the police station; I can understand that. But if you're seriously trying to tell me they were right with their fucking crap, then just keep it to yourself, okay? Nobody's going to tell me I don't have the right to kiss my date in my own car if we want to, or that there was anything wrong with that!"

She fell quiet for a bit as they rounded the band stand toward Colaba, apparently absorbing the fact of his intransigence. When she did speak, she sounded strained, as if she had to work to get the words out. "You're right. I agree with you."

But her face told another story, its muscles stiff, as if resisting her effort to compose it into an agreeable expression. He felt a wave of guilt, a sense that he may have bullied her into falling in line with him, the way he'd seen his father shout his mother down, even when Behroz was right. Viraf had always felt mad at his father for that.

There was something about the parking incident that reminded him of his parents at VT—his uncontrolled yelling at the cops, and Jer's pacifying efforts. Except that she'd pacified *them*, not him. And, unlike his mother, she hadn't been thrilled with his macho approach. But what was he supposed to do, just let the buggers act holier-than-thou about nothing and even arrest them? Maybe he could have bribed them instead. But damned if he was going to pay them for ruining his only contact with a woman in over a year and insulting the fuck out of them. For all he knew, it was a money-making racket.

When he dropped her off at Cusrow Baug, there was no question of a goodnight kiss. They went out again a couple of times after that, but the evenings were flat, both of them wary of something. After the second time, he didn't call again.

CHAPTER 17

Mill Workers' Strike

So the days slipped by, and by mid-July he found himself surprisingly ready to return. A week before his flight, he sat reading Olmstead's *History of the Persian Empire* off his mother's shelves. Jim Reeves' "Partners" played on her turntable, a moody song of gold-miners who swore to split the gold but were destroyed by it when they found some. Viraf remembered how, in IIT, he'd distanced himself from Reeves. He wondered if Rangan still deplored dhin-chak songs.

Unable to read while listening, he flipped to the photographic plates, chuckling at bas-reliefs of prominent-nosed, full-bearded Persian warriors. He was almost ready to grow out his beard like theirs. At least he looked more the part now, without glasses. He'd sounded the part, too, with the morality cops, though an ineffectually blustering one.

It didn't escape him that his father did fit the part. And that a Parsi, General Manekshaw, nicknamed Sam Bahadur or Sam the Brave, was the victorious head of the Indian army. Or that unflattering accounts of the first divide between East and West were based on Greek records. The Persian side of it had been sent up in smoke by Alexander.

The empire had had its ups and downs. It had spread all the way west to Greece and east to India by means of a gargantuan military—the first superpower. But Greek resistance and centuries of war with the Romans had softened Persia up for the Arabs' devastating knockout. The once proud Persians were among the first in history to have to bow to the Musulman sword. Maybe a hangover effect, even a thousand years later, made Parsis like his father so touchy, so belligerent. And others like Percy so paranoid, so suspicious of anyone not Parsi.

The wind howled at the door of the young miner, who'd just killed his friend for the gold, and as the needle scratched between numbers, Viraf thought he heard a muffled howling in his head. But his mother had heard it, too—she rose and scurried down the corridor. He followed on her heels. They stopped at Mamaiji's bathroom door, from behind which emanated cries weaker than her monthly screams when Behroz cut her toenails. Her disembodied voice informed them that she'd slipped and hurt her hip.

"Oh, Mummy," Behroz said, rattling the door-handle in a frenzy. "Why did you lock it? So many times I told you not to."

"Then anybody can walk in, Behroz," said the subdued voice.

"Nobody's going to walk into your bath, Mummy. Anyhow, that's beside the point now. Wait, I'm going to call Jadhav. Viraf, talk to her."

And she went off to the front door.

"I'm here, Mamaiji," he said lamely.

"Viraf, maru bachu, when you come inside, cover your eyes—I don't have any clothes on."

It wasn't an image he wanted to dwell on. "That's all right; Mummy will put on your bathrobe for you. But first Jadhav has to open the door. How's your hip?"

"Paining a lot every time I try to get up. Also, the tiles are all slippery and cold."

"Okay, don't try to get up," he said. "Just wait."

Behroz returned with the grizzled Jadhav, whose unofficial job description encompassed more than just liftman. A quizzical look now overlaid the perpetually tired smile. Soon he announced they'd have to break open the bolted door or climb through the slanted window above it.

"Oh Khodai," Behroz said, wincing at the idea of breaking the door down. "First try the window."

A curious Louise had joined them now, shaking her head, murmuring soft advice in her broken Gujarati as well as indecipherable comments in Portugese. Once they set up a tall stool, it became clear that Jadhav lacked the strength and agility to pull himself up into the window.

"Let me try," Viraf said, and got on the stool.

Those childhood pull-ups paid off—he hoisted himself into the opening and unlatched the window. Contorting his body, he dragged himself through. An acrid whiff of Phenol hit him. As he cleared the frosted pane, he glimpsed a shapeless length of flesh stretched across the tiles like a great stranded fish.

Then he was tumbling over and dropping to the floor with his back to the scene. It took only a second to slide the bolt, let his mother in, and get out of there.

"I'll cover her up, then we can carry her to the bed," he heard her say, apparently including him in the "we."

But he was already on his way to the other side of the flat.

Mamaiji's hip was broken, and in the time she'd lain shivering on the tiles, the cold had seeped into her lungs. They settled her into a room at Parsee General Hospital, and Viraf postponed his departure.

Life became a rotation of mornings, afternoons, evenings, and nights by Mamaiji's bedside, keeping her spirits up, calling in the nurse, or getting Dr. Udwadia's assessment whenever he came by. The top doctors, heavily in demand, were notorious for being short on time and even shorter with patients' relatives, so it was a matter of determinedly following Udwadia down the corridor with one's questions as he stalked away.

Sometimes it was Viraf, sometimes his mother, sometimes both of them, joined in the evening by his father and a small stream of friends and relatives. In a way, they were sweet times, long drowsy chats shrouded in the smell of Dettol, endless variations on a basic joke about hospital food, and the strongest sense of family he'd felt since their car trips during his childhood. Even Soona and Mehernosh cut short their honeymoon in Simla and joined the rotation. They talked of treks on the hillsides and going around a roller-skating rink while Hindi movie songs blared. At such times he could feel the forces of togetherness and light.

But in other ways, they were sad times, watching Mamaiji's body betray her the way she'd feared machines would, seeing her unable to carry out basic ablutions without help, leaving the room hastily when the nurses transferred her to a potty chair and her groans escalated. He could not forget that inert slab of a body on the bathroom floor, an image that undercut his idealizations of the female form, as if to say, That's where it's all headed. The antiseptic smells nauseated him, and in his head he heard the distant rumble of flatcars. At such times, the spirit of darkness overcame him.

So the days turned to weeks and the weeks to near a month, till at last she began to mend. He was glad when they moved her out onto armchairs overlooking the compound. Garden hedges defined a great bull's-eye drawn in varicolored shrubs. Green smells floated up from an enormous jackfruit tree.

The vista drew him out often to the coconut vendor by the old Warden Road gate. Mamaiji drank more fresh naryal pani than her system really needed. But it was the magic potion everyone swore by, so she sipped it happily and endlessly. For all she recalled, she was only on her first sip. Twice a day, he went around the corner to Snowman's, to fetch sandwiches, dosas, and softies, hurrying back before the softies melted. Mamaiji was not supposed to eat any of these, but she did anyway. It was hard to deny her.

On one occasion, he strolled along Warden Road to the US Consulate, Bombay's White House. He remembered how he'd stood in line, over a year ago, and how far the line had stretched. The distance to where he stood now was not the width of the road—measured the other way, it was the circumference of the earth.

July had melted into August, and the monsoon began, thunderclouds rolling ponderously over land. The air felt laden with humidity. He'd begun to worry about fall registration at UD, when Dr. Udwadia, looking like a minor thundercloud himself, steamed into the room one morning. After hovering over Mamaiji and snapping out a few questions, he took her hand in his and asked if she felt like going home. She nodded, evidently charmed. He set her discharge for Thursday and stalked out of the room.

For once, no one other than his assistant followed him: the Adajanias had the news they wanted, and felt unusually warm toward him and tolerant of his past elusiveness. Corridor legend had it that he'd been a child genius on the violin, but had given up his musical aspirations to study medicine, only pulling out the old Stradivarius for trusted dinner guests. Surely if he could make such a huge sacrifice in order to heal the multitudes, they could forgive him his lack of chattiness.

Thursday dawned gray but dry. By the time Mamaiji's bill was paid and sweetmeats from Parsi Dairy distributed among the nurses and neighboring patients, they were dangerously close to yet another hospital lunch. The prospect spurred them on in their packing and descent to the old Fiat in the parking circle. Govind pulled it around to where Mamaiji waited in a temporary wheelchair at the foot of the stone building. Even as he helped transfer her into the back seat, she made disparaging remarks in Gujarati about his reckless driving and her reluctance to put her life in his hands.

Viraf wondered if the wiry thirty-something man understood. But, either way, he didn't want to displace him this time for no reason. His return flight was booked again, and he'd no longer be available if she made it a habit to only enter cars driven by her grandson. He settled into the front seat, leaving her with his mother at the back.

Whether or not he understood, Govind seemed to consciously drive slow as he circled the great jackfruit and headed for the main gate. He picked up speed as they went through, emerging onto a narrow access road between dilapidated brown buildings.

And then he slowed again, for blocking the street about a hundred feet from the car was a throng of men—worker-class men in shabby cotton shirts and polyester pants. Under the overcast sky, Viraf could see their individual faces and bodies if he tried. But something bound them so they swayed and broke and came together like a single organism, a many-limbed creature that turned toward the Fiat and murmured like a mass of bees around a hive.

"Today is Bombay Bandh, looks like," Govind said nervously in Hindi to Viraf, recalling for him the mill workers' strike. "Aagé chalau?"

Should he drive ahead, in spite of the shutdown? In retrospect, Viraf would realize that the right answer was No. What would it have mattered had they put the car in reverse and backed off to the hospital, even checked Mamaiji back into the ward? But in the instant he had to answer, that idea didn't occur to him, as if the only options were to stop or proceed. Far more dangerous to stop. Also in hindsight, easy to see why Govind deferred to him, but he would wonder why the strong-willed women remained silent, leaving the decision in his hands.

"Chalao," he said, gesturing lightly ahead, his eyes on the workers, qualifying the direction with "dheeré sé." Slowly.

And their car crept toward the buzzing crowd, which showed no sign of dispersing to let them through. Viraf half expected Govind to brake as they came up to its periphery.

Instead, he leaned his upper frame toward the windshield, raising his left hand. His loosely spread fingers patted the air, as if to say, Wait, let us through, we're unarmed and docile.

Then they were crawling through a mass of moving bodies that didn't seem to move aside so much as be gently pushed, yielding little by little, for what felt like an eternity in a space of floating, brown, mustached faces pressing in on them.

Just as they were about to emerge into the clear, the Fiat nosing into nothingness, as if realizing it was about to slip away the milling bodies and faces descended upon it, thumping its sides, banging the windowpanes, and rocking it like a boat. The women screamed for the first time, Mamaiji shrieking in Gujarati. Viraf turned to catch the alarm on her face, as they continued to inch forward.

Then somehow they were through, and Govind was shifting gears rapidly while the workers ran after them, catching up to slam the trunk before he gunned the car up the street.

Soon they were on an eerily empty Peddar Road. A nervous silence prevailed inside the car, as if everyone was reviewing the event in his or her mind and uncomfortable with discussing it. Viraf, on playing the movie over, was struck again by the group dynamic that had swayed the crowd. It was as if the Spirit of Ahriman had come over them collectively. He felt their hands must have been stayed, at first, by Govind's placating palm and their recognition that he could easily have been one of them. Maybe they'd fallen on the car only once they could no longer see his working-class face.

In his mind now, Viraf could imagine how that self-fueling group dynamic must have spurred on the three in the Bronco. He could hear their shouts and curses—like his father's at the wheel—as they swung past the laboring Pinto. He put words to their angry mouthings as they came alongside and saw its brown-skinned driver. When he refused to pull over, he could see them spin around to one another. Who did the fuckin' dago think he was? He could see, for the first time, the comely young woman open her mouth.

Her tones would be silvery, in that sweet Delaware accent: You gotta teach him a lesson.

The contemplative mood held all the way home. That evening, over dinner, they told the story to Aspi, each correcting the other. Louise leaned against the sideboard to listen. When they reached the point where the workers had attacked, Mamaiji described in dark tones how one of them had flung a stone through the window at her.

Louise put a hand to her broad, wrinkled face and exclaimed in amazement and empathy.

"Really?" Viraf was startled by the revelation. "I thought all the windows were up and they were just banging on them."

"No, no, I'm telling you," Mamaiji said, affronted. "Straight in front of my face it went—like that!" And she gestured sharply, an inch from her nose and eyes.

Viraf wondered if they could find the stone and if she realized that the aging Fiat, far from being the dangerous threat she'd always seen it as, had shielded and protected them within its battered old body, then sped them away to safety. That, on the contrary, the danger had manifested itself in the shape of impoverished and angry human beings.

Had the windows been down, they might well have been stoned. But they would also have heard what that swell of voices was saying. Do you hear us, it might have cried, you rich seths in your fine clothes made by us, riding comfortably in your car? Do you hear us?

Yes, he wanted to say this time. I hear you.

Not until the next morning, when his father handed him the *Indian Express*, did he realize the extent of the danger they'd been in. Not only had stones been hurled at cars, taxis, and buses, but twenty-four BEST buses were set on fire, and the Morarji Mills, too. The Century Mills' showroom at Haji Ali was broken into and looted by hundreds with impunity. Ironically, the city bandh had been started not by the usually nonviolent workers, but by angry policemen, whose union leaders had been arrested that morning by the Central Reserve Police.

Seeing this, the workers had piggybacked their cause onto their erstwhile enemies', and the two factions even marched together from Worli Naka to Nana Chowk. Without policemen to enforce the law, anarchy—or Ahriman— took hold of the city. Hundreds were shot and a handful killed. For the first time since Independence, the state government had to call in the Indian army. Now Bombay was under curfew.

The talk among Parsis, his family included, was that Tata Textiles and Bombay Dyeing, led by "our own" Naval Tata and Nusli Wadia, were already paying the workers so much, plus pensions and so on. How could they put the companies at risk by raising everybody's salaries? Even then, they'd generously accepted the labor minister's proposal of a Rs. 30 pay hike for all the workers, magnanimously overlooking the illegal strike, which our Naval had rightly denounced as irresponsible. But the greedy workers had turned even that proposal down!

Viraf pointed out that an increase of little more than $2 wasn't really all that generous. But he was promptly told that a rupee bought just as much here as a dollar did there, and that the proposal included advance pay of Rs. 650. That was still only about $50 that they'd have to pay back anyway, but this time he kept his mouth shut.

The next week, when the family saw him off, Mamaiji refused to come along in the car. He had to hug her goodbye at the lift, as Jadhav stood there with his smile and "Salaam, seth." Viraf took a hundred-rupee note out of his wallet for Louise and another for Jadhav after he'd loaded up in the gully. Only once Govind swerved them out into traffic with his normal panache did they realize that Mamaiji must have been out on the kitchen balcony with Louise, ready to wave to Viraf.

"Look back, Viraf," his mother said anxiously, invoking an old superstition meant to ensure his return. "Quickly, look back at your home!"

He twisted around in the seat. But it was too late to see Mamaiji and the weathered Seth Building.

CHAPTER 18

The Penny Jar

Not so much in brick-and-concrete New York, that distant cousin of Bombay, but on Big Red again, rolling past barns and farmhouses asleep in the sun, Viraf had an aesthetic epiphany that said he was glad to be back. The rhythms of American voices over the drone of the bus were familiar yet fresh—more black people on board than he'd seen at any one time in Newark. Once the bus deposited him, even little Newark, with its white wooden houses and brick college buildings, was clean and pretty again with the beginnings of fall.

Nowhere to be seen, anymore, the streetside misery of beggars or of slumdwellers having to live in their own shit. And no Jadhav or Louise to be ordered around, in 101, H Building, of First State Apartments. It surprised him that the much-missed convenience of their services no longer compensated for that awkwardness—he felt an aversion, now, for the hierarchy Mamaiji thrived on. For hierarchy in general.

Next door, Doug and Ali looked preoccupied but not unhappy to see him back.

"How was India?" they asked.

"Great," he said.

"You stayed longer than you'd planned." Ali was even prettier than he remembered. He'd spent long enough in the land of silky black hair to have missed that splash of orange.

On the heels of that recognition came a wariness of circling back to the old Love Temple. Quickly, he explained about Mamaiji's injury.

"Oh, bummer," Ali said.

"So is she all right now?" Doug asked.

Viraf took that to mean they didn't want the whole story. "Ya, she's back home now."

"That's good," they said.

"What have *you* been up to?" he asked, and was told of veg parties at

Megan's, bong sessions at Bernie's, ceramics class for Ali, and the Moles' gigs in town. One coming up at Deer Park.

"Cool," he said. "Remind me so I can come."

Across from them, Lynette, still between housemates at the halfway house, was outside her door more than ever, swinging it and smiling flirtatiously at everyone going through the entrance.

"Want to see my penny jar?" she warbled the next morning, as he turned toward the front door. He'd gotten better at understanding her speech.

"Um...did you say 'penny?'" he said, turning around.

"Yeah," she said, "I'll show you," and ran inside on flip-flops, leaving the door open.

She returned, breasts heaving under an orange-on-white dress, holding a large cookie jar packed two-thirds up its glass walls with glittering copper and silver coins.

"That's nice." He'd sounded the way Megan had sometimes sounded toward him. "Must be quite a lot in there."

"Mm-hm," she said, batting her eyelashes and holding it out to him.

He took it in his hands, feeling the heft, exaggerating how much he tipped over from the weight of it. Her future life, all the way out, would depend on it.

"Wow!" he said. "You're rich."

She couldn't stop smiling after that. She liked his new beard, she said. He smiled back and thanked her. Not a good idea to keep it going, though. So he handed the jar over and made his escape.

The Pinto coughed only a little on starting up, despite the months without a run. But just getting in it brought some of the bad feelings back. And taking it out on the road jangled nerves he hadn't felt in all the craziness of Bombay's streets. He wondered why, with all that noisy dashing around, you saw more accidents here than there. It was almost as if the orderliness of driving here, its predictable progression, lulled you into a false sense of safety. Whereas in India, you had to be on the lookout for whatever the idiot next to you might do. All the honking, too, was good warning. The Bronco, he recalled, had never honked.

Something about the stale air trapped in the car was drying his contacts. He rolled his window down and turned up the air. Maybe after a couple of paychecks, he could look for another used car, one that wasn't a deathtrap. Sell the Pinto if anyone would buy it.

At UD, he avoided the lot behind Evans, parking near the lab instead. In the department office, Richard Danner, the bespectacled secretary, welcomed him with a smile.

Before leaving for India, Viraf had stopped by to see if there was anything he needed to do to roll the assistantship forward. Were there forms to be filled? His outsized face tired at the semester's end, Richard had said no, it would all be taken care of...did Viraf have plans for summer? And now that he was back it was, How was India? Great, India was great. There was no point talking about ailing grandmothers.

Up in the assistants' office, Will had his Plastic-Man legs stretched past his desk. He and Talaat Gamal were talking Middle Eastern politics. At another desk, Mark Myers was quietly at work. Viraf said his hellos as he settled onto his chair and pulled his books and files out of the drawers.

After reorganizing, he put drops in his eyes. The fluid seeped behind the lenses, while he tuned in to the conversation. Iraq and Iran were at war, and Talaat had heard that the US was playing both sides, with billions in aid and weapons. And Israel, suspecting Iraq of developing the bomb, had bombed an Iraqi reactor into oblivion.

Talaat, whose beard was cropped stylishly, had noticed Viraf's attention and wanted to know what the deal was with India's "peaceful" nuclear tests.

In spite of fuzzy knowledge derived from his father's grumblings while reading the front page, Viraf felt obliged to be an expert on Indian policy and also defend it. "Just think about the amount of military aid the US gives Pakistan, which has a history of attacking us. So we're just showing them we're still the boss in that area."

"Didn't India sign the non-proliferation treaty?" Will said.

"The UN treaty? No, because it's exactly those countries who have the bomb pressuring those who don't from getting it—what sense does that make? Just like what sense does it make for the US to aid a military dictatorship like Pakistan against a democracy like India?"

"The same way that in Iran," Talaat said, "British intelligence and the CIA plotted against Mossadeq's democracy and put the shah in its place."

"What?" This was news to Viraf, probably from before he could assimilate his father's running commentary. "Why did they do that?"

"Because Mossadeq nationalized Anglo-Iranian Oil and kicked the British out. You didn't know that?" Despite a stylized accent like Omar Sharif's, he said *didn't* like *ditn't*. "And see what the coup led to in the end: the ayatollah."

And the hostage crisis, thought Viraf. "Wow. Now I'm happy it's just military aid across our border."

Mark, gangly but not as tall as Will, looked up from his work with a frown. "I thought India got plenty aid, too."

"Not military. Loans back in Nehru's time that we're still paying off with interest. And with that hanging over our heads, it takes guts to resist the pressure to toe the line."

Mark shook his head disapprovingly. "So India's no longer the peacenik of the world."

It hurt Viraf to hear that.

That afternoon, he cut through on Academy to the Wilmington Trust on Main Street. His statement in the mail had shown no recent deposit from the department. And now the withdrawal receipt from the teller showed a significantly decreased balance after his trip home. The new car would have to wait.

Two weeks later, he made the same walk, fully expecting that the deposits would have resumed. The two courses left for his master's were in full flow. Dr. Reese, now almost exclusively at the computer science department, had not yet kicked their thesis project into high gear. So there was time enough to handle the courses. Even time to hit the tennis courts with Will, who was ambidextrous, switching to his left when extended. He got everything in play, and argued line calls with quiet belief in his judgment.

In any case, the FORTRAN simulator was almost ready, just a few modules left to write and debug. So all seemed well, in the cool of Wilmington Trust, until Viraf's teller of the day, a sandy-haired lady with a creased forehead, pushed across his receipt. It told him, inexplicably, that what had gone down was still plummeting.

He trudged back to Evans, tossing the mystery around, and visited Richard Danner. A small frown on his face, the department secretary squinted at paperwork and his computer through sober black glasses.

"Let me get back to you about this, Viraf," he finally said, which told Viraf nothing.

"But did you find what the problem is?"

"Um... Doesn't look like you're on the assistants' list anymore, for some reason." Then, seeing Viraf's stunned expression: "I'll look into it and let you know."

"But what 'reason,' Richard? Has to be a mistake! I asked you before I left if there was anything I had to do, remember?"

Richard paused to think, and Viraf's stomach tightened. The brown little room seemed to fall away, leaving only the man in front. Then the large head moved in a nod, and Viraf breathed again. "I'll look into it. Give me till tomorrow."

By the time he pulled into First State, Viraf was starting to feel better. It was just a clerical error that would soon be resolved. One of the freight trains was rumbling through again, and Lynette was outside, diddling around the flowerbeds. He waved back at her as he unlocked the entrance and closed it behind him, noting that her front door was ajar.

It was one of those evenings when he wished he'd bought a TV set or was still close enough to Doug and Ali to drop by at any time. But he passed time cooking rice and the watery concoction that was his version of chicken curry. Then he took out his contacts, opened his textbooks, and read until his eyes began to close. In bed, his mind drifted off to replays of Richard's words and things he should have said. It took some tossing around and counting to a hundred several times, but at some point he fell asleep.

When the phone jerked him awake and he scrambled off the bed, the first thing he noticed in the dark was the smell of chicken curry. A call at the dead of night had to be from home. He fumbled around the kitchen counter for the clamoring object and put it to his ear.

"Hullo... Viraf?" It was a metallic version of his father's voice, and immediately he knew that something was wrong—usually it was his mother first, before she passed the phone to the others. From then on, whenever he got a call after dark, his mind would rush back to that night in Delaware and the nightmarish day that followed.

"Dad," he said, fighting the feeling in his stomach, "it's me; I was asleep."

"Ya, it's your nighttime there, I know." The crackling voice was slow and considered. "Viraf, your Mamaiji passed away last night." It paused, but Viraf had no words. "Her pneumonia had come back, but she kept refusing to go again into the hospital. So we were taking her to the doctor every week and bringing her back. We thought no point bothering you there until she was all right. But now..."

Viraf's vocal chords stuck, but he worked them: "Should I come back for the...?"

"No, no; you don't disturb your studies." His father's voice was final. "We are making all the arrangements for the ceremonies at the dakhmo. Your mummy is a bit distressed, otherwise she would talk to you. And Soona is with her—she is staying with us for some days; Mehernosh will go back and forth. But we will all talk with you next time."

"Mummy's okay, though?"

"Ya, ya, just very sad, naturally. Little bit of crying."

"Okay... Give her my love."

"Ya, okay." Then Viraf could hear him doing so right away, off to the side, and his mother's voice responding and getting closer. "Here, she's coming, I'll give it to her. You don't worry, Viraf, we are taking care of everything. Here, I'm giving it to your mummy. Bye."

"Bye," he said, but his mother was already on the line.

"Viraf, maro dikro," she said, her voice shaking, "your dear Mamaiji is gone."

The phrase twisted his stomach. "Dad told me, Mummy. But how are you? Are you okay?"

"I don't know, darling...very confused. I keep on thinking how she was before your grandpa died and she became all bitter. She even stopped thinking she would see him again, after she saw those men jumping around on the moon."

He looked around in the dark, his eyes starting to pick out the refrigerator and couch and coffee table. "I know...when you and she went to the agiary."

"Yes, and now she is also gone. I know Zarthust saheb said we would all go to heaven after we die, but even he must have never thought, three thousand years ago, that people would be flying around in rockets." Her voice broke again. "In my heart I feel that my daddy was gone and never came back and now Mummy is gone, and one day we will also be gone, Viraf, and you and Soona must try to remember us, wherever you are."

He could hear his father's voice reproving her for saying morbid things to their son, so he spoke up hurriedly. "We'll all be together, Mummy, no need for remembering. As if we could forget, in the first place."

Then he could hear her crying and Soona's voice consoling her before it spoke into his ear. "Viraf, she's too tired, darling."

"No, that's okay, Soona, let her rest. You and Dad are okay?"

"Ya, of course, we're all fine. But you're the one who's on your own."

It was not something he could safely acknowledge to them. "I'm fine. I just feel sick thinking about Mamaiji."

"I know." Soona's voice seemed to drop and waver, and he knew better than to ask for details. He didn't want to know too much, in any case. What was the point of having images in his head of Mamaiji's face painfully contorted or something?

He felt thankful he'd hugged her one last time before leaving, but bothered that he hadn't looked back in time. What difference could that possibly have made, though? And yet, there it was: he would never see her again. A vision of her laid out flat, while the dasturjis chanted funeral prayers at the doongerwadi, filled his head. He'd never been on the reputedly lush grounds near Hanging Gardens, held in trust by the Parsi Panchayat. How she'd hated "Ole Turkey Buzzard." And now she'd be deposited in a tower of silence and left for the birds to pick her clean.

After saying bye to Soona, he stood in the dark with his hand on the phone. For a disoriented moment, he thought his voice had awakened Nitin. But no roommate's voice broke the silence. Soona was right.

Stumbling over to the couch, he slumped onto it. A heaviness in his head pulled him toward sleep. In a drugged state he saw Mamaiji at her post on Seth Building's balcony, overlooking the traffic on Queen's Road. He was looking straight at her, as if seventy feet in the air.

Government should pass a law, she was saying in her old woman's voice, make people just walk again. And this time he didn't go off to his comicbooks, leaving her to herself. I know, Mamaiji, he said, there should be no cars at all.

But her wizened face dimmed, and he wasn't sure she'd heard. He found himself looking in on Satput Singh in the passenger seat of their Fiat. The old driver lurched as he'd done during lessons with Viraf. But when the view floated to the driver's side, it was Mamaiji in her kimono, gears grinding as she mistimed the clutch.

Then he was looking, through her eyes, into the front grille of a lorry, a dilapidated brute that came groaning around the hill. He barely had time to yank the wheel before it was upon them. Its driver's eyes were blue. They scraped between it and a precipice, only to face another truck in a long, rumbling convoy. And then another, and another....

When light filtered in from behind the blinds to play on his eyelids, the thought crept into his mind that those manmade machines she'd abhorred were still rushing beneath Seth Building, while her body had broken down forever. She'd filled its tank with oxygen for the last time. The irony bothered him, and his head hurt.

After locking the door on his way out, he turned to face a common sight on the footpaths of New York and Bombay, but an unusual figure for Newark. A man with dusty black hair in clothes reeking of urine had descended the steps into the lower space—the entrance must have been left open. Probably by Lynette.

"Hey, man," the figure said, nodding at Viraf, who nodded cautiously back.

"How're you?" he said perfunctorily, shifting his weight to move along.

But the stranger lifted his hand to disclose a tinted bottle, and there was no mistaking the fumes. "Good," he said, then tipped the bottle toward Viraf, nodding some more.

"No, thanks." He shook his throbbing head, holding a hand up. And he took a step to go by.

A few words in a thick voice stopped him. It couldn't have been what he thought he'd heard.

"What?" he said, peering hard at the man in the unlit hallway.

And the stranger said it again, as normal and conversational as if asking the time. "Can I suck your dick?"

Viraf couldn't tell why he was threatened by the question—it offended his sense of manhood but there was more to it, something it seemed to state rather than ask. He had no idea what.

"Fuck off," he said, gesturing to the nearest door, the back door to the courtyard.

The man looked at him without moving. Viraf held his point a bit shakily, not sure what he should or could do if the stranger, as tall as himself and wider at the shoulders, refused to go.

Then the slightest forward tilt of the man's head indicated his compliance, and he began to drift toward the door. Viraf watched him until he'd opened it, then went out the front door.

CHAPTER 19

The Voice of Authority

At half past five, when the other assistants had left, the phone rang. It was Richard Danner asking if Viraf could come by the office. Sure, he said apprehensively. When he walked in with lifted eyebrows, there was no reassuring smile on Richard's face, just a sober shake of the head.

"You're not on the list, Viraf," Richard said. "No assistantship. And that means no tuition waiver either, I'm afraid." He seemed sympathetic at the consternation on Viraf's face. "Chairman Pickett would like to have a word with you about your situation."

He inclined his head at an inner door, one that Viraf had only seen closed. Now it was open, revealing another room.

"Okay," he said carefully, aware that their voices were reaching it. "Thanks."

He knocked with a tentative smile and a "Dr. Pickett?"

A bulky man behind a desk looked up over reading glasses. Putting them away, he rose with a surprisingly hearty "Hello there; come on in." A broad smile was on his face.

Viraf walked in, and they shook hands, exchanging the usual back-and-forth over the pronunciation of his name. *Adajania* was, as always, too much to handle, but a *giraffe* rhyme delivered his first name. His nerves began to settle. He'd never, in four years at IIT, exchanged so much as a word with the head of department, and now here he was, having a man-to-man conversation with the chairman. A conversation he would rather not have, but still.

"So tell me," the chairman said, "where did you get your undergraduate degree?"

"At the Indian Institute of Technology, in Kharagpur."

The chairman looked impressed. The smile spread again on his broad face under a receding red hairline. "Good. We're happy to have an IIT student come to us. Now, how's it going? I see you came here on a research assistantship—which of our professors have you been working with: Dr. Froley? Dr. Takagi?"

"No," Viraf said, smiling back. "Dr. Reese."

He almost missed it, but inexplicably there was the slightest narrowing of the chairman's smile. What had Will once said, about some tension between the two professors?

"Mm. And after the master's, what? Do you plan to get your PhD with us?"

Reminded of the line of questioning at the US Consulate, he shook his head. "Oh, no, just the master's."

But the smile had weakened further, almost disappeared. "I see."

This was a strange inversion: it seemed the chairman, unlike the consular official, would be happier if he stayed on for a doctorate. Maybe not enough Americans were opting for that. There weren't even a lot getting the MCE.

"After the master's," he said, feeling the need to elaborate, "I'll be joining my father's construction company back in India." He pulled his chair closer. "So I'm working on a site-management project, with Dr. Reese. For my thesis."

"I see," the chairman repeated, his face unreadable now. The panel light reflected off the bald part of his head. "And how far along is the thesis—almost complete, ready to write up?"

"No, no." Viraf was shocked by the implication that it should be or even could be. "Our investigative tool, a FORTRAN simulator I'm developing, is almost complete. But the research can't be done until it's ready."

"Well, what's taking you so long?" The smile was gone, and without it, the heavyset features and a disconcerting change in tone told Viraf he was no longer dealing with someone as easygoing as Ed Reese. "What have you been doing all year?"

He felt a complex mix of self-doubt, apprehension, and resentment rise within him. Will's almost-forgotten warning resurfaced: this was not a man to cross.

Viraf kept his own tone even. "I've been focusing on my course requirements, and I've finished all but the two I'm taking this semester. I have A's in all my courses, except for one B. And that was in Engineering Mathematics, my first semester." Taught outside the department, Engineering Math was notoriously tough. "It made sense to get it all done, and done well, after which I could concentrate on my thesis."

But Dr. Pickett did not look impressed. A glint came into his eyes, and now his tone was openly aggressive. "If that's so, where were you during summer session? You weren't here all summer, I believe! What stopped you from wrapping up your course load over summer?"

Suddenly Viraf understood. All this time, while the man had been smiling and asking questions like he didn't know a thing, he'd been waiting to spring this.

"No one told me I had to be here in summer! I didn't even know you could take courses in summer. Summer months at IIT were always holidays."

An unpleasant look came over the chairman's face. "So you just took the entire summer off! What did you do with it, you haven't said—how did you spend all of that time?"

The chairman's loud aggression, strangely familiar, was fueling Viraf's own anger, swamping his anxiety. Later, he would distinguish Pickett's overbearing tone from the cowboy's. This was the voice of authority.

In response to it, his own tone finally changed. "You want to know? I'll tell you. It's none of your business what I do in *my* time, but I'll tell you!"

He saw the chairman's eyes widen, but barreled on. "You want to know what I was doing in summer? My sister, whom I hadn't seen for a year, was getting married! My family, none of whom I'd seen in a year, wanted me home for her wedding. So I went. Then, just before my return, my grandmother broke her hip and caught pneumonia. We had to put her in the hospital. So I canceled my flight and stayed: she was in Parsee General for a month. *That's* what I was doing in summer!"

The chairman's eyes had stayed open during the outburst. But as it progressed, his belligerence seemed to give way to uncertainty. His voice was less strident, less assured. Yet it carried a note of skepticism. "Your grandmother?"

That was when Viraf lost all control. "She died!" he shouted, further incensed by the sudden pricking at the surface of his eyes. "Do you hear me? She's dead!"

And the chairman's eyes dropped momentarily. "Well," he said, and looked up again, "it's a good reason." He came close to sounding abashed. Then his voice picked up once more, and his jaw hardened. "But now what?" He spread his hands. "You're no longer on our assistants' roll; how do you plan to see your studies through?"

It brought Viraf back to the present problem. "I asked Richard before I left—" He gestured in the direction of the doorway and did a double take. For the first time since the interrogation had begun, he saw that Richard was still at his desk, had been there all the time, listening. It was an eerie sight, almost ghostly in its unexpectedness, this silent, bespectacled figure with the large head down as if reading something, but utterly still and alert. "—I asked him if there was anything that needed to be done to carry it over, any forms to be filled. And he said no, it was all automatic."

He held his breath, still half-turned toward Richard. But the man kept his head stolidly down and never so much as opened his mouth, let alone contradicted Viraf.

Nor did the chairman call on his assistant—he just shrugged. The two had clearly talked before bringing Viraf in. "Well, let me say this again: all the assistantship funds have already been allocated. And that's a finite amount—there's no more to go around. So there's nothing either you or I can do about it. The question is how do you intend to handle it? Here's my advice: take out a student loan, finish up as fast as you can, work at an American company for a while, and pay it off. That's what most people do."

Viraf shook his head. "I came all the way here on the assurance of a scholarship for my master's, not to get into debt in another country. And in any case, I'm expected back after the degree."

A challenging expression came over the chairman's face. "Well then, what are you going to do?"

Viraf shrugged; he was tired of the fucking thing. In fact, he was just tired, period. His head felt as if it had been sucked empty. His lenses felt encrusted.

"I'll go back," he said simply.

For some reason, though, the chairman didn't jump at that convenient solution. "You'll just stop, a year into the program, and go back?"

Viraf nodded. "I'll join my father's company, like I'd have done a year ago if I hadn't been offered the scholarship. It's a waste of a year, but anyway."

That brought the chairman to a boil again, his face scrunching up. "You have the gall to sit in front of me and call a year of our program a waste of your time?"

Viraf waved the misunderstanding wearily aside and made an effort to pick his words: "I meant a waste in terms of not getting the degree and not learning the ropes either. My father pointed out to me that there's a gap between class theory and what's practiced in the field. So if I'd started with him a year ago, I'd be a year of work experience ahead by now."

The chairman's voice quieted a tad. "So I'll ask you again: what do you intend to do?"

It was puzzling, not to mention annoying. He'd just told the man what he intended to do. There was something going on. He didn't know what, but it occurred to him that his honest reply didn't suit the chairman. Why, exactly, he had no idea. All the more reason, though, to stick to it verbatim.

"I'm going back." It felt satisfying, like some form of nonviolent protest.

The chairman looked distinctly unhappy with the answer. The last time Viraf was policed, Jer had advised him to try to see it from the other side. So maybe the chairman just didn't like to see a student drop out. If he'd been Doug's principal in high school, maybe he'd have talked him, too, out of it. But Viraf doubted that.

Maybe... And something clicked. Maybe the chairman didn't like a student from a top college to drop out: an IIT alumnus who'd leave UD without his master's. The word might spread among former classmates and professors that this was what a UD scholarship had amounted to in the end: "a waste of time."

The chairman eyed him, brushing a hand through thinning red hair. "What if we arrange an interest-free loan for you? No interest to pay, none, and we can talk about the period of repayment."

Viraf shook his head as neutrally as he could. "I'm not going to take on any debt. It's just not the kind of risk I grew up with: we don't have car payments in India, or mortgages. Not even credit cards until the last few years."

And then, leaning forward, the chairman said something quite bizarre, if entirely unoriginal. "Well, what *are* you going to do?"

What was wrong with the guy? Maybe he expected Viraf to lose his cool again and throw out an accusation in Richard's hearing—clearly the man was meant to be an observer, a witness—anything that could be turned against him.

The one thing he did know was that he didn't want to hear the question another half a dozen times. So he allowed his forehead to pucker, then lifted a questioning hand in a What-on-earth gesture. "I just told you."

The chairman sat back heavily in his chair at that. He looked stymied. It gave Viraf some fleeting pleasure to see that, took the edge off his tension.

Finally, the chairman spoke. "All right, here's what I'll try to do. No promises, do you understand? No promises."

Viraf nodded.

"I want from you a research proposal—a written proposal—for your thesis. And I want it fast. I'll try to put through a departmental proposal to fund the project with a grant. I'm talking a small grant, mind you, no more than two thousand. I don't know if we can clear room in our budget for even that. And if we can, it's a one-shot deal, no more to come. After that, you're on your own. If I were you, I'd wrap everything up this semester. Your remaining course load is small, and we're talking *master's* thesis here, not a dissertation: don't make more of it than you have to! Get all the research done in fall, along with your coursework, and write it up over winter. Then go home to your daddy's company."

Viraf, who'd been nodding quietly to it all, felt his face tighten at the final sneer. But he kept his mouth shut, grimly.

The chairman wasn't done. "You've said some things in here that I'm going to put aside, only because you're young. But you're not the first person in the world to lose his grandmother. And you won't always get off so easily."

It had the ominous ring of a threat or a curse, more than a prediction. Seething again, Viraf held the older man's eyes without even a nod this time.

The chairman arched his eyebrows. "I want that proposal on my desk first thing tomorrow morning."

Tomorrow morning? No time to consult Dr. Reese—in any case, who knew what his role had been in all of this. But what the fuck was supposed to go into a formal proposal?

"You'll have it," he said shortly and rose to his feet. He'd be damned if he was going to thank the man.

He glanced at Richard on his way out. But the secretary kept his head down over his papers, a silent observer to the very end.

Even the diligent Will had gone home. In the secluded hush of the assistants' room, Viraf collapsed onto his chair, none too sure he'd have it much longer. He put the coolness of drops in his eyes and took stock.

Then he got to work.

An hour later, when the light through the window changed, he drove home for dinner. As soon as he pulled into a slot near Building H, he knew something was up. The entrance door was wedged open, and people he rarely saw were either standing around talking in the evening light or going in and out. Brad and Russell, the undergrads on the upper-level who'd once told him the reason they didn't fraternize with Doug was his lack of education, were there. And inside so was Debbie, Lynette's supervisor, with an arm around her charge's heaving shoulders. Lynette was crying, a stream of snot trickling into her mouth.

Doug and Ali were between their door and Lynette's, looking uncomfortable and concerned, respectively. Viraf walked over to them, wondering if he should in his frame of mind.

"What happened?" he said.

"You missed the cops," Doug said. "Knocking on doors, asking questions, taking notes, the whole nine yards."

He resisted the impatience that rose within him. "Why were they here?"

Lynette was sobbing something out to her middle-aged supervisor, her words even more indecipherable than usual.

Ali spoke, her voice on edge. "Something happened to Lynette; we don't know what exactly. Some guy got into her apartment; you know how she leaves the door open." He nodded, instantly recalling the drunk. "She came across to our place afterward, just crying her eyes out. I couldn't tell if...you know, if the guy had done something to her. But I called Debbie, and she called the police."

He looked over at their childlike neighbor, who was blowing her nose with facial tissues handed to her by Debbie. That was not a shift he'd made yet, from handkerchiefs to tissues. Lynette's flimsy, orange-on-white dress was short enough to show her thighs, but it looked intact and all in place.

"My penny jar..." she was saying inconsolably, the rest of it garbled.

"That's about it," Doug said, sotto vocé, a stubble-faced Doug who no longer looked like Jesus. "Some guy took off with her jar of pennies. If it was anything else, Debbie and the cops would've taken her to a doctor long ago."

Ali seemed to turn her face away at that. She, too, kept her voice down, but she didn't look at him as she spoke. "They ought to've taken her anyway. She isn't capable of telling us, even if it did happen."

A short silence ensued. Viraf was picking up on some tension between them that he hadn't been sure of since his return. He'd heard her raised voice, recently, audible from their apartment as he let himself into his. But he hadn't thought it was angry, at the time, just unusually loud. And the one time he'd dropped by, her normally comical monsters, on sheets of paper by their couch, looked almost evil.

He felt obliged to fill the silence. "I think I saw the guy this morning, before I left."

Ali looked at him. "Really?"

He nodded, but didn't elaborate.

"You should let the police know, Viraf," she said. "They may need you to help identify him in a lineup."

"Ya, that's true," he said. "I'll go some time tomorrow. I've got an emergency at school right now—I'll tell you about it at Deer Park." If he was still in the States. "Where's the police station, by the way? I don't know where it is."

It turned out the station wasn't far, just past the old people's home by the railway line. Even with the lost assistantship on his mind, it bothered him to think that, had he known of the station, he could have stayed ahead of the Bronco for just another mile and gone to the cops. What would it have mattered, in the long run, if they'd fined him for not fixing the taillight?

He went inside, took out his contacts, splashed water in his face, threw an omelet on a frying pan, and opened a can of baked beans to go with it. After wolfing it all down, the hot and the cold, he reinserted the contacts in his mutely protesting eyes and went out again. What had Doug, swinging that blond mane, once said about adversity? "Builds character." Well, if he survived all of this, he'd have an abundance of character.

There was no one in the corridor anymore, nor was the entrance open. The large stone that had been used as a wedge lay off to the side. Dusk had fallen. He raised a hand toward Russell and Brad, who were still by the hedges, talking. They waved. Then he got in the Pinto and drove back to the department.

CHAPTER 20

Wanted

By the time he left UD, it was early the next morning. He printed up the detailed proposal and deposited it on Pickett's desk, surprised to find the office doors had been left open. God only knew what the man would think of it or whether he'd really push for that grant. But Viraf had done his part—now he'd have to see which side up the coin fell. Stay or go.

If he had to, he'd fucking go, but for now he wouldn't call home about it. He wouldn't pile another load on them, on top of Mamaiji's death, unless he had to. In any case, the only phone company here, AT&T, had its monopolistic rates so high per minute that he'd go broke now if he called India.

Fighting a scattered feeling, he looked around him. Facing away on the desk was a gilded photo stand. He was torn between the urge to look and an instant resistance. He went with the resistance. The darkened inner room still echoed with the heated words flung around it hours ago—enough time for him to realize the temerity of what he'd said to the chairman.

Still, surfacing only now that the need for single focus had passed was a growing satisfaction at how he'd handled himself, confronted by someone powerful enough to have crushed him had he slipped up at any point. He could feel deep in his gut, like a long-tied knot beginning to unravel, some vestige of his battered pride coming back. Had the men in the Bronco engaged him in a battle of words, of reason, of intelligence uncorrupted by brute force, they'd have lost. The big stranger in the faded checks must have realized this when he'd resorted to first shouting Viraf down, then bludgeoning him into ignominious flight.

Even so, reverberating around the office was something puzzling: his own voice shouting down the chairman with words curiously like his attacker's. "Do you hear me?" he'd cried, at Pickett's refusal to understand, echoing the blond stranger: "Do you hear me, you fuckin' dago? Do you hear me?" What was it that Viraf hadn't understood? What was the source of his attacker's anger, his frustration, his hatred? Ostensibly, the near-wrecking of his new Bronco. Was that it, then? But nothing had happened to the Bronco. And whose fault had it really been?

He headed back to First State for some sleep, thinking the other time he'd heard something comparable was when the stranger on Main Street had yelled, "Go home, you fuckin' I-rainian." Pickett had echoed the call with his sneer: "Then go home to your daddy's company." Doug, too: "So why don't you go back to India?"

And now maybe he would.

On his way back to UD that afternoon, he stopped by the police station. Its proximity still bothered him, but it helped to find it recessed and hidden off Main Street. Had he stayed ahead of the Bronco looking randomly for a police station, he would not have seen it.

The parking lot was flanked by trees, still mostly green. At the back of the lot, a gray stucco facade emblazoned with symbols and legends would have kept the men in the Bronco at arm's length. He pulled up along heavy black motorcycles and squad cars bearing the word *Sheriff*. He smelled eucalyptus as he walked over to the entrance and hesitated. It was a sanctuary too late. For him, if not for Lynette.

The officers at ground level had shoulder-patches and badges over their hearts. On their own turf, they did not look like he made them nervous. He was directed to one at a desk, no more than twenty-eight and almost black-haired like himself. The officer listened to his story, nodding quietly when he stumbled over the "suck your dick" part.

Viraf liked to think that the proposition was ironic: Am I even good enough to suck your dick? Subtly delivered. Smart. But he had a growing understanding that, although the stranger had never mentioned money, he was probably soliciting. What sequence of events had led to such a desperate state? Was he, like Jadhav, born into poverty, the multigenerational lack of an economic base? Or had he been a respected member of society, only to fall out of favor? Like Viraf had at the department.

Once the officer got a description, he made a reference to the drunk that Viraf hadn't heard before. "Would you recognize the homeless man if you saw him again?"

Homeless. An honorary Parsi. Viraf pursed his lips, thought back, and nodded.

"Good. Do you think you could help our sketch artist develop a composite drawing of the man's face?"

"Why not?" He didn't know exactly what a composite drawing was, but they obviously couldn't get anything reliable out of Lynette. "Um, was Lynette okay? Herself, I mean, aside from her savings."

The officer nodded reassuringly. "The doctor confirmed she was fine. No physical issues, nothing."

He felt relieved. Mostly for Lynette, but somehow also for the drunk. He couldn't shake the sense that he'd turned away from the man, and in the process antagonized him.

Once before, he'd had to deal with a plain-clothes' detective from the Kharagpur police station. Returning to Patel Hall for lunch, he'd locked his Hero at a stairwell, its black less glossy than when he'd bought it years ago. The mishmash of gluey rice, dal, and oily curry called for a snooze and a missed class. Ambling down for the next class, he saw that his bicycle, whose bar had on fifteen occasions been graced by Maya's bottom, was gone.

He'd trudged over to campus security at the main gates, to report the theft. Behind a red sign, POLICE, were officers in khaki and berets. Promised a follow-up and already too late for class, he went back to await action in his A Top room. Their sports prowess had earned Imtiaz, Rangan, and himself prime rooms in the very wing where Milind had once ragged them.

An hour later he heard a knock, and standing there in long-sleeves was a man no older than a student. He shook Viraf's hand and introduced himself as Detective Shekhar. More mild-mannered than Miss Marple, he exuded a quiet confidence, conducting the inquiry in a non-Bengali accent and jotting the answers on a notepad. Viraf took him to the scene of the crime. No, he admitted, he hadn't seen anybody suspicious. Did the detective feel they could find the bike? Yes, why not, there was always a chance. And his modest nod implied a host of secret resources that would now be set in motion.

After two weeks without word, Viraf inquired at the station. Detective Shekhar was unperturbed by the passage of time and still held out hope of recovery. But that was the last Viraf saw of the likable young detective. A week later he bought a second-hand Hero. He would soon leave it to rust in the bicycle shed, when final year ended. Newark and the Pinto were just over the horizon.

*

This time, in Building H, he *had* seen someone suspicious. The drunken stranger must have stopped the back door from shutting behind him, leaving an easy re-entry once Viraf was gone. The thought bothered him. If he'd watched the man until the door closed, maybe Lynette's savings would have been safe. And if he hadn't antagonized the guy, maybe he'd have just gone away.

The sketch artist on the upper level, a middle-aged man with scattered white in his hair, was more relaxed than the grave young officer on the ground floor. His mouth twitched upward in permanently humorous fashion. It was hotter upstairs, and Viraf rolled the sleeves of his shirt past his elbows as he sat across from the officer. With fall setting in, there was a chill outside. Before he learned his assistantship was history, he'd added a couple of flannel shirts to his diminishing wardrobe—his Indian shirts didn't fit anymore, tight at the chest. That the new ones resembled not only Bernie's but the men in the Bronco's wasn't as relevant as their warmth.

What, the artist wanted to know, was the shape of the suspect's face? And right away Viraf was at a loss, trying to picture it in his head and match it up with adjectives. He had a surprising amount of difficulty doing either. Rectangular? Oval? Square? No, not square. But what the fuck was it?

As if reading his mind, the officer opened a large wooden box and pulled out a number of outlines to spread on the desk. Centered on each page was a different face shape, hairless and without features. No simple ovals, but shapes that undulated at the hairline, cheeks, and jaw. Viraf stared at their blankness, glad to have an aid, yet confused by the almost inhuman configuration. Eventually, he picked out two that offered some resemblance to the shape in his floundering memory.

"They're too long, though," he said, adding with his newly discovered uncertainty, "I think."

"That might have to do with how he kept his hair."

"It was dirty and short. And dark underneath the dust."

Upon hearing this, the officer started to pull out and superimpose different hairstyles on the outlines, looking up inquiringly after putting each in place. Viraf kept shaking his head. He began to feel bad about his indecisiveness, and settled on one that looked too neat but was roughly the right length and had an indeterminate style. It covered none of the forehead—that seemed right— so it didn't help with the face length.

He went with the face that looked shorter, though it still left him uncertain:

something about the width, or one of the widths, since it narrowed and widened. Maybe the jaw line needed to be wider. Or maybe not. The original was shifting in his head like the faces in Longwood.

"It's okay if it's not exactly the same," the graying officer said, again reading his face. "Once we get more of it in place, we can go back and change it. Let's move on to the nose: what kind of nose would you say he had?"

"Um..." Viraf angled his eyes up to better envision, but it didn't help. "Average?"

"Well, would you say it was black? Caucasian? Asian?"

"What's Caucasian?"

"White."

"Oh. Never heard that. No, his skin was brown—like mine."

"Was he Hispanic?"

"Hispanic?" He was starting to feel stupid.

"Um, Latino. Like Mexican, Puerto Rican, Cuban."

"Oh. I don't know...hard to tell. Maybe. Or maybe black. Even Asian, come to think of it." He knew he'd sounded wishy-washy, and dropped his eyes to the outline.

"Really, Asian?" The officer's default start-of-a-smile gave way to mild surprise. Strong expressions seemed beyond the scope of his facial muscles. "So were his eyes Asian?" And he rummaged inside the chest, pulling out slanted or slit eyes.

"Not Chinese." Viraf wondered at the assumption. "But maybe, you know, Sri Lankan or Bangladeshi or certain kinds of Indians. He didn't sound Indian, though."

It was the officer's turn to look confused.

"So, not slanted," Viraf said, responding to the man's patience with his own. This inside view of the warden's office was starting to change his mind about "complaining" to one, if he ever needed to again. "But dark, yes. Like mine."

It was the second time he'd said that. Skin and eyes like his—and what else? Same height, from what he remembered. He'd mentioned that to the officer on the ground level: about five-ten. In the morning, he'd almost added, but it felt like something a kid would say.

What about the timing of the man's appearance, this desperate specter of pennilessness, in several ways his hapless counterpart? God only knew how the departmental meeting called by Pickett had gone. Had it even taken place?

Paying for rent and utilities himself, without Nitin's half, would quickly wipe him out. And then what? Go home to daddy's company, as Pickett had so tactfully put it? Better than being thrown on the streets and freezing to death. Homeless.

The sketch artist had reached into the kit again. The dissociated pairs of eyes he arranged in a row stared up at the popcorn ceiling like some kind of audience. When he placed the one picked by Viraf within the outline, the face looked creepy, nothing but eyes. But the eyebrows followed, and the nose, mouth, and ears, all largely generic, until at last it became a face with a full set of features looking up at them.

Viraf stared back at it, shaking his head. But the officer said, "Give me a couple of minutes," and turned away, presumably to earn his title of sketch artist, not mere assembler of parts.

The sun poured in through a window behind the officer's chair, lighting his work. Viraf could see sky and the brown wall of the old people's home. From time to time, a distant bird flew in and out of the picture. He felt shaken by the difficulty he'd had with the process, his inability as a near eye-witness to accurately picture the perpetrator. It occurred to him that the older image of the men in the Bronco burned more fiercely in his head: the flare of the blond man's nostrils, the startling blue of his eyes, the look of anticipation on his brown-haired accomplice as he waited for the moment.

Twenty concentrated minutes later, the officer swiveled back, and with evident pride, his mouth turning up again, offered Viraf the finished sketch. He examined it with some surprise at the transformation: not patchwork anymore, it was a single, unified pencil drawing pulled together by skillful shading that made it startlingly three-dimensional. This was a real face looking out at him.

The only problem was it was not the face of the man who'd offered him a swig.... Apart from the inexact features, he wasn't sure how the look was different: maybe too young, too neat. A kind of vigor emanated from this face, an apparent strength and vitality. Nowhere in it the wretchedness from which had issued that spectacular non sequitur. What had led to that, he wondered, what unknown sequence that had continued in Lynette's apartment?

"I don't know," he started reluctantly, not keen on either revisiting the process or squashing the artist's sense of accomplishment. "Something about it—"

The officer's expression and nod said he understood. "Hard to get it exactly right. It can't function like a photograph; we know that. But it'll give us a rough idea of what we're looking for and tell us if we're in the ball park when we have a suspect."

Viraf nodded back, relieved they weren't going to put it up on a WANTED poster. He didn't want it to lead to the wrong man, still less someone in crushing poverty.

They shook hands, and he went out to the Pinto and back to campus.

CHAPTER 21

The Browning of America

In the assistants' office, students were drifting in to consult the TAs. During lulls there was silence, everyone at work. Yet Viraf had the feeling that they knew his situation, at least some of them. And that they, too, now questioned his right to be in the room. On the phone with Dr. Reese, he limited what he said to yes and no and setting up a meeting.

On his way out, he turned to Will to test the waters: "Tennis on Saturday, Will?"

"Yeah, man." Will's manner was routine enough. "How about at three? The wife's got evening plans for us."

"Sure, no problem." Viraf lifted a hand as he left. Good enough: even if they knew, they weren't talking about it. Not in front of him.

Tennis felt like a good idea—slam the shit out of the balls, maybe turn the tables on Will, who'd won narrowly, the last few outings. Their last match had turned on Will's line calls, which Viraf, at the opposite end, had seen differently. If the disputed points had gone his way, it could have changed the outcome.

Unlike the eucalypti at the police station, the shade trees on campus had exploded into orange, starting to carpet the mall. It struck him that, after over a year, he had no idea what kind of trees they were. On cross-country drives in India, his father would stick his hand out of the window, pointing to a sprawling banyan or teak or gul mohr. The great jackfruit at Parsee General had been an endless distraction for Mamaiji.

He'd learned of the sour gum from Ali, but apart from that, all he knew were names he'd read in books: elm, ash, sycamore, maple, oak, and so on. No idea what they looked like. Maybe there really was a purple variety that grew around Longwood. A few steps along, he shook his head: no tree could go from green to purple and back and forth in a matter of minutes.

He went up the steps of Smith and navigated to Dr. Reese's office. Once again, Viraf wondered how his advisor had figured into all of this.

Ed Reese's face, when he answered, was as bloated and red as ever. His expression was a nervy combination of concern and conspiracy. He ushered his charge into the little room, musty from books, cluttered with papers, bookcases, and folders, then shut the door and motioned Viraf to a chair. The professor bustled around to his own, preceded by his belly.

"Now," he said in his New York twang, "tell me everything. I wish I could've been with you when you met with Dr. Pickett. I hadn't heard a word, so it was a shock when it came up at the departmental meeting. But tell me exactly what was said between the two of you."

Viraf, relieved to hear of Reese's uninvolvement, did so at length. His voice rose as he described how the chairman had drawn him in, then sprung the summer-term issue. His advisor sat quietly through it all, taking it in, nodding from time to time, his eyes occasionally widening.

At one point, he sighed before interjecting: "You got caught up"—he said it like "quat up"—"in some things that have nothing to do with you, things that have been festering between me and my old department for a while now. But go on...."

Viraf's eyebrows lifted at this hint of a supportive perspective. He felt encouraged to open up. If his argument might be conveyed by Reese to the chairman or a departmental gathering, then he had better state his case as strongly as possible. At any rate, it felt good to air his grievance without having to worry about repercussions.

"It's very unjust, Dr. Reese," he said, working himself up at the thought of it, "to come all the way from India on a scholarship and then have it just cut off like that!"

Ed Reese nodded, his baggy eyes satisfyingly grave.

Recalling the impact on Pickett of his decision to go home, Viraf started to speak with his hands. "They can't do things like that and expect students from top international colleges to still come here. Who would come, if they knew? And then where would the department be? Three-quarters of the grad assistants are from abroad—the whole assistantship program would go down the drain. And it would serve them right; they don't deserve to get the best students if they act like that. There in India, people are complaining about the 'brain drain,' and here they're cutting off the best students? How can they afford to do that? Even Dr. Pickett knew they can't!"

He'd begun to feel like a striking mill worker demanding just treatment. But the professor's look of agreement was replaced by one of alarm.

"For God's sake," he said, falling back in his chair, "put away that arrogance. This is no time for it—just put it away!"

The word took Viraf by surprise; it sobered him up and left him uncertain all over again. He'd been aware of being angry and loud, but anger wasn't arrogance.

Maybe it was the "best students" comment. He hadn't been a topper, not with how much he used to bunk class for tennis or badminton or just an afternoon nap, something he'd learned he couldn't get away with here. Too many regular assignments, not just mid-terms and end-terms. And if the GRE had not been an aptitude exam, he wouldn't have scored in the 90 percentiles, UD wouldn't have given him a schol, he would never have come to the States, and he would not have to decide whether or not to go back.

"Listen," the professor continued, less apoplectic, apparently perceiving in Viraf's dumbfounded reaction something that soothed his nerves. "There's more to this than you know."

This time Viraf nodded, accepting the advice. It was obvious by now there was a whole lot about the world he didn't know.

His advisor leaned forward. "Adam Pickett and I, we haven't always agreed on things, and there's been some resentment over my doubling up at the computer science department. They've been leaving me out of the loop, when assigning assistants. When they selected you, I don't think they anticipated that you'd hook up with me instead of one of them."

"The secretary, Richard, sent me to you when I said I wanted to work on site management. He told me you were the management expert."

Ed Reese nodded, his face relaxing as he glanced at a textbook atop a pile of assignments. Viraf recognized the Engineering Systems text authored by Reese himself. Viraf had consulted it before the Daylight Savings Time fiasco. How long ago that seemed: circa one month BB. Before the Beating. Before the world went Bad.

"Richard Danner's a good man; I'm afraid he's in some trouble over this. I might be, too, but it won't matter much longer." The professor seemed centered again, calm. "Once they commit to taking care of you—which, if you don't rock the boat, I believe they will—I intend to leave the engineering faculty and devote myself fully to computer science."

Viraf's mouth fell open at that. "Are you sure? I hope it's not because..."

He didn't even know how to finish that. He was suddenly aware that his was not the only life that had been shaken up. And yet the professor's concern had been less for himself than for Viraf. All the more reason he didn't want to see his ally leave the department.

Ed Reese shook his head. "I don't like the way they've handled this, and I feel partly responsible—I should've seen it coming. But it has opened my eyes. I've stayed on too long, out of loyalty. I need to get on with what I started when I joined this fledgling department: it's just too much, trying to do both. This is the work I want to be doing in the coming years—it's the future."

It wasn't the far future that worried Viraf. "How about my thesis, Dr. Reese?"

The professor nodded. "I'll see that through with you. Soon as we get the official green light, let's get cracking."

And now there was nothing left to do but admire his advisor's stand. As for that prediction for the future, maybe he was right. Back in IIT, armed with a Japanese calculator, Viraf had never used his father's old slide rule. At the computer lab, they'd submitted their programs on punchcards, just handing the stack over. It had waited in line to be fed into the Russian mainframe that awed the seniors.

So when he arrived at UD, the rows of terminals in DuPont's basement had impressed him. And by his second semester, every assistant in the department had his own terminal. Things were changing fast. Mamaiji would have bemoaned the idea of a future that revolved around computers. Ed Reese, on the other hand, couldn't wait.

That Saturday afternoon, pulling into Will's subdivision over a speed bump, Viraf heard something in the Pinto creak. He wasn't sure if he'd imagined it, in the growl of the motor. But he laid his racket on the hatchback, and lowered himself to look under the chassis.

Keeping his T-shirt and shorts above ground, he peered at the sooty maze. Rust spots and a slight smell of fuel. But the gas tank looked as sound as one could expect on a '71 model. Of the treacherous bolts in Will's tale, there was no visible evidence. Still, he was seized by the old foreboding.

He straightened up and made his way through the children's park, amid squeals and laughter. It took him out of campus troubles and the solitude of First State. The kids were on molded plastic tractors, swings, and toffee-colored slides, their corners rounded for safety. The slides went from low and straight, through higher and convoluted, to a corkscrew twister that had them screaming as they slalomed their way down.

Built into the set were revolving blocks with animal parts or alphabet or noughts and crosses on them. The letters were currently turned to SUN, FUN, and YES, while the animal parts made a cow, bunny, and kangaroo. The honey-colored cow had a bloated udder, and a baby 'roo peeked from its mother's pouch. Someone had abandoned the noughts-and-crosses at the end game, with the X's poised to go out either vertically or diagonally, no matter which line the O's blocked. As his father put it, damned if you do and damned if you don't.

A basketball half-court signaled the grown-up section of the park. He'd arrived ten minutes early so he could hit some serves before Will walked over from his apartment. On a couple of occasions, "the wife," whose name was Shona, had come by to watch. She was an elementary school teacher, sweet and cultured. Viraf liked the almost Indian sound of her name.

She had fresh lemonade in the refrigerator, she'd announced once, if they were in the mood for it. They were, sweat dribbling down their faces, T-shirts drenched and heavy. The walls of the cooled apartment were in more solid shades than in First State. Will had a keyboard and 8-track on which he recorded near-professional rhythm and blues with a black flavor. The beats were intricate and jumpy, foreground rather than background. In no way dhin-chak.

He felt at home with them in a way he didn't with others anymore, even Nitin and Judy. It was hard to drive over rural 896 and Porter Road without his mood souring. He felt wary of anyone from that area, even Judy. She sounded like the people in the Bronco. But at Will and Shona's, the international camaraderie of the assistants' office blended with the female touch into a comfort zone, one no longer possible with Doug and Ali.

Viraf entered the screened court through a squeaky corner door. There was something soothing about the enclosure's symmetry, billowing blue backdrops around a green court, its varicose cracks visible when picking up balls. Soon there'd be a brown-skinned man on either side. It was like a protected little world, yet open to the sky and smell of trees. Maybe this was his perfect place.

He opened a tube of old balls and began to practice his serves, drawing yellow lines through the air less precise than the white ones. Hard to hit the corners or down the T without missing the service box or finding the net. But if he went safely to the center of the box, Will was all over it with his octopus reach. Lately, he'd had a hard time holding serve.

They'd always played each other tough, but when they first began, Viraf had the upper hand, rarely dropping a set. In those days, Will was the one disputing calls made on Viraf's side. "I don't think that was out," he'd say, shaking his head, upon which Viraf reversed his calls. It wasn't worth the argument—he was winning anyway. For the same reason, he hadn't bothered to question calls on Will's side.

But session by determined session, Will's game had stiffened, until through sheer consistency, he began to grind out some of the sets. It infused his game with confidence, loosening him up, allowing him to go after his shots, pushing Viraf back with newly discovered power. That began Will's string of wins, and now it was Viraf for whom every point mattered. He was the one who started to question the close calls.

Will had been increasingly touchy about that. In their last session, when Viraf said he wasn't sure if Will's shot had stayed in, the normally composed big man had seemed ready to erupt. Adrenalin could do that, but something else seemed to be going on as well.

Finally Will had said, not without a dash of sarcasm and a couple of air quotes, "From here on, if we're 'not sure,' let's just call it 'good.'"

And that made sense all around. Viraf shouldn't have spoken, just played it as if it were good. So that was how they would play it today.

He rotated his serves around the court, rocking back, then leaning into them, starting to feel the rest of the world fall away. About five after three, Will walked in, stooping through the door with a "Hey, man." They shook hands, remarked on the great tennis weather, and began to smack the balls back and forth, working both flanks.

Viraf could feel his attention close around the little objects flying at him, could feel himself slip into a trance that excluded everything else. Mamaiji and Pickett, Doug and Ali, Broncos and Pintos, Lynette and the drunk, Maya and Rangan, all gone, blanked out by the imperative demands of each shot.

Once they'd warmed up, Will popped a fresh tube of balls without asking if Viraf had bought one. He hadn't, and though he'd been spared the embarrassment of saying so, he felt a cloud cross his consciousness. It was a sign that the other assistants knew of his fall from grace. But, not for the first time, he noted his friend's decency.

Calling up or down, Will spun his Prince, bringing Viraf back to the moment. He called up, but the *P* fell inverted like a *d*, giving Will the serve. Viraf twirled his T2000, and they started a set.

They held serve through 4-all. Light sweat sprang up on his forearms, and he was in the moment, his twinge of anxiety forgotten. Even the fur on the ball was visible as it flew, so well was he seeing it today. The *fwop...fwop...fwop* hit his ears like a drumbeat. Then at 30-all on his serve, he broke open the rally with a forehand that looked right on the line, a rare clean winner past Will.

But Will called it long.

Viraf said nothing, though it put him down break point. At times his contacts blurred on the run, as if a lens had shivered before centering itself again. He didn't think that had happened just now, but who knew? In any case, the call nagged at him, breaking his trance. When the balls came at him now, a part of his mind was still on the call. He dropped serve, and Will, uncoiling at the top of his height, served the set out.

Viraf's game continued to slide in the second set. At 0-2, love-15, he was in danger of going two breaks of serve down, which, against Will, would mean the end. He lined up on the ad court and went into his service motion, trying to recover the rhythm he'd had at the start. It worked: he pounded one down the T. 15-all, he thought, starting to move over to the deuce court.

But Will didn't move. "Can't say for sure, but I think that was long. Play two."

This time, Viraf made no effort to be quiet. "I thought you said if we weren't sure, just call it good."

Will looked affronted. "You saw it good?"

"Ya, I did."

"All right: just take as many first serves as you need."

The pause had caused sweat to break out on Viraf, streaming down his face and forearm onto his grip. He tried to wipe it off on his shorts, but they, too, were sweaty and the racket slippery in his hands.

"That's not good enough," he called out. "You weren't even close to the ball, so it should be my point, period."

"I didn't move for it, because I thought it was long." Will's touchy tone was back. "Now, I don't question your calls, but you're pretty much saying I cheat."

Viraf moved to the net so they could talk without yelling. "You *have* questioned my calls, and I'm *not* saying you cheat. All I'm saying is when the game gets close, your calls get tight."

Bad choice of words—he should have said "our calls." Too late: Will was already gathering his balls and putting his gear away.

"You won't have to worry about my calls anymore," he said.

Viraf went over to him on the sidelines. "Come on, man, Will, you're overreacting."

Will was calm but withdrawn, eyes averted, his face a wall. "Listen up," he said tersely. "I called it the way I saw it."

Viraf was realizing he'd overreacted, too—just crossing over to that reserved face was enough to make him rethink his certainty. Try to see it from the other side, Jer would have advised.

"I know. Sorry. I should have said *our* calls get tight, not just yours. It's just that you said yourself if we're not sure we should give it to the other guy. And I agreed."

But Will was shaking his head. "No, man. You as good as called me a cheat."

"I didn't mean anything like that. I swear! I'm sorry it even sounded like that."

But Will shook his head doggedly. He'd made up his mind, and nothing was going to sway him. When their talk petered out, he picked up his kit and stalked out of the enclosure. Its screen door clanged shut.

Back in the Pinto and smelling of sweat, Viraf mulled the incident over. How in the world could two honest people see the same event so differently? Pondering this kept him from the sick feeling that their friendship was over. The psychology of it all was too much to figure out, but he felt he ought to be able to solve the physical mystery—or what good would he be as an engineer? Had sweat trickled into his eyes, coating the contacts? They were clear right now, the street signs sharp. And the contacts never fogged up or streaked the way his glasses had.

He took a turn without slowing—and there it was again, the creaking or groaning that made his heart jump. From the back, he felt, taking a swift glance in the rearview. Nothing but street. In vanishing perspective, as Mr. Gonzales used to put it in drawing class at Campion.

And then, like the board duster once hurled at him by Mr. Gonzales, it almost hit him. Vanishing perspective...vanishing perspective... What about it, though? Not much to do with the limited length of a court. And yet...

He had the crazy urge to shut his eyes in order to think, resisting it as he neared an intersection, closing just the left eye instead. With only one eye, he felt the Pinto was about to run into a tree that was safely on the side of the road. What was the other term Mr. Gonzales had used? Depth perspective. His depth perception was compromised.

That was it! More about depth perception than vanishing perspective. When he'd hit that serve, he'd seen it bounce off the back of the service line and away from himself. In. Whereas Will, seeing it come at him from the opposite side, saw just the front of the ball hit unpainted green. Out.

Or else Will, nearer where it bounced and six-foot-three, saw a flash of green between the yellow and the white. Out. Whereas for Viraf, half a court away and forever short of Mr. Ahmed's prediction of six feet, that pinch of green was so compressed as to be invisible, bringing yellow and white into apparent contact. In.

Of the two scenarios, it was hard to tell which was fact. Probably why McEnroe and Connors could argue themselves red, in accents like Dr. Reese's. They were simply describing what their eyes had seen. But this much was clear: there was a fifty-fifty chance that Will had been right.

Viraf scrunched his eyes at the realization. For an instant, he felt himself moving through darkness.

CHAPTER 22

Deer Park

That Friday night on his way to the Deer Park, the rear of the Pinto erupted. The deafening sound jerked his foot off the gas. A metallic din followed. Craning to see the fire, he yanked the Pinto over. But the racket slowed with the car, and the explosions—repeated backfires, he realized—switched off with the engine.

He sat there as headlights swept past, reluctant to ruin the silence with what he might discover. When he made his way around and dropped to all fours, he saw the muffler trailing from a broken pipe. Heated air pushed his hands back before they could close on the pipe. Exhaust clogged his nose. Straightening up, he dusted off his Levis, then paced the sidewalk as a boisterous group went by, clearly out to party, and the clock tower of Center Square inched over from 10:17 to 10:18. He adjusted his Seiko to match it.

By then, his hands were as cold as the night, and this time when he gripped the pipe, its warmth was welcome. He wrenched the rusted muffler off and threw it in the hatchback. Maybe he wasn't destined to die in a car after all.

The Pinto roared into the tavern's parking lot like a flatulent Harley. He caught looks from people out with beers in their hands. After finding a space, he waited a minute to dissociate himself from the racket before walking to the open porch. Its red-and-white frosting shone through the gloom. A lighted board proclaimed TUE BURGER NITE and WED NACHO NITE and DOORMAN WANTED. The buzz enveloped him. He unzipped his jacket as he went inside and climbed the stairway.

The upper level was jumping. A foot-stomping bass line and drumbeat hit his ears, and he made his way around the crowded bar. Beyond its stacked glasses, beyond the stag's head, Bernie was hunched over, goatee bobbing, arms flying, sticks and pedal driving holes in the drums. A wah-wah pealed over it all, pulling Viraf's eyes toward Doug.

Something was different: he didn't have his foot on a wah-wah. As he played his lead, he mouthed the wah-wahs into a tube running to a stack of amps. The wailing guitar was eerily human, as if man and machine had merged.

Resplendent in leather, Sean stepped up to the mike and squared his shoulders. "I wonder how you're feelin'," he sang.

Frampton. Looking around the tables, Viraf spotted them against the wall: Ali, Megan, and Taylor, with another woman. Doug's camel parka was slung over the back of a chair. Viraf made his way through the smoky room, grabbing another chair and returning Megan's wave.

It took barely a minute after the hi's and heys to pick up on some awkwardness around the table. The new face, a pretty brunette, introduced herself as Sarah. But there was a pause before anyone filled him in. Ali, next to him, had her shoulder turned away from the band and her eyes on the table, on her drink, on her fingernails.... Megan looked tipsy. Taylor spoke up, gesturing vaguely.

"Sarah came in from California," he called out. "The new talkbox they're using—she got it for them."

"Huh," Viraf said, tuning in again to the wah-wah. He raised his voice over the music. "It sounds great...like a musical android or something."

She laughed at that, her teeth even and attractive in a kissable mouth. "C-3PO, maybe."

He smiled. "Did he sing?"

A discussion ensued as to whether C-3PO could sing, and if he could, what would he sound like? Or better yet, R2-D2, what a voice! Even Megan joined in. But not Ali. She rummaged in her handbag for something that never emerged. Draped behind her, matching her hair, her kapok was as orange as a life-jacket.

Sean and the Moles had moved on to the next song. "Take it easy," he sang. "Don't let the sound of your own wheels drive you crazy." Viraf decided to take the Eagles' advice. He asked if anyone needed a refill and went off to the bar. By the time he returned with a daiquiri for Megan and a rum and Coke for himself, the band had broken into a number he'd never heard before. It had a rolling rhythm counterpointed by Sean's keyboard.

He sang of passing farmhouses, car dumps, and freight yards peopled by old black men. "Good mornin', America, how are ya?" he called out. "Say, don't you know me? I'm your native son." He was speaking for a train, it turned out, called the City of New Orleans.

Viraf leaned over to Ali and spoke close to her ear. "Which group is that?"

She looked up and into his eyes, as if the question had greater meaning. "It's Arlo Guthrie."

He sat back. The word *porter*, something about sons of porters and sons of engineers, had caught his attention. Pretty, but it reminded him of Porter Road. And how the pretty woman in the Bronco had smiled at his beating.

Ali was waiting for him to say something. "So what've you been up to?" she said, clearly trying to sound upbeat.

"No good," he said, making an effort in return. Leaning over again, catching a whiff of another variation on her fruity perfumes, he told her about Mamaiji.

Her face saddened. "I love my Gramps in Wilmington so much," she said. "I can't imagine how I'll feel when the day comes. He's so frail now."

He nodded, remembering Pickett's comment about grandparents. A vision of Ali's, a frailer version of the kindly, silver-haired optometrist at Delaware Vision Center, formed itself in his head. He'd heard, by now, how the death of a grandparent was a common excuse for a student's absence. No wonder Pickett had been skeptical. He recalled the family-photo stand on Pickett's desk and how he'd resisted looking at it, avoided the revelation of a different side to the chairman. But he could still hear the belligerent voice of authority.

Sean was striking up a familiar number on the keyboard, building from a tinkle and bass counterpoint to a pounding chord. Doug's lead sang out an unearthly whistle. Then Bernie came in on a cracking beat, Todd banged on the bass, Doug switched to rhythm, and Tull's "Locomotive Breath" was roaring down the tracks.

"They have a train thing going today," Viraf said loudly to the table at large. The rum had warmed him up nicely.

"Yeah," Taylor yelled back. "Exactly what Amtrak sounds like."

The others laughed, Ali too. The hammering beat seemed to be picking her up.

"So what else?" Viraf asked her, lowering his voice.

"Oh, this and that," she said, leaning close. "My ceramics class is really neat; I have to show you some of the stuff I've been making."

"Like pots and vases?"

"Yeah, that," she said, nodding. "And some of my own stuff, too: like my little dragons, you know? But in clay now. And glazed in these gorgeous colors."

So they were dragons, not ghouls. Maybe she had an Arthurian thing, growing up in New Castle County. Maybe her perfect place was Camelot. A place of the past, like Persepolis. She'd often spoken of a game called Dungeons & Dragons. The harmonies of "Puff, the Magic Dragon" had worked a gentle spell on him at Megan's, as Galahad tramped across creaky floorboards. It was a song of changing times, of vanished lands, of a childhood peopled by kings and friendly dragons.

The thought made him smile. Growing up on Queen's Road, a young Parsi reader had not been immune to that influence. "I like your dragons."

"Thanks." She looked suddenly shy. "I'll have to make one for you."

Sean had picked up a flute between verses and was huffing locomotive breath.

"How did you first start on them? What gave you the idea?"

"Oh, I don't know. I was pretty young then. I think everyone has to deal with their demons at some point. This was my way of taming them, giving them a funny face instead of a scary one."

He pursed his lips and thought about that, sipping at the rum and coke. Its sweet and sour piqued his taste buds. "What kind of demons?"

She looked down. "Nothing, really. Silly teen stuff."

He didn't push it. Now that he thought of it, the light dapple across her nose was kind of pointillistic.

"Remember I told you I was dealing with an emergency at UD?" he said after a second, to change the subject.

"That's right, I forgot!" She looked up at him. "What happened?"

He gave her an abbreviated account, toning down his altercation with Pickett.

When he got to Dr. Reese's revelations, her eyes widened. "That's so establishment," she cried, "to screw you because of their politics with your advisor!"

It felt good to see her jump to *his* defense, just as she'd leapt to Doug's at Lums Pond. And if Pickett was the voice of authority, then she was the nonconformist.

"I'm sorry those assholes cut your assistantship, Vir." The blue-gray eyes were as soft as they'd been cold in the Galaxie.

It was a long time since she'd called him Vir.

"Thanks." A note of relief entered his voice: "The good thing is they came through with that grant for my thesis project. Might see me through."

Pickett, he had to admit, had been better than his word. He'd delivered what he'd been careful not to promise. The man could have said good riddance to Viraf, instead of which—for whatever reason—he'd saved him. The one-time grant wouldn't last very long, but it would keep him in the game. And in the States.

"Cheers," he said, lifting his glass.

"Cheers!" She touched her margarita to his rum.

"What're you guys toasting?" Megan called out, stretching across the table to add her glass, clinking it before they'd said a word.

Garbled explanations went back and forth, congratulations and commiserations were yelled—couched in phrases such as "your pig of a boss"—and more glasses were clinked. Something in Viraf felt released and overwhelmed to see their happiness for him, to hear them side with him over their fellow American.

"Thanks," he said, over and over. "Thanks."

Sean announced the last song of the set, and some people came off the floor. Bernie started a pattern on the cymbals, all chak and no dhin: chakachaka chakachaka. Doug came in on some nimble picking. "World turning," Sean cried, and the Moles chimed in.

"Man, that Stevie Nicks is something else—right, Viraf?" Taylor yelled, earning a disparaging look from Megan.

"Is that a Fleetwood Mac number?" Viraf said. "Yeah, she's sexy."

"Oh, you guys," the newcomer Sarah said, smiling. "That's not even a Stevie Nicks vocal."

Only Ali was quiet again.

Doug and Bernie took the band out with guitar licks over a bongo, then laid their instruments down to applause. The buzz of fifty voices took over. Doug and Bernie ambled across, pulled up their chairs, and listened with big smiles to effusive exclamations.

Doug's look had changed again: even the stubble beard was gone, disclosing a chin. The radiant hair was still long, but the Jesus look was history. His face was alive with an exhilaration the beard must have hidden— he soaked in the praise as if he lived for it.

Ali offered none. Some, more low-key than Megan's, was delivered by Sarah, and he looked like he couldn't get enough. He hunched over their corner of the table to respond, while she listened, rapt.

Between him and Viraf, Ali looked down at her drink. Her expression was an attempt at unawareness. It surprised Viraf that it hurt him to see this. All held in and stoic, unlike Imtiaz over Maya. More like himself.

He leaned toward her. "Another margarita?"

Her eyes were clouded as she glanced up at him. "No, I won't be here much longer, Vir. Thanks, though." The eyes cleared and she continued, now obviously of a mind to be distracted: "So how's Nitin? Have you seen him and Judy lately?"

"It's been a couple of weeks," he said. "They're doing fine."

This surprised him even as he said it. Contrary to his doubts, they only seemed to be growing closer, like some manifested coupling of their countries. If the overriding thing that drew Jer to him or Maya to Rangan was their shared background, then how could one tell the full strength of their connection? So in spite of Judy's neighborhood, something within him had begun to pull for her and Nitin to make it.

"Oh, good," Ali said. "I haven't seen you around much, either. You haven't been at work all day, have you?"

"Well..." He didn't want to sound dull. "Gotta do it, Ali; the pressure's on. Never done a thesis before, you know. And now suddenly I'm expected to wrap it up in a couple of months, on top of my remaining coursework."

She nodded.

"But I've been getting out for some tennis." Not anymore. Will had his head turned away, at the assistants' office. There would be no perfect place at Laurel Walk again. "And I grabbed a couple of beers at Jimbo's last Saturday night."

He'd gone there the evening after his argument with Will. Unable to focus on work and dogged by a feeling of isolation, he'd felt the need to be among people, even strangers. So he'd gotten in the Pinto and rolled out to Paper Mill. The bar was by a rushing creek, its bed strewn with rounded white stones. The sight relaxed him.

"Jimbo's?" Ali cried. "But, Vir, that's a meat market!"

She sounded half dismayed and half entertained.

"A what?" he said. "Oh. No, it was an older crowd, just there for a drink. Me, I like the area, that's all."

But at Ali's cry the others had turned to listen.

"What's this about Viraf and meat markets?" Megan said with a knowing smile, her words slightly slurred.

"Vir has been picking up women at Jimbo's," Ali said, still aggrieved, tossing her marmalade hair.

Either she could feel possessively about two men at the same time, or this was her way to diminish what was happening at the other end, maybe even make Doug jealous. At all events, Doug did turn his head.

"Did you say at Bimbos'?" he said with a smirk, getting a laugh out of everyone. And votes were cast as to whether or not Jimbo's really was a meat market.

Viraf hadn't gone to meet women. But maybe because of that, he'd met one. She'd taken the bar stool next to his and ordered a vodka. In the welcome hubbub around them, he just sat there with his beer, didn't even check her out before she spoke.

"Haven't seen you here before," she said.

He swiveled his head. Late twenties—an "older woman." Short honey-blond hair.

"It's been a while." Since Nitin had stopped needing company, to be exact. They talked about nothing for a few minutes, a social skill he'd improved.

"I'm Carrie," she finally said.

"Hi, Carrie. I'm Viraf."

"Oh, that's different." Brown eyes that seemed to like what they saw. "Say it again?"

"Viraf. Rhymes with giraffe." Maybe he could make a limerick out of it: There once was a man named Viraf, who rode around on a giraffe.

Nice smile. "Viraf... Is that South American? Like from Venezuela or something?"

Ah. He aimed for Venezuela, but was such a silly fella, he ended up in... Hmm. America? India? Persia? "No, it's Indian."

"Oh!" She seemed unusually delighted to hear that, and he felt encouraged. Until she followed up. "Which tribe?"

The anticlimax made him laugh, and her expression stiffened. But when he tried to stop, it kept sputtering out of him.

"What's so funny?" Her forehead furrowed.

He managed to stop. "Nothing," he said. "I'm Indian Indian, not American Indian." Indian Indian. He had to shake his head at that. "I'm from the place Columbus tried to find, not where he landed."

"Oh." She didn't sound impressed by his little witticism. "Well, I have some Lenape in me, so I'm from the place where he landed."

"Really?" He stared at her, trying to see it. "American Indian?" He was glad he hadn't said Red Indian to start with.

"Yeah." She looked annoyed now. "Also Brit and Irish. And that's probably not all."

"Huh," he said. "Lenape..."

"It means 'original people.'" She took a sip of her vodka.

"Wow," he said. "You're my first American Indian."

He'd wished he really felt awed, but it was hard in the presence of her blond looks.

Ali waited until the band was a couple of numbers into the next set before she stood up with a little hand-wave around the table and put on her jacket. Even Sarah tried to talk her into staying, but she smiled back and shook her head. The margaritas had given her a headache, she said, and she really wanted to rest. She looked and sounded to Veer like an adult, no longer a college kid.

Viraf watched her navigate the tables to the stairwell, feeling the bars of that old Love Temple snake around him all over again. Twice, she turned her head in the direction of the band. But Doug's eyes were nailed to his fretboard.

Viraf stayed where he was, separated by the width of the table from Megan and Taylor, and by its length from Sarah. He could see the potential for trouble if he got to know her too well—best to stay out of it all. But she moved around to sit where Ali had, right next to him, and struck up a conversation about moviegoing in India. She wanted to know if American films such as *Star Wars* were just as popular there.

He said yes, with the more Westernized audiences, but not if you were talking movie audiences in general. They were most of all into Hindi fillums, more of which were made each year than Hollywood films in America. Oh ya, he assured her; that was a fact. Sure, they were good. Good for a laugh: that was what he and his pals went for. Heroes and heroines singing duet after duet while dancing and running around trees. Followed closely by villains who duped or outright abducted the heroines and impregnated them en masse, while the heroes crooned their sorrows into the moonlight.

He got some gratifying laughs out of her. His sense of humor was back. And it was hard, in the face of such pretty laughter, to dislike her. He was on his third rum, by then, and a sucker for feminine charm.

Eventually they sat back and listened to the music. It was bongo-backed and funky. Bernie swayed over the bongos, his hands beating out an elastic pattern. "Feelin' alright?" Sean wondered, in the mood to change his scene. Sarah, who thought the number was a Joe Cocker original, was impressed when Viraf told her it was actually Traffic. Doug leaned in to harmonize. Then, bracing his feet, he launched into an opening, weaving lead that repeated, building resonance, drawing whoops of recognition. They were back full circle to Frampton.

"Do you feel like I do?" Sean sang out, bringing back for Viraf the times they'd played the marathon anthem in Imtiaz's A Top room. But some of the words felt new: they told of crashing into a taxi after being busted, of the need to play music or break down.

The song hit a lull. Bernie, back on the drums, swung into an easy chukchuk chikachika, and Sean introduced him to the crowd. Todd came in with a brooding bass. Then Doug on rhythm, to cheers and applause. And Sean himself on the keyboard, to more cheers.

Doug picked up the talkbox tubing and placed its end in his mouth. He struck up an unmodulated, piercing lead that played over the bass and the cymbals. Then he moved his mouth around the tubing, and the lead began to shape-shift and wail and to scat funky phrases. Eventually, it spoke.

"Do you feel...?" it inquired.

And Deer Park answered, "Yeah!"

"Do you feel...?"

The effect had the hair on Viraf's arms standing up. Just as it had years ago in Patel Hall.

"...like I do?"

The tables and waitresses, bartenders and barflies, the whole crowd said it did. Sarah waved her arms in the air.

．

After the robot-Doug voice intoned its goodnights, and last calls went out from the bar, the band put its equipment up and strolled over to the buzzing tables. Then the human-Doug voice said, "Did she leave already?" He sounded honestly surprised.

He took his chair on the other side of Sarah, then downed the remainder of his tequila. They kept their conversation low, leaving Viraf to relubricate his contacts. Blinking to spread the drops, he turned to Taylor and Megan for small talk. Galahad was eating well, apparently. Maybe too well; he was passing a lot of gas. They were changing his diet, but in the meantime they'd probably have to invest in gas masks.

"So now, if a thief comes along," Megan said, "he'll collapse from the fumes even before he sees my big baby and dies of fright."

"Hey," Taylor said. "I'm not that scary."

Viraf laughed. Megan kissed Taylor and said, no, he wasn't. Doug wanted to know what he wasn't. Megan said it was a shame, though, that Lynette had been robbed of her penny jar. Then Sarah asked who Lynette was and what had happened. Everyone tried to fill her in at the same time. When they were done she looked thoroughly confused, and of all the names mentioned, Ali's hung uncomfortably in the air.

Viraf considered telling them about the homeless man and his composite sketch, but thought better of it. What had become of that sketch? Probably gone the way of the bicycle detective, and a good thing, too.

Doug leaned around Sarah to ask Viraf for a ride home, since Ali had taken the Galaxie. He said sure. Sarah didn't need a ride; she'd driven all the way from LA. And that probably meant she hadn't come into town for just a week or two.

In the emptying parking lot, he and Doug stowed the guitar in the hatchback. Light glinted off more metal inside, and Doug was amused. "What's your muffler doing in the trunk?"

"Wait till you hear the car now; it's a hot rod."

Doug chuckled as he positioned the guitar. Then he straightened and stretched in his fur-edged jacket. "So, what did you think of her? Isn't she great?"

The quick irritation this aroused in him took Viraf by surprise. "Who, Ali?" he said dryly.

"No, wise guy. Sarah. She and I hung out a lot in LA."

Viraf closed the hatchback carefully. He was tempted to stay out of it, let the damned thing run its course the way it had with Imtiaz and Maya. But he couldn't shake the expression on Ali's face every time Doug and Sarah had leaned close. He stood there, watching the breath issue from his mouth.

"Listen," he said, finally. "It's not my business, and there's no question she's very pretty and nice. But you've already got an incredible girl...."

Doug looked at him for a moment. Then he nodded and spoke in so mild a tone that Viraf was nodding back before the words registered.

"I know. But I never pretended to be monogamous: she knows that."

He could only stop mid-nod and stare. Maya's impassioned self-defense—that her boyfriends had heard what they wanted to hear—had not been so very different. But stated so quietly, Doug's blunt reason had the force of a philosophy. Of a lifestyle choice, one that Viraf had only half believed ever existed.

Leaving it at that, they got in front. But when the Pinto roared to life, the sound made both of them smile.

"Take this baby to Daytona!" Doug cried, rolling his window down to get the full volume. Unfiltered exhaust blew in.

"Daytona?" Viraf had to raise his voice to hear himself.

"The Daytona 500, man. Florida, here we come!"

He pulled out of the space ahead of a car that followed them. They rolled up to a still busy Main, and Viraf looked for an opening to cross it.

The car behind them stopped to their right, short of level, needing room to come all the way up for a right turn. It took a second to hear him over the Pinto, but the guy at the wheel was calling out officiously. They turned to listen.

"You're blocking us." It was a burly young guy in a Blue Hens jacket, pointing at Viraf. In the car were more undergrads. "You need to be over to the left!"

Viraf could feel his mood darken.

"Fuck you," he said, lifting his voice over the racket.

The outraged jock spun around to his pals and made a quick move to come out of the car. The others corralled him and seemed to be talking him down.

The road opened up. Viraf moved the Pinto out, one eye still on the other car. Doug just sat back and laughed. A loose, easy laugh, no worry, no anger. It was infectious, and Viraf cracked a smile. But not until he saw that the rearview was empty did he start to laugh, too.

CHAPTER 23

Cute Dragon

After that night, the snows came, and Newark frosted over. Viraf settled into a steady grind: scrape off the windshield and hatchback; drive cautiously to Evans, the Pinto muted by a new muffler; grab a sandwich at Pete's; walk over to DuPont; run the simulator for new sets of variables; tabulate the results; browse the bulletin board for students' tours abroad; slip and slide to First State in the dark; open a can of Campbell's or a packet of Oodles of Noodles; clean the contacts; work on course assignments till midnight; crash.

When December arrived and the coursework was over, so too, after rent, was the grant. He would finally have to call in the cavalry, or as Pickett put it his "daddy," to wangle some dollars from the black market. With all the needed course credits in the bag now, and only the thesis to complete, he could drop a remark about the assistantship being over without his parents suspecting too much.

In the meantime, he expected any moment to be evicted from the assistants' office.

One Sunday as he sat at work, the politically minded Talaat walked in, looking enigmatic under his crisply trimmed beard, crooked his index finger, and said, "Come with me."

Aware that the dread moment had arrived and he was to be exiled by, who else, an Arab, Viraf wanted to know where. But the slim Egyptian just put the same finger to his lips and, with his other hand, pulled Viraf to his feet and out into the corridor. Without a word, he led him down the stairs and to the office of his advisor, Dr. Tindale, a graying man with old-world manners and an accent described by Talaat as Southern.

Robert Tindale, it turned out, had begun a five-week undergraduate course in structural design and needed a grader. A grader wasn't paid as much as a TA, but would Viraf be interested?

Yes, he would, thanks! Not a word of his situation was breathed by anyone in the room, nor did Talaat, now revealed as his savior not evictor, ever allude to it afterward. But finally Viraf had confirmation that it was common knowledge among the assistants. Yet they'd treated him no differently, bless them. Even Will had loosened up again. And for whatever reason—maybe Pickett had his differences with more than one professor—Dr. Tindale viewed Viraf with approval.

Scarcely had the last of the assignments, bringing back more about I-beams, T-beams, rivets, and trusses than he cared to remember, been graded, than he received a call at the office from Dr. Tindale. A course in engineering systems had just been added to the professor's spring schedule; would Viraf be interested in being the teaching assistant for the course?

That was a clue—Engineering Systems had always been taught by none other than the author of its textbook, Ed Reese.

He asked Dr. Tindale if he could think about it and call him back. Then he dialed Dr. Reese at the computer science department.

After bringing his advisor up to speed, Viraf came to the point. "Did they take your course away from you, Dr. Reese?"

There was no hesitation across the line. "Oh, no. I declined to teach it anymore, as I'd told you I would."

"Well, then," Viraf said, pushing against his instinct for self-preservation, "should I turn down the offer to TA it? Let the department manage its own mess. Serve them right."

"No, no, no," Reese said. "I'm very glad they're taking care of you. You're the logical student to TA the course, having helped me with it in the past. And Bob Tindale's a good man. You should just go right ahead."

So Viraf did. Dr. Tindale was also an interesting man. He hailed from the small town of Jasper, near Birmingham, Alabama. Jasper had been named for an ancestor of his, a Revolutionary who'd died when trying to raise a fallen flag. He told Viraf stories of a confusing array of preachers, circuit riders, sheriffs, barbers, homesteaders, farmers, doctors, and Sacred Harp singers who'd built and peopled Walker County, surely a name after Mamaiji's own heart.

There was a certain kind of person who figured often: the "mean drunk," who was fine until he drank and fine after he stopped, except that in the meantime he'd been up to no good. The same ancestor who, when sober, punched out a couple of rowdies harassing a traveling salesman, got drunk and put a slug in the thigh of an incompetent barber. And did time for it. Cold sober again after his release, he went straight to the barbershop to apologize to the barber. But that worthy, understandably, could find no forgiveness in his heart.

Having grown up in Alabama, the professor had stories of the civil rights' movement. He'd marched for it, as a young man, whereas his sister, he said, was still leary of Afro-Americans. She thought the blacks were out to get back at the whites, now that they could. As evidence, she recalled being crowded off the footpath by a group of belligerent young blacks marching shoulder to shoulder. From what Viraf could tell, this had happened almost twenty years ago.

Soon, as if the universe had decreed a complete turnaround for Viraf, emergency funds from his father arrived in the form of a check written by a family friend in Chicago. He was relieved and thankful, to say the least. He had spending room again. The first thing he did was to visit the Delaware Vision Center and, as he liked to think of him now, Ali's silver-haired Gramps. True to Dr. Hansen's prediction for himself, the dapper optometrist was now minus his bifocals.

"Yes," he said. "Soft lenses will certainly make it easier for you to keep your contacts in longer. They'll need more care, but there's something to be said for the added comfort."

After the semi-permeables, it was almost like there was nothing in Viraf's eyes. Mamaiji would have been horrified at the idea of sticking a piece of plastic in her eye, but in fact it was 80% water.

One thing he'd noticed, that spring semester: Ed Reese was not the only person missing from the civil engineering department. Richard Danner, the departmental secretary, was gone.

Reese had predicted trouble for him, in the wake of Virafgate, but there was no way of knowing what exactly had gone down. Pickett had already replaced him with a young mother who had the irritating habit of gazing at Viraf with soulful eyes, as if she felt mightily sorry for him. Why, when she didn't even know him, he had no idea.

He, on the other hand, felt bad for Richard. What about his family, after, at the risk of his job, he'd stood quietly behind Viraf's account? The man could have sacrificed Viraf to Pickett and saved his own skin by denying the conversation they'd had before the assistantship was cut off. But instead he'd chosen the honest route, and look where it had gotten him. Or had he resigned in disgust? How tenable could his submission to authority have been, after he witnessed its inability to bully a mere youth?

Ed Reese, at any rate, was now exactly where he wanted to be. And yet, he stayed just as engaged in Viraf's thesis as before. It was far from over. Pickett's instruction to not make too much of it was proving easier said than done. For one thing, simulating even a simplified, repetitive-unit construction project was inherently complex. A number of variables were involved, including probabilistic task completion times to mimic real-world uncertainty. For another, conducting a thin investigation was alien to Viraf's nature. So the more output he tabulated and the more trends he fitted with predictor equations, the more scenarios he found he still needed to run through the program.

For a third, the program always did exactly what it had been coded to do; in that sense it was incapable of error. But its programmer, the code's writer, was not. Already well into the research phase, he caught the simplest of bugs that had eluded all his preliminary debugging: an imbedded loop counter he'd initialized at 1 instead of 0. When he swung through the loop mentally and saw that the bug had skewed every bit of output data, he put his head in his hands and sat frozen for a minute.

He reported to Dr. Reese in his cluttered office at Smith, its bookcases stacked with texts less alluring than those Viraf had devoured as a boy. On the desk he noticed the picture frame of a young woman roughly his age and bearing a subtle resemblance to his advisor. Bringing his attention back to the problem, he thought it best to prepare the fatherly professor before breaking the news.

"Okay, Dr. Reese," he said, making cautionary motions with his hands, "I have some bad news."

"What is it now?" Reese exclaimed, sitting up in his swivel chair.

"We have a big problem."

"Good God, man, just tell me what it is!" The paunchy professor, not concerned with looking professorial in pants cinched beneath the belly, had turned red in the face.

But when Viraf told him, Reese fell back in his chair with a huge expulsion of breath. "That's all right," he said. "That's a problem we can solve—just fix the program and run it through all the iterations again. I thought there was more trouble at the department!"

Understandable, although Viraf was the one who'd have to redo all the work, not Reese. Still, he was moved again by his advisor's concern, even now when the man was free of the civil department.

So it was back to square one, and the winter wore on.

In all this time, Doug and Ali were scarcely to be seen, even less so together. Or it might have been truer to say Viraf was scarcely at First State. He rarely saw Lynette anymore. She had a new roommate, an older woman, and their supervisor Debbie dropped by more often.

One snowy evening, after he'd finally begun to draft an opening chapter for the thesis, he skipped the lab and drove home. He'd generated enough data to analyze, and the entire thesis was taking shape in his head. For the first time since Pickett's orders, its completion seemed less an open question than a matter of time.

As his thesis acquired the texture of reality, so did the related matter of going home. Despite his belated look back at Seth Building, he could see its brown façade over the dry-cleaners, flanked by the church and hobby center, its balconies overhanging the Irani restaurants and the pork shop. All fine with him, even the rank smell of pork.

But also increasingly real were the dusty factory sites like Percy's, the crooked site-manager's shacks, the scintillating company or lack of any, the outdated surveying instruments, the half-naked, dust-covered workers, the dozy atmosphere, and the unending, flat-line tedium. Not really endless, he told himself, just for a couple of years. After which, he, too, would be based at the office like his father and Cyrus Uncle, setting out now and then for an excursion to the sites.

Conversely, Newark and its bricks and mortar had begun to take on an air of unreality, its edges less defined, its odors bland, its colors starting to fade. Or maybe that was a function of the snow falling lightly over Main Street. Klondike Kate's looked appropriately Alaskan—it was hard to recall its true colors. Were those roof shingles blue? And the awnings green? The color still showed on anything vertical: the deep oak of the doors, the beige of the façade. The wrought-iron railing was still black, as were the chairs at its outdoor tables. He ought to buy a cheap camera and take photos before it was too late.

He was surprised to detect, in spite of events he'd rather forget, a feeling of impending loss.

Back in 101, he turned on the heat, flipped the light switch, and yanked up the blinds. Then he settled on the couch to prepare a solution sheet for

Dr. Tindale's latest assignment. No sooner had he lifted his pen than Ali came knocking.

"You need to stop working so hard," she said at the door. For some reason she had one of her hands behind her back.

"Come on in," he said, only too glad to put his papers aside.

"I've got something for you," she said coyly, going past him at an angle so her back stayed hidden. "I made it last fall in ceramics class."

She held out a small object. The motion recalled for him the wild flowers she'd picked in Longwood and held out for him to sniff. A Biblical move. The offering, this time, was a six-inch figurine of one of her Yodalike monsters, sitting up on a fat behind.

"Wow, that's fabulous!" he said, taking it and turning it from side to side. It was surprisingly heavy, its glassy skin splashed with color. "It looks so cool in 3-D like that."

And in fact, the creature seemed wackily alive, pot-bellied and web-footed, glazed in blues, greens, and yellows that spilled over and dappled each other. Spattered black specks recalled its pointillist forerunners. The gray winter landscape outside was more dismal than ever, after this explosion of color in his hands.

"Do you recognize it?" she said.

"Ya, of course," he said, wondering what she meant. "One of your little creatures."

"Not just *any* creature," she said. "Look."

At first he thought she was pointing to its head, a sort of pudgy dragon's head, mouth open in midspeak. But on closer inspection, he saw it had glasses and was adjusting them on pointed ears and an equine nose with a three-fingered hand.

"Is it me?" he said, his voice rising.

"Yeah!" she cried, equally delighted. "See how he's throwing his hand around as he talks?"

And sure enough, the other hamlike hand was flung out expressively.

"That's the first time anyone's made a statue of me," he said, leaning over to hug her, instantly conscious of her body and a faint fragrance. No fruity perfume today.

"Just a little figurine." She made an apologetic face.

"That's fine," he said. "No one's made a figurine of me either, Ms. Michelangelo."

"Oh, good," she said, her eyes alight, more blue now than gray. "So are you volunteering to pose for a David?"

Something of a variation on her question long ago, when she'd been covered only by blue fleece. About his attitude toward women in nudie magazines. He chuckled and patted the figurine's belly. "Ya, maybe you'd do me without a paunch and fat ass, then."

She glanced at her handiwork. "I think you make a cute dragon."

"Not too bad," he acknowledged, proceeding to admire some of the fine detail work: flared nostrils, buggy eyes behind the glasses, indented belly button, deep impressions of fingernails and toenails.

"Stop before my head swells," she said, and left him to stare unseeing at the solution sheet.

By the time she came over again, winter was easing up. The research phase was over, and chapter drafts for *Computerized Simulation of Multi-Unit Construction* were going forth to his advisor. Dr. Reese returned them crisscrossed by arrows and scrawled over with dry formalizations of Viraf's language.

When Ali knocked, he was shaking his head over a passage that now read, "Inadequate managerial policies can result in consequences ranging from the inconvenient to the disastrous on project costs and completion times. Unfortunately, for any project at any time, there will usually be a range of strategic choices, which likely leads to a non-optimal policy." Like sitting around in Thana for weeks, waiting on wooden forms, he wanted to add.

The gloom must not have left his face, because she asked if she was disturbing him.

He said no, come on in, but she stayed outside, looking uncertain but pretty in a black woolen top. It set off the flare-signal of her hair.

"I just have a quick question," she said. "I'm going to the Grateful Dead show in Philly, a week from Saturday. And I've got an extra ticket. Do you want to go?"

"Wow, sure—fantastic!" he said, brightening up immediately but wondering about the extra ticket. "Thanks! Are we going in the Galaxie, like for the Moody Blues?"

"No, it's just me. I meant to ask: would you mind driving us there in your Pinto?"

"No problem," he said. "Absolutely no problem."

"Great," she said, smiling at last—a smile that blanked the words from his mind. Then off she went.

He settled back on the couch, putting the draft aside. And for the next hour or so, he pondered the latest development. If he was reading it correctly—which was a big if—then on the one hand, he hated the idea of betraying Doug the way Imtiaz had betrayed him and in turn been betrayed by Rangan.

Where would Doug be, for that matter, if not at the concert with them? Left to burn with feelings of jealousy and betrayal, as Ali went off with his neighbor and friend? Was this her way of getting back at him? On the other hand, it was clear Doug had already betrayed Ali. That was where he'd be, of course: with Sarah. And if *he* wasn't monogamous, why need Ali be?

PART III

NO SIMPLE WORLD

CHAPTER 24

No Simple Highway

When she came over before the show, Ali was very much the Deadhead in a tie-dye over long skirt, green bead-strings around her neck. No sooner had he opened the door than, aglow and excited, she reached up toward him with her lips. He turned his face down for the greeting peck, glad to get more than a hug out of the occasion. But she pressed her lips full against his before rustling in around him, and as they spoke, he could still feel the kiss.

"Looking nice," he said, recovering to lift his eyebrows admiringly at her ensemble. He gestured at his blue jeans and sweatshirt. "Same old, here."

"Oh, there'll be so much stuff you can pick up outside the Spectrum," she said, gathering up a pinch of her tie-dye. "If you want to."

He nodded again, taking in the splash of color. "Still a bit chilly for that, though."

"I know. I brought my wrap." And she threw a green knit webbing about her shoulders.

He doubted it would be enough, but didn't say so. Instead, visions of warming her up went through his head as he fetched his jacket. "All right, then. Let's go!"

It was a bleak day outside, patches of snow still showing. The front of the Pinto came alive as she settled in and adjusted the belt, her hair matching the rust and tan. Hard to tell what the perfume du jour was—it may have always been the same, altered over and over by her skin. Or his nose. He set the heat to blow as they pulled out past the sour gum, its branches bare.

She chattered about the Deadheads, how they followed the band around the country from show to show, some to vend memorabilia, some just to see the concerts and let their hair down, freed from the pressures of life. After months together on the road, more than just friends they were a big family.

"Wow," he said. "Sounds like fun. Would you do that? Chuck everything to follow the band?"

He was fishing, but she didn't really bite. "I might, some day. Maybe after I finish at UD—it's so hard to know right now."

Ambiguous in terms of her status with Doug. But it reminded him of his thesis, not far from the end now. And after that, what? As Pickett had put it, home to his daddy's company?

"Would you?" she added, turning the tables.

"Hmm. Can't tell yet," he said, intrigued by the idea. See those distant states, California, Florida, the Carolinas, riding the coattails of a band.

They were on Newark Christiana by then, heading east on 273. He was doing sixty-one in the left lane, six above the limit. Even so, in the rearview, a car was riding their bumper. Viraf inched up to sixty-four, beyond which they weren't safe from cops.

The car stayed hard on his tail. Its long blue hood and murky windshield filled the rearview: Doug in the Galaxie coming after them. Guilt grabbed at Viraf's stomach before he realized it wasn't the Ford.

Finally, room opened up on the right. But he was bothered by the arrogance of the silhouetted driver. Let the jerk go around them, if he thought he was on a racetrack. And sure enough, the car swung out to the right and moved alongside, a station wagon of some kind.

Ali was saying something about Phil Lesh and Jerry Garcia losing their voices. She interrupted herself to go "Asshole!" as the station wagon cut back hard across the Pinto's nose. Grimacing but prepared for it, Viraf took his foot off the pedal to give way. They slowed enough for the stern of the station wagon to go by.

Then three things happened simultaneously: Ali screamed; he saw streaming in, where nothing should have been, an open trailer behind the wagon; and his heart almost stopped. He stamped on the brake, jerking both of them forward. But the trailer was just halfway past and the other half swinging in heavily at them, inches away, when he drove the pedal to the floor, yanked at the steering, and fought for control as the car spun screeching out from under them.

The median came crazily at them and receded. They went spinning at cars in the right lane and barreled back into the left. Again and again, he lifted his foot and jammed it, turned into the skid and came out an inch from crashing. Side-on. Flashes of startled faces swung this way and that across the windshield. Over and over, the tires shrieked.

But gradually they lost speed. And at last, he straightened out.

They were a hundred yards or more behind the trailer now. His head was on fire. Ali was leaning forward, one hand on her chest, the other against the dashboard. But when he gunned the engine, and the Pinto lunged after the trailer, rocking her back, she found enough breath to cry, "No! Just let it go!"

She might as well have been whispering. As they came rapidly up behind it, he could see the misshapen bulk of equipment covered by a tarp on the trailer-bed. The wagon, too, had been picking up speed, but, burdened as it was by the trailer, he flew past on the right, blaring his horn. Then he cut viciously ahead of the blue hood and jammed on the brake.

He could see in his rearview the wagon lurch to avoid hitting, and he released the brake. As soon as a gap opened up, he hit the brake again and watched the wagon lurch. Dimly, he was conscious of Ali yelling at him, her hand at his shoulder. But he was too intent on the rearview to tell what she was saying or to care.

The wagon pulled into the right lane to go past, but he sped up and got in front of it again. It swerved back into the left, and again he blocked its escape, elated by the ease of it and the control he had over the bastard. Swinging his wheel like a madman, he waggled the hatchback's rear in the face of the station wagon.

At some point, through the craziness and rage and exhilaration, he could hear Ali's voice, shrill with its own set of emotions, "Stop it, Vir! Stop it!"

He stopped the waggling, but stayed ahead of the station wagon, which had lost its zest for the dogfight and fallen behind. His heart still hammering, he cut his eyes over for a glance at her. Shaken, looking straight ahead. None of the vicarious pleasure that had soured the face of the woman in the Bronco. Not even the tacit approval in his mom's demeanor, when his dad shouted down the VT passenger.

"Sorry." He sounded hoarse. "Not a good idea—waggling the rear end of a Pinto in front of a homicidal driver." Then, miffed by the lack of a response, his blood still high: "He could have killed us, you know."

"He's a jerk," she conceded in a shaky voice, "a dangerous jerk. All the more reason not to react like that."

No way to explain it all. It was best left alone.

Up ahead, cars were slowing for a light, and he coasted up to them.

Hard to tell if he was imagining it, but the last car in the right lane had seemed to drift over to block him from going through on yellow. From that guy's perspective, if he'd caught only the most recent action in his rearview,

Viraf must have appeared very much the villain of the piece. He eased to a halt, keeping one eye on the mirror. The station wagon came up slowly behind them, then moved over into the right lane, one car back.

He turned to look over his shoulder, but Ali's hand was at his face, pushing it forward—almost intimate. "Don't look," she said, still tense and disapproving.

He turned his eyes back to the rearview. The door of the station wagon had opened. "Too late for that. Here he comes."

He cut the engine and snatched at his seat belt.

"Don't go out!" she cried.

He had time only to shake his head without meeting her eyes—too hard to explain. Then he was out, his pulse racing, slamming the door and stepping away. This time he would not sit back.

The figure coming at him—only one, this time—was in some way like the somber customers in the Rising Sun. Older, around forty. Beneath the second-day stubble, and despite the grim expression, it was a good-looking face. And automatically one he hated.

He spoke before this stranger could get in his face, and his words came out hotly like an echo from the past. "What kind of stunt was that? You almost killed us!"

The man pulled up in front of him. About the same size as himself—no looking up into manic blue eyes, though the brown eyes were anything but friendly.

The voice was as hoarse as his own. "Listen, you motherfuckin' spic—I don't have all day to get where I'm goin', behind people who don't know to ride in the slow lane."

"And that gives you the right to ram your fucking trailer into them?"

"Damn right it does. Beat your fuckin' head in, too; what're you gonna do about it?" And the man made as if to step up to him.

"Try it, you fucking asshole!" He was shouting now, bellowing in the guy's face like his father at VT, almost out of control, his fists clenched. As if Ahriman had taken over. "I'll knock your rotten teeth out. And *then* I'll call in the cops!"

At the very mention of cops, for some reason, the man's eyes fell away. The rigidity went out of his frame. He looked back at Viraf, and some of the anger was gone from his eyes.

"Listen." The voice, too, was not as angry, even the slightest bit tired. "I had a bad day, you understand?"

But Viraf could not have let up if he'd tried. "And that gives you the right to call people anything you want! And to lay your hands on them!" The words were tumbling out of him. "Because you had a bad day!"

The man opened his mouth to speak, then closed it. A sullenness crept into his eyes. Cars slipped out as the light opened up, and the cars behind them started to honk.

The words were still pouring out of Viraf. "I don't have to do a damned thing to you." He wasn't sure where the realization was coming from. Certainly the fact that the stranger's violence had found violence in return and would find it again in others. But also something else. Something to do with the lines on the man's face, with his worn brown overalls like those of the mechanic who'd soldered the Pinto's sideview back on. "Life will take care of someone like you!"

He nodded grimly at the instant understanding that sprang into the man's eyes; there was no need to expand. Here was the American counterpart of the frustrated mill workers.

Mercilessly, he said it again, stabbing his finger at the guy. "Your own life will take care of you."

The eyes glanced away, and the man fell to muttering. "Yeah, yeah, yeah," he said, as he turned to the station wagon. But there was no conviction in his voice. He seemed to wander in the general direction, while car-horns blared again. Engines revved irritably, spewing exhaust.

Still heated to the point of explosion, Viraf turned back to the Pinto. He could see Ali bent toward his window, following everything. Anxiety still all over her face, she straightened up when he got in.

"Sorry," he said for the second time in five minutes. He turned the car on. "It's okay."

But he could tell that it wasn't.

Yanking the seat belt across his body, he moved out past the light. The station wagon, so recently in such a hurry, seemed content to stay in the right lane and behind them. Viraf pushed up past sixty, then changed into the right lane. But the station wagon didn't move up to pass.

"How were you planning to get the cops?" she said eventually.

He glanced over at her.

"It didn't come to that, Ali. Maybe because I said that." Invoking the sheriff at last had worked perfectly. The stranger must have had trouble with the law.

"You should have seen how his face changed."

"I did.... Stupid redneck."

Fitting payback for the stunts he and the Bronco guys had pulled. But Viraf registered the scorn in her voice. "What's a redneck?"

"Oh, some country folk. Ignorant, uneducated, right out of the boonies—that kind."

There was no point trying to pin down what the boonies were. And he didn't want to get into what a spic might be—he had a good enough idea. Clearly, though, she saw her own background and upbringing as very different from the stranger's. When he'd thought of the Bronco trio as just another group of young Americans like her, Doug, and Bernie, that was his unfamiliarity with America at work, his inability to tell one American from another.

"You could tell all of that from just looking at him?"

He'd drawn comparisons, too, but it was her turn to glance over. "And listening: the way he spoke, the things he said."

He left it at that. It made no sense to sound as if he were taking the guy's side, even if the last girl he'd been on a date with—Jer—would have liked that. And yet, through all the scattered thoughts, there was something about the way the man had turned away, so defeated, that bothered him.

When he took the exit for I-95, the wagon stayed on 273. He'd come as close as possible to a crash without it actually happening.

"There he goes," he said, with a tilt of the head. "You can relax now."

"I'm relaxed," Ali said.

He took the I-495 bypass, from which a gray and brown Wilmington looked dismal passing by. Better not to comment on her hometown. Her mind was probably there, thinking about her family or something, and they lapsed into silence.

The man's voice played in his head as he drove: "I had a bad day, you understand?" And this time, in that flash of insight, he'd understood only too well, at a level that had taken the guy unawares. More like a bad life, that was what it was, a life full of bad days and, if that wasn't enough, bad days still to come, stuck inescapably in a life going nowhere. He'd done worse than point that out; he could hear the grim intonations that sounded less like a recognition than a curse. Like Pickett predicting that he wouldn't always get off so easily.

He hadn't intended it as a curse, but he'd taken huge satisfaction in seeing the vision and imparting it. And he could imagine it playing over in the guy's head from now on, every time things went wrong for him. Where Mamaiji cursed an unconscious machine for taking her husband's life, her grandson instinctively targeted the person in charge. But his curse had this added logic: the man's penchant for violence would spark violence in return. Or, as Doug had once put it, what goes around comes around.

What, then, of the men in the Bronco, those violent cousins, he now knew, of the man in the station wagon? Did he now, by extension, know more about their lives? They were younger than this man, their car unlike his just "one month off the lot," a matter of pride for the big stranger, inordinately protective of it. Maybe it represented his hope for change, for upward mobility. He must have gone deep into debt to get it and would be paying it off for years. He'd certainly shared this stranger's need to get somewhere faster, resentful of whoever came in the way.

But maybe he was on the same road to nowhere, just not as far along it. And maybe he had a sense of that, from what he saw of his elders. Every man in the Rising Sun must have known it, so steeped in rumination.

Though there was a limit to "understanding," Viraf could almost understand their territorial disposition. The merit system in Patel Hall, rewarding extracurricular prowess with points, had spurred its residents to earn prime real estate such as the rooms in A Top. But it worked under the powerful constraints of a seniority system. Final-year residents got first go and could bid for any room. Third-year residents could bid only for rooms still available, second-year residents had an even narrower choice, and freshers had no say in the matter at all. Their inescapable role within the system was to accept their allotted ground-floor rooms. Any inclination to act above their place was swiftly ragged out of them.

That, then, was the lesson the men in the Bronco had tried to beat into him: don't cut in front of us—get back in line.

Still, there was a difference between the mechanic's "I had a bad day, you understand?" and the blond stranger's "Do you hear me, you goddam dago?" The latter a demand. To pay the man his due—attention, deference, even submission—to know your place in his world or have it beaten into you. And there was a big difference between both of those and the ultimately accepting nod from the man at the Rising Sun.

CHAPTER 25

Uncle John's Band

When a sign said they were in Pennsylvania, he tried to pick up the broken thread of his conversation with Ali. "So Garcia and Lesh actually lost their voices?"

"Mm-hm, Jerry's just for a while—they had to cancel when that happened." She didn't sound too upset with him anymore. "But Phil's went out for years; his singing voice, I mean. Lucky he only did harmony."

"Huh. Did he get it back?"

"Just last year, I heard." She leaned forward to twiddle with the radio, its crackle competing with road noise. "We should be able to pick up the Philly stations by now; maybe one's playing the Dead. Like a run-up to the show."

Sure enough, one of the stations was playing "Scarlet Begonias," and she perked up perceptibly. Garcia's curiously unsteady voice filled the car, singing of a girl with flowers in her hair. It was obvious that Ali could relate. She came up with more Dead trivia: the missing finger on Garcia's strumming hand, chopped in half by his brother's axe while cutting wood. And Bob Weir's undiagnosed dyslexia, which got him kicked out of school. Unlike Doug, Weir *had* made it big.

The deejay interrupted to say, "The Candyman's in town, folks. Be there or be square!"

"We're there," they yelled back, starting to laugh for the first time since the station wagon had tailed them.

They were, almost. To the melancholy strains of "Candyman," they climbed the city's serpentine flyways. A song he'd never heard, "Stagger Lee," started up, and they took the exit for Broad Street. Only half his attention was on the song, but it sounded like there was a lot of shooting going on. First Stagger Lee shot some guy over losing his Stetson at dice. Then, when cops were too scared of Lee, the widow shot him in the balls, no less, and brought him, presumably staggering, to trial. "True story," the deejay said, "St. Louis, 1895."

The Spectrum was dwarfed by sports arenas. They parked and gravitated to a section full of rainbow-painted trailers and a temporary marketplace. It was peopled by what looked like a distinct breed: psychedelic T-shirts and kaftans, long skirts and sandals, frizzy hair, women in head scarves, men in hats, women with bells on their fingers and rings in their noses, reminiscent of Indian women, even guys with nose-rings. And weed in the air.

Alongside Dead paraphernalia in stalls, embroidered patches of the Stars and Stripes and peace signs abounded. A purple banner said, I'M RUSSIAN AND I'M NOT EVIL. Across from it, another said, MAKE LOVE UNDER THE STARS, NOT STAR WARS. It reminded him of the times they'd played RISK at Doug and Ali's, while Nitin was still at First State. Once, when Imtiaz was on spring break from Columbia and Bernie was there, too, there had been enough players to form American and Indian alliances. After it got a bit heated, Ali had refused to move her armies exclusively against the Indians. And, without her, the weakened American alliance found itself slowly but inevitably surrounded by Indians whooping it up over their victories. Back in 101, Imtiaz, shaking his head, confided: "Man, that Ali—something about her...."

There was something about all the women around them now, but even in their midst, she attracted more than her share of male looks. She, too, seemed distracted, looking around as they spoke. Viraf insisted on paying for a set of beads she liked; he didn't want her spending on top of the ticket. They drifted to where a bespectacled girl in baggy dress outside a tent was strumming an acoustic guitar, singing "Uncle John's Band." Her voice was sweet and a little off pitch. "Woh-oh, what I want to know," she sang, "will you come with me?"

Off to the side, a full-bearded man with a receding hairline and long yellow hair was horsing around with a group of squealing children. A couple of the kids were black, their hair cut close to the scalp. The man picked one up and swung him over his shoulder, where he kicked and wriggled in delight. The other children clamored around the man's waist, begging to be lifted, too. And all of a sudden Viraf had to turn away, disconcerted by a stinging at the back of his eyes.

When he got hold of himself, he could tell that the swirl around the stalls was thinning. Ali was still listening, rapt, to the girl at the tent, who'd moved on to a song he'd never heard. They weaved their way out of the marketplace, her voice growing distant. "We will get by," she sang over and over.

They joined the throng winding up the stadium steps. The volume of chatter was high. Here and there, someone broke into laughter. As they poured into the ring, people began to move to the music coming over the PA. By the time they located their section and then seats, the enormous covered space was swarming like a beehive.

They were at an angle to the stage, far from the milling in front of it. As they took in the setup, featuring two sets of drums, Ali told him of the Dead keyboardists' curse. Whisky-loving Pigpen had died of liver failure at 27. Keith Godchaux was killed in a car accident at 32. The question was how long would Brent Mydland survive?

Viraf's mix of guilt and triumph over the curse he'd placed on rednecks came over him again. A woman in a dress like a pumpkin crossed in front of them, mercifully distracting him. He asked Ali if she thought the woman was pregnant, getting a giggle out of her. From within the sea of torsos in the middle section, a tom-tom started and was taken up by rhythmic clapping. They joined in and kept it going. Then at last the band members were streaming onto the stage, guitars and drumsticks held high, to the deafening approval of twenty thousand fans.

The funk of "Shakedown Street" filled the stadium and set all those feet to dancing. Ali was into it, though when the band sang, "Maybe the dark is from your eyes," she didn't do a lot of mock-peering into his. In any case, it was fun—made no sense to find fault when at a Dead show with a girl like Ali. More or less a perfect place.

Halfway into "Fire on the Mountain," she took her seat and so did he, ready to just take it all in. Rangan would have been ecstatic over the double drums: between Kreutzmann and Hart, there was no room for dhin-chak. Garcia and Lesh, it turned out, wore glasses. And the cursed Mydland looked on fire—or something—as he pounded the keyboards, hair reddened by the lights. They launched into "Me and My Uncle": cowboys in a shootout for gold, the rough intensity of Weir's vocals rendering the outlaw perspective.

And when they chorused, "If I had my way, I would tear this old building down," Viraf knew they weren't talking about the Spectrum. The song was about that old demolisher of houses, Samson, and his coal-haired seductress. Again and again, the chorus declared its desire and the crowd roared its approval.

*

Out in the swarming ring space, they split up to visit the restrooms. In a corner of the men's room, three guys had improvised a bong out of a soda can and were passing it around, overpowering the smell of pee. In line he pulled out his eye-drops to lubricate the contacts. Then it was his turn, and his darkened piss spattered against the yellowed porcelain.

Washing his hands at the mirror, he liked the gravitas of his beard. He'd trimmed it with Ali in mind, but it must have told the redneck he wasn't dealing with a boy. He hadn't felt like one in a while.

Another piece of his pride felt restored by how he'd faced the man down, thought on his feet, and backed him off. He was grateful he'd found it in him when the need arose, resurrected some of the old warrior spirit in his genes.

Out in the circle, a woman twirled to the tune of "Ripple," her skirt flaring around her knees. "There is a road, no simple highway," Garcia sang, "between the dawn and the dark of night."

Ali was already at a concession stand they'd agreed on, talking with a long-haired guy. Before his eyes could really tell, Viraf knew who it was. Then the figure turned in mid-speak, revealing golden stubble. He must have grown it out after Deer Park.

The sight scrambled Viraf's brain. It felt like Doug had not only appeared out of nowhere, he was intruding where he no longer had the right to. At the same time, there was the uneasy feeling of being caught in the wrong.

They swiveled their heads as he approached. But he waved and moved into one of the lines at the stand, leaving them to talk. It gave him time to come to terms with the sudden turn the evening had taken. He should have known: her mixed signals, the two tickets, her glances around the marketplace, searching. And Doug would have known, from his original ticket, which section they were in.

Viraf angled his body in line so he could see them. Behind the surface reserve on Ali's face, or maybe in it, he saw the depth of her feelings for Doug. It was the kind of expression his mom wore after his dad was quickly past a fit of temper while she still had to get over it.

Doug, doing the talking, looked up and ceased as Viraf approached with a pizza box and drinks. They nodded and grinned and kidded around awkwardly. But even the simple act of Ali taking one of the glasses from Viraf seemed freighted with significance.

Not for long. "Vir," she said, "Doug's with a friend in town, and they're having a party after the show." She hesitated. "Do you think you could drive us over? I know the way."

He nodded. "Sure." At least he was still her safety net.

When Doug went striding off along the ring, they returned to their seats amidst the crowd noise. Neither of them seemed to know what to say. The old fleece blanket between them had appeared to be lifting—and now it had fallen again.

The band kicked off the second set with "Truckin'." The crowd went nuts, singing along. Viraf tried to get into it, but all of a sudden it was painfully apparent that the lyrics were hardly as upbeat as the tune. Lousy things were happening to the people in the song, things to which he could relate. "Sometimes the light's all shinin' on me. Other times I can barely see." It felt like he'd played his cards, as Weir and Garcia said you should, yet lost anyway.

Another perfect place had proved anything but. The pizza tasted like the cardboard box it came in, and Ali looked subdued. Out on the stage, the band swung into "Man Smart, Woman Smarter," a rousing calypso he recognized from his mom's LPs. When he leaned over to tell Ali, she brightened and was curious. She'd never heard of Harry Belafonte. What he didn't tell her was damned if Belafonte's version wasn't a hundred times better.

Clearly his perceptions were now jaundiced. There was a lot of scurrying around and setting up on stage. A *third* drum set was added. Accompanied by percussion and wind instruments, they started a self-conscious intertwining of beats. Rangan would have been in paradise. But after a while it began to feel like a prolonged exercise. Kreutzmann's short-of-spectacular solo was a welcome transition. The guitars and keyboard crept back, then took over. But they rambled on, going nowhere, and the constant play of psychedelic lighting didn't help. Viraf felt a headache coming on, whereas others in the crowd were having audible orgasms.

Even when the jam gave way to "Morning Dew," it was almost too mellow for him. Garcia's tremulous vocals bordered on sentimental. But the set improved with "Wharf Rat," and restored his faith, if not his good humor, with a quiet "It Must Have Been the Roses."

He stood with Ali and hollered for more, as lighters flickered around the darkened stadium like stars. Eventually, the band members filtered out for a hand-clapping, foot-stomping sing-along to "U.S. Blues." And the show was over.

*

As they streamed into the chilly night, Viraf was accosted by an Indian guy in denim overalls. There was something incongruous about the combination, and it took him a second to recognize Mohan Bhagia of the perennially tight pants and pussy-licking claims.

If the outfit had changed, the flirtatious flower child who clung to him and the keen eye he cast on Ali said maybe the lifestyle had not. He spoke in the comfortable Hyderabadi accents of old, and homesickness swept over Viraf. They introduced each other to their companions—the flower child's name was Holly—and raved over the show before catching up with their news. Mohan was doing well at his Philly firm and had settled nicely in his rented digs. Not alone, he managed to imply with a smile at Holly, which she returned happily. Viraf told him what he knew of Ritesh Thadani: their flight back to Bombay, his presence at Soona's wedding.

"Good guy, yaar, good guy," Mohan said. Unlike his old friend, he would not return to India. "I must call him up. You know his number there?" Viraf shook his head. "I've got it somewhere, no problem. You give me yours."

They exchanged numbers on Mohan's address book and a grocery receipt in Viraf's wallet.

As they parted, Mohan managed a suggestive wink at Viraf and an approving thumb in the air. He had no idea how to respond—it was too ironic.

CHAPTER 26

Snow

Aside from the arena complex, the only part of town he'd seen before—on a day trip with Nitin and Judy, no longer a stranger from Porter Road but an established friend—was the historic area. The tall ships at full mast upon the Delaware, colonial horse-carriages circling the riverside park, and, in its yoke, the cracked Liberty Bell that had rung out the States' beginnings. Now, in the streetlit gloom, the city seemed a succession of old-fashioned brown-and-white buildings with nothing much to distinguish one from the other.

Beside him, Ali looked pensive, in her Deadhead look. Probably thinking it over about Doug. The radio was in a nightlong tribute to the Dead, and they talked some more about the show. She thought it had been great, all of it, so he kept his little criticisms to himself, sticking to the numbers he'd loved. By and large, they focused on finding the way.

A light snow began to fall, as they approached a building and circled the block twice before finding a spot.

Ali threw her wrap over her tie-dye and drew it about her, as they walked up to the house. They climbed a stairway with faded banisters. The door she pushed at opened into a sparely furnished hall with a balcony overlooking the street. The few people in that space seemed only to be crossing it, either into doorways at its sides or coming out of them. Ali stopped a guy in a colorful kaftan and introduced him to Viraf. They shook hands, saying great show. The guy made a hash of Viraf's name before moving on to one of the doorways.

Ali began to peep inside them. Doug appeared at one and stood and talked with her. There was something about the way they looked together, just talking. Then she turned in a half-wave at Viraf, who'd stayed where he was. He lifted a hand in reply, and she disappeared through the doorway with Doug.

Viraf looked around the decaying walls for a second, then made his way to one of the doors on the other side. Inside the room, people were clustered in small groups, more men than women. A lit bowl was going around one of the clusters, glowing when someone pulled on it. Its vapors reached him as he gravitated toward a trio he could hear talking about the show. But the chatter was mostly about friends in the audience or how the show compared with other Dead shows they'd seen. Pretty well, apparently.

After a while, he wandered out into the hall again and onto the balcony. The cold air refreshed him. He leaned against the old balustrade and watched the snowflakes drift onto car-tops and vanish. A thin layer had begun to cover everything. One flake drifted under the overhang at an angle, and he reached out and let it splash into his hand. He left it wet until his fingers began to freeze, then wiped it off on his jacket.

He'd begun to feel like Mamaiji standing watch on her veranda, when he heard his name and turned to see Ali poking her head out. He went in to where she stood.

"I thought you might have left already," she said.

Redundantly, he shook his head.

"Vir, I hope you don't mind," she continued, her voice hesitant, "but I'm going to stay here for the weekend—Doug will take me home."

"Okay," he said, nodding. Another piece had fallen into place: her request that they use the Pinto and not her Beetle, so he could make his own way back.

She may have seen the thought cross his face. "You can spend the night here, if you like. Our friend won't mind."

He shook his head. The "our" wasn't lost on him. "Thanks. I'll just go back, if you're okay."

"I'm fine. I had a great time at the show."

"Good, I'm glad. Same here."

She pushed at a stray hair across her face. "Is it still snowing?"

He nodded.

"A lot?" She looked worried.

He shook his head. "Nah."

"It might get slippery after a while, so drive carefully."

"I will." He tried to sound reassuring.

And still she hesitated. "Can you find your way back? You have to get back on 95."

"Oh yeah, no problem." He had no idea how to get back onto it.

"Okay." She teetered on the edge of a hug, but he had no desire to revert to that, after the kiss. So he mustered a smile instead. It surprised him that he could.

She smiled back, the worry or whatever still in her eyes. Then she went inside.

He watched her return to Doug's room, then went to the room where the bowl was going around, the smell heavier in the air. One of the guys in the trio was now at the perimeter of a larger group, his curly beard imparting a benevolent look like Garcia's. Viraf crouched by the side of his chair and asked if he knew how to get to 95. Easy, the guy said, but soon lost Viraf with easts and wests.

His request for lefts and rights, instead, seemed to jar the man—he rattled off what sounded like an abbreviated set of directions and turned back to the group. When Viraf tried to repeat them, the man kept his head turned. He said petulantly to the group, as though Viraf weren't two feet from them, "Who is this guy?"

That was it. There was a limit to how much a man could take. He stood up, before anyone could speak, and left the room. The front door, stairway, and entrance couldn't arrive fast enough. If he wasn't a fuckin' I-rainian, he was a goddam dago. If he wasn't a goddam dago, he was a motherfuckin' spic. If he wasn't a motherfuckin' spic, he was a bothersome foreigner who didn't know his way around.

And always, he was the stranger.

Well, he'd had it with being the foreigner. They could keep their precious country; in fact they could shove it up their asses. He was finally taking their advice—he was going home.

It took a few rounds in the falling snow before he found the Pinto, not so recognizably orange anymore. When he started it up, the radio was playing "Sugar Magnolia," and he turned it down. The brown and gray Philly landscape was dappled over with white. He kept the car in third while deciphering street signs, hoping for familiar names.

Right up against the windshield in order to read past the wipers, he could feel the temperature dip, chilling him through his clothes. He switched on the heat and warmed his hands against the vents. When finally he hit Broad Street and turned onto the empty artery, he sat back in relief and shifted into fourth. The road would take him back to the Spectrum, and from there he knew the way.

But for some reason it never opened up into the vast arena complex. The snow was falling hard now, in thick flurries, and he eased up on the gas. At one point, he saw the flash of a red-and-blue shield for 676 against the burgeoning white. Turning his high beams on, he spotted another for 95 and merged just in time.

Then the snow fell like a curtain. He nudged the wipers up to maximum, but for all his peering, he could barely discern the road. He should not have been too proud to ask Ali. But he couldn't really blame himself—he'd wanted that conversation over. Eventually the high beams picked out a sign for Camden, New Jersey, and he knew he was lost.

He drifted to a standstill on the right and started his emergency blinkers. The radio became audible, playing "Casey Jones," while the wipers continued to sweep. He switched on the reading light. It glowed yellow like a candle. Then he opened the glove box and unfolded his map of Newark. Flipping it over, he found a box for Philly.

From what he could tell, poring over it, he'd gone the wrong way on Broad Street and wound up on 676, not 95. He cursed out loud, then sat there for a minute in the chill. The Dead were doing it again, portending a train wreck to a cheerful tune. He switched it off and turned back to the map.

As he searched, angling it to catch the light, he heard the wind blow, rocking the car. There was another box for the New Jersey area near Newark. If he turned around, he'd have to deal with the city again, and the conditions would only get worse. But if he kept going, assuming he could see the way, he would merge with 76 and 295 on the other side of the river—the side he was now on, apparently. The wrong side.

The sooner he got back on the road the better, before it iced over. He switched off the light, and the Pinto fell into darkness between its headlights and the flashing red. He put it in gear.

The next stretch felt timeless, the wipers sweeping hypnotically as he pushed through a surreal world. There were phases when he wasn't sure he was on the road, when the falling snow met the drifts in an uninterrupted blank canvas, when even the road lights disappeared, the car's hood was coated white, and its headlights ended in a few yards of dense flurry.

Then the tires struggled to turn, and the aging engine whined against the load. Glancing at the temperature needle as it inched toward the red, he let up on the gas, afraid to pull over and be unable to get rolling again. In Jim Reeves' "The Blizzard," a cowboy stayed by his lame pony and froze to death "just a hundred yards from Mary Anne." There was no Mary Anne waiting for Viraf, but for the second time in his life he wished his tank were full. It was a cold, empty tank that would get him in the end, not one on fire.

At other times, the churning wheels met only slush and the car leapt ahead, threatening to skid. And each time, in his head, he saw over and over a replay of his afternoon heroics, when he'd kept himself and Ali from crashing. So he looked for the times in between: a steady grind against surmountable resistance. That was when he became conscious of the wipers, and time settled into neutral.

He felt numb, inside and out. Shivering as cold overpowered the air from the vents, he twiddled with the radio and found varying degrees of crackle before clicking it off. He was left replaying "Casey Jones": "Trouble ahead, trouble behind."

At one point there seemed to be less snow coming down. He wondered if he was imagining it. But, slowly, the skies began to lift. The headlight beams lost their conical definition, and road lighting that had disappeared began to glow through the haze.

When the flakes finally ceased, an arctic landscape lay in twilight for as far as he could see. He switched off the emergency lights. A hush had fallen. The crunch of his wheels felt unnaturally loud and the wipers beat like metronomes. He clicked them off, wondering if this was what they called the eye of the storm. There was a sense of being the only creature alive in a bleak yet ethereal new world.

He continued in this trancelike state for eons, before awakening to the sound of wind picking up and a light swirl of flakes. Peering ahead, he had the suspicion there was something on the horizon. It grew, as his wheels churned, standing out against the snow in a plain coat of green, lifting its shoulders until he saw they were the towers of a bridge. Then the signs said he'd been right about the map—he was on 295, and it had brought him faithfully to the New Jersey end of the Delaware Memorial Bridge.

There was a symmetry about it, as it filled his windshield, identical half-mile bridges side by side. Each lighted tower mirrored the other. Then he was rising, and the wind buffeted the Pinto across the snow-spattered lane as if it were a toy. It didn't obey his steering. As he rose onto suspension spans, the wind had a hold of the cables, moving the very road beneath his wheels. It was like being on a gargantuan seesaw. Between the straining verticals, he saw a gray stretch of the Delaware, and across the twin bridges, a gray sky.

The closer he came to the towers, the steadier the roadway became. But as he moved past them toward the center, it swayed again and the wind blew him around. The road felt like ice, but he kept the Pinto drunkenly within the center lanes until he reached the next set of towers. Then he drifted right, toward a guardrail beneath the tower, and stopped.

He switched the headlights and the car off, pulled the hand brake, and set the emergency lights flashing. The wind wailing around him, he reclined his seat. Then, sitting back, he took stock. He was spent. Even if the bridge iced over, he'd be better off once the wind settled. In normal conditions, he was just half an hour from Newark. In the meantime, he wasn't in anyone's way. In fact, he was the only fool out. And if other cars did come along, they had three lanes to pass him. A lamppost just yards behind ensured they'd see him.

Everything seemed to check out, but his teeth had started to chatter and his beard felt frosted. With the engine off, the cold was setting in. So he switched it on, and the air began to blow, its warmer currents mingling with the cold.

It was obvious now that his time in America was coming to an end. There was no Ali to keep him here. The thesis looked good, no more scribbles from Dr. Reese. Once he graded the spring exams for Dr. Tindale, his obligations at UD would be over.

And certainly, now, no magical mystery tour with the traveling Deadheads. His time up close with the hippie life was almost at an end. Instead, he could put the remaining money toward another tour. He'd had an eye on a brochure pinned to the department's bulletin board. The American & European Student Union's bus tour. Seventeen countries in forty days, dirt cheap. See more of the world, since that was the idea in the first place, before finally going home.

Maybe then he'd be content to twiddle his thumbs on Thana construction sites, not, God willing, in Percy's company. Beyond that, it was fuzzy. He knew better than to try to predict. If there was one thing he knew about life by now, it was this: there was way too much he didn't know.

CHAPTER 27

Destiny

When your father has waited all your life for you to join his company and continue his work, but you find that it bores the shit out of you, what do you do? You lie. You say while you were overseas in Delaware, working on your thesis, writing code, running your programs on the DEC 10, you caught the computer bug. That way it isn't personal—it doesn't kill him.

"I need to work with computers," Viraf said, echoing Dr. Reese. He didn't mention the professor's forecast—his father had never liked the sound of him or the influence he had on his son. As it was, the new photo of Mamaiji, at Rustomji's side again, had a disapproving glint in her eyes. Maybe it was a reflection of the hall lights, above a startled Aspi's head. Or of the fragrant garlands that Shobha, Jadhav's daughter, strung daily around the frames. Either way, Viraf didn't let it stop him. "That's what I want to do with my life."

Aspi was wounded anyway; Viraf could tell from his silence. That was worse than losing his temper. The sunburnt face was expressionless, as if he didn't know what emotion to bring to the fore. Maybe he was thinking of the risk he and Cyrus Uncle took when starting up, years of building the business, the reputation so dearly acquired, never scrimping on materials or taking bribes, always meeting schedules, project after project. He certainly seemed blank about whatever it was that had weaned his son away from him. With amazingly bad instincts, he'd deliberately posted Viraf at Percy's site to "learn" under him. Even Viraf hadn't anticipated just how much he'd resent having to answer to the guy.

He tried to make it real for his father by pulling out the clothbound thesis from the old VIP that had been around the world in forty days—well, Europe anyway, where English speakers were the handicapped ones. He handed the thesis to Aspi to feel the heft of those 128 pages. (*Just* a master's thesis? Ha, fuck you, Pickett!) Aspi looked impressed by the family name in gold letters: *Viraf Adajania — Computerized Simulation of Multi-Unit Construction.* His eyes glazed when flipping through pages of symbols and charts, but he said nothing about the gap between theory and practice. Viraf told him there was a copy in Morris Library signed by Dr. Reese, the chairman, and the dean. And another copy in the university library system of America.

The senior partner of Adajania Construction made noncommittal sounds and shook his head. Finally he looked Viraf in the eye: "You know you're killing the goose that lays the golden eggs."

"Mm." Inappropriately, Viraf was reminded of his father's old eggs-sucking metaphor.

"Percy is too smart to do that." As hard to stomach as that was, he was relieved to hear the edge in his father's voice. "Your Cyrus Uncle is getting ready to make him a junior partner."

"Mm," he said again, thinking Percy was welcome to it. He was pretty sure his uncle had wanted him out of the picture all along, so Percy could inherit the firm.

His dad shook his head again glumly and walked away.

Behroz, looking puzzled and sad—she'd grown painfully thin after Mamaiji died—took Viraf aside to tell him how disappointed his father was. He could only say he understood. He felt as guilty as hell about letting his dad down. She, too, was disappointed, it was obvious; no more jokes about paychecks and Impalas.

It hit him now that he'd squandered half a dozen years of engineering studies, never mind a cushy family job. Now that he hadn't gone home to his daddy's company, as Pickett had so charmingly put it, he knew he'd better find another company to join.

When he walked Mahatma Gandhi Road now, a part of him still saw Main Street, knowing he'd never walk it again. The crush of pedestrians here was too real, the traffic too blaring, the shopkeepers too cavalier, the beggars too miserable, the smells too solid, the colors too vivid to block out.

The lack of an occupation amplified his sense of being out of it, like an idle ant in a colony crawling with worker ants. And time felt as fractured as at Longwood. Home was different without Mamaiji and Soona. The looks from his parents drove him out into a subculture of idle playboys, jaded housewives, and rich retirees at the club's tennis courts and billiards room. He didn't have to feel any guiltier than them, and his game was improving. In more ways than one: with their husbands at work, younger wives were given to flirtation. But there was a dry feeling of ennui to it all. Or some similar malaise.

Weekends were better—everyone was off. Still, he was uneasy in the company of Rangan and Maya, now married and expecting, or Milind and Veena or even Ritesh Thadani, all climbing their respective ladders during the week. The one refuge he could count on was at Mehernosh and Soona's. She could not have cared less if he never worked, or, for that matter, cleaned latrines for a living.

A sister's love, he was learning, may be the most unconditional there is.

Soona still read romance novels by the score and he teased the hell out of her for it, but inwardly he had to admit she'd done better than him in that department. And Mehernosh, to his credit, was as phlegmatic about Viraf's career problems as he'd been about his own. Now he was in line for a junior partnership at Jamasji & Antia, a baby whale in Behroz's approving eyes.

In their happy company, Viraf could unwind and re-assimilate. One starlit night in Cooperage, at an open-air Shakti concert, he sprawled with them in a free float like coming down from the acid trip. With Campion just a sprint away, he was overcome by the feeling he'd once had on spotting the US Consulate across the road. Instead of strolling from school to the show, he'd gone the other way, tarried first in Bengal, then America, and come around full circle.

Zakir Hussain's rapidfire tabla rolled over him as he lay on the earth so redolent of childhood, reclaiming him as an Indian. But Hussain's virtuoso question-and-answer with John McLaughlin on a streaming Gibson took Viraf back to the double-drums at the Dead concert. And he realized there had been a similar fusion at work inside him.

So he joined a software consultancy, Tata Burroughs, a collaboration like him between India and America. At the Santacruz Electronics Export Processing Zone, he tailored software packages for a Swiss firm.

His parents were not unpleased. They could balance their admission to friends that America had put strange new directions in their son's head with the boast that he now worked at the venerable House of Tata. "No, no: no use of influence; he got in all by himself."

That didn't spare him from comments. During dinner at Nanking with Cyrus Uncle and family, flanked by elegant black-and-gold tapestries of Chinese dragons, Rhoda Aunty remarked on how shocked they'd been to hear that Viraf had left Adajania Construction.

"Why shocked?" he asked curtly, as his parents stiffened.

She made a face that said the answer was obvious. Her features were birdlike and still pretty behind translucent pink glasses, but her expression wasn't pleasant.

Soona jumped to his defense. "Viraf's so smart he can do anything he wants."

He found it deeply satisfying to see how happy she and Mehernosh were in his family flat near Haji Ali, after all the dire predictions. They hadn't needed a fucking mansion, nor she a whale. It was a welcome reminder of how wrong the elders could be.

Aspi focused grimly on his plate while Behroz looked from face to face, clearly dismayed. Viraf ladled more American Chop Suey, crisp noodles topped by fried eggs, a dish he'd never actually found in America. The bracing odor reminded him of Mamaiji's fried eggs and toast.

Percy, typically, was having none of his cousin's silence. He promptly inserted his oily tone. "So, congrats," he said with a smirk. "You found a way to go back to America."

"You be quiet," Cyrus Uncle said. His hair had thinned since Viraf had last seen him, and, not surprisingly, so had his patience with his blabbing son.

"That's not what I had in mind," Viraf said between mouthfuls, but he knew no one would believe him.

On weekends now, after all the early tensions, it was a relaxed life in South Bombay. Lots of good Parsi and Goan food made by Louise. And without saying much to the family, he'd been going out with a fellow trainee at TBL. Incorrigibly cheerful, she laughed endearingly at every joke he cracked, even the lame ones.

His Parsiness, it seemed, was actually a plus for her, though he wasn't too sure her dad felt that way—nor how his parents felt about her. And his layer of Americanness acted on her like an aphrodisiac. She loved to hear the soft *T* when he said her name: Namita.

Before long, though, she was assigned for a full year to a software project in London. He missed her, but it was okay—he was increasingly accustomed to the idea that women would come and go.

His sense of America, now, was more evenly derived from the two years he'd spent there, than the night when it all went wrong in a hurry.

But one horrific morning, the headlines screamed of mass death and suffering in Bhopal, at a Union Carbide pesticides' plant that had stopped production and let its safety measures lapse. An abandoned but unempted storage tank exploded, spewing twenty-seven tons of gaseous methyl isocyanate and hydrogen cyanide into the air.

A white cloud descended over the city. People poured into the streets, some in just their underclothes, shouting, Run, run, their lungs on fire, eyes burning, froth coming out of their mouths. By the end of the week, the dead filled fifteen thousand body bags, and a hundred thousand more had been poisoned or blinded.

In the enormous common lunch hall at SEEPZ, Viraf and his colleagues were buzzing about the horror for weeks, the terrible images on distantvision. At home, his mother insisted that Ahriman and the forces of darkness had begun their predestined onslaught upon the world.

Cyrus Uncle remarked to Aspi that the self-indulgent '60s and '70s were eventually bound to catch up with American business. Furious though he was at Union Carbide, Viraf found himself speaking up.

"Americans may play hard," he said, recalling the phrase, "but they work hard, too."

His elders heard something in his tone and nodded hastily, conceding they'd based their perception on movies such as *Woodstock*. He wanted to tell them his best American friends were hippies. That their subculture had stood conscientiously for Thoreau and Gandhi's principle of civil disobedience. And that even from a business point of view, Woodstock was a pioneering and massive piece of organization. But he let it go. Their approach to business dealings was staunchly parochial.

"Only Parsis can be trusted from the start," they advised him gravely. "With other Indians, be careful first."

There was no hiding his exasperation. "What are you talking about?"

"You're used to your IIT and TBL friends," Cyrus Uncle said, nodding understandingly, "but don't think all Indians are like them."

It was hard to miss the irony, if he'd really been angling to make Percy the sole heir at Adajania Construction.

Violence still got to Viraf in a bad way. In the middle of the blaring frenzy of a Mad Max film, he stood up and walked out of Regal Cinema, pulling a puzzled Mehernosh and an unquestioning Soona with him.

He had a bad moment, one evening, when enjoying the Marine Drive air by the gymkhana grounds. Within the stream of cars, compact red Marutis mixed with the old Fiats and Ambies—unlike the project's founder, the People's Car was still alive.

Nearing a small police kholi on the pavement, he heard terrible cries from inside, interspersed with sickening thuds. Some smalltime crook was being mercilessly beaten.

Torn by the sounds, Viraf slowed. An attractive young woman in a paisley dress was coming the other way, probably from the women's hostel. They crossed in front of the shanty. Her head turned toward the horrific sounds and, stunningly, a small smile flitted across her lips.

After a year on TBL's in-house projects, he was unceremoniously assigned to one in Iowa, returning him willy-nilly to the world at large. At times he'd felt that people went about their lives unconscious of a larger reality. For unspoken reasons, his family and friends encouraged him to go. And to his surprise, he felt a surge of anticipation.

It was jumbo-jet time again—not such a safe way to get around anymore. A month earlier, off the Canadian coast, the *Emperor Kanishka* had broken up in mid-air, blasted in half by a Sikh militant's luggage bomb. Over three hundred people had died. The same month, Muslim gunmen hijacked a TWA jet to Beirut, before freeing the passengers. Under various aliases, Ahriman was notching up point after point.

Under what alias had he begun? And when? The Sikhs would say he'd first possessed Indira Gandhi when she ordered armed forces into their Golden Temple. Had she lived, she'd say Jarnail Singh Bhindranwale had left her no choice by leading marches against her, then stockading himself in the temple. Had *he* lived, he'd say she should have rightfully returned the city of Chandigarh to Punjab. Transitioning from one analytical profession to another, Viraf had no illusions that some unearthly demon targeted humans malevolently. He'd come to believe in their own reactive, territorial, bestial inner natures.

So this time when he was searched by Heathrow security, he understood why. He still had the black beard, and he wondered how it would go over in the States. He got to see Namita again, at the airport, but now their hug was cautious, their kiss short of passionate. Already he felt as if he were being returned into that larger reality, and though she was a full member now, sophisticated in linen jacket and heels, there was no telling when their paths would cross again.

A prop plane, on his final leg, touched down at Moline, Illinois. He took a cab over the gray, rolling Mississippi into Muscatine, Iowa, so small a river town it had no airport of its own. A chill in the back seat fought heated air from the front, putting him back in the old Pinto on his desperate push through the blizzard. Queasy old feelings from Delaware swirled around him like a spell. He had a complicated sense of being back, of having moved to America for the second time, without even trying.

Ironic, he realized, when so many people scrambled to get in but failed. It was hard not to think this was destiny.

His next project was for that erstwhile manufacturer of Pintos: Ford Motor Company. Talk about destiny. Had the idea come up during Will's crash course in corporate management, they'd have laughed themselves sick. And sicker still to think Ford would prove one of the best employers he'd ever work for. Will, whose fathers, mothers, sisters, and brothers, with their indomitable courage had made possible Viraf's rights in this country, would have liked the diversity around the Plymouth Plant in Detroit. The project leader in Data Processing, a family man in his forties with wispy facial hair and sharp eyes, was second-generation Mexican. One of the team members, a woman in her late twenties who could have been Persian, for her curly dark hair and the length of her nose, had a coquettish manner that reminded him of Ali.

She was second-generation Greek. Detroit's large Greek numbers were reflected by Greek Village. When she married her mainstream American boyfriend, his ancestry less apparent, they invited Viraf with the others to a long but beautiful ceremony in her Greek Orthodox church. Nobody cared that he was descended from an enemy empire.

Popular phrases around the plant were "the work ethic" and "the dignity of labor." Viraf recalled the general absence of such dignity in India—Jadhav would not have had a clue as to what it meant. Though its membership peaked in the '70s, United Auto Workers was still a powerhouse at the first mass-production car company. The plant had a noisy common cafeteria, whose steaming meat, potatoes, and pasta lunches acted on him like sleeping pills. It seated everyone, suits and overalls, side by side or across from each other at long tables.

Rough, friendly people struck up conversations with him, then introduced him to paths around the plant where he could walk off his drowsiness. Single women asked about his marital status and suggested he "just go with the flow—that's what I do." Elderly folk, including grizzled men who reminded him of the Rising Sun, wanted to set him up with their daughters.

The plant's corridors were lined with close-ups of every employee, whether plant manager or assembly-line worker, in no perceivable order. Despite these signs of community, Viraf doubted they'd add a contract employee on their walls. He was wrong. In time, a company photographer came by his desk, and his close-up joined all the others. In it, his smile had more than a tinge of accomplishment. Whenever he passed the portrait, he looked as happy at his workstation as anyone on the walls.

CHAPTER 28

Respect

Motor City was a good place to live, except for one thing: its long, cold winter. After five US winters, he would finally conclude that a Bombayite wasn't cut out for the cold. Will had been right, all those years ago in Delaware. The prettiness of snow wore thin after months of digging out his Taurus, then scraping off the windshields while his fingertips froze right through the gloves. Months along the slick roads to work, never knowing when his wheels might slide out from under him. He often had to inch around scattered vehicles in a chain reaction, the impact sending one sliding into another and so on, like bowling pins. It felt like a metaphor for something, maybe his life. Maybe life, period.

So once he got his green card—officially an "alien registration card" that dubbed him a "resident alien"—it was here comes the sun. His letters went out to companies in California, Arizona, Texas, and Florida: "out west," mostly, as if he were turning into Doug. He wondered how the Moles were doing. And Ali. Sometimes he wasn't too sure that old Love Temple had released him. He still had her multicolored figurine of him, the only thing remaining from Delaware.

Ali's innuendo about the pussy willow and the flicking of her tongue at the Love Temple had projected an air of experience. But he could recall another remark on genitalia that should have told him her experience was limited to Doug.

It was probably a couple of months BB, when Megan and Taylor had the First State gang and the other Moles for a jam session and veggie snacks. Their little home down the county roads was a simple white-boards' affair under a gray roof, like the one on Judy's house off Porter Road. A dormer window peeked between the branches of a tree in their yard, its base circled by white rocks. A perfect little place.

But Judy and her house and Porter Road didn't exist for them yet—Nitin hadn't met her and was there by himself. So was Bernie, though Sean and Todd had brought company. The centerpiece was Megan's chipped and faded piano, at which Sean quickly settled to bang out some blues. Doug played along on his Martin—he had his Jesus look then. There was a moment in the singalong when Viraf heard Ali's voice separate out, a bit shaky but sweet.

Once the echoes died, you could hear the floorboards creak as Galahad padded across the room like a little pony. As always, Viraf was taken by the huge fellow's gentleness when he nosed at them one by one. He was also capable of the most evil farts, but luckily was not in form that evening. Megan fussed over him for a minute before bustling off to set up her freshly baked spinach dip and sandwich buns spilling alfalfa sprouts. A yeasty smell came off the bread when Viraf leaned over to dip it.

Beer and wine began to flow, and the conversation was raunchy. Sean had his shirt on for a change and his dark locks made him seem a counterpart to Doug. In his nasal speaking-voice, he described a rehearsal at which they'd all dropped their pants to compare penises.

"And whose do you think," he asked, looking around expectantly at the women, "was the granddaddy of them all?"

"No comment," said his friend, a strawberry-blonde femme fatale, coolly sipping her Chardonnay.

"Aw, woman," he said in mock disappointment. "Have you no faith in my manhood? Well, it so happens you're right. Will the winner please raise his hand? Not your cock, please, just a hand will do."

Titters ran around the seated circle, as one by one, Todd and Bernie made false starts with their hands. Once Bernie pulled his back with a rueful smile and shake of his head, all eyes turned to Doug. Knowing sounds and commentary filled the room, and, a huge smile on his face, he flourished his arm at a Heil-Hitler angle.

Finally the laughter abated, and Ali was heard to say, "Oh my goodness! That must mean *I* have the biggest you-know-what, right?"

That set everyone rolling around again. Sean, grinning wickedly, said, "That's right, Ali." He added something about sluts, and she leaned over and smacked him. She was flushing so hard, the dapple across her nose had disappeared.

"That's not true, you guys." Megan sounded none too sure. "Is it?"

"Well," said Doug, only too willing to string her along. "It's a good thing we've got some educated people here. Let's get the engineering skinny on this baby."

And now the eyes turned to the duo from 101. Viraf was having a hard time keeping a straight face, but Nitin, still shaking like Jell-O, pointed weakly to him. He was the designated technician.

"It's called elasticity, Ali."

"Well, don't stop there, Vir," she said wryly. "Spell it out."

He chuckled. "So it's one size fits all, right? And when you're done, it comes back to the way it was."

"Oh, thank goodness," she said, exhaling in relief.

"Until you have a baby," he said, grinning. "*That's* when it's stretched past the elastic limit and can't totally recover."

"Oh no," the women all groaned in unison.

"What did I tell you?" Doug said happily, obviously no fan of having babies. "That's why they'll be paying him the big bucks some day."

"Out West" was no more in Viraf's destiny than it had been in Doug's. The first response to his job apps was from a consultancy in Florida. California, fine, his friends in Farmington Hills said, but not Florida. Why not, he asked. They won't like you there, they said, shaking their heads soberly. He didn't ask why not. He'd applied to Systems Solutions because Nitin worked there. He, too, had become a systems analyst—all roads led to computer systems now. Dr. Reese had proved quite the prophet. Viraf called SSI in the city of Jacksonville, and after a telephone interview, they flew him out to interview with their client, Jacksonville Transportation Authority.

The interview was a breeze. Florida's license plates proclaimed it the Sunshine State. The weather was as warm as he could have asked for, and the coastal city sprawling and green. He spent a relaxed evening with Nitin, Judy, and little Nina, their brown-haired and toffee-skinned five-year-old, in their suburban home. Nitin was contracted to Jacksonville Electric Authority, next door to JTA's data processing shop in City Hall. So they drank to reuniting. They laughed while Viraf recounted his misadventures with women.

When the talk came around, inevitably, to Delaware, he asked about the Pinto, which he'd left with them before returning to India. They said they'd left it behind when they moved, had it towed to a dump after trying to sell it. Ambivalence tugged at him when he heard of its fate, unwanted and discarded. It had carried him through tough times, even a blizzard that would have killed him on foot. His mind flew back to when he'd drifted off inside it on the Delaware Memorial Bridge.

They pulled out an album with pictures of their wedding, at Judy's Methodist church back in Newark, and for the first time he saw what he'd looked like in a gray tux. A bit plastic. Thinner. A badly shaped beard. But, he recalled, handsome according to Ali. Doug, Bernie, and the other Moles were in a group shot, all dressed up and neat under long flowing hair. Judy's side, too, looked awkward in formal wear, her widowed mother pensive. Lynette's chubby face smiled out at him inanely; he wondered if she'd ever made it out of the halfway house. Megan and Taylor looked cute together in retrospect, and, in aquamarine taffeta, Ali was radiant.

Just as inevitably, under the warming influence of a Merlot, he was reminded of what went down on an eerie night in Delaware, when to the sound of crickets and the scritch-scratch of boots, he saw his destiny approach with a deliberate swagger. Nothing could have said more emphatically, *You're not accepted here.* He'd still never spoken of it to anyone. Its impact had receded during his year and a half back in India, when surrounded by only Indians. But over the three and a half years since then, in the constant company of Americans, it had reared its dragon head from time to time.

After his contract ended in Iowa, he'd driven all day to Detroit.

The gas indicator on his old Volvo dipped toward empty. Night fell. Loaded American cars traveling the other way seemed an indicator, too: the Motor City was struggling.

He took an exit to a Shell, its red-on-yellow like a beacon. Other travelers had done the same; the pumps were all taken but one. He rolled into the space at the same time that a pickup with a Michigan plate tried to back into it. Furniture and moving boxes stuck up from the pickup bed. A bulked-up, brown-bearded man leaned out of the driver's window and glared. On the other side, so did a middle-aged woman. Presumably husband and wife. If they'd seen his boxes and out-of-state plate, it must have felt like he'd displaced them twice over.

The truck didn't move away, and the pumps were pay-first. Returning from the cashier, Viraf saw the big stranger emerge from the truck on a collision course with him. Or toward the cashier, but every cell of his body snapped to attention. There were things that by now he knew not to do. He didn't break stride, and he didn't lengthen it. He didn't look away. He didn't change expression, not even to match the grim one coming at him. The only thing he did was to visibly slip his far hand into the pocket of his hoodie.

There was nothing in it, and the big man didn't seem to notice. So Viraf braced himself as they came abreast. They brushed up against each other, bearded men in the night.

But then he was past, and they kept going. He left his hand in the hoodie while filling up, gas fumes waving hazily. His adversary coming back didn't even look at him, just got in the truck and pulled up to another pump.

Settling into his new home, Viraf was proud of his ruse, thankful he'd thought of it. It even felt like a little payback for the trick the man in the Bronco had once played on him. He could just hear the woman say, aghast, to her husband, "Did you see...?"

"Sure did," he'd say, still grim. "The sonofabitch was packing."

And wherever they were, they'd tell the story of how close the man had come to being shot...or knifed. By a hood.

Now, with his old friends from Delaware and less burdened by youthful pride, Viraf was tempted to finally loosen his tongue. But each time he tried to get the old story out, the habit of years intervened, and the voice of caution said it could wait some more.

Judy dug out a scoop of ice cream for little Nina, who scooted back to an episode of *Family Ties*. Later, they'd slide a Hindi movie into the VCR. And while Judy would need the subtitles, her daughter would not. She was adding layers of gray matter before their eyes, and it was reaching her through a couple of mediums. What worried him, though, were all the layers she would only be able to acquire through trial and error, some of it too late to save her the pain. Too bad it couldn't all come out of a box, however magical.

In the meantime, they'd begun an account of their visit, last Christmas, to Judy's mother, Ruth, in Newark. He'd met her once, a war widow who'd sat in the background toward a dim corner of their living room, nodding solemnly without speaking. Her worn expression said it all. When she did speak to him, she'd lifted her voice as if she had to get through to him across an enormous distance. There was a shy, almost girlish quality about the slight woman in her fifties that surprised him. She'd been an athlete in high school, Judy told him, never mentioning college. She still had her medals in long jump and sprint.

She and Judy's dad had been high-school sweethearts—they hadn't kissed, Judy added, until months after their first date—and had married when he joined the army. On the mantel, now, stood a browning picture of him in his uniform, light-haired and handsome, a brash little Judy posed in front of him, and his arm around Ruth's waist. It moved Viraf to see how pretty Ruth had been.

Deer Park, Nitin said, was still the same, college kids sitting around the peppermint porch even in winter, the Blue Hen and Poe raven in their showcases. But in First State, Building H was occupied by strangers—even Lynette was no longer there, so maybe she'd made it all the way out into the world. They'd bundled up little Nina for a day trip to Longwood, and it was huge now, more than a thousand acres. She'd gone crazy, running from plot to plot in the conservatories.

And for old times' sake, they'd swung by Judy's old rental home off Porter Road, its old-fashioned dormers still looking out, all bug-eyed, at them. It was taken, of course, a truck and car in the snowed-over driveway. So they couldn't go in.

"But would you believe that old rural 896 has been widened to four lanes?" Judy added, in that sweet New Castle County accent. "Two each way, and even a traffic light at Porter Road."

"Huh," he said, trying to picture the intersection, opened out now and lighted all the way. Cars going through side by side, as many as four abreast. He could see a Pinto turn onto what was now the slow lane. Were it to happen today, the Bronco would be in the fast lane and would speed on in a parallel world where nothing went wrong and no one was beaten up.

In the mist of his dreams, sometimes, he saw that Bronco hurtling toward him. Sometimes he felt it whoosh past and was rocked again in its wake. Sometimes it hit, with splintering force and cracking sounds and the long-anticipated eruption of flames. They lapped at the hatchback, feeding on it. Sometimes it wasn't him in the Pinto but Rustomji, progenitor of the family nose, freshly garlanded and smiling in his photograph. Only, now, it was breaking up before Mamaiji's gaze, shards of glass raining upon the sofa.

Sometimes he saw her still keeping vigil over the cars on Queen's Road. Sometimes its width swelled, and the volume of traffic, until it filled his vision. At other times he saw a train, its compartments overflowing, spewing people from its sides as it rattled and swayed through Marine Lines.

On such nights, he awoke with a foreboding that the world and its inventions were still on track to collide. There was usually something physical bothering him: the temperature too high or too low; the mattress needing turning; a pillow too thick; a pillow too thin. But lying there in the dark, he was overwhelmed by the intangibles, the unanswerable questions: all those people on the road, day after day, going nowhere, headed for the inevitable crash at the end. For that great bulls'-eye on the Parsee General grounds.

Why? To what purpose? So as a whole they kept the world turning, like rodents on a treadmill. Or held it up like Atlas. But if he got out of bed and sleepwalked to the door, in a clear sky he saw a multitude of other worlds. Like glittering pins in an enormous cushion.

"Something once happened to me around that area," he said, feeling his way along, picking at a slice of Judy's blueberry pie, rivulets of ice cream slithering down its sides. "When leaving your place, actually. Not the most fun thing, so just thinking about that intersection still gives me the creeps."

He hesitated, remembering how wary he'd been of her for belonging to that area. They were looking at him quizzically. She asked the obvious question, and he told them in spurts, keeping it brief: the near miss, the chase, the beating, the smile.... It came out easier that way.

Their quiet nods seemed to say these things happened, unfortunately. Then he was done. It was out at last and, in an awkward pause, he waited.

"You can find ignorant and violent people anywhere," Nitin finally said, "just more of them among uneducated rednecks."

"That is so true," Judy said, sympathy in her eyes. "What a *terrible* experience!"

Viraf nodded, simultaneously touched, relieved, and uncomfortable. "Ya, but long ago—not a big deal anymore. It just popped into my mind when you mentioned Porter Road."

"You could have talked to us about it *any* time," she said.

"Thanks. I know." He nodded. "I should have."

When Megan and Ali had asked him at Lums Pond if something was wrong, that was the time to speak up and be helped. Instead, he'd walked away from them. They'd never known what was wrong with him.

Judy sounded tentative. "Why didn't you?"

He shrugged. "Young guys have too much pride for that." There was enough pride still left in him to have denied it was a big deal.

It was her turn to nod.

Nitin was silent again, in a contemplative sort of way. Finally he said, "North Florida's pretty much South Georgia, you know. We have friends and neighbors who love to joke about being rednecks, just like this stand-up,

Foxworthy. He goes, 'If you look for a date at your family reunion...you might be a redneck.' And our friends go, 'M' cousin Curtis does that.' Then they laugh their asses off. Good down-to-earth pals, is what I'm saying. We can always call on them in a fix."

Viraf nodded. "I know—there's all kinds. It took me a long time to learn that." Automatic trust in strangers was still beyond him, but by now he could give each new acquaintance a chance, gauge him as an individual, whatever his background. "Back then I couldn't tell one American from another."

There were reasons why, as a fresher in the New World, he'd confused the good guys with the bad. They'd all been working-class folk. Some, like Doug, had not finished school. Others, like Megan and Taylor, lived out in the country. Judy, right there on Porter Road, must surely have had neighbors who fit the insulting designation. Friends. Even relatives. Herself, before she took to college and, like Don Williams, began to sound more like the newspeople. She'd finished her degree and now was store manager at Toys R Us. It moved Viraf that she'd sided with him, agreed so readily with Nitin about the violence.

He, too, had blue-collar friends at Ford. He'd seen their family pictures, been to their homes, met their wives, husbands, parents, and children. Enough to know that not even the few there who didn't like him would beat him up. Nor smile to see it. Not a single one hated him and there wasn't a single one he hated. That took not knowing the other. It took being strangers. "Don't be a stranger," Doug and Ali had said. And how right they were.

"Did I mention I once dated a distant cousin?" he said, smiling. "*All* Parsis are distant cousins, there's so few of us. But she and I were kissing cousins, till the Bombay cops broke us up."

They laughed, looking confused.

A pointed look came over Judy's face. "You weren't the best driver, you know? Can I say that?"

"Well," he said with a wry smile, "you just did." It was the kind of phrase that would have made him mad back then.

But she was a proven old friend now. Ironic how he'd been depressed by the transitory nature of friendship when Nitin moved out of First State and in with her. And here they were, the very ones to come back into his life. Or the other way around. Ironic, too, how he'd always feared the return of Porter Road. And ironic how he'd doubted their compatibility, as his parents had doubted Mehernosh and Soona's. Their happiness had proved him wrong.

In any case, it was a relief to feel the ease with which he'd taken the remark, even if it assumed he was the driver at fault. "I think, basically, I was just a Bombay driver on Newark streets...in more ways than one."

"That's true." She looked penitent. "I shouldn't have said that."

"Nah, that's okay."

"I've been a Newarker in Bangalore, and it's not easy. Not even for a visit." She was nodding now, her eyes wide with meaning. "I respect you, you know. I really respect you both for making your way here, so far from your home."

She continued to nod at him. And he nodded back, not sure if she was done.

"Thanks, Judy," he said finally. "Thank you for that." He hadn't known just how much he'd needed to hear it from someone.

She wasn't done.

"Wish I'd been there, in the parking lot." Her expression hardened, and she sounded like her old self again. "I'd have told that bitch in the Bronco off."

And something that had its teeth in Viraf all those years loosened its hold at last.

"Hey, you know," Nitin said, changing the subject, "I couldn't find either Doug or Ali in the directory. So I dropped by the Ho Jo. Well, Taylor still works there, in an office now, like senior manager or something. Suit and all. He and Megan got married, couple of kids. So they had us over—same old place in the country, same veggie grub, good old Galahad on his last hairy legs, I'm afraid. Nina had a blast playing with him and their two boys."

"Wow, very cool."

"Ya. They asked about you, you know. You should come with us, next time."

He nodded. It felt good to know they remembered him. And he'd have liked to catch up. He could just imagine Megan now, running into other Indians and, this time, having none of the misconceptions that had generated tensions between them, such ready tinder sparked by her fellow Americans in a Bronco. If it wasn't Indian techies that Americans had come to know over the years, it was doctors. Or store owners. Motel managers. Restaurant owners. Yoga instructors. Writers. Financial analysts. Engineers. Even though Megan had never ventured beyond New Castle County, a small part of the world had come to her in his shape.

And yet, he wasn't sure he wanted to see Newark again. It was not his perfect place. And if he proved Poe's curse on the Deer Park wrong, maybe all the curses would be lifted. Lifted off lorry drivers winding around the Ghats to eke out a living. Off freshers lacking the experience to avoid danger. And off mechanics having bad days indicative of their lives.

"Well, anyway," Nitin continued, "Doug and Ali had moved to Oregon. They went to Portland first, and she's still there. School teacher, apparently."

"School teacher. What kind?"

"What kind do you think? Art teacher."

He couldn't imagine a better vocation for her, other than simply an artist. And with some luck her paintings would catch on. He wondered if they were still of hobgoblins in a varicolored, pointillist world. Or had those served their purpose, tamed her childhood dragons once and for all? Or had Doug slayed them for her?

In any case, Viraf was one of her first fans. Her dappled little figurine, still his only artistic likeness, had gone everywhere with him and now adjusted its glasses and flung its arm about on a corner table in his living room.

"What do you mean *she's* still there?"

"Well, he's in Eugene now. Cuts precious stones for a jeweler."

A jeweler. With a glass to his eye. A craftsman, at any rate. Better paid than a cook—Doug had always been grateful for his day job. And "out West" at last. Just the Northwest instead of the Southwest. Distant, fabled, rainy land.

But what about the light-fingered genius on the guitar and his dreams of stardom? Had the world finally cut his hair? Clearly, in terms of a livelihood, it valued his utility more than the artistry he'd tried to give it. Hard labor was what it must feel like, cutting stones, compared to the rush up on stage.

"He still has a band, though?"

"I asked the same thing. New band—it's called the Trees."

Ah, from the Moles to the Trees.

"So why didn't she go with him?"

"She did, initially. Apparently, there's a hippie commune still thriving in the woods there, can you believe it?"

Viraf shook his head mutely.

"So they went there for a summer." An ironic smile crossed the dark features. "And you know Doug...."

Viraf lifted and dropped his eyebrows. Sure: Adam in the Garden of Eden. So in some ways the guy still had his hair.

CHAPTER 29

Hindustan

There was a new term, like African American, for desis: Indian American. Easily confused with American Indian. Viraf liked the inclusive logic of it. By now he had his identity limerick, begun back in Jimbo's:

There was a young man named Viraf
whose Pinto was a bit of a laugh.
He started in India
then went to America
and found he was now half and half.

It struck him that life had been a dizzying series of disorientations and reorientations. Motion sickness in the extreme. And yet, each new place had been a microcosm of the whole. There were patterns that recurred.

When he flew to India now, Bombay was Bombay, no longer recalled through tinted glasses. Not a perfect place, but no place ever was. In any case, it was in his blood forever.

At another Nanking dinner with Percy and family, Rhoda Aunty asked him which he preferred—living in India or living in America.

"That's a complex question," he said. "I like both."

She frowned at him through her pink-tinted glasses, as if he'd said something stupid. "You can't do both!"

"Why not? I remember the people at TBL went back and forth all the time."

"In the end," she said, "they'll have to pick one."

One bright Sunday morning, his mother took him to the towers of silence, where Mamaiji had been placed. Govind drove them to the Doongerwadi near Hanging Gardens. He was no longer the newest servant—horrible word. There was another liftman now. Jadhav was dead—of what, no one knew; maybe emphysema—and his replacement was, if possible, an even more rundown personage.

Viraf missed Jadhav's all-forgiving smile; in some ways it haunted him. Saraswati and their daughter cleaned the flat together now. Shobha refused tips in an offhand display of independence and equality. It touched Viraf that she trusted him enough to flirt scandalously right in front of her mother. Mamaiji was not around to scold them anymore. Only the bust-length photograph next to Rustomji's remained of her.

Saraswati and Shobha still lived in the garage's annex, so the new guy had to sleep on the steps with the hashed-out regulars. Viraf's brief stint in the purple haze was nothing compared to their permanent residency in the twilight zone. By now he knew how the acid—lysergic acid diethylamide, to be exact—had shorted the synapses in his brain. Those trees, faces, and flowers had not changed. The world and its transmissions were the same—*he* was a different receiver. Same reality, different perception. Still very much like being in a different reality. One that had "existed" all along, hidden until he could tune into it, then revealed in all its crackling, electric, seductive splendor.

Back in the States, Ben & Jerry's had introduced a new flavor, Cherry Garcia, that reminded Viraf of the Dead show all those years ago in Philly. The ice cream wasn't bad, not even too cherry. Creamy chocolate-chip with the odd split-cherry thrown in, packaged in matte red tones that reminded him of Ali's hair. But Garcia would have to abstain, having fallen into diabetic coma for a while. And the curse of the Dead keyboardists had claimed its third: Brent Mydland, so on fire at the Spectrum, was now dead of an overdose. He was only thirty-seven.

Viraf could see, as if it were yesterday, the makeshift marketplace at the Spectrum. He could hear the bespectacled flower child sing what he now knew was "Touch of Grey." It was all over the radio, with the release of their new album, *In the Dark*. He knew better than to overly romanticize them and their followers, but he couldn't help feeling that for the most part they'd radiated light. And he didn't mean psychedelically.

The car had to be left at the Doongerwadi gates. Viraf was a bit stunned by the grounds' idyllic appearance: pathways lined with flowers, no sound of traffic, everyone walking. Just as Mamaiji would have liked. Her perfect place. Even the air smelled fresh, after the city pollution. It felt like the Making Wonderful, resolving eons of war between Ahriman and Ahura Mazda. He'd been dipping into Olmstead's *History of the Persian Empire*, and it made reference to an ancient Videvdat, an Antidemonic Law. Demonic "attacks," Olmstead paraphrased, "could be prevented only by rites of aversion." Maybe, in this land of no cars, Mamaiji's demons had been laid to rest.

As for his own, they'd receded, the wounds scarring over. Leaving Delaware, he'd packed Ali's ceramic dragon with his clothes in the old VIP. It survived his transatlantic jaunts, but not unscathed. The outstretched arm and a donkey ear cracked off. His dad, who loved to fix broken items, put aside his feelings toward the prodigal son and pulled out a tube of Fevicol. Amidst fumes of epoxy resin, they kept pressure on the cracks with rubber bands and cellotape. The bonds held, leaving hairlines where microscopic bits had chipped off forever. And now it was a gentle, light-hearted presence on Viraf's mantelpiece in Jacksonville.

His mother, visibly emotional, pointed out the prayer house where they'd gathered around Mamaiji's stretcher. They followed the central path. Old folk with prayer caps swayed piously on its benches. At the end, they reached a clearing ringed by greenery. Behroz directed his vision up at the tail of a perched peacock. No vultures in sight. Within thicker foliage stood one of the towers, discolored and squat, not towering but certainly silent. No akashvani, no voice in the sky.

As if sensing his disconnection, his mother took him back along the path into an almost empty hall. On a table at the center was an enormous open book, as wide as the table and as thick as three Webster's Unabridgeds. Flipping the huge old pages back, she showed him Mamaiji's name in blue ink: Persis Elavia, nee Sheriar. It was the book of the Parsi dead, across three centuries in Bombay. She kept turning until she hit an entry, in the same blue scrawl, over a quarter of a century old: Rustom Elavia, the grandfather he never got to know. The sole man in Mamaiji's heart to the day she died.

In the same book, at least, though who knew if in the same place. But a whole sheaf of giant pages between them reflected the high death rate after generations of inbreeding. Heart disease, infertility, mental illness, even suicide, all taking a toll. Once Behroz saw that she'd had the desired impact, she flipped forward until she hit blank space.

"I wonder, haa, Viraf, after three more centuries, will the book run out of pages or will the last name be written?"

He acknowledged her reference to their dwindling numbers with a noncommittal grunt. Give her the slightest encouragement and she'd be matching him up with more Jers. His very cells questioned the wisdom of perpetuating the cycle. They walked back to the gates.

On the flip side of the coin, Soona was due. At Parsee General's maternity ward, a few wings from where their grandmother had lain, his sister gave birth to a seven-pound baby girl. Naming her was a no-brainer: it was plain to see she was a Persis. Mehernosh, his hair receding prematurely, joked that she was a better-looking baldie than Persis Khambatta of *Star Trek: The Motion Picture* fame. Behroz was relieved that her nose hadn't skipped a generation only to land on Persis. Fingering his replica, Viraf reminded her that it *hadn't* skipped a generation. Everyone laughed, except Aspi. He wasn't over his son's refusal to inherit the firm.

In any case, Viraf Uncle was fascinated by the pastime of watching little Persis. The play of expressions over the tiny features, the shifting of her eyes, their open astonishment, the wriggles and jerks, the vocabulary of sounds expressing discomfort, delight, surprise, need, and contentment. The absolute innocence.

He'd received a message on a dazzling new phenomenon called e-mail. It was from Imtiaz, at an R & D division in San Jose. Like some labyrinthine railroad junction, the world was coming together in ways Mamaiji could not have imagined. But Dr. Reese had. They'd entered a magical new digital era. Imtiaz was working on an Artificial Intelligence project. Intelligence, he wrote, is an accumulator of information that can build upon itself. Viraf felt he was watching the latest-model Persis, no shortage of oxygen, gathering her info at every turn and growing layer upon layer.

Maya and Rangan, too, had a child: a little boy, Prasad. They prompted him to say hello to Viraf Uncle, but he was too shy to say anything. There was a difference in the way Maya regarded Viraf now, very composed and affectionate. Not passionate, affectionate. Motherhood had put a cap on the first, but he was still a part of her past. And she a part of his. It was kind of peaceful—and sweet. Rangan, who was her past and present and presumably future, seemed okay with those vibes. Even he clearly came second to Prasad in her world.

One evening, Milind the Everyman and his dainty wife Veena had Viraf over for dinner.

On the roads, a change had taken place. Driving to Shivaji Park, Viraf saw Hyundais, Chevys, Scorpios, Skodas, Mercedes, Marutis, Hondas, Tatas,

Mitsubishis, Peugots, and Fords. Apart from taxis, his Fiat and the odd Amby were now the rarity, not the rule. Free market reforms under Rajiv Gandhi and Narasimha Rao had clearly had an impact. Viraf's made-in-India cotton shirt was not from Colaba but JC Penney. He wondered if the export boom was trickling down to the mill workers.

Still, in various ways, Mr. Pande's hopes for India were finally coming true.

In Milind's living room, though, he and a couple of friends were trumpeting the praises of BJP. A baby-sized, cherrywood Ganesh watched from a showcase. Looking prosperous, Milind turned to his IIT junior for confirmation. Viraf nodded diplomatically.

"BJP's platform is a bit bigoted," he said quietly. It was the understatement of the century. The Ayodhya mosque controversy was already brewing. Before long, it would literally explode.

"Bigoted?" they chorused. "Why bigoted?"

He spread his hands, puzzled by the denial, wondering if for the nth time he was wrong but unable to see how. "What's Hindu nationalism if not bigotry?"

They all raised their voices to tell him what. Veena came around from behind the counter to say, "Please talk about something else, or it'll come to blows."

Viraf was incredulous. "Between us?"

She smiled at that, reassured, and went back to supervising the preparations.

The smells of vada-bhat and khichdi wafted into the hall, as they dipped pakodé in chutney. Milind's other guests worked for him at Bharat Petroleum, where he'd risen to Area Manager. Oil was big in a decade that had kicked off with a deadly chain reaction in the Persian Gulf. IITians were doing well, the men at least: Rangan had shot up the ranks in Hindustan Lever, whereas Maya hadn't cracked a glass ceiling. Though she doted on Prasad, she'd put off having a second child to concentrate on her advancement. Rangan, on the other hand, couldn't wait to have a little girl "just like Persis."

One of the BP managers, a fair-skinned, sharp-featured guy who could easily have been taken for a Parsi, had a question for Viraf. "Have you seen how shamelessly, at cricket matches, the Muslims cheer for the *Pakistani* team over our own team?"

He shook his head. "I haven't seen any cricket in a long time." There was no point elaborating—they could not have imagined a world where people had barely heard of the game.

The other BP guy had lit a Wills, and was offering the pack around. Smoking still had a worldly aura about it here. "Have you read," the man said, exhaling contemplatively, "of the Hindus who have been murdered by Pakistani terrorists?"

"Terrible thing," Viraf said, "and they must face justice. I'm the first person to say that. Don't forget my ancestors were among the first victims of Islamist militancy in history. But my ancestors were militant themselves when they built their empire. And what was the big point of it—where is that empire now? I'm sick of the whole vicious cycle."

He paused to weigh what was pouring out of him. Friends like Imtiaz and his old benefactor, Talaat, had taught him not to demonize whole populations. And the felt weight of even small violence had left him intolerant of all violence, except in defense or for justice.

Even those had their limits. "I'm not talking about only BJP or excusing Congress," he continued. "I don't put blind trust in any party anywhere. I've also read of India's human rights' violations against the Kashmiri Muslims: beatings, torture, murder. How come we always forget that two wrongs don't make a right, never mind three or four or five? There are more than two sides to a story; it takes someone from three countries to know that. This is supposed to be a secular country—it's written in the constitution."

The man's mouth twisted. He tapped his Wills on the brass rim of an ashtray, and its tip glowed again. "This land has always belonged to Hindus."

Viraf bobbed his head ironically. "Ya," he said, making scribbling motions with his hand. "It's written on the ground."

The BP guy took a puff and exhaled. The smoke dissipated slowly.

The others, too, were silent, until Milind spoke, equally ironic. "So then why is it called Hindustan?"

Viraf sat back and crossed his legs, smiling hopefully. "You're just helping me make my point, right?"

But the Patelian shook his head, frowning. "No, I mean it; this has always been Hindustan."

The air went out of Viraf, and his head dropped. He could no longer meet Milind's eyes.

"Then it's over," he said, tugging at the crease in his pants. "It's over. If even educated people like you can think that, then Imtiaz and Percy and all the cynics are right: all of us non-Hindus should get out of your Hindustan while we can. Actually, all North Indians should get out too: give it back to the South Indians. While you're at it why don't you give Iran back to the Zoroastrians—kick all the Muslim families out of their homes. Give California and Texas back to the Mexicans. Then give them back to the Spanish. Then give them and all of America back to the American Indians. Kick all the other Americans out."

There was silence again.

Then the irony was gone from Milind's voice, as reedy as when, a decade and a half ago, he'd ragged a very green fresher in Kharagpur. "He is right, we are a secular country.... Let us go eat dinner together and forget about politics."

CHAPTER 30

A Man of the World

In Jacksonville, he drove a Mitsubishi Galant. Its coat was a deep chocolate. He was drawn to it by commercials in which it zipped around a course for 30,000 miles without breaking down. Mamaiji's kind of car, if such a thing existed.

When what passed for winter slipped into spring, he drove to Metropolitan Park for an annual festival called the World of Nations. An attendant waved him to a space beneath the highway. The Gator Bowl hulked to one side; the city was big on football.

Long, long ago, in 1564, it had been Fort Caroline of New France, the French Huguenots' historic arrival point in America, marked by the reconstructed fort on the bank of the St. Johns. During the Revolutionary War, it was known as the Cow Ford, for the obvious reason. In 1822, it was renamed for Andrew Jackson, after the frontier general wrested the lush state from the Seminoles, the British, and the Spaniards. The infamous Trail of Tears had led through Jacksonville to dingy prison cells at the St. Augustine Fort.

To this day, the city's native population referred to the Civil War as The War of Northern Aggression, their sense of defeat and occupation reminiscent of the Parsis' eternal feeling of dispossession, of India's postcolonial hangover and its underlying history between North and South. Viraf heard echoes of Bombay English in the y'alls and easy cadences. The luck of the draw had first deposited him smack on the dividing Mason-Dixon Line, in Delaware.

During the Civil Rights Movement, River City, as it was called, was infamous for Ax Handle Saturday, when a mob of armed white men assaulted black demonstrators who'd staged a peaceful sit-in at Grant's whites-only lunch counter. The city's blacks rioted in protest. A pickup full of Klansmen roared through a housing project, shooting into black homes, which shot back. Pulp mills mushroomed along the river, emitting sulfurous, rotten-egg fumes that gave Jacksonville another nickname, Armpit of the South, even as it grew into a prosperous port and naval base.

Before Desert Storm broke, the self-described Bold New City of the South lived up to that motto by electing a second-generation Lebanese American to be its mayor. True to his campaign promise, Tommy Hazouri cracked down on the chemical emissions, restoring clean air to his constituents, but sparking the ire of the corporate "fat cats" he called out in public. Months after the Gulf War, the city denied him a second term.

This event, every year, was when Viraf most loved his adopted city. At the World of Nations gate, a towering departure board reminded him of the one at VT. But its destinations were Kuala Lumpur, Nairobi, Warsaw, Lyon, Saint Petersburg, and Shanghai. At the ticket window, he was handed a slim book whose gold letters said *Passport*. Women in colored robes, head wraps, and stone necklaces stepped through a gateway to Nigeria and Ghana. The world was sprouting cornrows and dreadlocks to the amplified beat of bongos.

The grounds opened up onto a circle described by a stage to the left, lawn on the right, and a riverwalk. The crowd milled toward a ring of national pavilions. Children dashed from one to the next, holding their passports out to be stamped.

Adjusting his Gators cap to block the sun, he skirted a martial arts' demonstration at China. A parasol booth at Vietnam was doing brisk business with the women. A girl with black hair to her waist twirled a jade parasol sprinkled with flowers. Her silk pantaloons billowed under an ao dai, slit from her hips to her knees. A log-throwing contest was under way at Scotland, its contestants in kilts, and a ring of people circled in a folk dance at Poland.

He headed for India on the far side.

A line led to trays full of samosas and pakodé. He smelled chutney. The strains of a Gujarati song emanated from speakers. Children in dance dress clacked their sticks in time. Among them, young Nina looked at home, a brown plait swinging behind her. A bindi bloomed on her forehead. In Jersey City, it would have marked her as a target for the Dotbusters. They'd terrorized Indians, shouting "Gandhi Go Home!" until the Indians marched for peace and New Jersey led America on hate crime legislation.

Nitin and Judy stood proudly on the side. Viraf gave Judy a hug and clapped Nitin on the back. His old friend looked prosperous in golf slacks and T-shirt. He hadn't applied for citizenship yet, holding on to his green card so he and Judy had a foothold in both countries.

Viraf had done the same. He'd read in *India Abroad* that, someday, India might allow dual citizenship. To his expatriate's mind there was no contradiction in being both Indian and American. He disliked the idea of renouncing all loyalty to his motherland at a "naturalization" ceremony—dual allegiance felt natural enough.

Naturalization would feel a little like the swearing-in of Patelian freshers after ragging. Enraged by the number of Patels in their phonebook, the Dotbusters had randomly picked a local pharmacist, Bharat Patel. Impersonating cops, they knocked at his Heights home. When he trustingly let them in, they bludgeoned his head with a metal pipe.

IIT's social microcosm was still full of parallels for Viraf. The title of "best country in the world," claimed proudly by both countries, great nations among many great nations, reminded him of every hostel's claim to being the "best hall in IIT."

By virtue of her parentage, Nina, who came running up with friends, anklets jingling, would have her choice of either nationality. And if she personified the browning of America—or the world, for that matter—then its future looked good. As for the present all around him, it reminded him of Ali's multicolored Yoda, which sat, fat-bottomed and jolly, on his mantelpiece.

The sun poured down on them, lifting the river water into the air. It felt like Bombay in June, the spirit of light all around, ready to wash them clean. Viraf raved over Nina's performance, patted her on the head, and left them to explore the Caribbean along the riverwalk.

A small crowd encircled a dance troupe on stilts, as a Haitian band belted out heady mizik. People thronged the jetty to ride the *Annabelle Lee*, a seafaring cake in its reds and whites. Around it, the river sparkled. Perched on a dock post, a dappled gull watched its fellows flap over water.

At Dominica, a hand-painted menu distinguished between Island Punch and 3 Island Punch. Viraf waited until a girl in green-and-yellow head wrap turned to him across a table.

"Hi," he said. "What's the difference between the Island Punch and the 3 Island Punch? The second one's also from Trinidad and Tobago or something?"

"Oh, no." She broke into a smile. "The first one, you get a tall glass o' ponch. The second one, you get *three* small ponch for five dollars."

"Ohh." He smacked his head and smiled back. "I'll get the tall one."

She turned to the mixer, then turned back. "You don't mind a little ginger in it?" Her dark eyes meeting his, she put the tips of her finger and thumb together. There was a bit of Maya in those eyes.

"I love ginger," he said, and proceeded to tell her how much they used it in Indian cooking.

When she handed him a glass, he promised to return for jerk chicken, though his mind was set on goat curry at Ethiopia. He'd circle around to it after he'd seen everything else. The punch was a watermelon red, and when its cool hit his palate he could taste the piquant ginger. Bob Marley T-shirts ringed Jamaica, and Puerto Rico was jumping to Boricua reggae. At Lebanon, belly dancers undulated and shimmied to Middle Eastern music. Outside both Turkey and Palestine, at a judicious distance from Israel, dancers linked hands and circled in variations of a kick-kick-step-right-and-kick. No Iran, but close enough.

Past Aztec motifs, giant cacti, and Frida Kahlo tapestries in Mexico, the riverwalk opened out into the South American section. The smell of fried plantains wafted from Cuba, and the sun flashed off trinkets in Colombia and Panama. Flamenco dresses flared and Latina hips swiveled wherever he turned. It made a guy just want to shoop.

There was something to be said for Doug's philosophy, after all, some advantage to being uncommitted, free to drift where he wished through this riot of sexuality. Even Charles and Diana were seeing others—so much for the wedding of the century. As for Viraf, it felt like he'd finally found his way out of the Love Temple. After hearing where Ali was, he'd considered calling her in Portland. But he felt no desire to come second to Doug forever, in her mind.

He turned the corner, past gladiators and bullfighters to his right, Vikings on the left, and Port-O-Lets in line like blue sentinels. Every year he saw more pavilions, and the crowd, too, had doubled and tripled, all less the strangers for it. No one was a minority here. Or everyone was. In the midst of it all, he felt more at home than anywhere else. A new term was catching on: the global village. Here was a larger allegiance that felt natural: not to manmade divisions, but to the world.

It was the perfect place.

America, this year, had a multiple theme. Indians in leggings offered feathered memorabilia, while on the Buckaroo Stage, a girl in boots stomped to a bluegrass tune. Alison Krauss & Union Station's "Steel Rails." Its streaming mandolin poured over him. He could see the multitude of tracks at Kharagpur

Station, as if the world were converging. A bunch of kids, black, white, and brown, waited impatiently to ride a mechanical bull. The sweet smell of barbeque ribs drew him to its table—the goat curry could wait.

A girl with punk hair was serving the ribs. She looked bored with a pimply young guy at the grill. He was trying to chat her up, while she pointedly looked away.

"Hi there," she said in flirtatious tones, interrupting him. "Are you enjoying the festival?"

"I sure am." Lifting his punch, Viraf sized her up. Up close he could see the diamond-point in her nose. Too young, though not jail bait, as Doug would put it. "How about you?"

"Oh, God, I love it," she said, her eyes opening wide. "I wish I was foreign."

He smiled at that. The innocence of it—or maybe the gray in her eyes—reminded him of a girl, long ago, with marmalade hair. How they'd taken him in, she and Doug and their friends. Back when he was first, and most, the foreigner. Into their homes, their lives, their world. They were all that had stood between him and the forces of xenophobia. In such a place, it wasn't hard to feel that their voices of love and peace had won the battle in his head.

"Well," he said wryly, "all you have to do is go to another country. And you'll be foreign."

She pouted, obviously suspecting him of humoring her. "No, I want to be foreign *here*, in America."

He chuckled. Just like a woman, to be difficult. "So then," he tried, "after a while you can come back. And you'd be a little bit foreign. Here."

It got a laugh out of her, and a nod that said she had an idea how that went. He could see that. It was probably what had drawn Doug and company to him, their sense of being outsiders. Clearly, their breed wasn't dead yet. Maybe it could still win the world over.

Funny how his thoughts went back to them, after all this time. Or maybe not. When you moved across the world, to make your way in a new country, it was like having to grow up all over again, to learn to swim in the unfamiliar stew of its cultures. To realize there were differences—that it was not a homogeneous solution—then learn to recognize those differences was a long channel-crawl toward understanding. There were those who helped you swim and those who pushed you under. And both of them would stay with you for the rest of your life.

The ardent young griller made a show of shoveling fresh ribs on the girl's tray. Viraf winked encouragingly at him, and the boy grinned back. When she served them up, the ribs were smoked and juicy. Viraf sat at a table and dug in, listening to the kids yell as they rode the bull, its massive shoulders dipping and rolling on slow.

By the time he'd wiped the stickiness off his fingers, one of his favorite acts, Inca Spirit, had struck up a Peruvian melody. He drained his punch and returned to their section. The musicians in rainbow-stripes came in from Miami every year. They played standing up, under a trellised gateway overflowing with vines.

He stood by and listened, a sense of peace and belonging coming over him. A handful of people drifted closer. The dark-eyed musicians breathed into Andean panpipes and bamboo flutes, and out came a slow, rhythmic huff, as of a train starting up. From conch shells and rain sticks, the coolness of breaking rain enveloped him.

The chuffing built, and, closing his eyes, he found himself back at Victoria Terminus as the Howrah Mail began to move. String instruments broke into a trill. A maltas flute lifted its voice like a songbird, and he was in Patel Hall, hearing "El Condor Pasa" on a Simon and Garfunkel tape. The first time he heard "Kuntur Pasa," he'd done a double take.

Now the rumble of hide drums quickened, the Madras Mail carrying Maya steamed into Kharagpur, and the Moles huffed locomotive breath at the Deer Park. Then the wind blew again, a gentle rain fell, and he came awake in a snowbound Pinto on the Delaware Memorial Bridge.

The windshield and windows had fogged over completely. It felt like sitting in the middle of a cloud. His head throbbed; the contacts stuck to his eyeballs. He fished out his eyedrops, and when he put them in, the lenses floated free again.

He cut the heat and turned the wipers on. They swept robotically. Through the clearing arc and lamplight, he saw a girder running alongside. Its I-beam showed green through patches of snow, riveted in patterns he recalled from Structural Design. No scope for design where he was headed, on factory construction sites at the outskirts of Bombay.

The cables had stopped straining. The wind no longer screeched around the window edges, and the roadway didn't behave like a seesaw. A guardrail above the girder indicated a walkway beneath it. He lifted his forearm and peered at his Seiko. Almost five in the morning. He ought to push on into

Newark, and now it looked as if he could.

Still, he was inclined to stay in place, freeze time right here on a bridge between two states. The line from "Casey Jones" still played in his head. "Trouble ahead, trouble behind." Out there, he knew, was a world full of flowers and shit and everything in between. And he was very much of that world. Leaving the engine running and the emergency lights on, he zipped up his jacket, pushed at the door, and got out.

The gloom outside was leavened by the lamp-glow. The chill cut into his airway, but his footing felt steady. He stepped carefully around the snow-covered hood toward the walkway.

The bridge tower loomed to his left like a colossus. He stood at the guardrail and followed the great box-shaped assembly of plates and rivets, all the way up to where the suspension lines peaked. An undifferentiated gray hung over it all. Looking down, he saw it reflected in the Delaware, whose gray expanse stretched endlessly. Behind either opacity, he could see nothing. But he stood there for the longest time, peering into the river.

At some point, the idling of the Pinto roughened, bringing him back to himself. The chill had cut through his jacket and sweatshirt. He straightened. The air seemed clearer. High above the tower, the lightest pink now streaked the sky. He took a last look over the rail, up and down the breadth of the river. Faintly, in the distance, he could see both sides.

ACKNOWLEDGMENTS

My thanks go out to members of my writers' group, Jean Shepard, Charles Feldstein, Mary Treyz, and Robert Gentry, and to my readers, Matt O'Keefe, Boman Desai, and Susan Muaddi Darraj. Mary Sue Koeppel, Matt Lany, and Nancy Richard-Lany weighed in early on. I'm grateful to Yaddo and Escape to Create for the time and place to work exclusively on the project. And to *Slice Magazine, South Asian Review, Crossborder Journal, Bridge Eight, Fifth Wednesday Journal,* and *The Normal School* for publishing excerpts. Also to Slice for the Pushcart Prize nomination, and to *Writecorner Press* for republishing "Distant Vision." To Marge Piercy for guest-editorial suggestions on "The Summer of the Strike" at *Fifth Wednesday Journal,* and to Vijay Lakshmi Chauhan for guest-editorial suggestions on "Country Roads" at *South Asian Review.* Altaf Tyrewala, too, provided feedback on "The Summer of the Strike." Thanks to Randa Jarrar for editorial suggestions on "Hood" at *The Normal School.* Thanks also to *Glimmer Train* for selecting "Hood" earlier no less than four times as a finalist for its Very Short Fiction Award. Thanks to the Sewanee Writers' Conference for the Walter E. Dakin Fellowship in Fiction, and to the conference workshop under Alice McDermott and Claire Messud for early feedback. To Susan Muaddi Darraj and her Writing About Ethnicity summer workshop for feedback. And to Susan for her discerning editorial eye. To series editor Michael Griffith for selecting *Go Home* as a finalist for the Yellow Shoe Fiction series at LSU Press. And Tim Schaffner of Schaffner Press for selecting it as a finalist for the Nicholas Schaffner Award for Music in Literature. And New Rivers Press managing editor Nayt Rundquist for selecting it as a finalist for the Many Voices Project Prize. And editors Rebecca Schwab and Lisa Graziano of Leapfrog Press for short-listing it in the Leapfrog Fiction Contest, and Black Balloon Publishing for the Horatio Nelson Fiction Prize. And editor Nan Kavanaugh, art director Christine Tarantino, and photographer Roxie Lute of *First Coast Magazine* for the photograph that became the basis for the author's portrait. Thanks to Noli Novak for that fine artwork. Thanks to Niloufer and Feroz Shapurji, my dear sister and brother-in-law, for help with research in Mumbai. And to Cindy and Sunil Prakash for help on Newark, Delaware. And Howard Denson for help on Jasper, Alabama. To Diane Johnson, Bob Shacochis, Deepak Singh, Margot Livesey, Jeffery Renard Allen, Irene Skolnick, Bapsi Sidhwa, Frank Green, Cheri Peters, Nancy Holmes, Peter Meinke, Boman Desai, Tamina Davar, Tenaz Dubash, Peter Mayshle, Karan Mahajan, Howard Denson, Michele Boyette, David Poyer, Becky and Marty Khan, Lynn and Steve Masciochhi, Sharon Cobb, Bill Ectric, Laura Lee Smith, Mary Anna Evans, Brad Lauretti, Solon Timothy Woodward, Tim Gilmore, Larry Baker, Teri Youmans Grimm, and Jim Wilson, thanks for your support of this project. Thanks to my dynamic literary agent, Priya Doraswamy, who knows the transnational experience from the inside out. And to my artistic publisher, Knut Knudson, who wears his long hair well. A.T. Olmstead's *History of the Persian Empire* was a useful resource, as was Rodney L. Hurst Sr.'s *It was never about a hot dog and a Coke!* To the musicians mentioned and the ones I've known, thanks for the music you brought into our lives. And to my friends and family, thanks for everything.

CPSIA information can be obtained
at www.ICGtesting.com
Printed in the USA
LVHW051021220722
724051LV00007B/340